WITHDRAWN

# FOREIGN BODIES

*Also by Barbara Grizzuti Harrison*

OFF CENTER
VISIONS OF GLORY

# Foreign Bodies

## Barbara Grizzuti Harrison

DOUBLEDAY & COMPANY, INC.

GARDEN CITY, NEW YORK

1984

I wish to thank the National Endowment for the Arts, Yaddo,
and the MacDowell Colony; their help was inestimable.

DESIGNED BY LAURENCE ALEXANDER

*Library of Congress Catalog Card Number 83-16553*
*Copyright © 1984 by Barbara Grizzuti Harrison*

*Library of Congress Cataloging in Publication Data*

*Harrison, Barbara Grizzuti.*
*Foreign bodies*

*I. Title.*
*PS3558.A664F6    1984      813'.54*
ISBN *0-385-19295-9*

for Sheila Lehman

*Love means: I want you to be.*

SAINT AUGUSTINE

*Couldn't you like me—just me, the way I am?*

"Vertigo" (ALFRED HITCHCOCK)

# FOREIGN BODIES

# Part One

What right have I to swear
Even at one A.M.
To love you till I die?

W. H. AUDEN,
"Songs and Other Musical
Pieces," XVI

# *Chapter One*

Suffering puts a gloss on certain women. I am one of them. Perhaps that is why I need to rehearse what happened with Devi when I am feeling drab—though, when all is said and done, unrequited love's a bore. At the time, and for a very long time after, I needed him to love me, as someone else said, to make up for all those who didn't. I needed to love him for all those (and one in particular) I didn't love enough. We outlive superhuman loves—they are the probation subduing the heart to human joys. I believe this; I am proof of it. Sometimes, when I dwell in the past, I forget it. The past is a sorry country. When I visit it—when I return to the scene of the pain—I deny, once again, that I caused Devi any harm. I do my best to remember that I was a responsible actor, not a victim, in this farce. Sometimes I forget. (We are not free to choose those whom we are free to love.)

Do you see how I play with words (not all of them mine)? "All your too many words," he said. That was the night he called me Bette Davis (no compliment intended), and laughed when I tripped on the stair and sprained my ankle—well, twisted it. That's what he hated—that I played fast and loose with words, that I played fast and loose with him. I didn't think I did—not until the very end, when I understood the harm I had done him.

Though even now . . .

Oh how I wish he were here.

I did not mean to set such an elegiac tone. I'm not Cole Porter or Noel Coward, after all. He'd like me better if I were.

I read in the paper today about a TV show I could watch if I
didn't have a date tonight. I read that I could watch a documentary about a seventeen-year-old girl who was "battling to
gain her independence from a loving but demanding mother
who is terminally ill with cancer." Oh dear, how we would have
gone at that one. Terminal cancer doesn't take its time. The
girl might have possessed her soul in patience, she'd be independent soon enough. That's what he'd have said—or I'd have
said (the sound of two voices clapping). On the other hand, he
might have rooted for the seventeen-year-old brat. "Loving
and demanding mother, just like you," he might have said;
"your daughter would be better off without you." He says
things like that. He doesn't mean to be unkind. He is perverse.
And I do mean perverse, not unpredictable, though he is that,
too. If a perverse man is good enough to love you, it convinces
you—what else can?—that you are also qualified for ordinary
bread-and-butter human love. (Oh how I long!) Loving a man
who is perverse has this advantage: It means, if he returns your
love, that he loves every side of you, even those you have
disowned, those you disavow, those you are frightened of,
those no one else has ever found and never loved, those no
one else could possibly love. If a perverse man loves you—
well, it makes up for a lot. No better way to feel safe.

Or so I felt at the time.

I have to keep reminding myself that his unpredictability
provided me with the intensity I crave—that it was, in fact, a
bizarre form of fun. Fun is not, generally speaking, a word I
use in connection with him. Of course it is true that the lines
between fun, intensity, and pain often become hopelessly
blurred with me; I tend to confuse phenomena. For example, I
have confused love and need, desire and desperation, goodness and the will to be good . . . in which I am not unlike
most people, always excepting the happy and the saintly.

Of course sometimes I think it is all nonsense, the idea that I
loved Devi because he was perverse, that because in his perversity he ferreted out the bad, phony, dopey parts of me and
loved me nevertheless. Sometimes I think we are doomed to
love certain bodies; all the answers lie in the flesh. To what

secret parts of my nature did Devi speak? This was not a question it occurred to me to ask then, my capitulation to him having been so total, so instantaneous. Often travelers in a foreign country will feel that they have come home, they have arrived at where they belong to be; nothing can explain this sense of familiarity, this recognition felt keenly as a sword. Lovers are travelers in a foreign country.

But you were not an innocent, friends say: Stephan's world prepared you for just such an unlikely infatuation, and taught you, too, to deny yourself the indulgence of it. In that world, there were other men who were beautiful, other men who were charming and perverse. How could you have taken an offering from Stephan's world, and why Devi? How do I know? Lovers are always innocents, I say. Nothing prepares one for love. Or everything prepares one for love. Suppose it had been in my power, after my first meeting with Devi, to lay my childhood out before me like a map. Perhaps at some forgotten intersection, some remote corner of that shaded landscape, I might have found reasons, a reason, the reason, for loving Devi. I might have found reasons, a reason, the reason, in my torn marriage, in my mother, perhaps even in some small forgotten cruelty perpetrated on me in the first grade—or in a man who loved me and killed himself (but not for love of me), even, perhaps, in Lucy, my daughter; who knows? I loved him without a backward glance.

When all is said and done, one loves because one loves.

It is also true that I am very stubborn.

Now I am back in the country of the past.

I dream, sometimes, that I am in a walled garden, curled against the sun-warmed stone; there, breathing the scent of old-fashioned flowers, I am silent, I do no harm. My flesh—this body which has brought me, and him, so much misery—relaxes slowly into its own ashes, dust to feed the roses, a silent, useful occupation. But I know: In real life, a child would wander into the garden, a repairman come to mend the wall; and my rhythmic silence would be broken. The sun would open the petals of the rose; and my body would warm to new desires, which are always the same desires, always the desire for him.

He knows: "Just to be alive," Devi says, "is a form of cohabitation."

"Then why bother, Devi?"

"I suppose because there's always the chance something delicious may happen tomorrow."

"Always provided one gets out of bed."

"So say you. Actually, it's much more likely that something delicious will happen in bed. As you well know. And suicide is not an edifying spectacle. It sets a bad example for the children."

I tell him my dream.

"Is one part of your clever mind always commenting on the other part of your clever mind?" he asks. "Must you always play parlor games in your head? If you are feeling melancholy and stale are you always noticing it and getting high on it? Do you always turn your pain into profit?"

"Yes," I say; meaning No.

"No," I say, "I'm actually much more simpleminded than you are, I keep telling you."

"Yes? Well of course I wouldn't know. I'm just a simple Wog. . . . Talk to me."

I am thinking: Doesn't he do what he accuses me of? And why is it wrong? And what in fact is he accusing me of? How is it possible to answer his questions truthfully when I do not know what his questions mean?

Nor do I know what he means when he tells me that I have damaged him more than anyone has damaged him, even his mother, "that bitch." I have implored him to tell me in what ways I have done him harm:

"I do not want to have this quarrel, Angela."

"It isn't a quarrel, Devi. It would help me if I knew. . . ."

"Help you? Who is the *you*, who is the *I* that makes these demands?" Now he is very angry, the skin of his face looks taut, and bruised. "Do you know *Thou art that?*"

"What?"

"Buddhist. It means you can see in someone else only that

which you yourself are. . . . Do you know I sometimes talk to this bed where you are lying because there is no one to talk to?"

"It is no wonder you have no one else to talk to if you talk all that Zen crap. Anyway you're Hindu. Just tell me how I've hurt you. . . ."

"*You.* Always *you.* You exteriorize everything. All your too many words. I never speak when you're not here, why should I? And I never think of you when you're not here, it is a waste of energy."

"*Exteriorize?*"

"Is there something wrong with that word? I am not, by the way, Hindu. Your wonderful missionary schools colonized my psyche beautifully. How dreary you are, I don't want to have this discussion. I was quite content to be unhappy before you came. . . . Ah no, don't cry. I haven't hurt you, you can't be hurt. You know that if I hurt you, I hurt myself. You can't allow yourself to be hurt by me. That is why I love you. My sweet, my precious," he croons. "My love."

Now all the tension has bled from his face, the hard black look is gone; it is once again the familiar, beloved face, impossible to renounce.

He kisses me full on the lips.

"I am safe with you," he says, "because you can't be hurt. Only you know how wonderful I am. You know I am wonderful?"

"Oh yes," I say. "You are wonderful. Wonderful."

He says, "I love you. I have loved others more."

If we could have foreseen, when we met, how it would end (how it would never end)—if I had known how much pain there would be, if he had known how much happiness there would be—would we have behaved any differently? We liked each other so much. And were probably, even from the beginning, pursuing our own separate ends. For he, wishing perversely to be an outcast, manages not even an effort toward the intention of joy; he seeks not to be in a state of grace. While I, muddled and stumbling, seek happiness; I long for the shadow of a great rock in a weary land. He would deny this. ("Balls. Impertinence.") He hates my definitions.

He would say, has said, " 'Falling in love,' horrid. Toppled and imbalanced. Surely it isn't necessary to 'fall' in order to prove to oneself that one is in a state of love. Maybe love under the System—of course I'm only a Wog and you're a capitalist so this won't make sense to you—maybe love under the System has become so disfigured, such an anxiety-ridden state that entering into it is invariably accompanied by a state of debilitation or falling. Why not 'I've *risen* in love'? Of course I always do fall, I always have done, no matter what I say. Impossible to make love with Europeans. Bed is always a battleground—a loving battleground but a battleground nonetheless. I used to think playing was winning. Now I see it's not. Not in bloody England it isn't. I mean, playing for fun was having fun which you were winning by playing, not by winning—your prize was fun. But all you Europeans are obsessed with end products. And I, of course—thanks in part to you and Stephan—have been corrupted too. And another thing: I thrive on the delicious anxiety of being a weaker vessel, while in fact I'm tougher than old boots, playacting a dependency to give myself an extra buzz, constantly testing the commodity to see if it will survive. You are a Westerner, you understand all about commodities, love is a product to you. Maybe anxiety has become the last surviving sensation. . . . Of course I haven't your way with words. Why do you force words from me? I talk to amuse you, of course. Regard it as a form of hospitality. Ah, Angela, I am babbling. I love you. I love you. Only you know I deserve to be loved. Why doesn't love save?"

He would say, has said, that I fell in love with him to satisfy my need for melodrama, and because he was the perfect sacrificial lamb. I deny this.

I will start where it began for me, though love belongs, not to time, but to eternity, in which time does not exist. (That is why to say that God is love, and that a thousand years are but a moment in His sight, is to make a precise emotional and mathematical equation.)

It was August, late afternoon, as hot and airless as a pharaoh's tomb, and I was trying, in my large apartment in Brooklyn, to apply one of the things I'd learned from living in India: To surrender to the heat, to abandon oneself to it, is the wisest, least enervating course of action. When both one's air conditioners have ceased to function on the same day, it is also the only possible course of action. My surrender to circumstantial necessity had been preceded by a proper Western temper tantrum that could not have been more satisfying had there been anyone at home to witness it, and by a brief, unsatisfactory sleep. I awoke bathed in greasy sweat. The pillow next to mine was covered with gray clotted cats' hair; I rolled it up into a furry ball and tucked it under the bed. Beginning to enjoy the prospect of homely household chores performed languorously, I put on a pair of underpants, not altogether clean, and an old bra; luxuriating in the heat, the sweat, even in the stench of decaying garbage that reached my third-floor window from the street below, I changed the kitty litter, which had maggots in it. Surrendering to inevitability always makes me feel self-righteous, and—I don't know why—clever. I began to defrost the fridge. I carried pots of boiling water from stove to fridge; I sloshed in water, the soles of my feet black with the dirt of the kitchen floor, sweat dripping into my eyes, sweat trickling down my back and between my breasts, my thighs slipping and slapping together in a parody of sexuality that became, finally, sensual in fact.

The phone rang.

It was Stephan.

"Angela, dear, how are you? You must come over for dinner, you'll never guess who's here."

"I'm fine. Hot. Who's there?"

"Whom would you most adore to see?"

"Al Pacino or the ice man. Who's there?"

"Three guesses, dear."

"Stephan, I just got back from the country, I haven't unpacked my bags, my air conditioner is broken, I give up."

"Devi."

"Who?"

"Angela, don't be difficult, he longs to see you, you're the only person in New York he wants to see, and it will do you good to get out of Brooklyn."

Stephan lives on Sutton Place.

"Do I know him?"

"Are you with someone?"

I could imagine Stephan pursing his lips in prissy disdain. Middle-aged and seldom without a clamorous young lover, Stephan takes a very dim view of sex. He does not like bodies. He is far too fastidious really to enjoy the more generous—and messy—sins of the flesh. All his lovers have been so thin as to be practically nonexistent. He worries about losing his hair. When I am inclined to dislike him, which is often, I think of him at the 1968 Chicago convention, marching in a Cardin suit he bought for the purpose, a suit that was later stained with blood from his own bludgeoned head, and with Grecian Formula hair dye.

"I'm alone with the cats. Who's Devi?"

"You met him"—Stephan was beginning to sound both syrupy and peevish—"in my flat in Juhu when you were serving tea for Madame Gandhi."

"I remember pouring tea for Mrs. Gandhi, but—I'm sorry— I don't remember anybody called Devi."

"And he came to visit you when you and That Person owned that brownstone in the East Village." Stephan always refers to my ex-husband, his second cousin twice removed, as That Person. "He has just been reminiscing about your squash."

"My *squash?*"

"He was very fond of your squash, Angela, he said it was the best squash he'd ever eaten. And very fond of Lucy, too, he says she was the most charming child he'd ever seen. . . ."

"Well, she is, and what's more, she's good."

"And he thinks you're wonderfully earthy and wildly original, so you had better come over for dinner."

"Dear me. Why aren't you in the Hamptons? Is he a composer?" Soft beads of dirt were forming between my breasts.

"A painter, dear. You remember you admired his paintings."

"You know so many painters, Stephan."

"They are not all named Devi. And they do not all paint six-foot oil canvases of the English countryside. I remember specifically your commenting on his brilliant use of ashy mauve. Rather boring, I thought, the mauve, the more so now that he has chosen to make it a trademark, but then you did seem to enjoy taking a lofty tone with him. I remember quite clearly your agreeing with him that he ought not to do book jackets or commercial art. A very tiresome conversation, in fact, about selling out. Now you will remember him."

I did not.

"And he will be devastated," Stephan said, "if he hears this conversation, he thinks you're beautiful, perhaps he'll paint you. We'll expect you at six?"

"Seven-thirty," I said, having no intention whatsoever of going. "I'm defrosting the icebox, Stephan. I'm filthy. And my father has just had another heart attack" (this was a lie) "so I have to stay near the phone. A minor heart attack."

"One doesn't defrost the icebox, Angela, one allows the refrigerator to defrost."

"Well, one does if one has been away in Maine for six weeks and if one is Italian and if one has neglected to turn one's icebox off in one's absence. I had to pour hot water on the freezer door, Stephan, just to get it open, the ice had sealed it shut. I think I may have torn that rubber stuff around the edges. You can't imagine what it's like in here, there's water all over the floor, and it will take hours."

"Good. It's settled then. I'll call you at seven, dear, to be sure that you are showered and ready to get into a cab."

I suppose everyone has friends he doesn't really like, friendships that survive largely out of inertia, propinquity, and the simple fact of longevity. I wasn't at all sure that I really liked Stephan, but he had been in my life for such a long time it seemed pointless to force a quarrel and terminate the friendship; and Stephan's tenacity made it impossible for me to allow our friendship to suffer death by attrition. Besides, he had been my neighbor in Bombay, and there were certain streets, certain expatriate states of mind, I had explored only with him; to lose him would have been in a way to lose India. And I had begun birth contractions in Stephan's flat on Marine Drive; he had so far overcome his squeamishness as to behave calmly and almost entirely sensibly when my water broke all over his best Persian rug. (He called the bearer, propped my feet up on a pillow, rang the hospital, put in a trunk call to my husband, and asked me if I should "loose my stays.") Stephan had been the first man to see Lucy (not counting That Person) after her birth; I could not bring myself to sever a connection with someone who maintained so early an image of my beautiful daughter. He did genuinely love Lucy. Certainly the gifts he gave her were impressive—and expressive of love, in that Stephan tends to measure love by the cost of a gift and the label on a package. By the time Lucy was eight, she had amassed a large collection of boxes and shopping bags from Tiffany's and Bergdorf's; and she had begun, at ten, to enjoy his parties, where she was spoiled and petted and allowed to drink champagne.

There have been times when I have felt real affection for Stephan. The time, for example, when Lucy was five, and he brought her backstage at Carnegie Hall to meet Margot Fonteyn. Fonteyn, gracious to a fault, asked Lucy how she had enjoyed the ballet; and my daughter, with the remarkable talent for honesty she has not yet managed to lose, said, "I liked it a lot. I liked everything but the dancing." Stephan was mortified, but he took Lucy nonetheless to the Russian Tea Room, where he ordered for her two cranberry creams and a Shirley Temple in a champagne glass.

When I am casting about for reasons to like Stephan, I remember the night we were arrested for trespassing on private property. We'd cut across a construction site to get to Stephan's Mercedes after dinner at Giambelli's, and when a security guard asked us, not overly politely, to retrace our steps, Stephan dropped his affectations, struck a manly pose, and said he'd be damned if he, a West Pointer, would be pushed around by a soft-bellied toady of the privileged class. (It pleases Stephan, who works out in a gym every day, to pretend—even to himself—that he works for his money even as you and I. Whereas the fact is, so far as anyone is able to see, he toils not, neither does he spin.) Within moments we found ourselves in front of a desk sergeant in the police precinct at 54th Street and Ninth Avenue, in the company of six lethargic hookers. Stephan was terribly solicitous of my welfare—exploitive, however, too: "My friend is a writer, you'll be on the front page of the New York *Times* if I'm not permitted to call my lawyer immediately." When we were released, at six o'clock in the morning, Stephan got behind the wheel of his Mercedes and cried. He told me about the time he'd waltzed with Hedda Hopper at an Academy dance. Then he drove all the way to Newport because he remembered a cliff walk where one could smell the briny sea spray and the fresh sweetness of wild roses. It was November.

I know enough about Stephan to feel contempt for him. I know too much about Stephan to have contempt for him.

That August afternoon, I found the thought of spending an evening in his company a vexation. I could not imagine transferring my body, which had begun to smell ripe indeed, to the sterile perfection of his ordered, cool apartment. His call, however, had disturbed my peace. What had been a sensual wallow had become a necessary discipline. (I whacked the ice with a carving knife.) I was in a mood to despise his mannered nonsense, but it had, nevertheless, the effect of making me feel vulgar, also poor. I took refuge in a calculated departure from charity, from which I knew I would later suffer revulsion, which would, in turn, land me directly in a taxi, a form of penance that would nicely dovetail with Stephan's plans. Stephan usually manages to get his way.

His dinner parties, I thought, are always the same. Either he serves peasant food on seventeenth-century pewter plates (I remembered once having boiled beef and turnips on exquisite Meissen porcelain he'd bought at a Sotheby's auction, another time having lima bean soup in translucent Sèvres bowls), or he serves beluga caviar and steak tartare and cold lobster and *fraises des bois* with white wine on peasant plates ("some amusing pottery I picked up in Sardinia, my dears"). In his lac-

quered gray living room, bushes of unblemished waxy white
camellias, coaxed into unnatural perfection, bloom perpetually, unaware of changing seasons or of time's vicissitudes.
Barcelona chairs. A black leather hammock. Erotic wood carv-
ings from Southern India; Steuben glass sculpture, one black
Nevelson, a Calder mobile, Mogul miniatures. Arguably pornographic drawings of men wrestling balletically, framed in
old Venetian silver.

I thought, as I attacked the ice, of Stephan's seal-point Sia-
mese cats, which match exactly the lacquered gray of the living
room, the windows of which look out to the East River (and
garbage scows, ha-ha. *Whack!*). A miniature orange tree in a
lacquered purple (*"eggplant,* Angela") bathroom (photographed in *Vogue*). A lacquered white kitchen, glass shelves,
glossy tiles, pots of anemones (photographed in *New York* magazine: "How New York's Seven Most Desirable Bachelors
Cook").

How irritable the heat was making me, how mean. And all
poor Stephan had done was invite me to dinner with what's-
his-name, Devi—whom, try as I might, I could not remember.

I had known, of course, that I would go from the moment I
told the lie about my father (a lie I usually reserve for my
dentist). I was beginning superstitiously to believe that if I told
that lie one more time, my father would really have a heart
attack, and my irresponsibility would be the cause of it.

("Superstition is after all a primitive form of faith, not entirely to be despised," said a Jesuit Stephan entertained one
evening, the priest's austere, elegant profile averted, all the
night, from the silver-framed wrestlers, to which Lucy's guile-
less gaze had wandered. "Do men do—you know—*it* with
other men?" she asked after a hard look at the athletic two-
some. "No, of course they don't"—Lucy frequently answers
her own questions—"but what are homosexuals, Mommy? I
forgot." "Have another lemon ice, dear," Stephan said.)

At seven Stephan called.

"My father's OK," I said. I had drawn the rice paper shades
and was now naked, sweaty. "I'm all dressed. A taxi's on its
way."

"I've made boiled beef with turnips and cabbage and potatoes. One cooks the beets separately, of course."

"Of course." Dear God, a truck driver's dinner on the hot-
test night of the year. I wondered whether we would get the
pewter or the Meissen plates.

I had not remembered him; but I recognized him. Devi
grasped my hands, and in that moment established himself as a
fact of my life—a fact of my past, my present, my future. My
memory, which had not been stained by facts and opinions,
came alive in his presence; he was immediately, dearly, familiar.

He was wearing a white embroidered kurta, loose white
pants, *chappals*. Through the fine cotton of his kurta, I saw the
warm breathing brown flesh. Into a room of artifice and con-
trivance, he brought life. I touched the pulse of his neck. He
kissed me. It was the kiss of a man who is both shy and generous, eager and tentative. "Are you happy?" I said. He smiled
as if the question were a reward. And Stephan preened because his dinner party had begun propitiously.

I have read that there are people who try, in the absence of a
lover, to summon up an image of his face and find other faces,
other images, swimming up through memory unbidden while
the desired face remains illusive, obscure. How frightened
they must feel! I cannot imagine such deprivation. His face is
indelible to me; I can summon up a photographic image of him
at will. (When I dream him, I am not lonely; it is impossible for
me to believe that if I am dreaming him, he is not also dreaming me.) Sometimes I think that a physical transference occurred that August evening: his image was burned on my ret-
inas, as the image of Christ is said to be branded on His
shroud.

Devi's physical beauty is like a character trait; one cannot
think of him except in relation to it. Our flesh is the flesh of our
souls, my confessor says. Devi's beauty amounts almost to a
kind of goodness; it nourishes and astounds. His physical presence inspired me with joy—and I mistook that joy for wisdom.

"Not a perfect beauty," Stephan said. "There is that scar."

"A perfect scar, perfectly placed, and I suppose you would manage to find fault with Michelangelo's David."

"No, dear, I'd buy Michelangelo's David if I could."

"And are you going to buy Devi?"

"Don't be crude, Angela."

"Well, are you?"

"I have told him he could stay in the guest apartment while I find him a dealer and a gallery."

"In other words, yes?"

"One might say so, yes. Although there is a regrettable tendency toward chunkiness there, have you noticed?"

"Are you happy?"

"Oh what a good question. I knew you would ask me good questions. Will you help me find the answers?"

"Do you really remember my squash?"

"Oh yes, and the way you held Lucy, and the questions you asked."

"What questions?"

"You asked me if I were happy."

"Do you know Italians cook the yellow flowers of the squash? You dip them in batter and fry them, don't you think that's a nice idea?"

"You grew up eating flowers."

"I grew up eating blood, too. My grandmother went to the wholesale market with a bucket and collected the blood from chickens' necks. I think it was chickens. Then she made a pudding of it. My grandmother was a terrible person. It had raisins in it. It was really very good—until you knew what it was, of course. Does it sound horrible?"

"My mother cooked spleen. Curried spleen. Does that sound horrible? And she gave me a spoonful of yogurt every time something terrible was going to happen, for luck."

"Like what something terrible?"

"Like the day I got circumcised."

"How old?"

"Ten."

"Oh dear. Did she tell you what was going to happen?"

"No. Just the yogurt and then the doctor and then snip."

"And weren't you scared? Didn't it hurt?"

"Do you think I could write a song about you? 'Blood and Flowers'?"

"Are you laughing at me?"

"What do you think?"

"I think you like me."

"The beets," Stephan said, "are cooked separately."

"Oh, I do remember! I remember a large seascape—acrylic?—and Lucy said she wanted to fall into it."

"Oil, actually."

"Lucy," Stephan said, "has been seductive and provocative since she was three."

"So what."

"It's odd," Devi said. "I wasn't particularly keen on that painting, I'd lost interest in it till Lucy liked it. Perhaps I'll draw her pictures of the sea and she will like me—would that please you? Will you cook me some squash?"

"Have some turnips," Stephan said.

"And you sing, Devi, I remember."

"I sang in the choir at Christ Church, yes. Will you come with me to Oxford sometime?"

"Yes. Of course. Yes. But how long will you be here?"

"You will tell me that. For as long as I am happy, is that a good answer?"

"There are practical matters—have another ice—like money, one assumes. Dealers and galleries," Stephan said.

"Stephan, I wish you believed in chocolate-chip cookies, how about petits fours? Can you make a curry, Devi?"

"I shall do for you, yes. Would you like me to sing 'Jesu, Joy of Man's Desiring' for you?"

"Chicken curry, please. Do you know how to make chicken tandoori? Stephan, do you remember, in Bombay we used to eat chicken tandoori and *nan* and cheese-and-peas curry at the Shalimar. Oh, Lord, imagine. I am nostalgic for the smell of jasmine and cow manure. Do you find that offensive, Devi? It must be awful for you to hear people go gaga-goo goo over India, like being patronized by your inferiors. How did you know I loved that song, by the way?"

"I know you, isn't it?"

" 'Isn't it' is not idiomatic. No educated Indian uses that expression, Devi, one would have hoped you had learned not to at Oxford."

"But I like to pretend I'm a simple Wog. Besides, Angela likes it, don't you, Angela?"

"Yes. I don't know why I like it."

"You like it because you are part peasant—all peasant?— too. And because I do it."

"Yes."

After dinner Stephan took a long phone call in his study. Devi grimaced—"A dealer? A gallery?"—and grinned shame-facedly, a reaction I perfectly understood, having all my life been unable to resist the temptation to run with the hares and chase with the hounds. I recognized the source of Devi's dis-comfort, having, all my professional life, not known how to deal with my resentment of people who have helped me be-cause there was something in it for them, accepting their help nonetheless. I am far from scrupulous; my work is the best part of me. It knows much more than I know.

"My work is much better than I am," Devi said. We were sitting on a black leather sofa with his portfolio balanced on our laps, our thighs grazing. "Do you know many artists?"

"I only meet them with Stephan, I can't say I know many. My husband used to drink sometimes with Franz Kline, but he didn't like it when I joined them. Once Kline drew a portrait on a paper napkin to prove to some drunk that he could do more than make blotches. I wonder where that napkin is now, it must be worth a fortune."

"We know where it is."

"We do? Oh dear."

"Stephan is waiting for exactly the right moment to sell." We giggled guiltily. We were holding hands and pretending not to be aware of it.

"Were you in love with him?"

"Who?"

"Franz Kline."

"No, of course not, Devi. I was married."

"How funny you are. Are you in love with somebody now?"
Our hands began to know what they were doing.

"I have a question for you. Why is it wrong to say, 'I know
what I like but I don't know why I like it'? Because I always
know what paintings I like, but I always find it difficult to say
why. I can't find reasons."

"No, but you're right. The reasons come after the love and
don't usually go very far to explain it. Most people talk too
much anyway. Do you know Rilke? 'A work of art is not to be
criticized but simply to be loved. It cannot be grasped by
intelligence; it can only be grasped by love.' "

"I talk a lot."

"You talk exactly the right amount for me."

When Stephan walked into the room he cleared his throat as
if making a declarative sentence. Our heads were together,
Devi's coarse wavy black hair against my skin. I was touching
his drawings, I wanted to see them with my fingertips as well as
with my eyes.

"I'll just go and have a pee," Devi said.

"Stephan, is he gay? He isn't."

"I don't know, dear. He was married once, or so he says. Are
you interested?"

"I love him."

"You'll come to Brooklyn Tuesday? Lucy will be home."

"Will it be a treat for me to come to Brooklyn?"

"It will be a treat for me."

I brought home a study in chalk and wash I had particularly
admired. (How generous he was in those days!) It was a drawing of two children of indeterminate sex in a playroom, their
pudgy hands grasping at window bars in a vain attempt to
escape, disregarding an open door through which they might
easily have gained freedom. On the nursery floor are dolls and
a rocking horse and blocks and scattered books, flyblown, their

pages blank. The children were so forlorn, their escape route so carefully marked and unheeded. That unenlightened misery convinced me of Devi's need for happiness—and almost seemed to guarantee me mine.

When Lucy saw the drawing, she said, "I can make two words from the letters on the building blocks—*gay*, and *sex*. " "Oh dear," I said; but it was already too late. Happiness had made me arrogant.

Happiness had made me ruthless. The morning after I met Devi I called to break a date with a doctor I'd been seeing, a man with all the proper qualifications except the ability to inspire love in me. I had spent a fruitless six months trying to persuade myself into the appropriate feelings, knowing that all I felt for him was a combination of affection and lust, insufficient to his needs and to mine. He loved me and I didn't love him; it is not at all to my credit that I find it more comfortable when it is the other way around. He called three times in vain appeal and in an attempt to wrest some clarity and kindness from me. The fourth time he called, Lucy hollered gaily from across the room, "Tell him you like somebody else better now!" I decided not to get angry at her, manners aren't everything. "You won't go to bed with him anymore now that you like somebody else better, will you?" Lucy said. I've always found it hard to live up to Lucy's standards of morality. This time I found it easy: "No, I won't. How do you know I like somebody else better?" "Because you look the way you look when you come home from church."

"Oh dear."

Stephan called to invite me to a party. I accepted knowing that Devi would be there.

"Where's Devi?"

"Out, dear. What a marvelous dress, is it new?"

"No, old. You ought to recognize it, I wore it when I was a character witness at your trial." Stephan had, several years before, been arrested by a plainclothesman in a bathroom in Macy's.

"I do remember thinking at the time that it was more appropriate for a cocktail party than for a trial, now that you mention it. Pity, wasn't it? that you weren't called upon to testify. And you'd come all the way from Brooklyn, such an effort."

"But lucky for you that the judge was bored and all you had to say was that you'd gone to West Point. Where's Devi?"

"I am not his keeper. . . ."

"I'm glad to hear it. . . ."

"But I think he said something about the Village. For a touch of low life, one assumes."

"Did he know that I would be here? Did he say anything about me?"

"No, my poor dear. He hasn't said a word about you, hasn't mentioned you at all. I am glad you didn't bring the doctor person with you, so hairy, hair on his knuckles. And so bor-ing."

"He's a very nice man, Stephan. With very short legs."

So Stephan and I settled in for a gossip—during the whole of which I enjoyed myself immensely and foresaw that I would later loathe myself—until his guests arrived. After dinner (champagne, caviar, steak tartare, Brie, watercress salad, bil-berries in cream), we all went to see a film at the Asia Society. It was the worst Japanese film I'd ever seen ("so *shibui,* dear"), possibly the worst film ever made, definitely the worst film ever made (oh, Devi!), what was I doing here with all these dressed-up strangers? A sixteen-year-old Japanese flower child leaves her aged mother to search for love and life in the big city. She begs for rice and writes haiku and joins a circus and becomes a prostitute and marries a rich man and gets a letter from her mother who is starving to death, and writes her mother the distillation of her earned wisdom: Only the spirit matters, she says, not the body. She herself yearns for the pure simple life she left behind in the shack with one cooking vessel, she can-not bear her present wealth; she implores her mother to look closely at the last morsel of food she has, to find beauty in a grain of rice and so to die happily, accepting her fate and the unity of the universe, along with a can of salmon (which the girl decides after all not to send her). The girl is last seen brushing a tear from her eye with the sleeve of her kimono;

flashback to the hovel (pastel colors, reeds). Running time: two and one half hours. Afterward we had bad champagne, and then we went in Stephan's Mercedes to an artist's loft in SoHo (photographed in *Esquire*). The artist painted nothing but shoes—giant oil canvases, all of them shoes: high-button shoes, sneakers, spike heels, workman's boots, babies' booties. I decided to make myself obnoxious. I stood in front of a painting of scarlet satin pumps, as if lost in a reverie (anyone can play this game), and said to the artist, my voice purring with falseness I was sure he would detect, "Oh, it's *brilliant!* It's a rose and a uterus and life's blood, of course you had the war in mind too. . . ." "You *understand!*" he said. "You *see* it! *God,* I was praying someone would! You *understand!*" I left the party without saying good night to Stephan.

Devi came on Tuesday as planned. I had, in the intervening days, been plagued by the twin demons of jealousy and posses-siveness (where in the Village had he gone? to whom?), which fled when I saw his face. (Always I had only to see his face for history and doubt to be wiped away.) Something else had happened in his absence (of course my love had multiplied in his absence): Devi himself contrived, in his absence, to impose restrictions on my otherwise overactive curiosity; he had presented himself in my imagination as someone both fragile and forbidding. The tenderness I felt for him precluded my asking questions. You will assume that this was because there were things I didn't want to know. And yet I am prepared to swear that there was nothing about Devi I chose not to know and also to swear that I believed I knew everything important that there was to know already (facts were not important). I kept my silence to give him peace; and because to do otherwise would have been to lose him.

I told him this years later. I said, "I was watching *Rebecca* on television last night, and it made me think of you—aside from the fact that you look like Olivier. . . ."

"Carry on. I don't, of course, at all."

"Yes, you do—like Heathcliff, exactly."

"I thought you said I looked like some Etruscan god at the Uffizi?"

"Well, a combination. You look like everyone who is beautiful."

"Yes?"

"Well, I was thinking what a ninny Joan Fontaine was. Why didn't she just say, 'OK, Danvers, what's up?' Why didn't she just ask her husband, 'Do you love me? Did you love Rebecca more? What's going on around here? What *happened*?' It really was exasperating, Devi, to watch someone agonizing when all she had to do was ask a few simple questions. Even Lucy said. And yet that was exactly the way I behaved with you. I had an editor once who told me I was an Aristotelian and not a Jansenist, so I had to have answers to questions, but I never asked you any questions, so I don't know what he could have meant. Which only goes to prove . . ."

"Oh, balls. You just like to create excitement for yourself. Besides, you have always known all about me. And Joan Fontaine didn't have the benefit of the Lib to tell her how to behave. Isn't that what you do? Write advice for the liberated women of America?"

"Who, me? When I think of all the things I still don't know about you . . ."

"I don't understand your attachment to the Uffizi. When I was at the Acropolis Museum—I must have told you this—I decided that if I could produce one, just one, piece of work as magnanimous and authoritative as that fifth-century B.C. relief of two lions ravaging a horse—I wish I had a postcard to show you—I should be happily drained of ambition forever. But I suppose I should still want to be paid an enormous amount of money for it—as incompatible a set of ambitions as ever there were. Like wanting to cross the street while remaining on the same side."

"I notice that you've changed the subject."

"I can always change the subject when I am with you because you know all about me and I know all about you."

"I notice that the subject always seems to be you."

"And do you notice that you always try to bring it around to you?"

I do not know what Devi thinks he knows about my past. I have had several versions of his past, some of them (I think) given me by him, at least one contributed by Stephan, and some, no doubt, invented by me: He was one of seven children, the others girls; his mother dressed him in girls' clothes and ribbons. He is an only child; his mother dressed him in girls' clothes and ribbons. All of his sisters live in India, three of them married to rich industrialists. All of his sisters are poor. He has three sisters; they live in Surrey. He has a brother. He has a brother and six sisters. He has two brothers. He has had no education. He was educated by Brahmins. He has had a rigorous Episcopalian education. He was a street urchin in Hyderabad, sought after for his beauty, seduced by a middle-aged Englishman, brought to England to study at the Slade. His father was a well-to-do businessman who sent him to Oxford. He was a virgin when he married, his marriage was arranged in Pakistan; he left the girl. He married a Muslim girl in England so that she could get working papers; the girl left him.

When, years after we met, I pieced the facts together—when his love for me was (or so he said, and I believed him) no longer the central truth of his existence, so that he was able, carelessly, to tell me the facts because the truth (he said) no longer mattered—the facts did not alter my feelings. He told me once that there was a village in India in which there were three crocodiles that had grown out of lice that had fallen from the beard of a Sufi pir who'd stopped there a thousand years ago. If he had told me that *he* had been spawned by lice or by a crocodile, or conceived by a saint, it would have made no difference to my feelings; there was a time I might even have half-believed that he believed his story.

He told Lucy, that Tuesday night, happy stories. He told her the story of Rama and Sita and Hanuman the monkey god, a story of saintliness and villainy, a love story Lucy had learned from her ayah before she was weaned, though she forbore to

tell Devi so, because she too felt immediately protective of
him, in part, at least, because of his beauty—"a lotus face,
Mommy, like in the Ramayana stories. I wish I had black eye-
lashes, can I try some mascara?" Lucy was always happy to
hear the story of Sita's long imprisonment by demons and
Rama's arduous search for her—although Devi dwelt rather
more on the demoness Shurpanakha than ayah had done:
"Shurpanakha said, 'Rama, Sita is unsuitable for you. If you
will become my husband, I will eat Sita up, and we shall be
happy forever.' So Rama's brother Lakshmana cut off
Shurpanakha's ears and nose. How not gentle our gentle
Hindu gods are! Like me, Lucy, so do I have a quick temper.
Am I not gruff? No? Yes. Though I fancy myself Rama, not
Lakshmana—the hero of course, not Tonto but the Lone
Ranger, though I fear I am doomed to be Tonto forever, what
do you think? No? Ah, lovely girl." Lucy—who always believed
she could somehow reshape the past, even though she was
sophisticated enough to understand how little control she had
over the present—was as shocked and dismayed as she'd been
the first time she'd heard the story when Devi got to the part
where the demon Maricha turned himself into a beautiful
golden deer to lure Sita away from Rama; and Devi, who was
holding Lucy's feet as he told the story—"wonderful bubbly
toes, like little animals, Lucy"—anticipated her and said, "But
the delicious golden animals always captivate us, Lucy, no
matter how clever we are, no matter how good. . . . Come,
Angela, it is only a story." And Lucy almost cried when the
demons cut off the wings and legs of the vulture Jatayu for
coming to Sita's aid; and she loved the noble stricken bird for
saying, " 'Despair not, Rama, for in that moment Sita was
taken from you, in that moment is the seed of your finding her
again.' . . . *In our end is our beginning,* isn't it, Angela? . . . All
empty were the groves and the caves and the forests without
Sita; and Hanuman and thousands of monkeys built a bridge
across the boiling ocean to where the demons had taken Sita,
who was heartbroken, Lucy, thin as a dime without Rama, but
always faithful. And the bridge remains, even the British
couldn't change that. And when they were reunited they were

as happy as we are now, and the land was ruled in justice, and never did the old bury their young. . . . She who listens to this tale with solemnity will live in amity with all and be freed from sin." Lucy said a solemn Amen, and we felt like a family.

A stranger, looking in that Tuesday night, insensitive to my suppressed excitement and to his, might have supposed that we had been comfortable lovers, even married lovers, for years. Devi with his sinewy arms elbow deep in sour cream and curry sauce, licking his fingers, offering me a thumb, then the palm of his hand, to lick. Devi drawing with Lucy. (I am looking at that drawing now. Outlined by him, roughly colored in and embellished by her, it is of a man muscular and naked to the waist, holding the reins of a giant bird, which he sits astride. Happy bird, happy man: he straddles the bird's strong neck, which looks like a huge, erect cock. Lucy has colored the cock orange.) Devi kissing Lucy good night, and giving her a spoonful of yogurt for pleasant dreams, and reciting to her the Collect for Aid against the Perils of the Night: "Lighten our darkness, we beseech thee, O Lord, and by thy great mercy defend us from all perils and dangers of this night." Devi playing Bach on the piano while I smoke the grass he has brought. Devi lying with his head in my lap watching television.

We are watching a documentary. A woman whose child has died is visiting a therapist. The woman wears a starched flowered housedress; her hair, false gold, is artfully arranged in corrugated ridges; her earrings, little bells, tremble when she speaks. Her daughter burned to death. "Josie died," she says, in a flat Midwestern accent, "when the forsythia was in bloom, and now I can never see forsythia, never, without thinking of her, and I can never walk into her room, and I can never see other children without thinking of her. I wake up every morning expecting to see her." The little bells tinkle as she sobs. "Never, never, never. Every day, every day, she is with me every day. Always, always, always." The doctor smiles. His ankles are neatly crossed. He has a goatee. In three days he will cure her of her grief. His manicured hands caress a paperweight. His cultured voice is soft, it beats against her sobs. "She is dead," he says. "You will never see her again, never. Say that, say those words. Say, 'I will never see her again. Never.' " "I-will-never-see-her-again-Josie-never. Never. Oh God. She had such a fresh mouth, she answered me back, I want to hear her fresh mouth again. I want her back." The doctor smiles, he caresses his goatee: "You will never hear her voice again, never. Say that, say those words: 'I will never hear her voice again.' " The woman rocks, holding herself, back and forth; the bells swing: "I will never hear her voice again." "Say, *'never.'* " "Never." It is the next day; she is wearing the same dress. On a polished table there is a ginger jar full of forsythia. The woman's eyes look like caged birds. "Do you use lemon wax?" she says. He smiles: "She is dead." "Josie is dead." "You will never see her again." "I will never see her again." "You will never hear her voice." "I will never hear her fresh voice. . . . There was a song she loved, she sang it all the time —'Raindrops Fallin' on My Head.' . . ." The doctor nods benevolently. His clothes are perfectly tailored. The woman produces a photograph for him. Her hands, like two small wild animals, disturb her sprayed and lacquered hair. "Look at the photograph," he says, his voice a whisper. "I can't." "Look at it." "Oh God." "Tell her how much pain she has given you. Send her away. Tell her you are sending her away." "I don't want to say good-bye." "You have to." "I cry when I make the pancakes. I don't want to cry anymore. . . . I don't want to say good-bye." "Tell her." "Josie, I don't want to say good-bye. I have to. You have to go. I have to stop crying." Her hands come to rest in her lap, her palms turned upward. She turns her face to the wall. Now it is the next day; on the polished table there is a photograph. "Oh God." She is wearing a polyester pants suit. Her hands are empty, they pick at threads. He plays a record: "Raindrops Fallin' on My Head." She listens, dry-eyed. "Thank you," she says. "I got sick when I knew what you were going to play. But I can listen to it now. It's a snappy tune."

Devi and I say nothing while we watch the news. I feel transformed; I feel as if the future is entering into me now, and that I am being prepared for some great grief. I am thinking, Where did her pain go? In church we are taught to offer our pain to God, Who will know what to do with it, and Who despises no gift. I am thinking: If she believed, she could keep Josie and give her pain to God. She could pray for Josie and pray to Josie. I am thinking of the first man who ever loved me, to whom I never pray. I am thinking of how he labeled—in that fine hand, which knew exactly what it was about to do—boxes and boxes of papers for me, his diaries; lines from a Whitman poem he loved handwritten on blue notepaper in an envelope on one of the boxes: "Know you I salute the air, the ocean and the land, Every day at sundown for your dear sake my love. I love you, before long I die. . . ." In the morning they found him, his brains blown out of his head. We are watching the weather report; the man who killed himself used to say that Hopper knew how to paint the weather, that you always knew what the temperature was in his paintings, and I am wondering idly whether to tell Devi this, while all the time I am thinking: Loss.

Devi sighs and rubs his forehead against my thigh, and turns to me: "You are so beautiful in this light, almost Indian. Have you ever loved someone who died?"

"Yes."

"Will you tell me?"

"Another time." I want to give him my pain. I want to tell him my life, I want him to explain my life to me. Not now. He brushes my hair from my face and kisses my forehead, my cheeks: "You have been crying." "Yes." He kisses my lips, soft, full, our tongues do not quite engage.

He says, "He was a silly man."

"The doctor? Yes."

"A bad man?"

"I think so."

"Shall we always agree?"

"I think so."

"When we are old, what shall we do? Shall we sit together on a porch in Kansas in matching rocking chairs and watch the corn grow? Would you like that? Would you be happy?"

"Yes. With you. Why Kansas?"

"For the ordinariness of it. But a villa on the Med if you prefer."

"Oh yes. A magnificent ordinariness."

Lucy cries out in her sleep. I go to her and kneel and gentle her. Devi watches from the doorway. I am covering her with a sheet that smells of verbena and I hear the sound of his light breathing and I am thinking: He loves me. He pulls me to my feet, embraces me, takes my hand. "Anywhere but London," he says.

"Why not London?"

"Because it's hard for me to be the person I am in London," he says. "It's so much freer here. The Village." I do not ask him what he means because I know what he means. "Though there are certain difficulties. Stephan doesn't like me to have friends in the apartment, he disapproves. Shall I get a flat on your street?"

"I suppose Stephan wants to go to bed with you."

"He will have to find other uses for me, he will find a way to fuck me over without bed, never fear."

"Would you like to sleep here tonight? There's a bed in the spare room."

"Another time—Friday, not now. I am too happy now to stay."

"Too happy?"

"How funny you are. When we are old, happiness will not matter so much, we will rock on our porch in Kansas and grow withered and gray and we will be so happy we will not even think of happiness."

"On the Mediterranean. I love you."

"I love you. Will you teach me how to be ordinary? Will you tell me my life?"

"Yes."

# Chapter Two

Devi told me he loved me; and I believed him. One of the few principles to which I have remained steadfast all my life is to believe what people tell me of themselves. You will think this is unimaginative of me; in fact, imagination never operates so freely as when one takes another at his word: I am given an outline of a person (which is all anyone ever really provides); I fill the rest in (to suit my needs, Devi would say). You will say that I err, erred, in not understanding that many meanings can be housed under the word love; and to that charge—the charge of simplemindedness—I plead guilty. I believed, then, that love implied action. I was innocent, and greedy, then. In my rage for happiness, I was prepared to sacrifice the simple joys that made my life an almost pretty thing.

I saw him two, three, sometimes four times a week, after that first Tuesday; when I did not, his absences went unexplained. Sometimes he spent the night, usually on the hard Empire sofa in the living room. When he slept in the spare room next to mine, I heard his breathing; on those nights I slept not at all. More often, he left me, his mood exalted—full-mouthed kisses, vows of love. On those nights, I did not grieve for desires unsatisfied; I slept as one drugged.

Of those first months with Devi, I remember bright images, cameos. I remember only scenes, not a life. He was my life. Lucy was the earth I drew nourishment from; he was the sun I inclined toward, aspired to. He blinded me. I thought I was seeing more than I had ever seen before. Years later, Lucy said to me, "Devi replaced God in your affections, that was clear." "How was that clear? I went to church." "Not always you didn't. Anyway, whose name did you say in church?" I said

Devi's name. "I prayed for Devi's happiness and salvation."
"Why not for mine?" Lucy said. "In those days I was lazy—as
to practice, not as to belief." "The two can't be separated,"
Lucy said. "You are not lazy as to practice now, and if you were
then, you were fooling yourself as to the sincerity of your
belief. You used it when it suited you." Of course she was right.

He is waiting for me in front of a theater. My taxi, caught in
rush hour traffic, is an hour late. He is waiting for me as if he
would happily wait forever; and as if he knows I will always
come to him, wild horses and traffic jams.
"Do you cry in the cinema?" he asks.
"I cry when I watch the Miss America contest."
"And not at funerals?"
"Not at funerals."
"No sad songs tonight."
"If you say so. Am I allowed to talk during the movie?"
"You take your lead from me. Don't be nervous, act as if I
were a girlfriend of yours."
"You're making me self-conscious."
"Good. It gives me the advantage."
*Notorious.* Cary Grant kisses Ingrid Bergman. Devi holds my
hand between his thighs, and: "Do you know why two Poles
couldn't make love? They were waiting for the swelling to go
away." "Devi, you are a racist Wog." His penis grows swollen;
my hand lies passive, in beautiful captivity.
Cary Grant kisses Ingrid Bergman; and he whispers, "Have
you heard the one about the two taxis that crash? The driver of
one shouts, 'Haven't you got a horn?' and the driver of the
other shouts back, 'What, looking at you?' " Ingrid Bergman is
dying. Devi squeezes my hand with his thighs, releases it, and
kisses my hair.
On the way out of the theater he pauses in the lobby: "I want
you to see one of the ushers. I had a lovely long look while I
was waiting for you. See? Isn't he cute?"
We go afterward to P. J. Clarke's for a drink; it is crowded,
and he can't make his way to the bar. He is all at once morose.
"I don't know how to do this," he says. "If I were at home in

my local, drinking with the boys, I'd know what to do. I don't know how to act the part of a man."

"I hate this place, Devi."

We walk silently for deserted miles, his encircling arm pressing me against his side. "Nobody knows how to behave well in those bars," I say, "except those that do, and they are the terrible ones." "You are good," he says. "Stephan took me to Elaine's." "And?" "I hated it, pretentious talk, trendy writers striking poses, everybody showing off, and bad food, and Stephan in a snit because he didn't get a good table and Woody Allen didn't bow to him. Nice to think of you real and safe at home. How beautiful this city is! Race me to the corner."

"I'm too old for that. Why didn't Stephan get a good table? poor Stephan."

"Old? You? Never. Look at that building, how beautiful it is."

In the taxi, crossing the Brooklyn Bridge, the skyline burns hot and icy; a white freighter, all dressed up and somewhere to go, is ablaze with light. "How beautiful this city is!" He sighs contentedly, rests his head on my shoulder, his hand lightly cupping my breast, and falls instantly asleep, snoring gently. When we reach my house, he wakes up as immaculately as a cat. "I'll stay tonight, if you'll have me." He stops at my door: "This is how it's done." He carries me across the threshold, traverses the narrow hallway, plumps me down on my double bed. "Put on your nightie," he says, "I'm going to listen to music." I fall asleep in the pale blue light of dawn, listening to the sounds of a Bach sonata. I dream of a ship that is a wedding cake, tiers of whiteness and flame. Devi and I are the porcelain figures on the cake, enshrined, like Donne's lovers, in an endless embrace; we are fuel and fire too. The ship sails off, alight, into the soft and welcoming dark. When I awake, he is gone. On the coffee table is a pastel sketch of me on lined looseleaf paper; I am smiling, wearing a flowing blue robe, a scepter in my hand. In his barely decipherable calligraphy he has left a message: "Read Gerard Manley Hopkins: 'The Virgin Mary Compared to the Air We Breathe.' . . . Lapis Lazuli ought to be a place, oughtn't it? Like Leptis Magna, or Paradise Lost."

Stoned on grass, we are watching a television documentary
about Blake. His head in my lap, he says, "The only visionaries
I've met who believe in the validity of their work are politically
committed ones. I, on the other hand, do not believe in the
validity of my work, am not politically committed to anything
—a soft-core Marxist isn't a Marxist at all—and have had only
one vision all my life: you. All the artists I encounter are cynical
or manipulative. The best of the lot are embittered. Whereas
you put your money and your mouth in the same place." My
mouth has only one desire now, and it is not to discuss the
relationship between politics and art. "Of course that's why
you're rare," he says, "or aren't you? I have never met a
visionary who wasn't fey, therefore boring. Do I ever bore
you? I move in degenerate circles. But I can't dislodge myself.
Are you in love with him?"
    "In love with who?"
    "Blake."
    "Jesus Christ, Devi, you do say the most astonishing things."
    "All those calluses collected along the way. Where were you
ten years ago?" He tosses his head on my lap angrily, like a dog
shaking off water. My vaginal muscles contract involuntarily.
He digs his fingers into my calf. Then he curls into a fetal
position and goes easily into sleep, smiling. In his sleep he
holds his genitals. I do not sleep. He awakens to the empty
buzz of the television, the station pattern "like a mandala," he
says. My neck and back are aching. He kisses me lightly on the
lips, his morning breath sweet and fresh. "Delicious sleep," he
says. "Do you know," I say, turning my face from him so that
he will not smell my sour breath, "that the French keep apples
near the bed to eat in the morning so their kisses will taste
good?" "And this is Eden," he says, "and you are Eve." He
cooks scrambled eggs and fries bread for me and Lucy, and
then he goes away.

# Chapter Three

On Lucy's twelfth birthday, Stephan gave a party for her at the Metropolitan Opera Club. Devi was not there. Neither Lucy nor I knew more than eight of the fifty people Stephan had assembled for the occasion. Opera singers gave Lucy autographed albums of their performances; a Canadian ballerina gave Lucy a pair of tiny red plastic ballet slippers and an 8 by 10 glossy of herself dancing Giselle. Stephan fastened a gold necklace with a single small diamond that burned with a pure, discreet flame around Lucy's neck and gave her a Bergdorf-wrapped Lady Remington underarm shaver, which she opened, to her intense humiliation, in front of a handsome baritone. The room was full of daisies. In a far corner stood a man, short-limbed, hunchbacked, whom nobody seemed to know, his deformities declared by a hot-pink tuxedo, a raspberry ruffled shirt, and a lavender cummerbund. Lucy warned me not to stare, because "he looks like a strawberry sundae, you'll laugh." He looked like Toulouse-Lautrec. I stared, and we were both overcome with funeral parlor giggles, whereupon Stephan produced Lucy's birthday cake: a WASP confection if I ever saw one, a bland white seven-layer cake with gritty sugar icing. Starving Lucy, drunk on champagne, told a coloratura about the meal her grandmother had prepared for her birthday—"antipasto, calamari in vinegar and oil, which are so pretty you can't eat them, and fennel which is Italian licorice celery, and manicotti that my Aunt Milly makes in a little machine—she never got married—and cannoli, and then we played poker, I had a full house." When the party dispersed, Stephan took us to an "intimate party of very dear friends," all of whom were male, none of whom Lucy and I knew. The living room of the house in the Village to which Stephan brought us had a mirrored ceiling, mirrored walls, plush turquoise-blue sofas, and black marble obelisks and spheres of varying sizes. A Filipino houseboy produced a seven-layer white cake with gritty white sugar icing and twelve turquoise-blue candles, whereupon Lucy vomited.

In the taxi riding home, presents piled around us, Lucy, pale with fatigue, allowed herself to be held like an infant. Huddled on my lap, her moist face buried in my neck, she said, "I think I'm getting too old to enjoy Stephan's parties."

I did not see Stephan after this party for three months, his martyred phone calls notwithstanding.

The morning after the party, Lucy woke me up looking both mysterious and confiding. She climbed into bed with me and we held each other while her first menstrual blood—bright red, unlike my own dull rusted-iron effluence—stained my sheets. We are like siblings now, I thought, twin planets circling each other; where she is, I have been, flesh of my flesh. Dear God, let her be happy.

"Mommy. Tell me about when I was born."

"You were beautiful, perfect, only five pounds, skin the color of an eggshell and thick black hair. When you were two days old I took you out on the terrace of my hospital room and held you up so you could see the ocean."

"Do you think that's why I'm a good swimmer?"

"Yes. Maybe. I love it that you can do all the things I can't do. The only time in my life that I wasn't afraid of anything was when I was pregnant with you."

"You're so good to me, Mommy."

"That's easy, there's nothing about you that frightens me. The doctor said you were too small to nurse, but the first time I held you, you just clamped your mouth on my nipple and sucked and sucked."

"Did it feel good?"

"Wonderful."

"It didn't hurt you when I was born?"

"Not a bit. You just slid out, you were in such a hurry."

"You weren't scared?"

"No. I knew you would be perfect. I used to be scared of everything, all the time. I was afraid that snakes would get me or bats or a tidal wave. . . ."

"Like now, you are."

"Yes, now. But when you were in me, all my fears went away. It was like being on a holiday from myself, do you understand? And I'm better now than I used to be, not so scared. When you were very little, you said to me, 'Your mother is afraid of everything, and you're afraid of a lot of things, and I'm afraid of some things, and my daughter won't be afraid of anything.' You can't imagine how I loved you for that."

"Do you think it's true?"

"Well, I think it was a gorgeous thing to say, and for you to have said it means it's at least partly true. I hope it's true. It gave me courage, anyway. Do you have cramps?"

"No. Do you think I'll have a happy life?"

"Yes." I crossed my fingers. I thought of something my father had said to me when I was only slightly older than Lucy: "The world eats up smart, pretty girls like you." I thought of Devi. I prayed that Lucy would, if just for this day, not have an inkling of the pity and terror I felt for her bright youth, for the goodness she wore like armor, for the compromises my sweet fierce daughter—with her sanguine curiosity, her need to believe in the goodness of the world—would have, someday, to make. I thought of how people would turn her goodness to their advantage, and I wondered, as one frequently does, whether goodness and happiness are the same thing. If they are, I thought, then nothing can ruin her.

"Mommy? Do you really think I'll have a happy life?"

"You'll have joy." That, at least, was not a lie. "Because you're good and you're brave and you're beautiful."

"So are you, but you were sad last night because Devi wasn't there."

"Oh, Lucy, I'm sorry. How terrible to be sad at your own party."

"It wasn't a party for me; it was a party for Stephan. This is a party. I think Devi loves you, though, because one night when

you were asleep I saw him take your shoe and he kept feeling it
and turning it around and around and then he kissed it."

"Oh dear."

"But Mommy, he's nice, but he's silly. He should grab you
and kiss you and hug you instead of boring, boring talk-talk,
paint-paint, sigh-sigh. . . ." Lucy was laughing hopelessly—
"talk-talk, paint-paint, sigh-sigh." She rained kisses on my face
so that I wouldn't think her laughter discourteous. Laughter
and wet kisses (my skin felt nourished by the meal she was
making of it), and: "So how do you know I'll fall in love with
somebody who loves me?" she asked.

"I don't. But I don't see how anybody could not love you."

"They can. Nobody liked me in third grade. But I think I'll
have a happy life. Do you die young when you get your period
old?"

It always amazes me when people fail to see the point of
children, the point of children being that they do no harm.

That night Lucy had a sleep-over party for seven girls. Devi
came, unannounced, with Japanese wind chimes and a sketch
of Lucy drawn from memory. He looked at the sleeping bags
that lined the living room floor.

"What's this?" Guarded panic in his eyes.

"Lucy's having a sleep-over. The girls are in her room."

"All girls? Seven girls?"

"Eight, including Lucy."

"I'll be leaving now."

"You haven't even said Happy Birthday to her."

"I just dropped by, no need to make a fuss."

"I'll call her."

Gales of laughter reached us from Lucy's room.

"Good night, Angela."

# Chapter Four

Why, a friend of mine asks, didn't you ever just grab him? It wasn't as if he never got a hard-on. Why didn't you just say, "I want to suck your cock." Why didn't you suck his cock?

One night I got very drunk; I had the flu. After our dinner guests had gone home, I staggered to bed, was violently ill all over the sheets, managed to find a clear space for myself in the mess, and fell heavily asleep. I don't know what I was aware of first, his voice murmuring my name, or the weight of his body on mine. His mouth was buried in my hair, he lay clothed between my legs, his hands, beneath my dress, had found my breasts. The room stank of vomit. He looked as if he were engaged in an intensely private rite. I, my dress rucked up around my thighs, felt like an interloper. My hand, like a leaderless army, reached for his sex.

"No."

"No?"

"No."

"Why?"

"I don't want to."

"Why?"

"You know what I am." His voice was only slightly reproachful. "I don't want to." He had traveled back very fast, very far, from the hot devotional world I'd surprised him in. He looked at me for a few moments quizzically, like a man emerging from a dark church into the brightness of a summer afternoon. "I don't want to."

If only he had said, "I can't."

I don't know why I thought, just then, of something Stephan had said: "Devi is really an Englishman with a brown skin.

Absolutely deadly, my dear. It allows him to want everything
and to despise everyone, especially himself. An exotic carnivo-
rous plant transplanted to an urban jungle. A very pretty man-
eating plant, of course, or one wouldn't trouble. Deadly. Poor
dears."

Did Devi despise me? He had only to look at me for me to
experience a transforming illumination. He was my familiar.
Not like the man I'd met in Cuernavaca after my divorce who
gave me yellow "herbal tablets"—speed—and then tried to
rape me, leaving on my stomach fingernail scratches that were
now delicate pretty pink splashes, the skin there like baby's
skin, more soft and tender than the surrounding flesh, as if
blessed, not violated. (My fingers often felt in the dark for the
soft pink rivers in the hard white flesh.) Not like the famous
and kindly sociologist in Chicago who made love to me so
expertly, so gently—and then, while I was still in love with his
hands, took a loaded revolver from beneath his pillow and
asked me to hold it, to aim at my image in the mirror. Not like
that; no.

Did he despise me?

The next morning, fever raging, I went to church, and tried
to pray, and, as had been the case since my divorce, made no
connection. Silence. And such a simple prayer: *Devi.*

I began to regard the evenings we spent together as normal,
as the particular reality reserved for me, better than other
people's reality, truer. I did not dream much in those days;
even my unconscious refused to analyze the data, as if to do so
would be a betrayal of him. I accepted what he gave. I did my
work, I loved my child, I waited for him. I confided in no one,
and spoke his name—the lover's disease, the need to utter—to
everyone. I cherished the thought that I had a great gift—the
gift of knowing how to love; and I saw this as humility, not
pride. I thought my love could heal.

To love such a man in such a way is idolatrous. Idolaters are
doomed; and in their doom lies the doom of the idol they
worship. I did not understand this.

Can lovers feed on air? I could not believe that my desire

would not ignite his own. I did my work, I loved my child, I waited for him. I learned to absorb the shocks he administered and still to stand upright.

Coming home from early dinner at our favorite restaurant we see strolling toward us a young man walking his poodle. A young woman, splendidly pregnant, walks by, regal with the casual arrogance of fertility. The sun and moon hang together in the sky, an oppressive late twilight, the sun casts no shadows, the moon no light; small children go to bed now, and women prepare meals. The young man stops nonchalantly, his dog's leash lax in his hand. Devi stops nonchalantly to admire the dog. I stand off to one side. This is not the air I breathe. On Devi's face there is an expression both furtive and bold as he and the young man exchange banal pleasantries; there is a look in his eyes I have not seen before, feral and conspiratorial. His tongue flicks against his upper lip; an answering flick from the young man with the dog. I feel as if I am floating far above my body, contemplating this scene through layers of protective mist. I reenter my body when Devi takes my arm, and sighs: "Do you love this time of night? I do." "No. It's a time for lovers or families and we are neither." He looks at me, frightened, and says quickly, "Of course we are. Both." Is it strange that I believe him? and that I am immediately comforted? and that I feel I must now comfort him? "Of course you're right; we are both."

We are walking along the Promenade, looking at the skyline, "How beautiful!" It is foolish to walk here so late at night; last week a woman's jugular was slit, the razor slice so fast, decisive, clean, she did not even know it had happened until she saw the blood gushing freshly and felt it warm and sticky on her blouse. But I am not afraid, because Devi is here; I will not die a New York death, sudden, violent, neat: Devi is here.

"What happened to the woman?"

"Someone found her just in time, and did something with a handkerchief, a kind of tourniquet, and took her to the hospital. The muggers only got three dollars from her purse."

"As you have found me just in time," he says, "and I have no loose change in my pockets, you have it all." While I am unraveling this sentence—am I his midnight mugger or his rescuer? or both?—three men run up to us and thrust a Gay Liberation pamphlet in our hands. Devi carefully folds his and takes mine from my blind hands, rolls it up, and with it slaps me lightly on the ass. "There's a locker room treat for you," he says. It is dark, he cannot see the angry tears that sting my eyes.

And yet we are congruous; how like a family sometimes! Lucy and I go with him to a gallery opening. The walls are covered with blown-up photographs of subway graffiti. Artists arrive wearing very much or very little. A famous writer known as much for his well-publicized brawls as for his books stalks and scowls in an impeccably tailored black tuxedo, searching for a famous enemy; a famous dilettante known for being famous wears paint-splattered jeans elegantly, and in a nasal Westchester boarding school drawl expounds on populist art; a famous rock singer arrives dressed in black satin toreador pants, black lipstick, and two giant white feathers pasted to the nipples of her very small breasts. Lucy sets her lips primly and clings to Devi. In the middle of the gallery there is one bare white wall; in front of it are two small black kids—fourteen? fifteen?—looking lost and angry, dressed in ragged clothes. Their sneakers have holes in them. The lighter-skinned kid has no socks; his ankles are dirty. They have been given two cans of spray paint with which to re-create subway graffiti on the walls of a Madison Avenue gallery. Black waiters circle around them, uncertain as to whether to offer them champagne. People mill around them, smiling brightly at a point just above their heads, and saying, *"Marvelous!"* though, so far, proud or defiant, the children have yet to make a mark on the naked wall. Lucy, her eyes hard and watery with shame and determination, approaches the black boys and says in a quavering voice, "I'm twelve, do you think they'll let us have champagne?" Devi says to them, in a loud, clear voice, as a patrician art critic walks by, "Bugger them all." One of the kids activates his can of orange spray paint, and, hushed expectation surrounding him, rapidly sketches a word on the virgin white wall: "FUCK." *"Marvelous!"*

"What should we have done?" Lucy asks.

"What could we have done?" I reply.

"Condescending obscene rich white bastards," Devi says. "Stephan's bloody foundation had its bloody hand in this."

I know Stephan had nothing to do with this, but I cannot convince Devi, who says, "That white bastard, of course he did," and glares at me.

"Will they go home alone?" Lucy asks.

"They won't get any money for their work—you can be bloody sure of that," Devi says.

"They didn't even get any champagne," Lucy says.

We ride home in a depressed silence.

In our kitchen, Devi, suddenly buoyant, says, drawing us together with his energy, "Curry!" Lucy chops onions for him, a slice of bread in her mouth. She has convinced herself that Wonder bread will absorb the odors and keep her from crying, although her tears are dripping on the mushy white bread. I mince cucumbers for salad, careful first to slice off the stem end and rotate it against the flesh of the remaining whole; the bitterness—I learned this in India—all goes into the severed end. Lucy says, her voice muffled by gluey bread, "You're not like those other artists, Devi."

"No? Good."

"Why do you paint?"

"I used to paint because I loved to paint, then I learned I could make money at it. Then I hated the things I had to do to make money, and the people—you saw—but now everything has come right again because of you and your mother. I am making money for our old age."

"And making beautiful paintings, too," says Lucy, to whom old age is a mirage. It is as difficult for her to believe that some day she will be old as it is for her to believe that Devi and I were once young.

"Yes, sometimes even beautiful paintings," Devi says. We are all very happy.

During dinner, Devi sets out to make Lucy laugh: "Have I told you about my English dealer? She pretends she's Cockney when she's not pretending she's from Liverpool—actually she's the daughter of an earl and she lives in Mayfair—and she

brays: 'We don't give a fuck about middle-class bourgeois val-
ues; we're very up on Women's Lib, and we swear a lot.' She is
touchingly old-fashioned, sweet thing, like someone out of *The
Forsyte Saga.* 'I hear you're a freaked-out weirdo with ideas and
that's a compliment.' . . . Do you like my accent, Lucy? . . .
I met her at a gallery opening full of people in spike heels and
green nail polish. The trouble is, I disliked her as much as I
disliked the others, because anyone who has to wear her liberation on her tits—sorry, Lucy—is a bit suspect by me, though
suspect of what I don't know. Probably of nothing more than
not doing it my way. Which is after all quite some crime, yes or
no?" Lucy, to whom little of this makes sense, says, "Don't you
ever meet any nice normal people at parties? People who don't
wear liberation on their tits? or feathers? Sorry, Mommy."
(But she is delighted with her contribution to the conversation.) "I did at that party, yes. A nice Polish lady who was
illustrating a book on children's games. 'I must molest ze
children on ze streets,' she said, 'so they show me their games.'
She told me her life story, all about being in a camp and how
she could never return to Warsaw because of the bloody Com-
munists—they said she was a Fascist—and she asked me to go
to Poland 'and brink me back a handful of memories from
Warsaw where beauty and sorrow exist site by site.' Which I
doubt they do. That's the second accent I've done for you,
Lucy. Next I'll do a Brooklyn accent, shall I?"

He did. Badly.

"That's not a Brooklyn accent, Devi; that's an Indian accent.
Mommy can do a Brooklyn accent." And Devi indeed is mov-
ing his head in that lolling Indian motion that means Yes/No/
Maybe.

"Well, never mind," he says. "If things get too awful, I'll go
to Warsaw. We'll all go to Warsaw, would you like that, Lucy?"
Lucy wants to know how it's possible to be nice and a Fascist
too, and how much does it cost to fly to Warsaw. When she
leaves the room, Devi's mood plummets. "That child is growing up too fast."

"Mostly what she extracted from that conversation was that
you wanted to please her. She'll wake up in the middle of the

night and ask me how it's possible to be a good person and a Fascist, I don't see what harm thinking about things like that can do her. I don't even think taking her to the gallery was a mistake. She's too smart to be impressed by flash. You saw she understood that what they were doing to those black kids was disgusting."

"Rich white bastards . . . I think I'm a bad influence on her."

"Nonsense," I say, my voice lacking necessary conviction, wishing, for one treasonous moment, that Lucy could awaken each morning to the sight of a man in striped pajamas warm from my bed. I have never seen Devi brush his teeth, she will never quarrel with him over who gets to use the bathroom first, she needs a daddy.

"At least I'm not as bad as Stephan?" Devi says.

"Don't be silly, no comparison, you're good," I say, beginning to feel like a panderer. I sometimes wonder if he reads my thoughts.

"Of course mostly I take Lucy for walks in the park and cook curry for her, that's healthy, isn't it?"

"Of course."

"And she doesn't know what I am."

"I wouldn't be too sure of that, but so what if she does?"

"I make a fool of myself when I talk too much. The best thing for Lucy and me is to draw quietly together, no words."

"You do like her?"

"How funny you are. I love her."

"Well, then."

"Love doesn't increase one's capacity to behave intelligently."

"I don't agree with that, I think when you really love somebody nothing you can ever do can ever be the wrong thing. In the long run."

"Hmmm. Not true. Do you teach Lucy that nonsense? Perhaps I am good for her after all. As an antidote to you. You are as sentimental as Stephan."

I chose to ignore this. "Lucy," I said, "is at this very moment telling her diary how good life is. Most of her life is as ordinary as bread, take it from me."

"You are not ordinary."

"Oh yes I am."

"Perhaps you are, perhaps that's why I love you."

Lucy and Devi did the dishes. He taught her to sing "All Things Bright and Beautiful." I felt wonderfully ordinary because I am tone deaf and I couldn't follow their sweet high voices and they made gentle fun of me and we were all very happy again.

# *Chapter Five*

The wages of gratitude are hostility, I should know. My ex-husband, That Person, was so busy being grateful to me for extricating him from awkward situations he had very little time left over to love me. Perhaps I should not have allowed his problems to humiliate me, certainly I should not have used my charm to get him out of trouble. (But "should" is a word that operates very strangely within a marriage, particularly when one is young; and I had been very young.)

My ex-husband had a talent for getting drunk with the wrong people. He was a sentimental bully when he was drunk, and craven when he was hungover. I've often thought that the reason he became a reporter was to weight himself down with facts, to give ballast to his seesawing emotions, which, left to themselves, were apt to fly in all directions, as unconscious as a hurricane, and as destructive. Once, when we were living in Algiers, he got drunk with junior members of the foreign press corps, and they took us to a nightclub. It was immediately apparent to me—but not to my ex-husband—that the only women on the dance floor were prostitutes. The stringers were having a wonderful time; I had a stomachache. They urged him to dance with me; obviously determined to regard this as a second honeymoon, he kissed me wetly and sloppily on the mouth. (I hated those winy kisses, a benediction that seemed so much like punishment; my grandfather kissed me that way when I was a child—smelly, winy person, he always pinched my cheek hard, after his kiss, twisting flesh between rough, gnarled fingers, while my uncles laughed.) My husband led me protesting (but not very loudly) to the dance floor, where he clutched and grabbed and did a flamboyant tango, out of step with the music, of course. The prostitutes were vastly amused; smirks and leers from the Algerian reporters. I was angry and humiliated but pretended not to be. His colleagues thought I was a perfect wife and that he was a dope, but not such a dope after all, because he'd managed to hold on to me; another woman might have made a scene. I hated them all. Lucidity arrived with his morning hangover, as did self-pity: Had he made a fool of himself in front of his inferiors? "No." Was he a Terrible Person? "Of course not." Would I arrange to entertain his boss that week? "Yes." And I would be charming.

I was charming. I counted the days. It usually took him four days to pay me back for an incident of this kind, then his anger would flame from the ashes of his gratitude. Four days after the nightclub fiasco, he flirted outrageously with a pretty Peace Corps volunteer and told her I had two false teeth. Then he picked a fight with me over my using his dental floss, which escalated into, How can you possibly be a good mother (I was pregnant with Lucy) if you don't take care of yourself, you're lazy and sloppy, all you really want to do is lie in bed and eat chocolates. (He was right; all I really wanted to do was lie in bed and eat chocolates.)

Stephan, who was convinced that my ex-husband was gay (he was convinced that seventeen out of thirty-two presidents, including Abraham Lincoln, had been gay, as were Pope Pius XII, Walter Cronkite, Robert Redford, General Douglas Mac-Arthur, and Jesus Christ), provided the occasion for That Person's greatest social embarrassment, and therefore for our divorce. He'd allowed Stephan to take him to a gay bar, whips and leather and chains, from which the man whom he was wooing for an important foundation job unfortunately saw him emerge. What a tap dance I did after that! I told everyone, including the foundation person, that I was doing research on gay bars and had used my husband as a surrogate reporter. I beat my breasts, produced so many tears and so many pitiful explanations that I very nearly convinced my husband's prospective patron that he had really seen *me* emerging from a gay bar. (I have always been a gorgeous liar, but I like to tell myself that I lie only in the service of the truth. Devi says that I am

therefore the most pernicious of liars, and perhaps he is right.)
I had everyone sympathizing with That Person. And then I had
to write the damn story as proof, and my husband wanted to
know why the hell he had to take care of Lucy every night, till
the story was in print; then he was so grateful I was terrified.

He paid me back. The night he paid me back our marriage
ended—though he didn't notice it till three months later when
I found the courage to ask for a divorce. Three months later he
chose to have a political fight with me in the presence of my
Aunt Milly, a Goldwater Republican who'd never spoken the
names of the people who'd lived next door to her for twenty
years (she preferred to call them "those Jews"), and who firmly
believed that my daughter would grow up to be a hatchet
murderer because I'd not stopped Lucy from looking at a
photograph of John Lennon and Yoko Ono taken in the nude,
and because Lucy had once, when she was five years old,
demonstrated to Aunt Milly how pleasant it was to sit naked
with your legs crossed under you; you could tuck your heel
inside your vagina, which felt terrific. "You," my husband said
to me, "are a cynical bitch because you won't vote for Hubert
Humphrey. When you are more mature, you'll understand
that it's possible to have friends who support the war in Vietnam. The kind of political principles you have, you'd sacrifice
Lucy for the Jews next door if you had a choice."

"I want a divorce," I said.

There is very little more I want to say about my marriage
except that I met my husband when I was on a Catholic Worker
picket line supporting prisoners in the Women's House of
Detention; after the march he bought me lilacs and said that
my voice reminded him of Laraine Day's, and two months later
we were married. In all the seven years we were married, he
never once managed to kiss me on New Year's Eve; at twelve
A.M. he was always dancing with another woman or he was in
the bathroom. Sometimes he patted my head, as if I were a
dog, or an unhappy child; I asked him to, I wanted a maternal
husband. The gesture never quite succeeded in comforting
me. Sometimes I squeezed his pimples: I wanted to be a maternal wife. I was lonely all the time I was married to him.

On the other hand, I was not able to forget the time when Lucy was two and ran out of a beach house in Cozumel and reached a stretch of burning sand and screamed and screamed, terrified and unable to move. I did not run to her rescue—I was cowardly, and wasted precious time looking for my sandals, while Lucy, in her little red bathing suit, screamed and screamed, "Mommy, Mommy!" He ran to get her without a thought for himself—an incident that probably prolonged my marriage by about three years, and rightly so.

Devi's social ineptness was of a different order from That Person's, it existed solely in his perception of himself. The social insecurity that he bemoaned translated itself into an appealing modesty, his tentativeness into an aura of mystery, a graceful reserve that only added to his attractiveness. Shyness, in an extraordinarily beautiful person, is counted as a virtue; he borrowed from it a dignity and a stature he did not believe he had. It was not unusual, when we were out together, for waiters to order for him, for the right wine to appear as if by magic; ushers rushed him to the head of ticket lines; taxis appeared for him from nowhere. In those days, when he spent evenings with my friends, I was perfectly relaxed—so unlike the frightened years of my marriage when I watched words forming on my husband's lips, wondering whom next he would offend and wondering, too, what I could do to forestall him. I knew that my friends would feel rewarded by any words Devi cared to offer. Safe in the knowledge that anything he said was bound to increase his value in their eyes—nothing he said was offensive or calculated to offend, his manners were perfect —I felt protected. And any departure from conventional behavior was attributed to his being an Indian and an artist in a country not his own; it served to make him more interesting in other people's eyes. I flowered in his company; he was the sun who warmed and eclipsed me. I liked it that way. He never understood the effect he had on people, the ways in which they sought to please him; he never believed in his own charm because (I thought then) he never consciously exercised it.

One night we had dinner very late in the Village.

"Did you notice how the waiter told me what to order?"

"Yes. Suggested. As obsequious as if you were a crown prince."

"As patronizing as if I were a simple Wog, which is what he thought I was. I am. A real man would know how to order wine."

"Don't pout, Devi. That's a perfectly silly way to measure the worth of a man and you know it. I don't think you begin to understand the attention you command when you enter a room."

"It is you who commands attention, you seduce everyone with your smile. What is it with you and men? I am safe with you," he said, just as a premonition chilled my happiness— dear God, don't let him feel that he has reason to be grateful to me. "You will never do me any harm," he said.

"And I am safe with you."

"Truly?"

"Truly . . . Will you hold my hand? I'm afraid of the stairs."

"No wonder men marry women, you make us feel so smart, how clever you are. Do you love me as much as you love Lucy?"

"Yes." I crossed my fingers. Well, I thought, I can afford to be generous. Sooner or later it is the question they all ask: Do you love me better, best? "Yes."

"You are good. Do you want to see my haunts?"

We walked down Christopher Street, his arm around me. A short, crewcut young man walked past us, supporting himself on crutches. He wore a black leather jacket, a black leather belt heavily studded with brass spikes, and tight black leather pants, one leg of which ended abruptly at his knee. "Never mind," said Devi, who often did read my thoughts, "you can be sure that someone in this flesh market is looking for exactly him, a one-legged leather freak. He is someone's fantasy and he will spend the night in what passes for happiness. People looking for nightmares always find them. The freaks of the world are lucky, they can always find a trick, it is the ordinary people who suffer, looking for ordinary human love." (And what of me, "Betrothed without the swoon God sends us

women?" He walks these streets in nihilistic abandon after he
has left me. If he leads me into self-pity, I will hate him as
surely as his gratitude to me will lead him to hate me.)

Motorcycles blasted down the street. He spoke with savage
softness. Street lights turned Christopher Street into a Maigret
landscape, yellow pools of imitation sunlight surrounded by
darkness in which darker forms moved, met, joined. Transves-
tites walked by glowering balefully at us. "Nasty, nasty, nasty,"
one whispered as he/she minced by. Men walked hand in
hand, arm in arm; in that world we were an anomaly, we were
freaks and voyeurs both. Groups of men giggled at our approach, their thin laughter menacing. As we neared Sheridan
Square, a man parodying Gene Kelly—"I'm Singin' in the
Rain, Just Singin' in the Rain"—stopped in midsyllable as we
approached and called very loudly: *"Whore!"*

"Those street lamps kill trees. The trees think it is daylight
all the time; they die for lack of rest."

"Don't be afraid," Devi said.

"I am afraid. I don't want to hate it here and I don't understand it here."

"Sweet bourgeois lady. I am in a place I do understand. This
is my jungle. Wolves, predators. Where do you think I spend
my nights when I leave you?"

"You are melodramatic, Devi."

"And do you not think they are wolves and predators?"

I did, of course.

"It is easy for you to be liberal sitting behind your desk,"
Devi said, "but you don't like what you see here." I hated what
I saw here.

"Nor," I said, "do you, apparently."

"I expect no mercy."

"Perhaps if you asked for it?" But of whom? I was of no use.

"And where is my peace?" Devi said, pursuing his own obscure reasoning. "I left London to come out of the closet,
horrid phrase, how filthy ideology is, how coarsening. And I
walked into this. And you  .  .  .  I wish you understood Urdu so
that I could recite poetry to you. . . . I walked into you as if
you were a building, lights in all your windows."

"But you have not entered me."

"But you have entered me."

On Sheridan Square we embraced, holding each other so tightly. This is the way lovers must die when bombs are falling all around.

"Angela, save me."

"Teach me how."

"Will you walk with me to Stephan's house?"

On the way, he said: "But one loves them all the same."

"Loves them?"

"The freaks, the one-legged leather men of the world. In a funny way, you know."

The taste of his kiss lingered on my mouth: "Loves them?"

"The freaks, the one-legged leather men of the world."

"Because of the danger they place themselves in?"

"No. One loves them because nobody could. So somebody has to."

"Divine of you," I said.

"I beg your pardon?" When he was angry or injured his consonants became almost liquid, in that Indian way; traces of Oxford vanished, the street boy spoke. And it sounded, that lilting inflexion, like the language of love: "I beg your pardon?"

"I meant that literally—the point of God being that He loves those whom nobody else could."

"Divine is a fag's word."

"Nevertheless. Anyway it isn't."

"You are being literary, isn't it?"

"No."

He kissed me.

It was false dawn when we reached Sutton Place, the river a pearly gray, birds singing, "and all the rich people asleep in their comfortable beds," he said. "Angela . . ."

"Yes?"

"Just I like to say your name."

We tiptoed up the stairs past Stephan, who was an early riser, "smug Episcopalian full of the conviction of sin, such a buzz for him. He gets up early to prove to himself that he is not decadent."

"He only goes to church on Christmas Eve. I think."

"And takes Lucy?"

"Yes."

"And receives Communion?"

"Yes."

"And what do you think of that?"

"His face looks the same afterward, that always surprises me. After church he has a party."

"To wash away the taste of God."

I had not been in Stephan's guest apartment since Devi had made it his own—or, more accurately, quite remarkably not his own. Only the dressing room that connected bedroom to sitting room bore his mark. In a rectangular space the size of a box room, an easel had been placed; in the built-in, half-opened rosewood drawers and on the rosewood shelves that lined the room were tubes of paint, pens, pencils, rolled up canvases, a heap of drawing paper on the floor. From the skylight, the sky, opalescent, streaked with amethyst and rose, threw watery blue light on to the waxed plank floor; the walls were washed in aqueous light. The sitting room, masculine and tweedy, which Stephan had furnished as conventionally and impersonally as if it were a room in a Hilton hotel, bore no trace of human habitation except for an ashtray filled to overflowing with Marlboros burned to the filter tip, and the pressed remains of the cigarettes Devi rolled himself. On a kidney-shaped blond table were two mugs of coffee on which a wrinkled white skin had formed; in one of them a fly had drowned. I was surprised that a fly could find its way into Stephan's house, it seemed so impertinent of it. In the houses in which I had grown up, sticky fly paper hung from tin ceilings. I used to watch the flies die, their final whine like a mating call. Sometimes they twitched for twenty-four hours. I had never told Devi anything about those houses, about my family. He did not seem to wish to know.

There was a framed rosewood photograph of Stephan's dead mother on the wall, totally unexpected, and out of place,

like a marble statue crying human tears. She looked dewy and
vulnerable, smiling gently as if to overlook a multitude of sins.
The photograph—his memento mori?—made me feel sorry
for Stephan, lying quietly in bed a floor below; it reminded me
that Stephan too knew how to weep, it made me feel guilty
about being here. Stephan had after all been my friend for
many years.

"Do you like my garret?"

"There's not much room to paint, is there? Couldn't you use
the sitting room as well?" I had no idea what financial arrange-
ments Stephan had made with Devi; I'd heard no more talk of
dealers and galleries. "Or move somewhere else? This looks
like a suite in a Hilton hotel." There was a garden apartment
on my block. . . .

"Paint in the sitting room? And spoil Stephan's carpet?"

"I spoiled a rug of his once, he didn't seem to mind. I think
we're being unfair to him. Anyway you can always roll it up."

"I am stuck here," Devi said, "like that fly in that coffee, have
you ever seen a necrophiliac fly? do you know that live flies try
to mate with dead ones? soon that fly will be joined by a live
one, having it off."

"There is a garden apartment on my block. . . ."

"Stephan has bought me for the price of this flat, cheap at
half the price—a phrase which, think about it, doesn't mean
anything at all. If I am bought cheap at half the price, then I
come expensive, or I am worthless, think about it. . . ." Devi
paces up and down, banging his fist on polished surfaces,
surely he will wake Stephan up. He has been swigging from a
bottle of gin, he slices a piece of hash with a penknife, crum-
bles it, mixes it with his tobacco: "He pays me for none of my
work—well, a pittance, sometimes. 'Please, sir, may I have
some more?' But I am supposed to feel satisfied in this elegant
prison, I am supposed to express my gratitude by performing
for his friends, the educated Wog who makes pictures. Because
I am black. No physical favors, of course. The sex was over
between us long before I met you." He glares at me, as if I am
responsible for those lost years. "Because I am black."

"Because you are black?"

"You don't think he'd treat a white man this way. I have never in my life trusted a white person or loved a white person, only fucked them and accepted favors from them, I have no right to happiness. A garden apartment on your block. And no money for it."

My head is spinning from the hash and the harsh tobacco and the gin, also from Devi's insistence that he is black, which, unless words have lost all definition, he is not. "Lucy and I are white," I say.

"Ah, you. You are the only one. 'Caught in the strong toil of grace.' "

"And I have some money, and as for happiness, can't you choose it? Why don't you have the right?"

"You'd give me the money?"

"Of course."

"Of course you would. . . . I have something for you. I've been saving it." From among a pile of socks in a dresser drawer he pulls out a paperweight, a magic world enclosed in glass: Two tiny children stand in front of an even tinier house, a still tinier fir tree, and when I turn the paperweight upside down, snow flakes fall on the children, the house, the tree. "How did you know? I've always wanted one. It isn't the sort of present one buys for oneself; it's perfect. I had one when I was a child, I loved it so much, how good you are."

"I do know you. Would you be happy in that world with me?"

Alone in the world with him. "Well, but Lucy . . . Yes."

I want to talk about his happiness. He says, "No more words," and leads me to bed. We lie atop the down comforter, arms around each other, and as we drift together into sleep, bathed in bright sunlight, I feel as if I am entering the happy childhood I never had. "Who washes your socks?" I murmur sleepily. "Were you happy when you were little?"

"I put them in the dishwasher," he says, "and I am happy now."

That afternoon, riding on the Staten Island ferry, eating hot dogs, "Life with you is so simple," Devi says, "so good, it cannot possibly be real."

"But it is happening—here, have some french fries—so it is real."

"I have a friend in London," he says. "We share a flat. We used to have a commune" (he is weaving his fingers through my hair), "till people started falling in love. That ended our happiness. I fell in love with St. John."

*"Sinjin?"*

"S-a-i-n-t J-o-h-n. St. John."

"Nobody is called that in real life. He made it up. He's probably called Bruce. Or Dennis. I have never known anyone good who is called Dennis."

Devi tugs at my hair. "I have never heard malice from you before. Bitchiness doesn't become you. He and I have nothing to do with you and me, how silly you are."

"I wish he were dead." I don't speak these words, but Devi answers them: "No need. He's just a sad old stuffy Cambridge nelly, he didn't choose to be in love with me, now we live together like two spinsters, but, oh, it would be so nice. . . ."

"What would be so nice?"

"If he were in love with me. Surely people can make that choice?" He looks at me as ingenuously as a child.

". . . love me back," Devi says.

"I'm sorry?"

"You haven't been listening."

I have been listening too hard. I have heard nothing, nothing but the cry in my heart that demands clarity, the silent dusty shout that overwhelms the spoken word. What do I understand of human conversation? The man who killed himself gave me what I am, taught me what I know: Clarity! he demanded, his fist battering the desk, the blackboard, the wall; sometimes the chalk snapped. He chose me because I listened hardest—I was a good pupil—and I heard everything but his intent, I heard every word as if my life depended on it, not knowing that his life did, until, in his last letter, in that fine small hand that knew exactly what it was about to do, he announced, with bitter final clarity, that he was choosing death. (I have never told Devi about the man who killed himself. I have never allowed myself to think about what his lack of curiosity might portend.) Women desperately in love do not hear the cry behind the words, or, like good pupils erasing past mistakes, they hear a cry when none is offered. I understand neither my silences nor Devi's words. Even his touch is not enough. It cannot teach me anything. Only my tears are unambiguous. When Lucy had her accident, she never cried at all, through all the months of hospital pain, the arm she almost lost, the clotted skin grafted onto her wrist, the rubbery patch of skin peeled from her thigh like a pointillist painting; only afterward at home, at night, she cried, "Mommy, Mommy, are my eyes bleeding?" She screamed into the darkness through a veil of bloody pain. Why has he never seen that foreign skin; why does he not ask about her pain? I feel Lucy's pain now; my eyes are blind, bloody with my heart's need: He loves me/he loves me not.

". . . back to England. 'Across the black waters.' Will you let me go?"

He is plaiting my hair.

I have no words. I curse my impotence. I have to believe that his carelessness masks anguish. What else is there to believe?

# Chapter Six

It was not the same after that. St. John, and England. Why, after all, should that have changed everything between us? I had known all along what he was, he had never attempted to deceive me. But to name him—St. John; all the difference.

There are small events that change one's whole perception of the world. When I was a child, I saw one day that it was raining on our side of the street and not on the other. I had a sudden sense of arbitrary boundaries and of differences. Whatever dream world I had constructed for myself in the name of reality did not include the possibility of this caprice— the world rent in measurable halves by a splintered curtain of golden summer rain.

"But you always knew," my father said, "that it didn't rain all over the world at the same time. You can see. There is the rain cloud, and on the other side of the street it is sunny."

"But I didn't know. Anyway I didn't believe it."

"But after all," Devi said, years later, "you knew what I was. What did you expect?"

"Love."

"I never promised you . . ."

"Oh yes you did."

"You knew what I was."

"Yes. But I didn't believe it. And besides, it wasn't right."

Looking back, it seems to me that I might then—*St. John, a sad old stuffy Cambridge nelly*—have cut the silver cord, and he would have found little to reproach me for. He might then have forgotten me. I might then have become nothing more than a footnote to his "American experience"; and all the harm done him would have remained undone. But I do not believe that even as I say it. Our most important choices choose us. One can't choose to fall or not to fall in love; one can choose only how to act upon that love. And I, because I had the power to kill without the power to die, chose not to kill. He tried, I think, to force my hand. Failing that, he appropriated to himself the role of abandoner. He felt so powerless, what else could he do? He grew wary. Having warned me, he waited for me to betray him . . . and with such an appearance of guilelessness. I loved the more.

I was never again to see him without wondering if it was the last time I was to see him.

On the surface, nothing changed. But I had waking nightmares: Standing on a supermarket line, my shopping cart piled high with food from all the major food groups, also Reese's Peanut Butter Cups, also wheat germ (in my mother's house, we practically lived on escarole and molasses; it gives me pleasure to see Lucy's tongue searching for the white mushy center of a Yankee Doodle) . . . standing on a supermarket line, oranges and Ring Dings, yogurt and Devil Dogs, I had waking nightmares: I saw Lucy in an airplane, I saw the plane spiral down in flames into black waters, she was wearing the little yellow mittens she'd worn once when, angry with her and unforgiving, I refused to take her outstretched repentant hand; and I saw Lucy dead in the oily waters. I held on to the shopping cart till the dry dizziness passed.

At cocktail parties, at PTA meetings, unbidden questions darted through my mind, like ragged jolts of electricity, in grotesque succession:

Why did Eichmann give the children chocolates before he put them in the showers?

Where is Joan Leslie now?

A South American dictator was brutally killed ("Good," Lucy said, and I slapped her face), and on the wreath his American mistress placed on his coffin were the words "I love you. Only death can part us." Only death can part us? What can she have meant? His shattered head was found three feet away from his bloodied torso. He will have a nice job looking for his body in the resurrection of the dead. Why did I slap Lucy's face? I hated him too.

The quality of innocence has always had, for me, a precise geographical location: Coney Island. What will Lucy's Coney Island be? When I was her age, it was so innocent, Coney Island, nothing more scary than the Skeleton Man, and we were warned against the hootchy-kootchy girl who belly danced in a beer-and-clam joint on the boardwalk. The hootchy-kootchy girl was Vice and all we knew of Vice (her navel had a rhinestone in it!), and our mothers warned us: "Don't go near the hootchy-kootchy girl!" A hundred million years ago. On hot summer nights we slept on the sand and had frankfurters for breakfast and talked about Tyrone Power. Once my friend Shirley and I saw a used rubber underneath the boardwalk. We circled around it as if it were a time bomb that might go off, we thought people made love standing up, they stood on opposite sides of the bedroom and then charged, and then, Bang! it was over—we were both fifteen. There is broken glass under the boardwalk now, and Lucy cannot walk there, the boys from the projects will yell, "Pussy!" and hot summer nights are times for muggings and only derelicts sleep under the boardwalks now; there are knives. What will Lucy's images of innocence be? She will be mugged, she will die. Why must Lucy have bars on her windows? Has she been inoculated against scarlet fever? Does scarlet fever exist anymore? Beth died of it—I read *Little Women* again the day after Lucy was born, but Lucy has never read it. When I took her to the Alcott house in Concord, she was bored, she reads Ibsen, how absurd.

Where is Priscilla Lane?

I live, now, so much in the unsafe past: In junior high school, we had a teacher who wore big soft floppy hats that covered one violet eye, and a ring that had a tiny watch covered by a cameo on the fourth finger of her right hand. How the girls adored her—cool, calm, violet-eyed geography teacher: Bolivia's principal export is tin. One day she halted midway in a sentence—*Bolivia's principal export is tin*—and wailed: *"Why* didn't I marry a doctor? He could have saved the poor little

boy. Poor little boy." She slammed her hand on the desk—the
cameo flew open with a little click—and fixed her violet eyes on
me: "There is no divorce in this state, do you know that?
*Adultery . . .* "She spat the word out. We trembled, waiting for
more, greedy for more; then she said, "Bolivia's principal export is tin."

Did Profumo's wife forgive him truly in her heart?

How much radiation is Lucy getting from the TV, and could
someone have given me DES without my knowing it?

I began to knit scarves for Lucy; I had never knit scarves
before, and she did not like them; but I stored them against the
winter, and I did not let Lucy know I was afraid she would be
raped on the F train. I plied her with Vitamin C.

A friend came back from bloody Cambodia, stories to tell.
"Is the food any good, there?" I asked. It seemed a relevant
question at the time, in any case a question, one has to say
something even if one is thinking only: Devi. Another friend
told me he was painting the stairs to his house: "Do the stairs
go up or down?" I said. It seemed a logical question at the
time.

Was it really my father's spiky handwriting I saw on the
subway posters of the Sea Beach Line? Why would my father
have written "FUCK" on the subway posters of the Sea Beach
Line when I was twelve years old? Is this something I have
invented?

In an old photograph album there is a picture of a house I
lived in when I was a child; next to it is a clearing, a yard
overgrown with weeds. When I look at that yard, I see a man
dressed in black, goose-stepping. Also I see a circle of girls—
ring-around-the-rosy. And I see my mother, pushing a baby
carriage; I am laboring to keep up with her. Who was the man?
Who was the baby? Did they exist? Something happened in
that yard. What?

Every encounter is a strange one: I go to the hospital emergency room, my doctor tells me to; I think I have cancer of the
nose. Why else would a nose hurt? My nose is black and blue.
Probably an internal pimple, my doctor says over the phone—
he is in Martha's Vineyard, and I have called him about a

pimple, which I know is cancer. But go to the emergency room because if it bursts you might get meningitis, he says, you'll need an antibiotic. I tell the young emergency room doctor I have meningitis. It's hard for women to talk about it when their husbands abuse them, the doctor says; he thinks I am a case. I'm not married, I say. Perhaps you fell out of bed? he says, giving me an out. . . . Without noticing it? My nose hurt before it was black and blue and I didn't fall out of bed and nobody beats me up. I have a pimple. . . . I thought you said you had meningitis? . . . Later I discover that my next-door neighbor, a woman I intensely dislike ("How *are* you?" she always asks, and waits for the answer), has given this very doctor at this very hospital Sensitivity Training—a coincidence that doesn't please me. So now, taught by her, they think all bruises come from bad men. I have noticed that the lives of crazy people are fraught with coincidence: the external world reflects the collision of their thoughts. Who is the crazy person?

I put the broccoli in the pot, I collect the mail, I sort Lucy's socks, I think of the oily darkness of the sea at night, the plane, like a mythic bird, entering silently my daughter's watery grave.

Devi came by soon after the day on the ferry: curry; drawing with Lucy; Simon and Garfunkel; the Late Show. "I have a friend in Baltimore. . . ." I glommed on to the television commercial, *springtime-fresh . . . no static cling . . . good for heavy loads. . . .* "Not a lover. But he owns a gay bath, what do you think of that?" On the screen, Marlon Brando, pigeon-toed and righteous, walked toward the shipyard owner, a violent epiphany, his free will and Eva Marie Saint's grace triumphing over corruption—*On the Waterfront,* our generation's *Our Town,* a sweet American fake. "Well, Angela?" "I wonder if he's meant to look like Christ." "The baths, Angela." "What about the bath?" "I could get a job there. Handing out towels, taking care of the locker room. Perhaps it would do me good to do some menial work, away from hypocrites and art-for-money's sake. Perhaps it would do me good not to paint, I

seem to have forgotten the point of art. If the point of art is
catharsis, then why should I be paid for it? Turning agony into
profit to line Stephan's pocket doesn't suit me, it's a fake."

"If art is a fake, then love is a fake, because presumably you
paint for the love of it." And I thought you said the profits
were going to support me in my old age, I might have added;
but did not.

"But if I love being in the baths better?"

"Is it so happy in the baths?"

"You place too high a value on happiness. . . . If art is put
to use there is no longer any use to art. . . . No. No one is
happy there—only sad and lonely, and why shouldn't I be sad
and lonely with them, why should I whore after happiness and
art? All this empty talk about happiness and art and love . . ."
Now he is talking about "compromises . . . psychic commodities . . . the guilt of selling out. . . ." If what he really wants
is to play with the queers at the baths why doesn't he say so.
"All the talk about detachment is fine in the abstract," he says.
"In the concrete, one pays for next month's rent with the
proceeds of last month's anguish. Boring old dilemma. Some
enterprising packager should market tailor-made compromises for people like me. Can't you see it. 'Two family size
compromises, please, medium rare, in dun, or any of the less
conventional shades' . . . A dealer in Paris wants my work."

What I see is that his chattering nonsense is a result of fear.
He thinks love is a fake; the more he loves, the more he is
alone. He is gripping my ankle as he talks. Soon I will be black
and blue. What I say is: "I wish I could see the problem, I wish
I were less simpleminded. Why can't you just do your work
without anticipating the consequences? Suppose nobody loves
your work in Paris, suppose everybody does, so what? At least
you'll have done it, you know in any case you'll never starve,
anyway I have money. It is a sin not to use your talent, I do
know that, all the saints say so: *Do what you do.*"

"Who?"

"Saint Augustine."

"Hmm. Very high-minded of you. Except that you expect to
be rewarded for holding that attitude. The trouble is, you can't

be meek and have it in the back of your mind that you're going to inherit the earth and that your day will come. If you're really meek, you're content to be so without expectation of reward, and you relish each and every inch of your gutter, consequently you've inherited the earth already."

He releases his hold on my ankle, and laughs. "What nonsense I talk. How do you put up with me?"

How do I put up with him, why do I love him? His beauty is more rare than truth. And, to tell the truth, I thrill to his conversation, the perversity of it. His shifting moods make me feel interesting. I enjoy being the repository of his craziness, which seems to me to speak to a sane part of my nature; how strange. I love, do love, the thrill of being misunderstood by him. If he understands the misunderstood me, then he will have encompassed all of me. If he gets the point of me . . . ! There is something exquisite in our mutual lack of comprehending—it promises.

He tickles the soles of my feet, then kisses them.

I say, "Well, thank God for that. I thought next I'd get the speech about how the people inside the loony bins are saner than the ones outside. . . ."

"Well, aren't they? I mean to say, look around you. You are in a perverse mood tonight."

"Just what I was thinking about you, Devi, and what indulgent crap. You can't think being crazy is fun. You must know better. I had a friend, well, no longer a friend, who told me she'd 'experienced' her madness and 'gone through it'—all in the space of ten minutes—holding on to a street corner lamp on Forty-second Street. Stupid woman. She gives Sensitivity Trainings. She also told me she understood the pain the Jews felt in Dachau when she experienced the pain of success— she'd written a dumb book about Sensitivity and she had to go on the Mike Douglas show. Another time she said she understood physical torture when her arms got tired of rowing ten minutes from shore. She compared herself to the North Vietnamese, can you imagine?"

"You have strange friends."

"But no longer a friend, I said. . . . When I think of what it costs me just to go down an escalator. I don't want to come any closer to panic than that, and I don't think my suffering on escalators is commensurate to that of the Vietnamese. I see your eyebrows are rising."

"I have always fancied myself King of Hearts."

"Oh very nice. I suppose you expect me to believe you'd enjoy finger painting with your own shit with R. D. Laing. Lucy did that when she was six months old."

"And now that I'm no longer a babe I must act like a man? I thought you loved *Morgan*, by the way."

"Up to a point. And only because he reminded me of someone I knew."

"There are times," Devi said, "when I don't think you have a logical mind. You certainly allow your affection to pervert your judgment. I don't see what you can know about it anyway, you are the sanest person I know, minor aberrations aside. You know of course that I am lost without you."

"So what about the baths?"

"Oh, bugger the baths. Here, give us a cuddle. I never meant that seriously."

"But I always take you seriously."

"Of course you do. You must. That's what I need you for. You do love me?"

"You know that I do."

"Astonishingly enough, I do."

# *Chapter Seven*

After that he began to spend weekends regularly in Baltimore: "Lovely chap, comfortable as old socks. Unfortunately I can't convince him that you're not like other women. Too bad. I'd like him to know you."

"But I am like other women. Whatever that means. Can you tell me why men think they're flattering us when they tell us we're not like other women?" In fact my vanity was fed; I did like to be singled out among my sex, but felt, on principle, obliged to protest.

"Are you accusing me of heterosexual behavior, you wonderful goose?"

"Of male behavior."

"Well, I do see the point. I wouldn't care for it if you told me I wasn't like other Indians."

"You often see the point. That's the point of you."

"I certainly see the point of you."

I slipped my arm into his. We were walking down Second Avenue, past singles' bars; young women, model-thin, suntanned in autumn, looked at me enviously (I had him, no predatory night ahead of me), and I allowed myself to feel pride of possession. I was not unhappy, though there is nothing sadder and more conducive of ennui than the clear light of a New York September afternoon, when every object is mercilessly defined; one's own confusions weigh so heavily in that revealing light. Skyscrapers rose competently and radiantly against the hard sky; I took note of my lack of unhappiness, feeling only slightly unreal; my feet skimmed the pavement, which rose to meet them. We were walking to the apartment of friends, about whom he had told me nothing. But of course, I thought, he means acquaintances. I am his only friend in this city, he has said so.

On Seventy-first Street we walked down four shallow steps to an iron gate covered with ivy, beyond that to a purple door, which was opened by Stephan, wearing a canary-yellow jumpsuit: "Well, Angela, dear, I see that you do consent to leave Brooklyn from time to time. What an extraordinary dress, how Peck and Peck of you. Devi." Stephan made a mock bow in the direction of Devi, who was immediately absorbed into a group of men and women, all androgynous.

"Stephan, who are all these people? Do you pay Devi a salary, he doesn't seem to have much money. I didn't expect to see you here."

"We have been friends for years, Angela, have you ever known me to do an unjust thing? My arrangement with Devi is perfectly equitable, naturally he complains, he imagines conspiracies. It suits him to believe he is ill-treated. Have an hors d'oeuvre. I am," he said, looking suddenly old and forlorn in his tight ultrasuede, "feeling forsaken. I never see Lucy."

"I don't know about an unjust thing, Stephan, but he doesn't seem to have much money. Who are these people?"

"Is it fair that I should not see Lucy?"

"Nothing prevents you from calling her up, Stephan. But she's in love with a rock musician who calls himself Neddy Nickle. She hangs out a lot. I don't see her very much myself."

"Your association with Devi," Stephan said, "has soured your disposition. You are my best friend, you know. At least I thought you were."

"Oh Christ. I'm not mad at you, Stephan. I don't know what the hell is going on—who are all these people? I love him."

"Is it helpless?"

There was no irony in his voice; all at once I remembered my reasons for liking him.

"You should know. Of course it's helpless. . . . Lucy said a wonderful thing the other night—she's been asking for you, by the way. She said she understood what dreams were; they were the thoughts our ancestors had when they were alive but were too dumb to put in words, so now she is dreaming our ances-

tors' thoughts. Nice, isn't it? She's been making dream drawings, you'll see them.'' I was looking for Devi.

"Devi will be going away soon. Come with Lucy to my farm
in Vermont, what you need is a good fuck with a simple
farmer."

Stephan meant well.

A pretty person—male, female, it was hard to tell—passed
by, looked me over, dismissed me, and joined a group of
people who were admiring a wall mural: Two naked children, a
girl and a boy, are standing on a rocky shore, the sea is pale
gray and the sky is pale gray, and the boy is looking toward the
horizon, at the ashy mauve kite he has loosed into the sky. The
girl looks toward land.

It must have taken Devi a long time to paint this mural. How
many evenings? Evenings away from me. And what of the
picture of the sea he promised Lucy?

The air was thick with the smell of pot and sandlewood
incense, the phonograph blasted "Carmina Burana," I could
not see him. A silver dish with eight lines of cocaine was
handed around. Stephan, who had made a decision to be kind,
draped his arm around my shoulder protectively. Devi appeared from the kitchen, wordlessly and with some force dis-
engaged me from Stephan, and led me to a chair; he sat at my
feet, his head against my knees. Poppers were being passed
around the room. When the cylindrical capsule of amyl nitrate
reached me, I inhaled the sick-sweet hospital smell deeply,
Devi's voice came to me from a great distance: "Don't be
afraid, I'm here." He held my hand tightly as I began the roller
coaster ascent into the most physical of all drug highs: my
head, red-hot, ballooned; my heart accelerated (I am too old
for this, I thought; my heart will crack, and besides this is
supposed to end in bed). There was a moment of total clarity
when I seemed to see every hair on Devi's head separately; I
ached for sex. I heard myself laugh. Seconds of blackness; and
I rocketed down. Time warped. I saw, without surprise, that I
was smoking one of Devi's hand-rolled cigarettes and drinking
champagne and *framboises* from a fluted glass. Stephan had
gone. The crowd had thinned out; only Devi and I and four

others remained. Someone inquired politely into the welfare of my daughter. The conversation—Ronald Firbank, Truffaut, Antonioni, Mick Jagger, Harold Nicholson—swirled around me, Devi against my knees.

Later, in the rain-fresh, cool street, "You were perfect," he said.

"Perfect? I didn't say a word."

"Perfect. They loved you. So do I."

"Loved me?"

"Insofar—here, are you giddy?—insofar as they understand love, whoever charms them they love. You were not what they expect a writer to be, you took them by surprise, you did charm them."

"How?"

"Do you think they're nice? I do."

"Yes," I said, lying.

"You are lying, you know."

"I'm lying."

"You think they're decadent and frivolous."

"No more than I am. I was stoned, too."

"So you're not going to cast the first stone? That was a pun, do you think there's something in the Eastern mind—our not understanding cause and effect, isn't that what you once said about Indians?—that makes it impossible for us to pun? Do you have to have a logical mind to pun? Though that wouldn't explain Zen koans, would it? They are," Devi said, "disgustingly frivolous and decadent, I am a toy to them; they wouldn't mind annexing you, too. They like my curries. I don't like any of them, really. I don't know why I go there, perhaps to remind myself that I am not you."

"That you are not me?"

"That I am not your life. Shall I not go anymore? You tempt me to be good. As if innocence were reclaimable. All the time I worked on that mural I thought of you. I thought, There is no real difference between being airbound and earthbound, they are relative differences and each is meaningless without the other. What right have they to judge you? I won't see them again."

"You frighten me, Devi. I am not good, I am not innocent, I am only ordinary. What was Stephan doing there?"

"That was a mistake."

"Whose?"

Devi was zigzagging along the pavement, skipping to avoid the cracks.

"How should I know?" he said. "The Archbishop of Canterbury's. Mahatma Gandhi's. Somebody's. Not mine."

"I wish I knew what you were talking about."

He had zigzagged his way five feet ahead of me; over his shoulder, he replied, "How often do I have to tell you that I love you?"

The next morning Stephan called: "Does your jaw ache?"

"Yes, and every joint in my body. I feel like death."

"Someone slipped some speed into the *framboises.*"

"Who?"

"Your guess is as good as mine, dear, too bad of Devi."

"Jesus, I thought I had some rare disease."

"You have the only disease that counts. You are being corrupted, my dear."

# *Chapter Eight*

Thanksgiving drew near. Days crisp and clear, as good as tangy autumn apples, alternated with gray, damp days marching as listlessly as armies of dour old men. Lucy and I pored over cookbooks—Lucy favoring a turkey stuffing of marshmallows and prunes—in anticipation of a Thanksgiving dinner for which we were planning a guest list; my birthday was on the same day as Thanksgiving that year, and I was determined to see my thirties out in style.

"Stephan or Devi?" Lucy asked, as she jotted down names.

"Not both?"

"You know they don't like each other."

"I know. I didn't know you knew."

"I'm not stupid. But they are, they live together and don't like each other. Why did you and Daddy get divorced? I'm old enough to know."

I recognized the symptoms: We were about to embark upon a quarrel.

"So who are we inviting, Angela?"

"Don't call me Angela, please, Lucy."

"So who, Mom?"

*"Whom."* Naturally I wanted Devi.

"Is this a good time to correct my grammar, Angie? Stephan's my uncle, and you have a complicated life."

"Are you telling me my complicated life complicates your life?"

"I'm telling you that Stephan's my uncle. You chose him to be my uncle."

"In fact he's nothing to you at all, only an honorary uncle, and your father chose. He's your father's second cousin twice

removed, like seventy-five thousand other people. What you
mean is, he'll bring you a present."

"Devi bought my birthday present at Woolworth's. Why do
you have to start in on Daddy?"

"He bought it at Azuma's, and you're spoiled."

I'll say this for Lucy and me: We never seemed to step over
the line where forgiveness was impossible and a tolerant ac-
commodation the best we could hope for. I would be damned
if I let Devi push me over that line. And I had a strong feeling
that Devi would make himself unavailable at Thanksgiving,
that he would pronounce it too Normal Rockwell for his taste,
which made me angry on Lucy's behalf as well as my own,
which resulted in my being snappish at Lucy, who said huffily:
"Your friends are weird. Why don't they like each other, the
way friends are supposed to?"

I sometimes think one of the pleasures of having a child is
that one can oneself behave like a child with one's offspring—
in my case a particularly delicious flirtation with regression,
since I had been a most earnest and unchildlike child, and was
therefore, in young middle age, prone to excess, and to a kind
of tit for tatting that becomes no adult. "You like Robin and
Lizzie," I said, "and Lizzie and Robin can't stand each other,
so why should I be any different?"

"Because you're a grown-up, and you're supposed to be
smarter than I am. I don't understand how you can like so
many weird people. Angela."

"Buzz off, Lulu." Lulu was her father's name for her, she
hated for me to use it.

To make peace with Lucy—to charm her—I told her that I
frequently had a fantasy that 250 people would come to my
funeral and they'd all think they were at the wrong place because none of them would believe they were talking about the
same person. I am different things to different people, a social
chameleon. I agreed with her that this was weird. My words
had the effect of unsettling Lucy, not pacifying her. She is as
apt an unconscious mimic as I; unlike me, however, she does
not suffer from self-loathing when she bends in an effort to
please. Lucy never really warps herself out of shape; I do. Age,

and motherhood—having constantly to be there for Lucy and true for Lucy—have lessened my proclivity to wear the appropriate social mask, to ape the people I happen to be with; but I still, sometimes, feel that both a diffusion of personality and a multiplication of personalities are my social mode: I forget, sometimes, when I am with other people, who I am when I am alone. Which is why my natural gregariousness is always at war with my equally strong tendency to reclusiveness; I am afraid that some day I will warp myself entirely out of the true—not so much out of a desire to please, but out of a kind of spiritual slackness: It is so much easier and less enervating to like people than not to like them, and, liking them, I am drawn into terms of reference that are not my own. I yield. I trade truth for comfort.

"Weird," Lucy said. "And Devi thinks he knows the real person you are, I suppose you think. That's insulting to me. What do I know, the person who pretends to be my mother?"

"That's a shitty thing to say."

"Well if you're My Mother, I want Stephan. He's my uncle. Angela."

"Stephan's whole goddamn life is a funeral procession."

"Then why are you nice to him?"

"I'm not."

"Fake!"

"You hated the party he gave for you."

"He's my uncle, and I think he's neat. Most of the time."

"You deserve to be ignored."

"Ignore me, what do I care?"

"Lucy, don't you like Devi? I thought you did. And do we have to have marshmallows in the stuffing? It sounds disgusting. Are you sure you know what you're reading in that cookbook? You don't like prunes."

"Are you sure you know what you're doing? You don't want me to have marshmallows because you don't want me to have Stephan. You're being mean."

"You're the one who's mean."

"You're being mean to me and Stephan. I hope you're not

going to invite grandpa and the cousins if you invite Devi. They hate fags."

"Lucy! Goddamnit! What the hell do you think Stephan is, John Wayne?"

"A fag you're in love with is different from a homosexual friend. It's abnormal to be in love with a . . . with him."

"Would you ever dare to talk to your father like this? Would you tell your father he was abnormal? Have you ever insulted your father? Do you talk to him like this?"

"Why did you marry him? He doesn't even care about seeing me at Thanksgiving. I can't fight with Daddy because he's always reasonable and he's never here, and you are stupid!"

Our yelling was interrupted by a wire from Lucy's father—the only person I know who has figured out that it's possible to send a telegram collect. He was going to be in New York for a week; he claimed Lucy for Thanksgiving Day. Lucy stomped off to her bedroom and slammed the door. I heard the sound of pottery breaking, then a long wail: "Stupid! Everybody is stupid!"

I went to bed.

Later: "Mommy? Please don't pretend to be asleep. Do you forgive me?"

"For what?"

"That means you don't."

"OK, come and talk."

Lucy's eyelids were puffy from crying, her delicate oval face swollen and flushed, the veins in her forehead pronounced. "Vines," she used to call them when she was little, "why does my body have so many vines?"

"Do you remember when you said, 'José didn't push me in the anthill?' " I asked. When we lived in Mexico, Lucy was delivered from school in a station wagon, and one day the station wagon stopped at our driveway, and inside there was no Lucy. Then I saw a hideous child with an enormous face, eyes swallowed in gross fat, dressed in Lucy's clothes; and then the child in Lucy's clothes said in Lucy's voice: "José *didn't* push me in the anthill." The hideous child was Lucy, swollen from the bites of red ants and protecting the boy who had done her harm; he was her best friend.

Lucy, curled in a fetal position next to me, had been sobbing in her pillow to muffle the sound of her cries. I remembered once having calculatedly and patiently wooed my own mother with my tears, having judged exactly how long and how much and how noisily to cry in order to wring guilt and sympathy from her without pushing her over the line into wrath. I'd despised her for her easy capitulation, and despised myself for having achieved such a cheap victory. Did Lucy despise me now? No. How much nicer Lucy is than I was, happier, too; she does not despise me. Does Lucy despise herself? Does Devi make her feel unworthy, unqualified for ordinary fatherly love? Was I prepared to sacrifice a jot of her happiness for him? What kind of love is it that requires human sacrifices?

"He didn't mean to push me in the anthill," Lucy said.

"Lucy, are you very unhappy?"

"Yes."

"Is it Devi? Tell."

"Yes. No. I want to feel like a family."

"And don't you with me?"

"I do with you. But then Devi comes, and he's kind and funny but then he goes away, and Mommy I can't imagine him with grandpa or the cousins, suppose they talk about fags. His feelings will be hurt."

"Oh dear."

"I want you to be in love with someone who won't go away and whose feelings can't be hurt."

"Me too. I want that too."

"And I can't say no to Daddy about Thanksgiving because his feelings will be hurt, and besides . . ."

"And besides you love him, and he loves you."

"But he's never here."

"He will be here soon."

Lucy was four years old when we were divorced, and her father, who claimed not to be able to find a job in New York, took off immediately for San Francisco, all the while protesting that I had stolen Lucy from him. Lucy had said then: "But

Daddy, you can sell hot dogs in New York, I'll help you, and you can be with me, we can buy a pretty hot dog stand, why do you have to go away?"

"Why did he have to go away?" she asked, hopelessly, knowing that as usual there would be no answer forthcoming— there was no answer. "I wanted to be with you on Thanksgiving. I always spend Thanksgiving with you. And it's your birthday. So I don't know what."

"You can have two Thanksgivings—one with daddy, and the night before, one with me."

"Can ours be alone, just the two of us? Can we see grandpa and the cousins that week too?"

"Yes. I love you," I said, tracing her blue-purple vines with my finger.

"It's hard to be good, Mommy."

"I've noticed. I was bad tonight."

"I hate it when you say you're bad. It makes me feel bad. You do bad things sometimes, but you're not a bad person."

"Lucy, I'm so sorry. Do you love me? I don't know how you can."

"That's what I mean. When you apologize to me so much I get scared."

If I were happy, it would be so much easier for Lucy to feel that she was good. Lucy wants me to be happy.

"I want you to be happy," Lucy said.

"Lucy, I'm sorry about Devi. I don't know what I can do to help myself." I didn't know what I could do to help Lucy.

"Not me, I'm not sorry. I have a very interesting life. He can come for Christmas. Anyway, he'll go away soon," Lucy said; isn't that what men did? "Are you mad about Thanksgiving? Are you going to be lonely?"

"No."

"Then can we watch *The Late Show* now?"

"Yes."

"Is Devi good?"

"I don't know. I think so. I think he wants to know what is good. I don't think he's bad."

"But that's not the same as being good?"

"Probably not, but being right isn't the same as being good, either."

"Give me an example."

"Oh dear. I'm not sure that I can. Well, think of Lizzie's mother. She's always right about everything, but would you say she was good? Do you like to hear her talk about Sensitivity?"

"Ugh. Lizzie's mother sucks. She never yells. I'd die if you were always right. But I still don't understand."

Poor Lucy. She needs a father.

"It's very confusing," Lucy said.

"You're telling me."

What do I know? It may, after all, be true, as theologians who espouse a pessimistic Christianity think, that because of the disfiguration and inner dislocation we call Original Sin, we cannot be good and we cannot be happy and that certain eternal achievements make happiness look like trash. But I cannot speak of sin to my daughter, whose flesh, sweet as flowers, is pressed against my own, and who is at this very moment watching Ginger Rogers and Fred Astaire; and, as all my achievements are ephemeral—Lucy aside—I choose the pursuit of happiness . . . in the only way I know, which must look to other people like self-destruction: Devi. Who is to say what goodness is? It has been said that even the betrayal of Christ by Judas might be considered wholesome if one considers the fact that Judas set the wheels of salvation in motion; the sin of Adam is the occasion of the Incarnation. And why am I foolishly inclined to believe that all these questions would unravel themselves if Lucy had a father? We would be happy, and we would be good.

Lucy has fallen asleep in my arms, her left leg flung over mine.

I know absolutely that when she is sexually awakened our sensual enjoyment of each other will be subsumed; she will no longer fall asleep with her left leg flung over mine, her perfect breast resting in perfect confidence against my side. How long?

Fred Astaire and Ginger Rogers flickered across the screen in the sanctified dark as I thought of that inevitable bereavement. I held my daughter closer.

# Chapter Nine

The next evening Devi came by. Lucy was formal and courteous and announced that she was going to hang out with Neddy Nickle, whose new group was called The Clap. He was working on a demo-single called "Katch It!"

"This weather doesn't suit me," Devi said.

"It doesn't suit anybody. How are you?"

"Have you ever been in San Francisco in November?"

"I haven't traveled anywhere to speak of in the last five years and especially on Thanksgiving."

"Hmmm. I wonder if San Francisco would suit me."

"I wouldn't like to spend Thanksgiving with strangers."

"It doesn't arise for me, Thanksgiving is not a Wog holiday, and I have spent all my life among strangers. In any case it is gross as well as delusional, like Norman Rockwell. Celebrating abundance with abundance while people starve. Think of all those poor Indians you robbed the land from while you're sinking your teeth into corn on the cob."

"I never robbed anybody's land that I'm aware of."

"I think San Francisco would suit me."

"I knew a man who fasted on Thanksgiving Day because of the war in Vietnam. He invited twelve guests and he carved the turkey—I think his wife even baked her own bread to make the bread stuffing—and then he sat at the head of the table and didn't eat. I gorged. So did Lucy. Even she recognized Quaker-chic when she saw it. We never went back to their house again. Lucy said he scraped all the butter off her toast one morning and reminded her that millions were dying in Asia. Actually it was margarine."

"You look very beautiful tonight. I have been reading some

Zen person on the virtue of detachment—doing one's work without anticipating the consequences or the rewards. I think I should go one step further and detach myself from work altogether. A week in San Francisco would do me good, I fancy it. Just that I don't have the fare. *Un*just. Stephan's bookkeeping. He'll give me a check after the hols, what a sense of timing. Four hundred and twenty one dollars on Pan Am. Must I make a case for my having to go to San Francisco? You understand that pleasure is a good enough reason for my doing anything, don't you? I never have to justify myself to you. Stephan would lend me money if I broke my leg or if I had to be bailed out of jail. The vulgarity of frugality, detestable WASP attitude, rich bastard. Only you understand that happiness is a necessity. And you allow me to choose the form my happiness will take. I really need only a hundred dollars, I have the rest."

I gazed at Devi's face, so beautiful (why would he never explain that scar?). I felt as if I were being blackmailed by his beauty. Totally without charity, I wrote a check.

Devi reached into his pocket and from a leather pouch pulled out a heavy gold ring with a large unfaceted diamond; cut and set in Indian fashion, it had only the dimmest watery gleam.

"What's that?"

"Ransom," he said. "Treasure from Golconda against my safe return."

"But it must be worth at least twenty times the amount of the check."

"How funny you are. I'm giving it to you, of course. Now you have the sum of my earthly riches, and you know you have my heart. You won't begrudge me the week in San Francisco?"

"I don't begrudge you anything," I said; which, the moment I said it, became true. I experienced these sudden shifts of feeling when I was with Devi; to have it in my power to make him happy was for me to be happy, and for me to feel enlarged: I was the caretaker of his happiness; and I did not know enough to know what danger that put me in.

Of course the diamond made its own contribution to my happiness, I have an acquisitive nature.

"Is that real?" Lucy asked. "Are you two engaged?"

"Engaged?" Devi said. "Whatever I have I give to your mother for safekeeping, she is incapable of doing me harm."

When Devi's back was turned, Lucy rolled her eyes, pointed at him, mouthed "crazy," and blew me a kiss.

Stephan called. "Did Devi tell you about our bargain? One assumes Devi tells you all. One assumes that you assume Devi tells you all."

"What bargain?"

"I took one of his large paintings and gave him a ring I bought in India. The diamond is quite extravagant. One does feel charitable as Christmas approaches."

"Properly speaking," I said, "you mean an exchange, not a bargain. I have a headache. You gave him a ring?"

"I have said so."

Devi sent me a garish picture postcard of the Golden Gate Bridge. "It suits me," he wrote.

It suited him so well, in fact, that he did not return until a week before Christmas. He brought me a pair of hand-knitted mittens, rainbow colored; and to Lucy he gave a pair of multicolored socks, which she promptly turned over to Neddy Nickle.

"Shall I help you trim your tree?"

"Would it please you?"

"The night before Christmas Eve I will decorate your tree and make you and Lucy fish curry."

"Italians always eat fish on Christmas Eve, twelve kinds."

"I know."

"How smart of you to know."

"Not really. There was an Italian in San Francisco."

"I don't know if it's twelve because of the twelve apostles or twelve because of the twelve days of Christmas or what. I really am a theological illiterate, a cultural illiterate too. Who was the Italian?"

"Hush," Devi said.

## Chapter Ten

The night before Christmas Eve, Devi called to say he had a stomachache, and could he beg off? Lucy was untangling skeins of colored lights; I was sorting ornaments. The enormous tree was sappy, still; the apartment was redolent of the soapy smell of pine, and of freshly baked cookies.

I wheedled, as much for Lucy's sake as for my own—Devi protesting that he would be rotten company, I insisting that his rotten company pleased me better than anybody else's good company. It was the first time I had tried to hold him to a promise; and I could feel him slipping like mercury from my hands. Mercury hardens. His voice hardened: "I haven't bought your presents as yet," he said, managing to make it sound like a reproach.

"You promised you'd come." Bach's *Christmas Oratorio* played in the background. I felt like a nag and a shrew. Devi, with ill-grace, conceded. I had won. Of course, the moment one speaks of winning in a relationship, the relationship is on its way to being lost. When two people genuinely love—always supposing the absence of fear—nobody loses because nobody needs to win, the prize (love) having already been secured. Devi himself was later to point this out to me over and over, his mistake, however, being to blame love itself for all the failures of love. Because Devi translates desire into fear, and naturally resents that which gives rise to fear, he is obliged to believe that every relationship between two people is a struggle for power and ascendancy. I contend that this is not so; Devi contends that I am living proof that it is so.

He arrived carrying a tiffin box of tired lamb curry—clearly the remains of an earlier meal—and looking rather grim. If

Lucy thought that was less than generous of him, she refrained from saying so, though she had all day been giving herself little pep speeches about fish curry, which she hated, but which, for my sake and Devi's, she was prepared to eat.

Lucy fussed over Devi, and under the warmth of her attention, he grew expansive, embracing her heartily, telling her her skin was like the flesh of a white grape—one felt one could almost see the light shining through it and from it, "and all the vines showing too," Lucy said. Devi shyly, almost demurely, accepted his presents with a bashfulness that endeared him to Lucy more than effusiveness would have done. She draped herself around his shoulders as he carefully unwrapped bottles of cologne from Caswell and Massey, bath oils from Kiehl's, beach glass Lucy and I had found one summer on the Cape, a kaleidoscope, a silver Victorian hairbrush; "fit for a queen," he said, and winked. Lucy dabbed two kinds of cologne on his cheeks and behind his ears. "Lovely," Devi said. "No one's ever given me cologne before, is it manly?"

"Yummy," Lucy said, pressing her nose against his neck the better to smell the leathery, sweet, spicy fragrances that emanated from him: "Delicious." It occurred to me that Lucy was a bit in love with Devi, too.

They trimmed the tree—Devi played a Suba Laxmi record on the phonograph (they laughed when I called it a victrola, "How funny you are")—and they were merry and acquiescent as I issued instructions from the Empire couch. I felt as if they were both my children; and I felt also as if they were mothering me. When the tree was a symmetrical glory of silver and gold, we turned off the lights and lit candles, and Devi's sweet clear tenor led us in singing (where had he learned them?) hymns: "Let Us Gather at the River;" "There Is a Green Hill Far Away/Beyond the City Walls/There our dear Lord was crucified/He died to save us all"; "I walk through the garden alone/ and the dew is still on the roses/and the voice I hear falling on my ear/the Son of God disclo-o-ses/and He walks with me and he talks with me and he tells me I am His own"; "Amazing Grace."

Lucy drifted off to bed in a cloud of goodwill and rosewater aftershave lotion.

Devi turned on the lights.

"Stephan is fucking me over royally," he said.

"How?"

"Talks about collectors, introduces me to collectors, collectors who don't buy. Trots me out at parties. All barbarians looking for a buzz. Condescending, patronizing bastard."

"Is it in the nature of a patron to condescend?"

"Took me to a pricey restaurant, I had to wear one of his old tuxedos, the waistband was under my arms and the sleeves kept falling in the soup and I had to be charming to an embittered old queen, who, I'd bet my last quid, wouldn't buy a painting from Rembrandt though he could well afford it. Stephan is a pimp, not a patron. All patrons are pimps, but he is more so."

"What about a gallery?"

"No point, as I'll soon be off. In any case Stephan discourages me from showing my slides around, he regards it as vulgar."

"When will you be off? Why? Why do you allow yourself to be discouraged? When will you be off?"

"It is vulgar, he has a point. Of course it also gives him control. Stephan is wrong even when he's right. And when he's wrong he's wrong for the right reasons—according to him. Bloody self-righteous prig. Yet he manages to make the world work for him. The people who make the world work for them are always the worst, aren't they? The people who can't cope are the good people. Despair is the only state of grace in this world. . . . Immigration. I haven't the proper papers to stay."

"No way out?"

"Only if I married an American to get my green card, absurd idea. And Stephan expects me to pay room and board, he's had enough of me—or not enough of me, as the case may be."

"Why do you stay?"

"A moment ago you were asking me why I meant to leave. Let's see the skaters at Rockefeller Center soon, shall we? It'll be a nice send-off for me. Bloody London, I love this city. I'll say good-bye to New York with you."

Later, after Devi had left ("marry an American, how absurd"), Stephan called: "Did you and Devi have that conversation?"

"What conversation?"

"Don't be coy, dear, so trying. He simply won't take advice, too bad of him. He won't do illustrations for the *Times*, he refuses to do book jackets—too low brow, one assumes—he only wants to woo rich collectors, he is too arrogantly all-or-nothing-at-all. I am exceedingly tired of trotting him around to rich collectors, whom he makes no effort to charm. One could so easily get him a job on a retainer basis at a magazine and all his troubles with Immigration would be over. Of course he refuses to allow one to use one's influence. One had to use all one's power to make him promise to talk to you about doing some graphics; it gave one quite a stomachache. One assumes you have influence over him. One is also justified in asking him to pay a nominal rent. Supporting him is St. John's job, not one's own. And one assumes that you did not take a lofty tone. I do hope," Stephan said, his return to the first-person singular a sign of his sincerity, "that you encouraged him to do commercial art, which you, after all, are in no position to deprecate—I see you are writing a column for the tabloids now —and to get off his goddamned ass."

"We had the conversation. He doesn't have to do commercial art. He's going to marry me."

"Absurd."

"Would you care to elaborate?"

"One assumes this is a temporary aberration, I wish to say no more."

Twenty minutes later Stephan called back: "Angela, dear, you know I love you. You know I love Lucy."

"I'm going to marry him, Stephan."

"And have St. John support you as well as him? . . . Don't be angry, dear. After all," he said pitiably, "I loved you first. And the boy is—don't be angry—a leech. . . . Midnight Mass tomorrow? As always? And presents afterward? You mustn't think me mean, I bought a painting of Devi's to give to you. It was meant to have been my great surprise."

"Yes, Stephan, Midnight Mass."

I was going to marry Devi.

Devi spent the holidays in Baltimore. His Christmas present to Lucy and me arrived after the New Year, an Elton John record and a Cat Stevens record, postage due. "He didn't even wrap them," said Lucy, who'd gotten a rabbit-fur coat, hat, and muff from Stephan for Christmas, "and don't tell me I'm being greedy." I didn't. We had spent a week rearranging the furniture and taking pictures from walls to accommodate Devi's huge oil, which dominated the living room. The ashy mauve of the painting clashed with the red of the Empire couch.

# *Chapter Eleven*

It was bitterly cold at Rockefeller Center. Devi wore only a light leather jacket; I was almost warm in an ankle-length seal-skin cape that Stephan had found for me in the attic of his great-aunt's mansion in Southampton and had relined in scarlet satin. Devi snuggled against my warmth as we watched the skaters glide. "Toasty," he said, as he wrapped his arms around my waist. "I got it at a thrift shop," I said, sniffing for a hint of the cologne we'd given him, and finding none.

"I thought Stephan gave it you?"

"As a matter of fact, he did."

"Then why lie?"

"Oh, because. I do lie. I never lie about important things, though."

"Quite right," Devi said. "A taxi to the Village?"

In the restaurant on Bleecker Street we were greeted with vivacity by the proprietress. *"Ch'é bel'uomo,"* she said, kissing me briskly on both cheeks; *"é come sta la tua bella figlia?"* she said, nodding and beaming her approval at Devi. She was always pleased to see me with a man, and, if the man charmed her, she sent her husband to our table with a copper dish of zabaglione: *"Mangia, mangia."* Once when I was having dinner with a Jesuit who perfectly understood seven languages, of which Italian was one, she asked if this was to be, *"allora é finalmente,"* Lucy's new papa, and, misreading my embarrassment, sent over a double order of zabaglione. I frequently wished I had a mother like her, she smelled so good and hugged so tight. My own mother never kissed me, nor did I her. My own mother had never acknowledged—no church ceremony—that I'd been married, had consequently never acknowledged that I'd been divorced. God knows where she thought Lucy had come from.

Over the zabaglione, I said to Devi, my heart pounding rapidly while the signora hovered:

"Devi, about that green card."

"Hmmm?"

"Would you really like to stay? Because if yes, we could get married."

Devi regarded me with perfect astonishment, halting his spoon halfway to his mouth. "You would marry me?"

"Well. Of course. I love you."

"You love me."

"It wouldn't bind you," I said. "You wouldn't have to live with me, I wouldn't be jealous or possessive." I would, though. I was. "I'd marry you under one condition: I'd never see you again. You'd have to promise never to see me."

If I could not believe what I'd heard my mouth say, neither, apparently, could Devi. I had, before, gotten no further in my thinking than this: I would marry Devi. Now I understood: Marriage to Devi meant separation from him. It meant that I would be married; he would not.

I saw the table silver reflected in the watery gleam of the diamond I wore on the fourth finger of my left hand.

"My mother's ring suits you," Devi said.

"Your mother's ring?"

"You love me," Devi said.

"You know I do."

"No one could love me."

"Devi."

"*In* love?"

"You knew."

"No. I thought . . . love."

"Well, how many kinds are there?"

"You know what I am."

"What has that got to do with it?"

"Everything, I should have thought, isn't it?"

"You don't have to be in love with me, I'm not asking you to be in love with me." I wasn't asking him to be in love with me, because I believed he was in love with me. And I was prepared never to see him again. So why was I feeling giddy with pleasure?

Devi's great brown eyes were liquid and opaque. He wagged his head in that ambiguous Indian way. The signora hovered. His eyes asked questions I could not read; who knows how long we sat there, silent in the chatter and bustle, remote from time.

"Shall I tell you a story?" he said. "Once a rubber inflatable globe came into Karachi and the Muslim customs man cut Israel out of it, very neatly, with a little scissors. It was meant to be a present for a child."

"Yes?"

"That's all. That's the story. He made a hole in the world."

"What does the story mean?"

"This sweet tastes like warm snot," Devi said. "Does everything have to mean something? . . . How do you know which are the important things?"

"What do you mean?"

"You said you never lied about important things. Who decides what the important things are?"

"I know that whether you stay or not is important."

"To whom?"

"Are you angry with me?"

"I feel as if I shall cry." And indeed his eyes were brimming over.

"I hope you're not feeling grateful to me, because . . ."

"I think you shouldn't tell me how to feel; I think we should not talk now." He kissed the palms of my hands. He said: "I do."

"Do?"

"Love you."

In the taxi, on the way back to Brooklyn, he said not a word. His right hand fretted on the seat. I wanted overwhelmingly to kiss it, to hold it. From time to time he looked at me and smiled. I sat very still.

When he reached my house, he nuzzled his head against the shoulder of my cape.

"Will you stay over tonight?" His thin leather jacket was no protection against the cold.

"No."

"Why?"

"Just not."

He reached across me, opened the door: "Thank you," he mumbled.

"For?"

"My life." He kissed me, a long kiss, and then said, "Mid-week? here?"

"Yes."

I watched him give animated instructions to the driver as the cab sped off. "Follow that car," I said aloud; I was drunk.

Inside, all the lights on, the phonograph blasting, Lucy was washing dishes and talking on the phone. She looked at me suspiciously. "You look like you've been making out."

"Making out! Jesus, what an expression."

"Guess what?" Lucy said. "I'm going out with Neddy Nickle."

"You're going out with Neddy Nickle? What do you mean you're going out with Neddy Nickle? You've been seeing him for months."

"*Seeing* is different from *going out.*"

"You mean like dating is different from going steady?"

Lucy hooted into the phone: "Mom doesn't know the difference between seeing somebody and going out. She wants to know if I'm going steady!" For some reason this inspired her to bellows of laughter.

As I left the room, I heard her say, "Mommy's so retarded she's cute. What can you expect? She didn't Do It till she was twenty-two."

"Lucy! Does going out mean sex?"

"Relax, Ma, I'm only thirteen, and I'm not stupid."

Neddy Nickle, however, was eighteen.

## Chapter Twelve

The days passed. They always do, though that is a fact it is sometimes difficult to remember. I bought a lot of plants, saw friends, wrote a book review, and met Neddy Nickle, who, to my amazement, looked quite beatific (long brown ringlets and a smile of disarming sweetness) in spite of the silver safety pin that dangled from one ear. He was exceedingly, however, dopey. And he had an amazing appetite. And had four sisters and a drunk for a father, all of whom lived on welfare. He had very few words, no discernible opinions or ideas. All of Lucy's friends were jealous of her conquest.

Neddy Nickle mooned ("oh, Ma, they don't call it that any more, mooning's something else now") over Lucy, who, so recently abjectly infatuated, was to my surprise entirely self-assured in his presence, teasing and preening and bubbly and absolutely adorable, why shouldn't he moon over her?

"He's not too bright in the head," Lucy said, "but he is cute. Sometimes he has to pick his father up from a saloon floor."

"And what do you do then?"

"I wait."

Midweek, true to his promise, Devi came.

In his absence I had contrived to see it all very clearly, the austerity and beauty and simplicity of it: I had it within my power to give Devi freedom. I would be joined to him even as I released him. The grief I felt at the prospect of never seeing him again was indistinguishable from joy. By marrying him— and renouncing him—I would take hold of my goodness. To make love with anyone but Devi was unthinkable; as I could not have him—and to whom was it given to be so happy as I would be if Devi loved my body?—to choose celibacy would be not a sacrifice but an affirmation. I would no longer confuse and confound him with my sexual desires, which, in the intensity of my greater desire to subdue them, would soon be burned away like chaff. I felt like a nun about to take vows. I would create an invisible wall against the clamoring flesh; and, already, dimly, I apprehended the peace and amplitude, the sweetness that awaited me in the walled garden into which no stray desire would ever find its way. I would subdue my will, and all my desires. I felt a presentiment of the calm I was about to enter.

The moment I saw him I wanted fiercely to make love with him.

My avidity knew no bounds; I admitted of no obstacles.

*Why* not.

How beautiful he was.

At the door, he hesitated, I hesitated, and in our awkwardness there was an omen—though of good or ill, I could not tell: Lovers are awkward just before they are unashamed; voyagers are awkward, too, no words before the parting ship pulls out to sea.

We brushed each other's cheeks.

Beautiful; and tonight so shy.

I was shy, too; how could such turmoil be contained within this placid shell? I wanted to grab, hold, possess. I sat still. (And yet a hungry man will smash a bakery window to seize a loaf of bread and we will judge it not a crime, but necessity.)

He sat down without removing his leather jacket, placing himself on the most uncomfortable chair, which was also the one farthest from me. No words. His large oil now dominated the living room, and his eyes were drawn to it as if its presence in my house were a metaphor, an explanation, or a mystery.

"I have something for you," Devi said, and on the coffee table that separated us he placed an envelope—inside, five $10 bills. I had quite forgotten I'd lent him money to go to San Francisco.

"I'd forgotten I gave this to you," I said, as he resisted my efforts to return the bills, which crackled in our fingers.

"I think," Devi said, "that you will never forget anything. For example, where I am sitting, what I am wearing, the way the light falls on my picture, the plaster on your left knee, the first words I said to you, and the last."

"I will remember," I said, "the important things."

Devi smiled. "Important to whom?"

"Or perhaps the unimportant things—the Band-Aid on my left knee. . . . It sometimes works like that."

I would remember the hiss of the radiator that occupied our silence, the silvery smash of an ornament that dropped of its own weight from the limp branch of the tree we should have thrown out long ago, the way the cat jumped on Devi's lap and Devi stroked, stroked, stroked.

"And what will you remember?"

"Your dress—like claret—and the way the street light comes into this room, the streak of silver where your hair waves to cup your chin, the way the light falls on my picture, the noise the radiator makes, your face as it looks now."

"How?"

"Sad. Lost. Like Lucy's face when Lucy is asleep. And the first words you said to me, and the last."

"What were the first words I said to you?"

"You said, 'Are you happy?' "

"And what shall be the last?"

Devi didn't answer, he stroked the cat.

"Eileen and Jim would like us to spend a weekend in the country with them," I said. "Next weekend." Eileen was my best friend. Jim was her husband.

Devi's face brightened. "A weekend in the country? Long walks in the snow?"

"Yes."

And a room of our own.

"I can already remember remembering those walks," Devi said, his head bent to the purr of the cat, his voice a shadow of a voice.

"Oh, Devi." I turned my face from him.

But now he was holding me in his arms, kissing my cheeks, my hair, my eyes, rocking my body, which felt as if it had been bludgeoned, his hot tears mingling with mine. "I can't," he said. "I can't."

"Why not."

"I can't marry you."

"You don't love me."

"So wise, and you understand nothing."

He slipped his jacket off, and held me to his breast. I kissed the hair on his warm brown chest. "You *do* love me?"

"Can't you recognize terror?" It was difficult to make out his words, anger muffled sound.

In his anger I recognized the first faint alarms of victory. "We could try," I said, my mouth at home in the wiry hair of his chest.

"And suppose it should be terrible?"

"It wouldn't be terrible. The first time always *is* terrible. It would be wonderful."

"It might," he said; "it might be wonderful, and that might be terrible."

"But why?"

"I have a history."

"So do we all."

"And you were not meant to be in the story."

"I am however in the story. You put me there."

"I should make you unhappy."

"No."

"I am not a man who stays. . . . You look like a madonna."

"Do madonnas sniffle when they cry?"

"How funny you are."

"We could try, Devi."

"And St. John?"

"Is he important?"

"To whom?"

We were like two exhausted children, limp in each other's arms.

"I've never been faithful to anyone," Devi said.

"Perhaps because no one has ever been faithful to you?"

"Have you ever tried to imagine my life? My life away from you?"

"Yes."

"All of it?"

"Yes."

"And still you want to try?"

"Yes."

"And you're quite sure you're not making any of the usual mistakes? You're not confusing tenderness with love? You don't regard me," he said, turning his gaze again toward his painting (a palette like that of Matisse, "so un-Indian," Stephan had said; "one would never guess his origins, a changeling boy"). "You don't regard me as an interesting experiment?"

"No. I'm sure."

"No," he said, more to himself than to me, and as if in dialogue with his painting, "she is not trying to annex me, I am not her fascinating Wog. You don't," he said to me, "have the soul of an imperialist."

"I hope not."

"You don't acquire people."

"I don't think so. Devi, why do we need to talk so much?"

"And if," he said, "I should need a night out with the boys? You wouldn't mind my bit of pleasure?"

"Perhaps you wouldn't need to?"

"And if I should?"

"Devi, I wouldn't mind anything ever again. I wouldn't mind being in a burning building, deaf, dumb, and blind, provided I were with you."

"How funny you are. I should flee, of course, from a burning building. I should abandon you, no immolations for me." But he laughed. And put my hand where it longed to be. And just as quickly removed it, though he was ready for love, and my hand, never happier in its life, had begun eagerly to demonstrate its happiness.

"No," he said. "At the weekend. While it snows. Perhaps it will snow forever, and we shall grow old and old."

"And tonight?"

"Tonight you go to bed and I sleep in here, with my picture, and the street light shining in. And tomorrow morning you shall have bacon and fried bread and tea in bed."

At five I awakened. I slipped my dress over my nakedness and, as glad and apprehensive as I had ever been, walked to the living room.

Devi was awake, clothed, smoking on the Empire couch. "There is," he said, taking in at once how little lay between him and my nakedness, "no bread."

"Too early for bread," I said, sitting at his feet.

"Too early for talk," he said. "Too many words," stubbing out a half-smoked Camel and lighting another one. "I have a hangover."

"You only had two glasses of wine."

"Nevertheless."

I rested my hand on his ankle. He swung his leg down. He hadn't even taken off his shoes.

"I promised you breakfast in bed."

He'd promised me everything.

"There's an all-night deli around the corner," I said.

Next weekend, while it snows.

"I fancy a walk," he said; "Will you lend me a quid? Off you go, under the covers"—frowning at a glimpse of thigh.

"I can't sleep."

"You have a hangover from your too many words. Sleep will do you good."

"Don't sound like a nanny."

"A nancy, I think, is the word you're searching for."

Oh, Devi!

"I'm off."

At ten I awakened again; the house smelled of bacon. I put on a bra and underpants, a robe, I walked through the kitchen into the living room.

"Devi, are you in the bathroom?"

On the stove the bacon was growing cold in its fat. Thick slices of bread on the breadboard, on the kitchen counter a note:

This morning, for the first time, I felt freer in the street than in your home. I realise my "haven of peace and sanity" is about to become a prison despite everyone's too emphatically socialized good intentions. So sorry to have to say this, what choice is there? It's true. I would prefer not to come to Eileen and Jim's at the weekend. I don't feel I shall enjoy it, so there is no reason to.

If you go, have a good time.

Thank you for my Christmas goodies. I shall enjoy sitting in my room, wearing the cologne, controlling the kaleidoscope, seeing perfect patterns splinter—an exile fit for a queen.

I wish you a peaceful week. I need time for myself, perhaps we can meet after you get back.

Love to Lucy,

D.

# Chapter Thirteen

At Jim and Eileen's house that weekend, the snow fell, and Devi's prophecy came true, though not in the way he had meant it: I grew old and old.

It is said that thinking is simply an intensified form of feeling, but when one's feelings are a violent formless welter, one is incapable of thought, one is robbed even of intuition. And violence is its own anesthetist. The numbness it induces feels very much like calm.

The snow fell, and only occasionally was my calm disturbed by a violent spasm of feeling, a thought that contained no other thought, a question that did not admit of any answer: *Cruel, he is cruel. Why, why, why. His face.*

Eileen sat up very late with me, endless glasses of wine. I had shown her his note. She was blessedly silent; she treated me like a convalescent—though I was as yet only at the portals of my illness, my grief. Jim's words were like stones dropped in the silence—"he's frightened, he's selfish, psychopaths are often charming, he thinks you have manipulated him, he'll come back. . . ." Eileen silenced him. At last Jim left us, two women alone together, in a glass house, while outside it snowed and snowed and I grew old and old; and my dearest friend mothered me—blankets and tea and wine and new logs on the fire, and her gracious silence. She had no theories to propound, for which I thanked God.

"God is all very well," I said to Eileen, who had been a nun, "but the trouble is I want Devi, too, not just an abstraction in a substance." And I wanted a mother, not mine. Eileen was carrying her first child. I envied her. I wanted to be a child, and

I wanted to be a mother again. Dully I wanted Devi. *Why is he so cruel.*

"If the baby is a girl, we'll name it Lucy," Eileen said.

Lucy. The real world. Nothing was real but the snow, the fire, the teacup in my hand. Tea laced with brandy. Eileen was good.

"Will it end?"

"Will what end?"

"This."

"Some things never end, one never recovers, one only acts as if one has," Eileen said; she was knitting.

"Lucy needs new clothes for spring."

"You'll buy them," Eileen said.

"Yes," I said, "and brush my teeth." Orthodontists, supermarkets, sitters, magazine editors, the kitty litter, plants to water, cats to feed. Lucy. Lemon oil on old wood, gossip and diets and subways and bills, *The New York Times*, the Middle East.

"It's hard to believe there is a real world outside," I said.

"This is the real world, too," Eileen said.

Why doesn't love save.

"Come here," Eileen said, and she pulled me to her and I rested my cheek against her stomach and felt her baby kick.

Lucy.

## Chapter Fourteen

Devi sent me a note from Baltimore, written on a scrap of butcher paper in red ink:

> I trusted you. If I have ever led you to believe by word or gesture that my love for you was anything other than that of a brother for a sister, I suppose I must apologize. You exaggerated all my gestures. Perhaps you need to get out in the real world more. I am having a peaceful time here with my pal, nothing more to disturb me than dirty socks lying around the living room. Nobody here on an anthropological dig of my psyche. Perhaps I should thank you for having advanced my notions of art: I have become a confirmed minimalist—in life, as in art. Large canvases don't suit me any more. By minimalist I mean something entirely different to "Minimalism." True minimalism is representational—draw a daisy, draw a cat. Nothing that can be misunderstood, nothing open to (mis)interpretation. Small enough to be tucked in a drawer, not available to the untutored gaze of pretentious vulgarians—or, worse, to the tutored gaze. . . . Smoking good hash. Love to Lucy, D.

I found bloodstains on Lucy's silk bedspread. She and Neddy Nickle had spent the afternoon closeted in her room.

"Lucy, I found bloodstains on the good bedspread."

"I know. It's awful. Can the cleaners get them out?"

"What were you doing in there? That was my grandmother's bedspread, and nobody got bloodstains on it for eighty years, as a matter of fact it was a wedding present to me, the lace was handmade."

"I know. I'm sorry, can the cleaners get them out?"

"The point is, what were you and Neddy Nickle doing in there?"

"Nothing I feel guilty about."

"Why don't you tell me what you were doing and I'll tell you whether you ought to feel guilty. Jesus Christ, I was right in the next room typing."

"So what are you worried about, the bedspread or your privacy, or what?"

"Idiot."

"Thanks a lot. Now I really feel like telling you what I was doing."

"What were you doing? I'm concerned about you, idiot, not the bedspread."

"So that's why you call me names. Why don't you just call me a slut?"

"Thanks. Would you explain the bloodstains, please?"

"I have my period. We were Fooling Around. I was not Doing It. Take back the idiot."

"You're not an idiot. I am."

"So where's Devi, nowadays?"

Devi, according to Stephan, was living in Baltimore, having cleared out of the apartment on Sutton Place, "leaving nothing but paint on the carpet and a child's toy."

"A child's toy?"

"A kaleidoscope. Quite appropriate when one thinks . . ."

"I don't want to think, Stephan."

We were having dinner at Lutece.

"My dear," Stephan said, "I am so truly sorry."

"Can you help me understand?"

"Only at the risk of offending you."

"Oh, I'm beyond that."

"One has always regarded Devi . . ."

I interrupted Stephan with an exasperated sigh.

"*I* have always regarded Devi," Stephan said, "that is to say

. . . he is like a brilliant imitation of a minor masterpiece. Of course one wishes to possess it—him, but one eventually feels soiled and uncomfortable, to say nothing of cheated, living with a charming fraud."

"I was not uncomfortable. And I never regarded him as a fraud. A fraudulent *what?* He is not a painting, Stephan, to be bought."

"Do understand metaphor. He is not a painting, but he can be bought."

"Not by me, he couldn't. And in any case, if I understand what you're saying, it would explain my leaving *him.* But I didn't. He turned on me. As for being bought—he's so independent he won't even expose his paintings to what he calls the vulgar view."

"He has, however, accepted money from collectors for paintings—which are now, one supposes, adorning the walls of a gay bath. So like him—a gesture of spite, think what the steam must be doing to those lovely oils."

"You like the paintings?"

"How could one not? It is he who is the fraud, the paintings are first-rate. His work is the best part of him."

"He says so too."

"So naturally—given his perversity—he gives them a home in a steam bath. It is enough to make one weep."

"You don't *know* that they're in a steam bath. And I am not weeping over art, Stephan."

"Have you questioned him closely about St. John?"

"I've asked very few questions."

"Tact? You are not well known, dear, for your tact."

"Yes, tact. No, fear. I don't know. He's not a person one questions."

"He is not a person one asks questions of, but he does expound. On the Meaning of Life and Art, on Politics-and-Art, quite boring and not at all to the point."

"The point being what? He doesn't expound. He talks. *We* talked."

"Yes. One can see the appeal for you, you yourself are quite interested in Politics-and-Art. It's rather interesting how many otherwise intelligent people are."

"Keep it up and I leave before the fish."

"Forgive me. One has so seldom seen you in pain one doesn't quite know what to do."

"Start with St. John."

"St. John is wildly in love with Devi. . . ."

"That isn't what Devi says. Devi gave me to understand that if anything it was the other way around."

"That," Stephan said, "is exactly to the point. Devi cannot receive love. Devi cannot perceive love as love. It is quite beyond my poor powers to understand the convolutions of his mind. St. John could grovel before him—he probably has—and Devi would protest that he is being dominated. Devi is intent on casting himself as victim, you must have observed."

"I thought Devi loved me."

"Quite."

"You think he did love me?"

"I think your great mistake was to let him know that you loved him. He likes to live on meager rations."

"How could I have loved him and not have made it known? I don't understand."

"You persist in being reasonable. We are not talking about logic, we are talking about Devi, and Devi is quite mad. . . . Is there something wrong with that sauce?"

"Not clinically mad?"

"I shouldn't be surprised."

It was some time before I took this in.

"Explain to me," I said, "why I feel crazy. I am used to understanding things."

"Devi is not to be understood. He defeats all efforts. He rejoices in being misunderstood. If you made any progress toward understanding him . . ."

"I thought I did."

"Exactly. If you made any progress toward understanding him, he would damn you for it."

"You don't think—now it's my turn to risk offending you—you don't think that it was just as simple as 'What does this ridiculous woman think she's doing? She knows I'm a queer. She's misinterpreted everything and made me miserable because she wouldn't settle for a loving friendship—she had to make it into sex'?"

"My dear, I would venture to say that your gender was almost entirely irrelevant. Devi turns on anyone who loves him. And he can't help being seductive, any more than you can. Only with you, one assumes, one gets the payoff."

"Am I seductive?"

"As is your daughter, my niece, whom I haven't seen, due to your seclusion in the vale of tears, and your obsession with a madman. Whom *do* you see, by the way? A hothouse existence never suited you before, and now—"

"I leave before dessert."

"One . . . *I* have always been seduced by your charm. When you choose to exercise it. Do, please, sit down."

"I never think of myself as seductive."

"The mark of the true seducer. One has sometimes wished . . ."

"One has sometimes wished what?"

"I think it might be rather pleasant to go to bed with you. One knows, of course, the appropriate technology."

Oh dear.

"You wouldn't like it, Stephan. You like skinny men."

"All this suffering has turned you into a wraith."

"I'm glad to know it's been good for something."

"My offer stands."

"Thank you, Stephan. You are kind. Tell me about his apartment. St. John's."

"May one know why?"

"I want to place Devi. I want to be able to see him there."

"Belgravia, Chester Row."

"But isn't that very rich?"

"He will have told you that St. John does something in the City. On the Exchange. Very rich indeed."

"Funny, I imagined a mews in Southwest Ken."

"What *do* you and Devi talk about? You are in command of remarkably few facts."

"Describe the apartment."

Stephan warmed to his task. Nothing gave him more pleasure than talking about porcelain and objets d'arts; and St.
John, it appeared, was impeccable as to taste.

Later, at Studio 54, I irked Stephan by refusing to dance. In
the space of five minutes the dancers—all of them—looked
fluid and sensual, then jerky and marionettelike, then like ro-
bots, alternately pelvically engaged and totally self-absorbed. I
was forgetting how the body speaks; this is what it means to
grow old. Because I could not read Devi's emotions, I was
losing my ability to understand the language of the body; it
frightened me. The skin is an organ; I wanted to be held.

Stephan's chauffeur drove me home.

"He can't help being seductive," Stephan had said; "I would
venture to say your gender was irrelevant." So had there been
other women? I did not believe that. I was as sure of that as I
was unsure of everything else. Nothing cohered.

I gave a moment's thought to taking Stephan's chauffeur—
who gave every indication of being amenable—up to bed with
me. I dismissed the thought.

I wanted to be held.

I knocked on Lucy's door and asked her if she'd like to watch
television in bed with me. But Lucy was watching *Random
Harvest*, and—oh dear, she was growing older—wanted to cry
alone.

I settled for reading a feminist analysis of transsexualism,
which succeeded in explaining nothing to me, though the
writer had many words to say, and I tried to imagine what I
would be like if I were housed in a man's body. I saw certain
advantages: Swimming trunks, for example, would be easier to
pull on than a bathing suit, one wouldn't have to worry about
breasts. It would be nice to enter the water like a sword. And
less flesh to grow withered and flabby and old. I imagined my
male body poised at the threshold of a room full of strangers;
but my imagination could not propel my body past the threshold, and, listening to Frank Sinatra croon "Try a Little Tenderness" on the radio, I fell asleep.

I dreamed I was abducted for having refused to sell some

property that belonged to me; my trial was held at Sotheby's. Everyone was very well-mannered, very kind. I was sentenced to death. My judges and inquisitors sat me at a refectory table on an oceangoing vessel and tied a straw around my neck and strangled me; just as I was about to black out, they untied the straw and told me I was to be allowed to live, but not for long: A stumpy brown man, leathery, with a square-shaped head and little pigs' eyes, was assigned to be my rapist. His arms swung loosely as he described, in measured, cultivated tones and graphically, how he would bugger me to death. I took the news very calmly, I knew that there was no torture I could not endure. I offered up my pain to God. Lucy stood on the shore in a long white Victorian summer gown; they told me, smiling, that she would be killed, too. But Lucy did not believe in God, for her He did not exist, so how could she go to Him, and why could I not reach her hand? I cried for Lucy in my dream, and I woke up crying for Lucy, who did not believe in God; and I prayed to the God in whom, in my dream, I had so unequivocably believed; I prayed for the calm I had achieved in my dream and I prayed for Lucy's safety and salvation. But the God who had so willingly received me in my dream retreated as my consciousness returned.

Out of this dream I formed a deep conviction that I had done Devi inestimable harm.

And for several weeks a pinched nerve in my lower back rendered my body nearly dysfunctional.

# *Chapter Fifteen*

In February, Devi called from Pennsylvania Station. He had some good hash, and could he come over?

Two hours later he called again. He had decided to return to Baltimore, he would come another night soon and bring the fifty dollars he still owed me.

All alone and quite deliberately I got drunk. I called to make an Amtrak reservation for a morning Metroliner to Baltimore; I called the sitter.

Coming out of the train station at Baltimore I slipped on ice and twisted my ankle and fell in a crazy heap. The taxi driver who came to my rescue told me that with thighs like mine I'd be a natural for sixty-nine. I told him to fuck off and limped to another cab. I had the address written in red ink on a scrap of butcher paper. The impassive driver drove around the block five times. Then we parked across the street, while I smoked twenty cigarettes. But the house told me nothing, an anonymous house on an anonymous street, and neither Devi nor his friend came out of it, nor was there any sign of life behind the blank, forbidding windows. I wasn't even sure I had properly read the scrawled address.

I had to use the bathroom at Pennsylvania Station. The old black attendant was mopping up somebody's vomit. I gave her a fifteen dollar tip.

Devi came early in March.

"You haven't thrown away the Christmas tree!" Nor had I removed the ornaments, or the colored lights.

"I've stopped smoking."

"Yes?"

"Yes, and it's made me depressed. Lucy and Neddy Nickle keep promising to throw it out, but they keep forgetting. How are you?"

"I thought half the pleasure of being a mother was to give orders?"

"Would you like a drink?"

"Here's the fifty," Devi said. "I see my picture is still here."

"Where else should it be?"

"Depression becomes you. You look beautiful tonight."

"It must be all the chocolate truffles I'm eating."

"Chocolates?"

"To keep from putting a cigarette in my mouth. I eat chocolates and lie in bed and watch soap operas." I omitted to tell him that I also cried, that I had grown so mistrustful of my body I went downstairs only to collect the mail, I ordered all my groceries by phone, Lucy bought me chocolates and vanilla fudge every night.

"And between chocs?"

"Work. The usual." In fact I had not written a word, nor had I accepted a dinner invitation, for over a month. I'd turned the telephone answering machine on and answered no calls, waiting only for one call, which I no longer had any reason to believe would come.

"You seem to be out quite a lot. I get the machine."

"There were no messages from you."

"No? Perhaps I just rang off. What are you drinking?"

"Amaretto with heavy cream."

"Too much of a muchness. Suits your personality, however. May I have a beer?"

I had asked few questions; I would not begin now. Devi gloomily consulted his beer, shifted uneasily in the uncomfortable chair he always chose, and addressed himself to his painting: "Lovely new digs at the Y," he said.

"Yes?"

"Near to Central Park. I am glad to be free of Stephan. Have you seen Stephan? He has fucked me over royally. Having appointed himself my dealer, he holds all the cards, which is to say all the checks. I am dealt out a pittance when it suits him."

"You've sold paintings?"

"Haven't I said so?"

"And the collectors have the paintings?"

"What it amounts to is that, having once had the use of me, he treats me as if I were annexed territory and talks vaguely about bookkeeping problems whenever I demand what is my due."

"I see." I did not see. According to Stephan, Devi's collectors were still waiting for the goods.

"You don't see at all," Devi said crossly—and it struck me, not for the first time, that when Devi was angry, his inflection became more Indian. When Devi felt himself to be cornered, he clothed his words in a foreign accent.

Devi smiled, in secret communion with his painting; and, with a warm glance and a sigh, erased history. "Shall I play some Bach?" *"Jesu, Joy of Man's Desiring."* "Shall we watch the telly?" I led the way to my bedroom and perched self-consciously on the bed, fiddling with the television dial to hide my confusion. He stretched out contentedly. "I think I'll hang my picture in here. To keep it safe from harm. I miss Lucy," he said, "we need her with us. Or not." He heaped pillows behind my head, and rested his head in my lap. "I am happy to be home again," he said. I received this with a dazzled blankness, and, as if this were a dream to be held on to, I fell asleep. When I awoke, he was staring at the ceiling, a sweet complicitous smile playing across his face: "You snore," he said, and surrounded me, kissing me lightly on the lips. "I must clean those windows for you. I like to see the dawn wash your face. What do you think of this?" He produced a penciled sketch of a woman holding a baby on her lap, a young girl leaning over her shoulder. The girl was Lucy, and I supposed the woman, though she was beautiful, to be me; but why the other child?

"Who is the baby?" I asked.

"How funny you are," Devi said.

# *Chapter Sixteen*

Weeks passed. It was an unusually gentle spring; the warm breezes caressed my skin, which, since Lucy had been seeing Neddy Nickle, felt winter-dry and hungry. My hands, unused, now, to loving, looked like an old woman's hands. I am vain about my hands, my fingers are long and well shaped. I found two liver spots. My hands looked like my mother's hands, hands she used to cover with cold cream and old cotton gloves at night, to no avail. (And of what avail those hands could have been to my father, I could not imagine.)

Devi was going back to England.

He had asked me to meet him at the YMCA. He wasn't there.

The lobby of the Y near Lincoln Center is handsome: Spanish tiles on the floor and walls, a mahogany reception desk, mahogany roof beams. It is gay, almost (in that other sense of the word), except for the gray men that drift by, their hungry eyes taking note of my femaleness and dismissing me; I am not what they want, my body is of no use. One knows what the anonymous rectangular rooms are like: a single naked ceiling light in a wire cage, a hard chair, a writing table, a cot too short and narrow for love. One wonders what the shower cubicles are like; one imagines slivers of dirty soap, sticky rubber bath mats stained with years' accumulation of transients' dirt and wasted seed; blind couplings of men, strangers, slippery with soap, the sound of water disguising the final cry of the act of love. Love? I tried not to imagine the couplings.

I called him on the house phone. No answer. I was of no use.

I am inured to pain, I thought; and it was over long ago. But I could not will my heart into numbness; I felt a physical pain in my chest. My brain was anesthetized, subdued by my will;

there was only that steady hurt in my contracting heart, and these labor pains would give birth only to new pain, renewing itself endlessly, feeding on itself. I am betrayed, I thought, by this red muscle, a pump, an intricate piece of plumbing in an empty house; I am an empty house, nobody inhabits me. For the first time in my life, I hated having my period; I would never have a child again, his child, I would give birth only to pain, my body was useless to me, its rhythms were mocking me, what good was it, was I? In seven days it would be Easter and Devi would be gone and in church we would praise the risen Lord. He died to give us life, but I do not want to live in this white despair; better for my flesh to feed the lilacs. Dear God, I am forgetting Lucy. In the midst of life there is death, and in the midst of pain there is the orthodontist's bill to pay, the graduation dress to buy. Dear God, forgive me for forgetting Lucy; who will straighten her teeth if I die? And now I will leave because he is not coming, I will never see him again.

When he walked in—leather jacket, jeans—I was laughing.

"You're laughing, why?"

"I was thinking of Lucy's teeth. She has to wear a retainer. Do you know what a retainer is?"

"Is it funny?"

"Yes, wires, very funny. Can you imagine poor Yorick's skull with wired teeth? You're late."

"The wires would decay before the teeth, I suppose—as irrelevant a detail as where my paintings are, why do you concern yourself with such things? Am I late? I was just saying good-bye. Sorry."

"Good-bye to whom?"

"To places. Are you feeling ill?"

"I have my period. My thighs are sticky. I am contemplating my mortality. With pleasure. Do you know that if you sleep on your left side it will shorten your life by a year? I read that. Your left side, where your heart is. Do you think when people are dying they remember that they haven't thrown the garbage out? Do you know that it's perfectly possible to feel your heart breaking and to wonder at the same time who will pay the dentist's bill? I had an aunt who died with the words 'whiskey sour' on her lips. I don't believe people see their lives flash before them when they drown. Not at all. I think they think, 'Oh God, my daughter will have to have a TV dinner tonight, will she remember to peel the foil back from the apple cobbler before she puts it in the oven?' Do you think that's funny? I once knew a man who killed himself and the person who found him said, 'He's dribbled egg yolk on his shirt.' Look at those people carrying palms—I left mine in the taxi—have you ever actually imagined Jesus eating a meal? Aside from the wedding feast and the last one, of course. Middle Eastern food isn't everybody's cup of tea, including God's, I suspect. He didn't know that he was God so maybe he was thinking—how do we know?—something silly when he died. I bet that never crossed the minds of those people with palms. Where are you taking me?"

He was steering me to a bar on the other side of Broadway, holding my hand exactly as if I were of value, exactly as if my body were of use.

"What am I supposed to do with that handkerchief, Devi?"

"Your face is covered with snot and tears." Broadway was a kaleidoscope of colors, I could hardly see. He was taking my hysteria very calmly.

"Blow your nose."

"Yes."

"How funny you are, thinking I could ever really leave you."

His words registered and didn't register; they felt like soft hammers, leaving no impression. They could mean anything, they could mean everything, they could mean nothing; I was too weary to decode. I behaved like a good and obedient child, mopping my face, which was occasioning many stares. "You should have been a nanny," I said, and at once we were laughing, hugging each other on a traffic island. Happiness always came to us like that, sudden and unexpected.

The bar he took me to was dark. The spring sunlight stopped at its threshold. For a long time we didn't speak. I don't know how many vodkas and tonics. I fed the jukebox countless quarters—Frank Sinatra, "Send in the Clowns." Devi didn't seem to mind.

"You know what you wanted?" he asked. "That big love affair?"

"Yes."

"Well, you have had it, you know. I am in love with you, I always have been. It was never New York, it was always you. You have been my reason for everything."

"Then why . . . ?"

"No, don't talk. I just want to look at you. You will understand everything."

"I don't understand anything. I look terrible." In fact I had to lose fifteen pounds, though why this should occur to me now was beyond my surmising.

"No," Devi said, reading my mind. "If you lose weight, I shall gain your weight."

"I don't understand you."

"And, in any case, your weight is amplitude, generosity. And my thinness is . . . you see? You must understand how not to disturb our balance."

"Well, I don't. Your face," I said. "How does it feel to be so beautiful?"

"Am I beautiful?" Devi said, bemused; and sounding a little frightened.

"You must know that you are."

"The trouble is, I can't see my face in a mirror. Shaving," he said, "can be rather difficult."

Dear God, and I would have said that he wasn't at all drunk. Now even my heart was numb: vodka, unanswered questions, unasked questions. I didn't even know how old he was, and now he was leaving. Or not? Younger than me, but by how much?

He left to go to the men's room.

"No," he said. "As always. I just see bits and pieces, my face won't assemble itself for me."

"I don't understand."

"It's very simple. When I look at myself my face fractures. I've told you. And you are my mirror. That is why I have to smash you. I told you you would understand."

Send in the clowns.

"Am I allowed to ask questions?" Stephan's words—"clinically mad"—were nibbling at the back of my vodka-besotted, pain-besotted mind; I dismissed them.

"There are no questions," Devi said. "I love you."

Afterward we went to Gaylord India Restaurant. He took as much delight in his food as a boy at boarding school who has received a package of sweets from home. I had no appetite. I ate so as not to spoil his pleasure. I watched his blunt-edged fingers, nails pared down to reveal a spatulate cushion of flesh, tucking neat little morsels of food into his mouth with that wonderfully economical movement Indians have. ("Hands more beautiful than Durer's," I'd once said. "Silly," he'd replied; but he too is vain about his hands. He is vain and I am vain—I wonder if the concept of twinning is itself mad.) From plate to fingers to mouth in what seems like one flowing gesture. His lips—a darker brown than the honey-olive brown of his face—showed a faint line of pearly pink, like that of the inside of a seashell, when he opened his mouth to receive the food. An image of what his mouth received in bed flashed across my mind.

"Beautiful dhal," he said, his thumb scooping lentils into cupped fingers. "Why is it that everything you do is perfect? I see that you are cruising the waiter. Do you fancy him? Don't protest, I like it, I like to watch men succumbing to you, it's pretty."

I hadn't even noticed the waiter except as someone who was there to serve Devi.

"I hadn't noticed the waiter."

"Nonsense, he hovers over you, he's ripe for the picking, what is it with you and men?" Devi chose *rasgullas* and *gulab jamuns* from a dessert trolley. "I am coming back of course," he said, licking rose water from his middle finger. "But not to stay at Stephan's house, that bastard."

"So at the Y?"

"Why would you think that? You'll find me a flat on your street, of course. I have business to settle in London. It's the asshole of the world, London is. I have to clean out my flat and negotiate with my dealer. Bloody London. Rain and bad food and everybody depressed, everything bleak, and supercilious upperclass bastards looking at my work, spoiling it for me. What England wants is another war to put a boot up its ass and set it going again."

"Then why do you go back?"

"I've told you: My flatmate wants me to buy a half-share in the flat, I don't want to, it has to be arranged. Though there is something to be said for tepid old London—very few buzzes, no excitement, but perhaps a spot of boredom would be good for my soul, what do you think? One doesn't have to make any choices there because there is nothing to choose among, isn't it? Everything seems to be of equal importance, or of equal unimportance, I'll stay a bit and see how it suits me. You won't put a curse on my plane, will you? I will arrive safely? You won't bend me to your will?"

Would I not if I could. Devi thinks I am a witch, he fears me. Some witch. I don't even begin to understand events well enough to manipulate them.

"You are a witch. A very nice witch, of course. You must wish for me only that which I wish for myself."

"If only you'd remember that I clean out the kitty litter and shop for broccoli—I am very ordinary, I keep telling you— you'd know better than to say I'm a witch. I haven't managed to seduce you. . . ."

"But that's the point, you have. Why doesn't Lucy clean out the kitty litter?"

"And I would bend you to my will if I could, but I can't. When will you come back?"

"Hmmm. Do you endure Stephan out of charity or do you enjoy the glimpses of trendy fag life he provides you with? White bastard. One of the reasons I go back to London is to kill Stephan off. In my mind, I mean. This hatred of him is bad for me; it spoils my pleasures."

"I've never understood exactly what he's done. Anyway he says he hasn't done it."

"Veiled his game in silence disguised as shyness, is what he's done."

"But what was his game?"

"He misled me into believing we were playing the same game. My idea was, Let's roll the dice and see what comes out, whatever happens it'll be a change and we'll turn it to our mutual advantage. He is a meticulous long-range planner. What I flee from is his I-only-know-I'll-get-what-I-want-if-I-connive-at-it-and-directness-is-offensive. A shuffle-gaited, maimed approach to something that could have been accomplished by a dozen direct words in the first week of my arrival."

Devi says these angry words, a speech, looking the picture of contentment, replete.

"What was his plan? What did you hope to accomplish? What dozen direct words might he have said?"

"You are Candida. You see the good in a Calvinist-Episcopalian prig who uses my art to line his pocketbook."

"Is this a loyalty test?"

"Of course the suffering you see in him," Devi said, "isn't there, it's just your invention. And adorable that you do invent it, so long as you always choose for me as against him. He has no pain, only fake angst. Your loyalty to him hasn't educated you. You, if you weren't you, would understand that manipulative Calvinist pigs have to be killed. In your case, it's just as much what you don't see as what you do see that makes you lovable. I have to kill him off in my mind. He is too unimportant to exist there, spoiling my pleasures, it is a wonder he hasn't been murdered already. There have been moments when I've wondered about your generosity, though. I do wonder if it isn't self-serving—do you get high on it?—and besides I want it reserved for me."

I do not like all this talk of killing. "Give me what you have in the inside pocket of your jacket—that one, on the left."

I do not know why I say this. From his pocket Devi produces, without surprise, indeed with a small show of pleasure, the key to Stephan's apartment.

"And do you still say you are not a witch? How did you know Stephan's key was there? You must promise only to think good thoughts of me, you are my good witch, you keep me safe from harm. Though of course I wouldn't have killed him." He kisses me, his mouth sticky with rose water. "Here. Wipe your eyes and blow your nose. Good coffee. Too bad we can't have pan. Will you come with me to India? Soon?"

"Oh, Devi."

"How funny you are, crying when I love you so much. Poor Western witch, you don't understand that nothing can separate us."

"I understand that you are going away."

# Part Two

*My love, my love.*
*Why have you left me alone?*

JAMES JOYCE

*Were Departure Separation, there would be neither*
*Nature nor Art, for there would be no World.*

EMILY DICKINSON

# *Chapter One*

Letter from Devi:

> London is beautiful, so clean and orderly and civilized. I
> feel like I'm on a health farm, all these tranquil people in
> the streets, smiling at the distance, nodding and deferring
> the right of passage to each other. . . . I wrote a letter to
> Stephan, a hideous letter, justified but hideous nonethe-
> less, saying too much and not enough. . . . Happy, here.
> Lots of love to you, high lady. And to Lucy, D.

Years later, I understood. I understood that I was a witch,
and that I had done him harm. I learned painfully, by reliving
Devi in the form of another man—by reliving Devi and by
reloving him. There are people it is not possible to love without damaging them. The only way to love them is not to love
them.

Of course—but this is hindsight—I didn't have to answer
Devi's letters, nothing compelled me to—except the fact that I
am a witch. . . . Well, acted like one. Writing to Devi was a
way to continue obsessing about him—imagine being the object of such an obsession! (For that matter, I could have torn
his letters up without reading them; the thought never entered
my mind.) If I stopped obsessing over Devi, he would stop
obsessing over me. Isn't that what I must, in my mischievous,
witchlike mind, have thought? That incredible false symmetry:
I wanted him to love me, to keep the habit of loving me, so I
had to obsess about him—even when the point of him threat-
ened to become illusive. I had to believe it was real, I had to
keep it real—and so I had to keep on and on about Devi in my
imagination. If my passion dwindled, I could not believe it had

ever been real. If I stopped loving him, where would I be when
he came to find me? He was right: I did believe I had magical
powers. I thought I could keep myself alive in his imagination
by keeping him alive in mine. I couldn't bring myself to be the
one who broke the vital connection. I prefer to be the abandoned, not the abandoner. This is not nobility of character—it
is pure stubbornness. It may even be wickedness: Obsession is
a sin against God because it disturbs the peace He offers us
(the peace I dutifully prayed for every week in church). I once
said to Father Caldwell, my confessor, to whom I returned
after Devi left for England, "If only I could turn this over to
God, if only I could rest quietly in the peace He promises us."
Father Caldwell just sighed. He thought I was going through
the dark night of the soul. He didn't know I was expressing a
fake pietistic sentiment—because in fact I didn't trust God to
handle this as well as I could (and also because I couldn't
convince myself that God—who does play with His cards
pretty close to His chest—was overly concerned). Father Caldwell didn't know, although he gives every appearance of being
wise, that I love the dark. The intense and fearful dark. I like
lightning, too. Father Caldwell thinks my besetting sin is lack
of charity, while in fact it is lack of patience—though that is
such a mean and niggling little sin, I let him believe that lack of
charity is my undoing; I do like people to think well of me. And
I do in fact prefer to be charged with large and messy sins—
perhaps because, as Devi says, I need to dramatize. Odd, how I
have come around to Devi's way of thinking.

The day after I learned that my mother's latest cancer was
inoperable, I drove to her house and proceeded methodically
to plunder her kitchen cabinets. Poor Daddy. He stood near
the sink, wringing his withered, palsied hands, and moaned as
I plundered. I wrapped art-deco highball glasses, and the de-
pression juice glasses I'd drunk from as a child, in the *Daily
News.*
   "Angie, oh, Angie, we'll have nothing to drink out of."
   "Never mind, Daddy, I'll buy you new ones."
   "You're a good girl, Angie, why are you doing this?"

Why, indeed.

I had that morning received a letter from Devi: He was gaining weight. (I was losing weight.)

Thank you for your two delish, nutrish letters. They were wonderful, and sounded just like you. What I miss most about New York is the pastrami and donuts I lived on almost all of the time. I confessed my longing for pastrami to a dealer who couldn't have been more horrified if I'd admitted to a penchant for necrophilia. So—with mental apologies to Carnegie deli—I went on to rave about my friend Angela's exquisite donuts, home cured but just like real, hole in the middle, paper napkin and all. . . . Everyone in England looks beautiful. . . . Till soon, D.

All the world's a hospital. I helped myself to depression-glass milk and sugar pitchers of deepest underwater blue, and I thought of how she used to paste pretty pictures, of kittens, of happy children, on the bottom of my milk glass—a new one every night, cut out from the *Ladies' Home Journal*—so that I should drain the glass to get my reward. I thought of how she'd smiled at my boyfriends coquettishly; she was never my mother: "I'm Angie's relative." She was beautiful. "Don't pass the salt to Angie, her body retains water." She prayed aloud for my salvation and my happiness, but she never kissed me.

I still wanted something from her, some gesture, some ac-knowledgment—forgiveness. Though of what I was guilty I did not know. I found stamped-glass salt and pepper shakers, Woolworth's. A woman who never threw anything away; and never gave anything away, either.

In a cracked restaurant cup I found a folded yellow page on which was printed: "Heavy flowers on a light wallpaper back-ground will give one the impression of falling. While to be showered with roses is not unpleasant, the constant expecta-tion with never a realization doesn't produce at all a pleasing effect." My feelings exactly.

"I'll need a shopping bag, Daddy."

All the world's a hospital.

I told Father Caldwell about the plundering. He told me

plundering—which he quite rightly called stealing—was not an unusual form of grieving, a protest against abandonment. This naturally brought the conversation around to Devi. Father Caldwell likes to make connections—he has had a sophisticated education—and he thinks there is some connection between my feelings for my mother and my feelings for Devi. My mother is to the point only insofar as mothers are always to the point, I said; also fathers. This is what I've decided, having had plenty of time in which to decide. Father Caldwell—who I sometimes think would absolve me if I admitted to hacking up my grandmother in twenty pieces and putting her body in a trunk (a fate which she well deserved)—says God is very much to the point: my loving a man as inaccessible as Devi, he says, is a reflection of my hunger for God, Who seems at times illusive to me. I tell him this is nonsense. God is available to me—why otherwise do I go to church every Sunday (well, almost every Sunday), and eat His body and drink His blood? Where God is concerned, I am the one who plays hard to get.

Sometimes I think my confessor takes a prurient interest in my affair with Devi, but that is a thought I immediately subdue.

"In what way do you think you have damaged him?" my confessor asks.

"Well, if a person says you've damaged him, you've damaged him, haven't you?"

"How?"

"By trying to force him out of his true nature, I suppose."

"But he gave you cause."

"Then by loving him more than he could stand to be loved. It is a form of idolatry. The idol is not responsible for the idolator's zeal. I am reprehensible, not he. And I lack any proof that I have made him better or happier. I have damaged his self-respect. That is what I think."

"I am concerned that your love for Devi is taking you away from the real world of real people. You make everything subsidiary to Devi. Listening to you, one would think no one else but Devi existed."

"Lucy exists. But what you're saying is exactly what I mean by idolatry."

My confessor sighs: "I think in some peculiar way you're enjoying this."

" 'An arrow in the side makes poor traveling, only not to run is a worse pain.' "

"Your love for Devi is stasis, and stasis does not belong in the natural order of things. Think of what he's keeping you *from.* "

"Sex?" I suggest mischievously.

"Healthy sex would be infinitely preferable to this. You may or may not be harming Devi. You are surely harming yourself."

"I am harming Devi."

"How?"

"He says so, therefore I am. I keep him from other loves, he says so."

"Is he capable of love?"

"He's not capable of loving me, apparently, and I won't let go. So I'm harming him."

"Is it possible that you enjoy thinking you have the power to harm? to diminish? If your love for Devi is a form of idolatry— a construction you seem determined to put upon it—then why don't you gently let him go?"

"It's entirely possible that my notion that I'm harming him is a form of vanity. That doesn't mean that I'm not harming him, however. As for letting him go—he keeps writing me these letters. I have to answer them, don't I?"

"No. You can't live in a hothouse forever," my confessor says.

He has a point.


Letter from Devi:

Thank you for your beautiful and loving letter. I was very happy to have it. A fling with a social worker has foundered on account of I could get his mind clicking away, analyzing my every move, "prescribing" himself for me. I suppose it's fair enough, but I got awfully edgy. I fall in love about every five years. I'm trying not to repeat the five-year cycle, but to live in a perpetual state of uncom-

mitted or undefined love with lots of (well, a few) people.
I'm thinking of pastrami and donuts a lot, but I still don't
know when I'll come back. I've finally decided to *like* rain,
cold, and overcast skies. I'm having trouble justifying doing any work, see no point. Being denied the true privi-
lege of being "ordinary," I see no point in making art or
forging connections between art and politics. If there are
no answers, what's the point of my getting steamed up, or
you? Do I *know* there are no answers, and is the steam
merely a way of adding "fervor" to the paintings? You see,
fine lady, wise and conscienceful friend, I am stoned,
hence talking a lot of claptrap. But I feel it strongly—feel,
that is, that there are no answers. And feel that if I lie to
you, I lie to myself—certainly at this stage of our friendship. Why doesn't love save? Love to you and Lucy anyway. D.

P.S. The social worker introduced me to one of his
clients, and said, "Don't get closer than three feet—he's
very friendly, but he hurts anyone who gets closer. Nothing personal—he just can't help it." I know *lots* of people
like that.

I said to Father Caldwell, "The thing is, I offer him false
hope. He thinks I'm sane. Which in a way I am, relatively
speaking. But the minute I get close to him I make demands,
and that makes him crazy, and he wants to hurt me—nothing
personal, he just can't help it. So the kindest thing—the only
kind thing—would be to leave him alone."

"Is it possible to be human without making demands?" Father Caldwell said.

"You don't know Devi, Father," I said.

"I'm not sure I know you," he said.

"That makes two of us," I said.

# Chapter Two

In his absence, my handwriting had come to resemble Devi's—my *g* and my *s* were nearly indistinguishable from his. What could this mean?

"What do you think this means?" I asked Eileen when she visited me that night.

We had settled in for a long evening. Eileen's here-again, gone-again lover was seeing another woman, a woman who had abandoned her children in order to study psychology and family life at NYU; we were planning menus. French, Italian, and Indian cookbooks were spread out on the dining room table. We'd set ourselves the task of writing thirty menus, duplicating nothing, before the night was out. It was the way Eileen and I dealt jointly with distress, and had been ever since the night she arrived, soon after her divorce from Jim, which followed fast upon her miscarriage, full of wild talk of suicide, and I'd fed her *pastina in brodo, pasta e fagioli*, and bread pudding with heavy cream. After she gorged: "What am I going to do?" she asked. "Plan menus," I'd responded; and Marcella Hazan, Julia Child, and Madhur Jaffrey overwhelmed her momentary infatuation with death. For many nights thereafter, we emptied the fridge of comfort foods and nursery foods and drank Amaretto with milk and competed each with each other to devise lovely meals (artichokes and quail; chicken and prunes). Eileen's birthday present to me had been an early edition of Mrs. Beeton (from which I'd more than once made blanc-mange, mostly because I liked the way it sounded—as lovely as the sounds of certain illnesses, melanoma, for example).

"What does it mean, Eileen?"

"I haven't told you my discovery," Eileen said, scribbling

furiously. "You'll like this. All those years I spent thinking I was searching for the perfect chocolate mousse—do you think it's a good idea to curry lobster?—well, I wasn't searching for the perfect chocolate mousse at all. I made this discovery in Purity Diner last week. I realized it was actually chocolate pudding I wanted. *Royal* chocolate pudding. With the skin on top. Like Mama used to make in Jersey City."

"Yes? So what does it mean that my handwriting looks like Devi's? . . . I wouldn't curry lobster—it's a waste. Just boil."

"There's a shrink at the New York Psychiatric Institute who says obsessional love is like an amphetamine high," Eileen said. "The loving brain releases a chemical called phenylethylamine into your blood sugar, and when the brain gets disillusioned, the phenylethylamine stops trickling or pouring, so you binge on chocolate, which is exactly like an amphetamine. . . . I'm planning a dinner for six, breaking all the rules, chicken-liver appetizer with cognac in it, chicken soup, chicken main course, I haven't decided how. And Royal chocolate pudding for dessert. Very frugal—except for the cognac—and not at all according to Hoyle."

"You can always take the chicken from the soup and braise it if you want to be frugal. Now tell me what it means that my handwriting is beginning to resemble Devi's."

"Are you depressed?"

"Moderately. I prefer anxiety."

I had met Eileen at a church bazaar, where, dressed as a gypsy, she was analyzing handwriting. She'd done mine ("not so accessible as she appears to be, flamboyant behavior but excessively private though apparently open"); and we had been friends ever since.

"The Environmental Protection Agency," Eileen said, "has approved a compound called Glossypure. It's a synthetic sexual lure. They sprinkle it over cotton fields to control pests. It's identical to the mating odor of bollworm moths. They lay a false trail with it, and the frustrated male moths give up in exhaustion, and the females—who are actually somewhere else—lay infertile eggs and die. I disapprove. I don't think unwanted species should be curbed by the disruption of their sex lives. My Superior once told me that the imagined delights of sex were like 'the sweet bait in the rat poison.' " She sighed: "At the moment I'm feeling like an unwanted form of life myself."

Eileen did not like to talk about Devi. Eileen did not like to talk about Devi because she claimed to see points of likeness between Devi and Jim, which was, as I often told her, absurd. The truth was Eileen, like so many other people, was terrified of obsessional love because it didn't yield to rational analysis. (The same people I might add—and did—who are up to their eyebrows in books about the Duke and Duchess of Windsor.)

"Eileen, I'm waiting."

"I don't know what your handwriting means," she said crossly. "Your unconscious behaves theatrically. It's a false symmetry. How long would it take to make some rice pudding?"

Stephan called: "What are you doing, dear?"

"Making rice pudding and planning menus. Eileen's here."

"Ah, gastro-porn, the last refuge of the sick of heart, a true perversion. Have you heard from him?"

"Not a word."

"I see that you have no time for me, you prefer to be bored by boring Eileen. We're having a cocktail party on Sunday, bring Lucy of course."

One never knew, with Stephan, whether he was using the imperial *we* or referring to his current lover-in-residence.

"Well, I don't know, my mother's sick. . . ."

"Then we shall provide you with welcome relief from the *malheur* of the sickroom. Dress up, dear, the Metropolitan Opera's coming."

"All of it?"

"Sunday at seven. *Ciao.* "

After the rice pudding, Eileen and I drank Amaretto with heavy cream and turned the ten o'clock news on. Coverage of a Gay Rights march; chanting: "Two-four-six-eight, How do you know your wife is straight? Two-four-six-eight, How do you know your husband's straight?"

"Sometimes I hate them all," I said.

"Then why did you fall in love with a homosexual?" Eileen asked, large amounts of Amaretto inclining her to discuss the dread subject. Eileen pronounced homosexual hom-o-ses-u-al, giving each syllable ponderous weight, as priests often do.

"There are as many reasons for falling in love with a homosexual as with a heterosexual, give me a break, Eileen."

"But you didn't fall in love with a heterosexual, you fell in love with a hom-o-ses-u-al." Eileen has a voice that I can only describe as Irish and nunlike.

"I don't know," I said. "Don't you wish you were one of those tall skinny icy blondes in the movies who say things like 'I don't know how to love!' Don't you? Don't you wish you were Tippi Hedren?"

Eileen laughed. "Not if it meant giving up rice pudding. All the same," she said, squashing three plump raisins between her strong white front teeth, "I'm glad Devi's gone, Angela. You can't live on letters forever," she said, with more hope than conviction.

Oh yes I can, I said, but I didn't say it out loud.

"Of course," Eileen said, "I cheer every gay man who comes out of the closet."

"Why?"

"Well, think about it. Every gay man who comes out of the closet is a man who won't marry a woman. Can you imagine Lucy caught in a marriage like that?"

We both thought of Lucy; and Eileen cried. Sometimes I thought Eileen never cried for her dead baby; but that may have been, as Father Caldwell pointed out, because I wasn't paying great attention to anything but Devi. I cried too. All the world's a hospital.

That night I dreamed of Luna Park and Steeplechase. Lucy and I rode the roller coaster. We wandered among the toy towers and minarets of the amusement park; and when we walked over a grating through which hot air rushed, my dress flew up over my head revealing twin empty cavities where my internal organs were—no womb, no heart—and Lucy laughed and laughed. Then my mother, dressed in the guise of a court jester, spun cotton candy around me; and I suffocated in a hot, pink, sticky shroud.

I struggled out of sleep—out of that appalling shroud—and called the hospital to ask my mother's condition: Stable. For a while I lay chain-smoking, reflecting on my mother's stability, and on my own. Then I read "Little Gidding," and then I fell asleep again.

I dreamed I was wandering among towers and minarets, and all the people around me moved gracefully, languorously; they smiled. Steeplechase and Luna Park had undergone a transformation: I was in the marketplace in Old Delhi, and in the middle of the marketplace stood the Taj Mahal. Then the landscape was obliterated, and Devi stood there; Devi stood next to my bed and whispered my name, "I love you," smiling, and kissed my lips.

Why do we think that what happens in dreams is less real than what happens in real life? I lived the whole of the next day in the afterglow of that nocturnal apparition. (Apparitions may not be real, but they are real apparitions: Devi had visited me, and my body felt loved.) That day I finished a book review two days ahead of deadline; there were invitations to three parties in the mail; I had lunch with an editor who charmed me as I charmed him—sexual electricity in the air, the more pleasant because I knew I would allow nothing to come of it; I took a long walk through Central Park and saw no lunatics at all; I got a phone call from an old friend in Oregon whose life was at last arranging itself well; Lucy and I cooked dinner together and listened to Frank Sinatra records, our quarrel over whether she could go to Studio 54 with Stephan forgotten; we curled up in bed together to watch *Jane Eyre*.

"The movie's better than the book," Lucy said.

"I don't know about that, but I've always liked *Wuthering Heights*—the movie—better than the book."

"Orson Welles would look terrible in color."

"Absolutely," I said.

"She should have let him buy her all those pretty dresses."

"Jane Eyre was a prig and Mr. Rochester was a sadist."

"Absolutely," Lucy said. "The movie after this is *Pride and Prejudice.*"

"You know you won't get up in time for school if we watch *Pride and Prejudice.*"

"I think Eileen is boring," Lucy said.

We watched *Pride and Prejudice.*

We slept till noon, Lucy fried bacon and bread, and then we took a taxi to the Metropolitan Museum of Art and marveled at the blues in the Islamic wing, and then we sat for a while in the outdoor café of the Stanhope, feeling pleased with ourselves, tourists in our own city, and then we walked to the Plaza for tea —Lucy ate sixteen dollars worth of tea sandwiches, I bought her a melon-colored silk blouse at the Plaza boutique, and we watched *The Thin Man* on television when we came home.

Life without Devi was bearable, after all.

That was Tuesday. On Friday my mother was released from the hospital. She called me to tell me she was making escarole salad; she told me how many more nutriments there were in escarole than in iceberg lettuce. "What kind of salad are you making tonight, Angie dear?"

"Romaine."

She asked me if I'd cut my hair. "Short hair is so much more becoming at our age, dear." She told me not to use salt, it was water-retentive. She told me drugs were being sold in school-yards: "Examine the pupils of Lucy's eyes, dear." I asked her how she was feeling, and she said her arthritis was better but she had an ingrown toenail. "Are you feeling it yet, dear?"

"What?"

"Arthritis."

"No."

"You will. At our age we begin to feel these things."

I told her I'd visit her on Sunday, but she said, No, Sunday was a day she'd set aside for prayer.

"Monday?"

Monday was her day to mop the ceilings, would I come on Tuesday. I said I had to interview someone on Tuesday. After a cold silence, she said, "Come whenever you have time for me, dear. Don't bring wine, it's bad for your father's condition. That man never listens to me. And never mind about the glasses you took, everything will go to you anyway.''

Life without Devi was unbearable.

After the telephone conversation with my mother I thought about having a haircut and decided against it. I hennaed my hair bright red. I spent the rest of the afternoon trying on clothes, all of which were too small or too large for me. Lucy came home from school in a sulk, demanding to go to Studio 54. I hurled a coffee mug across the kitchen; then she went into her bedroom, slammed the door, and blasted punk rock on her radio. I blasted Mozart on my stereo; and our downstairs neighbor called to complain.

I got my period.

I dressed for drinks—a dress I hated, black.

I met the respected editor of a woman's magazine at the Algonquin. "I celebrate my abortion every year with a birthday cake," she said. . . . "I got a photograph from a woman who has eight children. Her face is beautiful, but what does she look like from the neck down? . . . I'd want to know the sex of an unborn child; if it were a boy, I'd think seriously of aborting it. Does your child ever seem like a stranger, an alien, to you? That's what I'm afraid of, that I wouldn't like it, that it would be an uninteresting person. . . . One thing feminists can give one another for Christmas is a commitment to a mutual exchange of lies: You tell my boyfriend I'm with you, I tell your boyfriend you're with me—and we can have a weekend of fucking other men. Garage-attendant types who won't engage our emotions. . . . There are witches—serious feminist witches—who eat cookies made with their own menstrual blood." The editor counted seven salted peanuts and allowed herself to eat them after she'd consulted her pocket calorie counter. "The Church burned nine million witches, or was it fourteen—all herbalists and midwives—during the Middle Ages," she said, lifting her much-commented upon sapphire-blue eyes to the cross I wore around my neck. . . . "My God, look at that good-looking man. . . .''

At the next table, two women were engaged in conversation.

"I've had a terrible week," one of them said. "Yesterday a man I booked an around-the-world tour for died. A helicopter blade chopped his head off. I don't know why such awful things always happen to me." "I'm an elegant and sensitive person," her companion said. . . .

Life without Devi was unbearable.

I had dinner with my good friend Sylvia and her good friend Merri, who was one of the most beautiful women in New York. Merri slopped around the living room in a man's flannel robe, her hair disheveled, looking ravishing. "You two are so lucky," she said. "You both do terrific work and you have wonderful kids who love you, and what do I have? I'm thirty-six and no kids, what do I have?" At the moment she had Warren Beatty, and an apartment on Central Park West overlooking the reservoir. "I was talking to Jack Nicholson about it at lunch yesterday, and he agreed. He said, 'You're thirty-six and you have no kids, what do you have?' " She had a weekly television show, an income of $250,000 a year. "Steven"—a film writer—"wants me to commute to California, he'll pay for my shrink. But he's so neurotic. He's so dumb and so guilty about sex. And he expects me to be faithful to him. How can I be faithful to him if I only spend three days a week in Malibu? You don't know how lucky you are." Sylvia and I commiserated with Merri, murmured emptily when she asked us if she should have a child, and apologized for our own good fortune, while tears watered Merri's flawless skin. We washed the dishes in silence while Merri languished in Sylvester Stallone's flannel robe.

In fact I did feel sorry for Merri.

"You're a fucking easy touch," Sylvia said.

"Who, me?"

"I goddamn hate her."

"She's your friend. And in a way she's right. . . ."

"Fuck her! Fuck Warren Beatty and fuck Jack Nicholson and fuck Malibu. When was the last time a film writer offered to pay *your* shrink? My fucking husband's goddamn child-support check bounced this week. She doesn't want a kid, she wants a fucking lapdog. Goddamnit, I hate her for making me apologize to her because my kids love me. And you're a fucking coward for not telling her so. When was the last time you cried on Jack Nicholson's shoulder? *I hate my fucking kids!*" Sylvia screamed, loud enough for Merri to hear; and Merri began to bawl.

I went home to a fight with Lucy, who had appropriated my color TV: "*Why* can't I have one of my own?" She'd burned the leftover pasta and burned the pot, and left the black-and-white TV on in the living room, and now she was hungry and I told her to fry an egg and go to hell and give me back my television set.

Life without Devi was impossible.

# Chapter Three

Eileen—who disliked being asked (she had once been repri-
manded by her Superior for engaging in "mischievous nonsense")—consented to analyze Devi's handwriting. She swore
that she did not read for content, and I believed her. It would
take an hour to decipher a postcard of Devi's. I'd frequently
spent days puzzling over the configuration of one word . . .
always sure, of course, that I'd missed the essential word. It
was my idea that Eileen did not in fact analyze handwriting,
that she was in fact psychic, and read character through her
fingertips. I did not like to tell her so, this idea would have
alarmed her. It never took her more than five minutes to come
to her rapidly penned conclusions.

I gave her a letter of Devi's; one of my ex-husband's, That
Person; and one written me by a man I had chosen not to
marry for reasons that were still opaque to me.

A: Crazy-perverse-contradictory around sex
   Artistic
   Flamboyant and egoless
   Intuitive, very intelligent
   Subject to sudden severe depression
   Fights, struggles with limits, and also with freedom
      (not repressed, tho, in general; Yes in specific
      areas)
   Unselfish
   Self-indulgent
   Strong psychic element
   Lazy
   Ambition, but no consistent drive to achievement
   Idealistic
   Immoral

> Very stubborn
> Violent, wreaks havoc
> This person cannot make other people happy  (*This was Devi.*)

B: Religious overtones
> Not so stable, can be depressive
> Confession-compulsion
> Conflicted
> Intellectual self-image
> Selfish
> Good ability to concentrate, especially on detail
> Not very sexual, but bursts of negative sexuality
> Dishonest
> Cultured
> Can be very generous with money superficially, but not truly
> Does not like self  (*This was That Person.*)

C: Creative, original
> Intelligent
> Cheerful
> Uses all that comes to hand
> Open but controlled
> Idealistic
> People-oriented
> Well-coordinated
> Witty
> Even-tempered
> May start slowly but carries through on projects and relationships  (*This was the man I didn't marry. Why?*)

"What does it mean, Devi is both 'idealistic' and 'immoral'?"

"It means 'I see and approve the better, but follow the worse,'" Eileen said. "A more interesting question is why you aren't with *C.*"

"I'll think about that next week in California. . . . One of the reasons I love you is that you believe so much in the sanctity of the flesh."

"How can I not, when I believe in the Incarnation?"

"I'll think about that in California, too."

"It's remarkable how little theology you know," Eileen said.

"It's because I'm Italian. When I was little, my grandmother used to say, 'Shut up, make the sign of the Cross, and go to sleep.' I thought that was about it. And the rosary, of course . . . You have no sympathy for Devi at all, do you?"

"I sympathize. I don't approve. What frightens me is that you seem determined to regard him as a sad proud sufferer. What you forget is that he's chosen his torment, so there's nothing noble about it at all. He likes it. He invites sympathy, and he gets it."

"How can you possibly say that, it's wicked. How can you possibly know that? We all choose our own torments. You sound just like Father Caldwell. What he won't understand, and what you won't understand, is that I've chosen to make Devi my burden, and that's how I harm him—it's unfair to be someone's burden—unfair to the burden, I mean. You make him sound exactly like Milton's Satan, you know."

"Exactly," Eileen said.

"I notice you sign every Gay Rights petition that comes your way."

"There's no contradiction."

"Tell me more," I said.

"It's one thing to support Gay Rights. It's another to adore a man you know to be a homosexual, by which you make yourself miserable. By which you make *him* miserable. It's perverse."

"That's what Lucy says. So tell me, since what do I know, what does God think about homosexuals?"

"What do I know? I'm obliged to believe He loves them, they're deformed and they're freaks."

"Is that why He loves them? Is that something you would say to your homosexual friends?"

"It's something you would say if you understood your own religion. We're all deformed, we're all freaks in one way or another. Pain turns us into freaks."

"But they're more freakish than the rest of us?"

"Angie, don't go on so. Think about it in California."

"You know, Devi once wrote me that someone ought to figure out what there was about a well-tanned bride that turned gays on so. I thought about that for weeks. Then I realized it was a typo—he'd meant a well-tanned *hide*. But an interesting typo, no?"

Eileen gave me an unrewarding look.

"OK, I know. I'm going on. . . . I'll think about it in California."

# Chapter Four

The day after Eileen's visit, I got a long letter from Devi:

I love you, too. There's a room going here for the next two months, if you feel like a spell of me and a spell of London. Alternatively, I could come back for a spell. I keep saying that, but the conviction with which I say it decreases each time. I can't seem to dislodge myself. I need to talk to you, too. And I feel like crying.

Just back from a bike tour through Cornwall, quite lyrical. I roared through tiny country lanes with hedgerows slapping my face, shirtless—felt like somebody (Peter O'Toole?) in a movie, credit-titles on my back, theme music in my ears, and an Oscar for the most derivative screenplay always just around the corner.

Saw a one-act play by John Mortimer about two Englishmen who have separate car crashes in Italy and wake up in a hospital which has a baroque mural of heaven all over the ceiling. They think they're there—heaven, that is. The one, an atheist who has led a pure and boring life devoted to aesthetics and asceticism, is horrified at having to spend eternity having his life's work constantly rendered meaningless, more so because his wardmate is a fervently moralistic, thoroughly vulgar hedonist who has shamelessly manipulated the lives of—and joyfully screwed—everyone his life has brought him into contact with—and regards heaven to be his right as a consequence. A doctor arrives to shatter their illusion; the atheist, overjoyed at his stay of execution, swears to live as amorally as possible, seeking pleasure wherever he can— till his wife arrives to lead him back to the prison he has constructed for himself (some scholarly work about Byron and his little boys—'your life's work,' she lovingly reminds him). The hedonist, meanwhile—seizing the main chance for pleasure and experience—simply dies. Nice, no?

Before that—before Cornwall—a trip to Spain. The flight was the bumpiest I've ever had. (Or is it I'm older and that jolt in the pit of my stomach isn't quite the deliriously scary thrill it used to be? For example, I've also stopped falling in love!) We didn't so much land as fall onto the runway, and I heard one stewardess remark to another, as a pot of coffee, two orange-juice jugs, and a dozen sausage rolls hurtled down the gangway, "Oh that man, you'd think he'd have gotten the hang of it by now!" I turned to look at her, and amazingly she was positively starry-eyed as she said this, obviously liking her pilots— her men—flawed.

I need to talk to you.

Later . . .

Grief-stricken. Anger, frustration, lovelessness. All solutions are traps of one sort or another. Even freedom is a sort of trap, so that looking for a brave and logical "out" only death and insanity remain. Fear not! My courage is gone—impossible for me to pursue either of those two ends. Meanwhile, I feel surrounded by death, Why? Surrounded by people with eyes like glass beads. When I get the shakes, I drink. As now. Art was never my therapy—I *loved* it, I *opted* for it, it was my only route to sanity. I feel like a man who must send his wife—his boyfriend—out into the streets to whore for the night. I'm not turning into a drunk, I worry every time I produce one of these sweeping statements in case I've given you a fit.

Angela, how bloody lopsided this letter is. How bloody lopsided I am.

I love you.

I've decided St. John does love me. As a punching bag.

I called Devi. After many rings, his fuzzy voice answered, "Hullo?" I'd woken him up.

"Devi, I love you."

"Yes?"

"I said, I love you."

"Yes? I heard."

"How are you?"

"Oh. Sleepy. How is Lucy? Are you working?"

"Devi, I said I love you."

"Hmmm."

"I was thinking, about that play. . . . Are you there?"

"Just groggy."

"Now I feel silly about saying this."

"Go on."

"Well, that perhaps there's a bit of both those men in you. . . . I'm sorry, I'm being dumb."

"Go on."

"It's just that—Devi, why do you talk about death and insanity, you sound terrible, I love you."

"You give the wrong emphasis."

"What's the right emphasis?"

"You give too much emphasis."

"Devi, are you OK?"

"Yes, why not?"

"Your letter wasn't."

"I know"—Devi was sounding wide awake now—"you like to hear that part of me."

"What part?"

"The weak part. That's what you mean by loving me. You love the weak part."

"That's not true."

"No? Then why do you say you love me?"

"This conversation isn't making any sense."

"Talking about love never does. What is meant is not what is understood."

"But why, Devi? We speak the same language."

"I don't think so."

"So what do you mean when you say you love me?"

"I've said it. You've had it. Why so many questions?"

"Had what? Devi, are you drunk?"

"Asleep."

"Do you want me to hang up?"

"No."

"Are you working?"

"Teaching some squatters at St. Katharine Docks."

"Teaching?"

"I thought you said we spoke the same language?"

"Teaching art? Is that good? Are you happy?"

"They want to be taught. I teach."

"Are you painting?"

"No."

"Devi, why?"

"Are you about to tell me it's my life's work?"

"I think I'm about to cry."

Silence.

"Do you want me to come to London? You said you did."

"If you like. Very few party laughs, here. Nobody talks of anything but money."

"Come to New York, Devi."

"I think not. It's another trap."

"Why is it a trap? What did you mean, 'freedom is a trap'? I know what you mean, but did you have anything specific in mind?"

"This is costing you money."

"What does that matter?"

"Are you rich then?"

"Lucy misses you."

"Angela, don't wheedle. And don't try to save my life."

"I'm trying to save mine."

"Yes? Thank you for calling."

*"Thank you for calling!?"*

But Devi had hung up.

The days drift by, and I am not derelict in my duties. But I live without grace. There are two kinds of days—those days when I am aware of the internal bleeding and those days when I am gratefully aware that the internal bleeding has temporarily been stanched.

Lucy thrives.

Devi has been gone six months now. When all my New York friends talk—and they do, endlessly—about how hard it is to find a man, I say nothing. I have not had sex for over a year and a half now, but that is the least of it.

I am going to California to interview a movie star. Perhaps I will find a garage attendant type to fuck. At the Beverly Hills Hotel. Someone who looks like Sonny Tufts.

## Chapter Five

On the plane to California—first-class, I was damned if I was going to crash surrounded by polyester-clothed bodies—I read four of Devi's letters, which had arrived in a clump: He was very poor, he had just returned from two weeks in Ibiza where he had been blissfully happy: "Something nice about being perpetually surrounded by bare flesh, it puts carnality into its proper perspective"; his money situation was "appalling," he'd just seen four West End plays ("Depressed because of capitalist conditioning that insists if I were a good enough worker it'd show on my bank statement"); he was broke and had just spent a week with St. John in Cambridge, long walks in the rain, clotted cream for breakfast ("blissfully happy, except, alas, St. John casts me in the role of Misunderstood Genius, boring"); he was having a fling with a psychiatrist ("sweet, perhaps too sweet, I find my attention wandering, alas. . . . Also he insists upon casting me as Misunderstood Victim"). He was on his way to Turkey to escape from the psychiatrist and the psychiatrist's "definitions."

As I was flying over the Grand Canyon, it occurred to me that there were worse things than dying, and, drunk and tranquilized (forty milligrams of Valium, two vodkas for good measure), I readied my tape recorder, into which I proceeded to talk about death and dying, having convinced myself that I was having a mystical experience. When I played the tape back in my bedroom the next day, I heard nothing but drunken babbling. Liberally interspersed with Hail Mary's.

There is something worse than dying, and that is humiliation—at least so it seemed to me; I would rather have died than had anyone hear that tape. There had been a comic sitting next

to me on the flight—I'd seen him once or twice on the Johnny
Carson show; when I told him of my craven fear of flying, he
grabbed my hand, but his hand was damp and fleshy, there was
no comfort in it. Devi's hands were always warm and dry, one
could feel all his bones; I often felt, when I was holding his
hand, that I was loving the essential Devi, the mortal bones so
close to the surface of the breathing flesh. The comic left his
seat when I began to talk into the tape recorder, no doubt he
thought I was a loony, perhaps he'd do a routine about crazed
airplane passengers on the Johnny Carson show.

In my darkened bedroom at the Beverly Hills Hotel—a
closet, last time I was here I forgot to tip the maids, and they
keep scrupulous records—I cut the tape into snippets with my
cuticle scissors.

I decided to reward myself for not having died on the plane
with a walk through Forest Lawn Cemetery after I interviewed
Hollywood's latest attempt to re-create Marilyn Monroe; perhaps I'd drive to Nepenthe; I would somehow manage to justify the expenses to the managing editor who'd bribed me with
almost twice my usual fee to interview this insipid photogenic
creature—Devi has a point, after all, in refusing to do commercial art.

The blond exerted her considerable influence to move me
out of my closet and into a cottage near the swimming pool,
where, drinking a double vodka, dressed in a caftan bought in
the lingerie department of Gimbel's, and feeling very pale and
very short next to blond starlets in white bikinis, I met a man
who was very much better looking than Sonny Tufts.

"Do you always wear that caftan over your body?"

"It's nothing to get excited about," I said, "just a body."

"And you live the life of the mind," he said mockingly,
whereupon my nipples hardened. "I know who you are," he
said, and he said my name, which pleased me.

"What do you do for a living, park cars?" I asked. I was not
quite sober, and not quite hungover.

"I come from New York, too," he said.

Well, yes: A New York Irishman if ever I saw one. Tall,
muscular, a face like that of some aristocratic animal, red hair,

red mustache, and very blue, slightly hyperthyroidic eyes. He was drinking a double vodka on the rocks. His lean legs were tanned. It was eleven in the morning.

"Are you a bartender?"

"Are you usually so unpleasant? I know who you are," he said, "a New York journalist."

"Are you a bartender?"

"Why don't you guess?"

"No thanks."

"I'm a stuntman," he said.

"How nice for you."

He laughed. It was a good hearty laugh, a laugh that told me he would be good in bed. Then, without preamble, he sang an Irish sea chanty, very loud.

"If you're so smart," I said, "sing 'Jesu, Joy of Man's Desiring.' "

He did. Then he told me a story about the headmaster of the English public school he'd gone to, all about being warned against the perils of masturbation, and the headmaster— "blindness, boys, blindness"—wore glasses an inch thick. By the time he was through, having exhausted three dialects and fifteen minutes, he had collected an appreciative audience, and I was laughing hopelessly. He waved the blonds away. "Are you planning on spending the night alone?" he asked.

"Not if I can help it," I answered, much to my surprise.

"Your cottage," he announced; and, in the daylight, we performed exercises on the double bed, which smelled faintly of jasmine and chlorine, vodka and lime.

He was talented and inexhaustible. He wanted me on top: "Tell me what you are doing now . . . tell me what I am doing . . . say the words . . . what words do you like for it . . . is this hard enough . . . is it dirty enough . . . say the words for it." I said the words. In between, we drank vodka, and he told anecdotes, all charming and rehearsed, no kisses, no caresses. The phone rang many times, and I did not answer it. "What do you call this? Where are my fingers now? Tell me. Move your face here. I want your fingers here. Your mouth." He told me what I was doing with my mouth.

"Why am I on top?"

"So I can do it to you more often," he said. "Tell me—use the words—how it feels. I want this. Here."

Later, much later, he ordered food from room service. "I'm a drunk," he said.

"A drunk stuntman?"

"The studio doesn't know it, but my heart is bad. I'll move to New York if you like."

"Ridiculous. You've never even kissed me."

"I love your filthy mouth," he said. "What a fine appreciation of sin you have, it's generally lacking in California. They think this is all right to do."

"And you?"

"I know it's dirty. And so do you. I knew you would love it right away."

"I have a lover in New York," I said.

"No you don't," he said. "You haven't done this for a very long time."

"Fuck you," I said.

"Good idea."

I had not brought my diaphragm—moldy, now, in any case, no doubt. I was sitting on top of him. "I want a baby," I said. He cupped his hands around my buttocks and lifted me off. He showered while I lay smoking a cigarette.

"Do you want it again?" he asked. His heart may have been bad, but his flesh was more than willing. "I won't come inside of you," he said.

"I want a baby," I said.

When he left—to catch a plane for Hawaii, he said—I realized that he hadn't told me his name.

"I'll see you in New York, Angela," he said; which sentence I took to be false.

On my right wrist is a scar: When I was five years old, I pulled the glass eye from a toy teddy bear out of its furry socket and then, to punish myself, dug the iron prongs with which the eye was attached deep into the flesh of my offending hand. On my left thigh are the toothmarks, barely discernible, white against pink-gray flesh, of a rabid dog who bit me when I was seven. On my stomach are the marks left by a man who tried to rape me.

I felt these marks, and welcomed their presence; they assured me I had a history. I took a long bath and washed my hair, which was sticky with semen. I transcribed the tapes of my interview with the blond. I watched the late-night movie, *The Winslow Boy.* Why hadn't I married a man like Robert Donat, just, generous, kind? Or Leslie Howard, but Stephan says that he was gay.

It frightened me to think that my life might become so claustrophobic and so lopsided as this—what Father Caldwell called my hothouse affair with Devi, punctuated by precipitous lovemaking with unloved partners. If my lovemaking had been altogether the result of animal attraction it would have been in its way pure, a giving—a sin of the body not worth fretting over. But this was a taking, not a giving; this was not a sin of the body. This was my using another man to anesthetize my heart by flaying my body, an act in which hard calculation played no little part. This was a sin of the soul. I used him as one uses hard liquor, to blot away the world. Only it brought me no closer to the real world of real people, because Devi had become my world. And Devi was inside of me—I held the world in my body—no foreign invasion could root him out.

To be in the world and not of it—what an odd and scary twist I'd put upon those words. No one, seeing me do my work, watching me with friends, would have guessed how divorced I was from any true caring for anything or anyone but Devi. My limbs functioned, my brain worked away on the worldly problems set before it, my soul mechanically remembered there was God; but at the citadel, in my heart, Devi was enshrined. Who would have guessed, among my friends, that all my offerings were leavings, dry crusts? The best, the blood and honey, reserved for Devi; the flesh despised.

Lucy was real. I thought of Lucy as salvation. This frightened me.

I thought of the fastidious distaste in which I had held my own mother when I was Lucy's age—the stubble on her unshaved legs, the slightly sour smell that emanated from her when she stood at the kitchen sink in the morning in old pajamas that declared she had no use for sex. What does Lucy find distasteful in me? Life had given my mother few occasions for suffering, and so she had invented them, a martyr to her own unhappiness. My mother began to take an interest in my sex life—nonexistent—when she lost interest in her own. I was twelve years old at the time. I would not let my unhappiness become the occasion of Lucy's unhappiness, poor little girl, only fourteen.

Sex with the Stuntman had done nothing to revitalize me, it left me only more alone. And yet I would do it, if I had the chance, again. This frightened me.

I remembered, as I fell asleep, that I had promised Eileen to think about certain problems in California—and I reminded myself that I was a person with will—but I could not remember what it was I had promised her to think of.

I dreamed of the man who had killed himself. In my dream, he looked, as he had in life, like Leslie Howard, a slight, fair man with an aquiline nose and eyes of bitter luminous intensity, a mocking mouth, a drawling voice that managed to convey both irony and tenderness. In my dream we were back in the schoolroom again, and he was standing at the blackboard again (the blackboard was bloodred). "Angela is my best pupil," he said. "I have taught her everything I need to know." He was diagramming a sentence on the blackboard: *When the passionate girl with the beautiful voice stands in the light, her hair is the color of sun-warmed wheat and I will love her forever and she will be young forever.* I raised my hand. "But why don't you love me now?" I asked. "I am fifteen and I will love you till I am twenty-two, and then I will marry someone else. You ought to love me now." "You are lovely," he said, "but 'lovely' is a word used only by homosexual men, isn't it? Do you think I am gay? Some day you will be a writer, and you will go to Beverly Hills, but that will be after I have killed myself, and you will always remember the winy smell of the maple outside my living room and the window seat where you listened to Schubert. I taught you everything I need to know."

"I will remember," I said, "that you never kissed me."

"She will remember," the students chanted, "that he never kissed her."

"And what will they mean," I asked, "the walks we will take through the park years from now, your narrow bed, the poems you read to me now, the malteds on your porch in that house your mother lived in, the talks we will have about happiness and Mozart and God?"

"They will talk about happiness and Mozart and God," the students chanted; and the man who killed himself said, "You will never know what I mean. You will only know all your life that I loved you and that I never kissed you."

"Do you love me?"

"You are in a state of mortal sin," he said, "but that is years from now."

"She is in a state of mortal sin," the students chanted; and the man who killed himself said: "I love no one more than I love you."

Then we were in the principal's office; the man who killed himself was gone, and the principal said, "Now we must have a postmortem. Why did he kill himself? Angela will know." Other voices: "Angela will never know. . . . He left her his diaries. . . . She says they told her nothing, they were fables, they were weather reports, they were stories of the girls who loved him. . . . She loved him. Not enough. She never understood. The man who killed himself was gay." "That is a lie," I said, and they laughed. "Yes," I said, "he is gay, and he is in my closet at the Beverly Hills Hotel." Then the man who killed himself reappeared. "You have been searching for me," he said. "I flew to this place to find you. You are in a state of mortal sin," he said, his light drawl mocking me, a revolver in his hand, "but the damned forgive you." And he kissed me on my mouth.

*I have grieved for you all my life,* I said; I awakened myself with these words.

I called my editor and told her I would need three more days.

I called room service.

Three more days in this cottage, and what was it Eileen said I was to think of? The Incarnation and the sanctity of the flesh. My mind balked. And what else was I to think about? Why I had not married the other man, the man who was just and generous and kind, "creative, original, cheerful, witty. Well-coordinated." The answer seemed clear: *I have grieved for you all my life.*

Devi seemed suddenly faraway. Everything that had happened to me had happened when I was fifteen years old.

My fingers felt again for my distinguishing marks.

The next day the *L.A. Times* carried an AP report of a cyclone and tidal wave in Andhra Pradesh, Devi's state, the state where his mother, his sisters, his brothers, and his father live—or do not live, or have never lived, depending on whose version of history one believes or has invented. In one district, four thousand rotting human corpses "and numerous dead buffaloes" were still awaiting burial or cremation. The government's offer of twenty rupees' bounty to dispose of each body had found no takers.

I went to Farmer's Market. I ate tacos under an umbrella, next to a stall where a woman hand-dipped chocolate all day, hygienically sealed in a Plexiglas booth, like Eichmann.

I read the paper place mat on which my paper plate rested: "PHOBIA! *Anthrophobia—fear of human society.* (That would solve a lot of problems, but I don't have it. Yet. Or perhaps I do, look at the society I have lately chosen, admired for my filthy mouth. Indifferent to human society would be more like it.) *Sitophobia—fear of food.* (I only wish. I am never not hungry.) *Aichmephobia—fear of sharp pointed objects.* (No; but what is this dagger in my heart?) *Triskaidekaphobia—fear of number 13. Mysophobia—fear of dirt. Microphobia—fear of germs. Aerophobia— fear of drafts:* No. *Basophobia—fear of walking.* (Only sometimes. On days when there seems to be a cushion of air between my feet and the pavement, on days when I shop for myself alone, when there is no Lucy to cook for. I like Lucy to hold my hand when we cross the street, she doesn't know I need her protection, she thinks I am guiding her. . . . Only sometimes. When I am alone.) *Skopophobia—fear of spies. Chronophobia—fear of clocks:* No. *Phobophobia—fear of fear. Nyctophobia—fear of the dark. Pathophobia—fear of disease:* Yes, yes, yes. (All the world's a hospital.) *Acrophobia—fear of heights. Brontophobia—fear of thunder. Astrapophobia—fear of lightning. Agoraphobia—fear of open spaces:* Yes, in varying degrees. Some days I function quite well. In any case I do not have *Zoophobia—fear of animals,* or *Ailurophobia—fear of cats,* or *Hydrophobia—fear of water.* (At least when the water is contained in a faucet, controlled by a tap; the ocean, of course, is another matter—tidal waves. To say nothing of the people it carries away from one.)

I love and fear the dark. I love and fear the lightning that rips the dark. I say I want clarity; the truth is, ever since the first man—the man who killed himself—I choose men and situations remarkable for their ambiguity. I like, need, the intensity this provides. There is no name for this pathology. Not on the place mat, there isn't.

I felt a slight, wet weight on my sandaled foot and saw— though how it had gotten there I could not imagine—a dying sparrow draped around my toes. Are there sparrows in California? What a place. *Charophobia—fear of gaiety. Ornithophobia— fear of birds.* It did not seem possible to me that I would ever love a man again: Devi; and the man who killed himself. Always the same man.

I do not, God knows, have a virgin body. I have a virgin mind: always the same man—Devi; and the man who killed himself. It occurred to me that loving Devi was a way for me to become virginal again. His newness would be my newness. And I was willing to wait a long time for such a rebirth. I know nothing about the sex life of the man who killed himself. I know so little about the men I love. I love the mystery.

I went back to the hotel, changed my reservations, and flew out to New York that night, forgetting again to leave the maids a tip. I crushed the phone messages the clerk had collected for me and stuffed them in my purse without reading them. On the way home—first class—I vowed to stop smoking again if the plane should not crash.

# *Chapter Six*

Later, when I tried to put an exact time to it, it seemed to me that she must have died when I was flying eastward over the Grand Canyon. When I was drunk. When I was contemplating my own mortality. When I was thinking of sex, jasmine and chlorine, vodka and lime ("Here; put your mouth here"). She died on Monday, her day to mop the ceilings. My mother's last words were "veal cutlets." She sat upright in bed, they said, she called my father's name; she called the name of her sister, long dead; and then she said "veal cutlets," and she died.

She was laid out in my Uncle Johnny's funeral parlor—he who had once given an interview to the New York *Post:* "You can't even hear yourself cry for the loved one over the noise of the train," Uncle Johnny said; and throughout that long day, the stained-glass windows of the funeral parlor rattled, casting sheets of brazen light—red, purple, blue, green, yellow—over her dead face; the crystal chandelier shook and chimed as the elevated train racketed overhead.

Lucy touched her hand, kissed her forehead; I did not.

Daddy said, "She's moving, she's moving," every time the train passed by, and my uncles and my cousins had to hold him up.

"Be *good,*" my Aunt Milly said; by which I understood that I was not to cry.

I did not cry.

Lucy cried. Neddy Nickle, whom Lucy had stopped seeing, but for whom she had fond affection, came to pay his respects, one platinum safety pin dangling from his ear (causing Aunt Milly to glare).

Her white hair was rinsed blue. "I did a good job," Uncle

Johnny said, "God rest her soul." The lights from the stained-glass windows played in her hair.

When the train roared by, the flowers seemed to emit a stronger fragrance, as if a summer breeze had passed over nodding roses. A vaguely cinnamony fragrance, an ample, homely fragrance, like that of the kitchens of one's childhood, the remembered kitchens in which, however, one had never lived.

So many tuberoses. The flower that had adorned her wedding day.

Lucy, in my absence, had arranged for a spray of white roses to be placed across the steel-gray casket: "From Lucy and Mom."

"Daddy, where's her wedding band?"

"What? What did you say?"

"Where's Mother's wedding band, Daddy?"

"Be *good,*" Aunt Milly said.

The second day of the wake, Uncle Johnny met Lucy and me outside the funeral parlor. "It's standing room only," he said.

I wish I had a brother, I wish Devi were my brother, I wish Devi were here.

The man who killed himself was laid out here. A decade ago. Yesterday.

The priest intoned the prayers: "Our beloved sister . . . Hail Mary . . . Pray for us sinners . . ." "Angie! Angie!" "Daddy." I held my father in my arms, a great groaning from his withered, palsied body. "Daddy, I love you." His sobs drowned out the words of the priest: "Now and in the hour of our death." My cheeks were wet. "Be good," Aunt Milly said. "Let them alone, Aunt Milly," Lucy said. Her face was whiter than my mother's.

My mother. Esther, my mother, born on Easter day. Her body had given birth to me—when she was only five years older than Lucy is now, a fact I cannot assimilate. The old man I rocked in my arms had touched her, how? tenderly? hungrily? "License my roving hands . . . between, beneath, above, below. . . ." Not *that* body, not this flesh, mortified by Uncle Johnny's cosmetics, tortured into false peace, resting on white satin, purple nail polish, what had Uncle Johnny been thinking of? "I did a good job," he said; "God rest her soul." "Our Father, who art in heaven . . ."

In the limousine, on the way to the cemetery in Queens (it was a Holy Day of Obligation, and she would have no Mass that day), my father rested his head on my lap and sobbed. How pink his scalp is, like a baby's.

"Wipe your face," Aunt Milly said.

"What?"

"Wipe it."

Lucy cleaned my tear-stained face with a corner of her dress.

"There has to be some dignity, you know," Aunt Milly said. "Life goes on. After *all.* I can't be expected to do *everything.*"

The chapel in the cemetery looks like the TWA terminal at Kennedy. "Why are we here? Aren't we going to the grave?"

"Don't say *grave* in front of your father," Aunt Milly said. "I can't be expected to do everything, you know, I don't want *two* bodies on my hands."

"Why are we here? Aren't we going to the grave?"

"Sshh! We're saying good-bye to her here. No *grave.*"

"Who decided this?"

"I can't be expected to do everything. I mean, after *all.* There's a limit."

"Isn't this good, Angie? We leave her here it's like nothing happened, you'll see."

*"Something has happened."*

"Will you be *good?*"

Over the sealed casket a strange priest intoned a final prayer: "Our dear sister Eleanor . . ."

*"Esther,"* Lucy said.

"Oh my God, this family," Aunt Milly said.

"What happened?" Daddy said. "I don't know. . . ."

On Queens Boulevard we passed three prostitutes.

My cousin the cop, now an insurance man ("Don't worry, Angie, there'll be a little for you"), rolled down the window of the limousine and shouted, "Why don't you work for a living, you fucking cunts?"

"What did you say?" my father said.

"Oh my God, this family," Aunt Milly said.

"Lucy, who made all the food?"

"Aunt Milly."

"While you were in Hollywood," Aunt Milly said.

"That's not fair, Mom was working."

"You don't know what you're talking about, missy. She didn't answer her telephone once. Working."

Aunt Milly dropped two pearl earrings into Lucy's wine glass. "She wanted you to have these."

"Where's her wedding band?"

"Get your father a brandy, it's the least you can do."

"Lucy, where did all the liquor come from?"

"*Mommy.* You bought it. Don't you remember? You made the ham, too."

"I did, didn't I?"

"Oh, Mommy."

Daddy opened a closet: "Take something," he said.

"I don't want anything, Daddy."

"Take her shoes."

"I don't want her shoes."

"Take her shoes, Angie, please."

I took twelve pairs of shoes, all of them a half-size too small for me.

"We could watch a little television," Aunt Milly said.

"There are fifty people here!"

"Life goes on," Aunt Milly said.

Lucy grieved.

I did not grieve, unless remembering is a form of grief. I remembered: I remembered a black winter coat my mother wore when I was young, a coat with a border of ocelot fur, the only luxury she had ever allowed herself. Had her hands caressed it? I remembered her long chestnut-colored hair, which reached her shoulders and seemed to float when she walked, as if it had a life of its own (does it have a life of its own now? and what does a decade in the earth do? is *his* light brown hair alive?). Sometimes she covered the masses of rich brown hair in a snood; I thought she was more beautiful than any movie star. Once some kids threw a rotten eggplant in her shiny hair and in the meshes of the snood—it was the only time I'd ever seen her cry. She walked to church crying, the stink of rotten eggplant at early-morning Mass; that day she did not receive the Host, as if she thought the sin were hers; she did not approach the altar with that stink, as bitter and as acrid as original sin.

I remembered: A young seminarian crouched at her feet in the large sunny kitchen, putting red nail polish on her toes. His name was Anthony. The murmur of their voices in the large sunny kitchen as I did my homework in the attic room. He stayed for dinner that night. He said a very long Grace; her enormous brown eyes, flecked with gold, were fastened upon him all the time, her lips slightly parted. My eyes fixed on her face, a new face, one I hadn't seen before. (My hands shook when I raised the soup spoon to my mouth; Daddy thought that I was sick. Aunt Milly thought I had a crush on Anthony.) Anthony had two veal cutlets; we had one apiece.

I remembered: "That *thing* in his pants. . . ." She was talking to a woman from her sodality. "What thing in his pants, who?" I said. "They know too much," my mother said, though in fact I knew nothing at all. "Take your nap, Angie."

Once, in the middle of the night, I awakened to find her soothing my hair. Not soothing my hair—she was taking my curlers out to put them in her own. I pretended to be asleep while her fingers played in my hair. I watched her, rocking in her chair, putting the curlers in her hair, moonlight streaming over her beautiful face. She was humming, and her face the same new face I'd seen when Anthony was there.

"What are you thinking about, Mommy?" Lucy's face was bleached with crying.

"The way my mother used to braid my hair. . . . The mustard plasters my mother used to make for me when I was sick."

"What are mustard plasters? . . . Tell me more things."

"She used to paste pretty pictures on the bottom of my drinking glass. She bought me a pink angora sweater once that she couldn't afford. It wasn't even my birthday. The salesman

said, 'This sweater is just right for you,' and she gave it to me.
Salesmen always fell in love with her, she was so beautiful.
Once a bus driver said to her, 'Lady, I'd ride you anywhere.'"

"What did she say?"

"'A transfer to Bath Avenue, please.' She pronounced it
Baath."

"That's not the way she talks."

"No."

"Mommy, why are you looking through her closets?" Lucy
sounded irritable; I was caught off guard. "You're making
Grandpa nervous," she said.

"I'm looking for the coat with the ocelot collar."

"Do you have to do it now?"

"I guess not. I was just remembering."

"Remembering about Grandma?"

"Who else?"

"Did you love your mother?"

"I don't know yet."

Lucy's face hardened as if she were about to say something
unkind; then: "I never went to bed with Neddy Nickle,
Mommy."

"I know, sweetheart. When you were teething, you used to
try to smile with your fist jammed in your mouth and tears
running down your face."

Lucy slammed the closet door. "Stop telling me stories,"
she said. "Your *mother's* dead. I don't want to hear about how
cute I was."

"For Christ's sake!"

"I don't want to hear that, either."

Devi called.

"Devi, my mother died."

"You didn't like her, isn't it?"

"No."

"No, you didn't?"

"I didn't like her."

"I suppose that makes it worse?"

"I don't know. Worse for me doesn't matter. It's not I who died."

"I'm no good with other people's guilt. There's no point."

"Unless it's earned."

"There's no point. Every time I see my old mum, every ten years, she says, 'I always knew you'd come back to me.' Frightening. Witless psychopathic bitch who happens to be my mother. No guilt will have accrued to me when she dies, having a worthless black-sheep son tops off her life. Never fear. Your mum believed you loved her. They get their hooks in you, they think they have you on a pulley. . . ."

"How many brothers and sisters do you have, Devi?"

"This connection is bad, I'll write. . . . Angela? Angela, I love you."

"I believe you, Devi."

Stephan called.

"Poor lovely, you should have told me right away."

"I feel such sorrow for Lucy." In fact I resented Lucy for grieving more purely than I did; after all, it was my mother.

"Let me take Lucy to Newport for the day."

"I need her, Stephan."

"She was just on the phone with me, however, crying. Allow one to be of use."

"Take her to Newport, then. Why?"

"You need to be alone with your grief, and Lucy needs to be reminded there is a world."

"Life goes on," I said.

"Perhaps for the weekend," Stephan said.

"You want to take her for two days?"

"I am leaving you my Renoir when I die."

"Stephan, how many brothers and sisters does Devi have?"

"A terrible mistake to seek comfort from Devi. He flees from pain. Except his own."

"What shall I do while you're in Newport?"

"Lucy says you haven't cried since the funeral."

"I haven't."

"You might cry."

"I might."

I spent the weekend with my father, who frequently confused me with his wife: "Esther . . ." "It's Angela, Daddy." "My eyes are bad." "It's all right, Daddy."

In the dark, after the dinner dishes were washed and put away, we held hands and wept.

"When do the dead go away, Angie?"

"I don't know, Daddy."

I did know. The dead we have with us always.

To sleep is an act of faith. I slept in the old double bed with my old father. I held him; his body felt like an armful of dry leaves.

How strange. I am grieving for my mother, whom I did not love. I am grieving for myself, because I did not love her, and for her, because she did not love me. It cannot be as simple as that. Surely she must have loved me once? Else how could I, in even so twisted a way, have learned to love others? Daddy grieves too; Daddy has turned ancient in these days; and yet she didn't love Daddy, either. "That *thing* in his pants," she said. And yet he is lost and empty without her, is this what people mean when they talk about ordinary human love?

Stephan is right: Devi has no use for any pain that is not his own. My mother has performed quite a stunt: She has erased Devi. And I didn't even like her. Suddenly my world is peopled, not with phantoms. There is Daddy to be looked after, there is Aunt Milly clamoring for attention, taking notice, now, of all her aches and pains. I will not let Devi kill me before I die. I will be good.

When Lucy returned from Newport (three days), I said, "Lucy, I loved my mother."

"I'm glad," she said, and went into her room and closed the door.

When I called Lucy for dinner, she said she wasn't hungry.

"Lucy, what is it?"

"Nothing. I'm not hungry."

"Why are you angry?"

"She was my grandmother."

"So?"

"So you act as if everybody belongs to you."

"I don't know what you mean."

"How often did you see her when she was sick?"

Not very often.

"What nonsense has Stephan been telling you?"

"Nothing. I had a good time with Stephan. He took care of me."

"What do you mean, I act as if everybody belongs to me?"

"I can't help you with your problems, Mama. I'm not your mother."

"I didn't ask you to be my mother, Lucy. What's the matter with you?"

"You say bad things about my father. You tell me things I don't want to know. You expect me to understand everything. I'm a child," she said, with adult acuity and cunning, testing the words and my reaction, and also with unmistakable weariness. "I'm not your sister," Lucy said.

I wanted to slap her; at the same time I saw her point.

"Why do you always yell at me from the other end of the house?" Lucy said. "Can't you knock on my door?"

"I don't yell. I'll knock your door. What else don't you like about me, Lucy?" I wanted to slap her.

What is Lucy afraid of? What is it she thinks she knows? What is it that she needs to know?

"I hate that painting in the living room," Lucy said.

"Shall we take it down?"

"Do what you want. Are you going away again soon?"

"I was only in California for four days, Lu."

"You were away longer than that," Lucy said.

Oh dear, all this stuff I read, it is poisoning my mind, corrupting my instincts (I sound like Devi). If your mother didn't nurture you, you won't be able to love and nurture your daughter—stuff like that; how I hate it. But suppose it's true? Suppose some vital element is missing in my relationship with Lu, I'd be the last to notice, wouldn't I? That's what they say, that the sick mind can't analyze itself. I know she loves me. But since my mother's death, she carries with her a perpetual air of silent reproach—and I had counted on her pity, her charity. Perhaps my mother was right, a fancy education puts nonsense into their heads. But oh dear, I do count on Lucy when the chips are down, and now I wonder if in neglecting my mother I have neglected her, if in loving Devi I have abandoned her. Who is the abandoned, who is the abandoner? If Lucy abandons me, I will hate Devi, and I will never discover the love for my mother I have waited years to explore. It all comes of falling in love and reading too much—all these too many words, Devi is right. A poem should not mean but be; what nonsense. All the trouble in the world lies in words. If Lucy were young enough to cuddle, if Devi were brave enough to touch  .  .  . But salvation lies in the word, too. An ocelot collar does not tell me much.

# Part Three

*If the future and the past really exist,*
*where are they?*

SAINT AUGUSTINE

# *Chapter One*

Nothing is to the point, and everything is to the point.

The man who killed himself is to the point.

He loved me, and I loved him but not enough, and now he is dead.

I don't remember anything about breakfasts. Sometimes I took the bus to school. More often I ran—animal spirits, my mother called it, unable to grasp the principle, which was joy. Once I lost a penny loafer as I stumbled book-laden off the bus. Someone, laughing, tossed my shoe to me from an open window, an act of kindness. Strangers could not always be depended upon to be kind. (You slip on the ice as you go to your piano lesson, limbs akimbo, lesson books every which way in the slush, and they laugh, as if the spectacle were proof that children have no dignity—which is confusing when you have secret knowledge that your body is no longer that of a child. Then you blubber like a baby.)

The only picture I have of David Larrimar is a Xeroxed copy of a photograph taken by a boy who loved him. He is standing before a blackboard, chalk in his hand, smiling at a nice mathematical equation.

Everyone loved him. So you think they'd let him be. They can't. After all these years they are still clamoring, questioning. I do not want my memory of him corrupted by facts. I have respect for facts, but not where he is concerned. There is nothing new I wish to learn about him. Far less do I wish to hear theories advanced about him. What he is to me is what he was to me, and facts and theories will not alter that.

I am tempted, of course. From time to time someone will call and want to talk about him. Always they claim to have loved

and been loved by him. Sometimes they claim to have understood him. Meetings are proposed. I say I'll come. I never do. I
cannot imagine myself in a room full of strangers talking about
him. They want to approach him with logical minds, in sunny
kitchens, over coffee. I want only the information that comes
to me in dreams.

Once, though I am not accustomed to begging, I asked the
man who was his best friend, and who is now my good friend, if
David Larrimar had loved me better than he had loved anybody else. "Please," I said. "Didn't he love me best?" My
friend paused for a very long time—he is kind—and then he
said, "Let me say that he didn't love anybody more than he
loved you." That was the first time I ever asked a question
about him, and also the last.

I would like to know where he is buried, but I cannot imagine visiting his grave. I believe that heaven is a precise physical
location, as real as Amsterdam High School. I believe that he is
in heaven, now. I also believe that we shall be no happier in
heaven than we were in our happiest moment on earth. He was
happy listening to The Trout Quintet. He was happier when he
was teasing me. I do not wish to quarrel with him at his grave. I
do not wish to hear his light, drawling mocking voice inviting
me to examine the proofs—rats, earthquakes—that there is no
God; even from heaven he might so perversely argue (I'm sure
God would not deny him the pleasure). I do not wish to revive
this quarrel, his being in heaven having closed the books, as far
as I'm concerned, on all such arguments.

He loved me. What he was to others is of no consequence. I
tell myself that.

I find it difficult to say his name, even his name I hoard. I
would have given his name to my child, had my child been a
boy. He asked me to do that, in the last letter I ever got from
him.

Everyone loved him. The crippled school librarian loved
him. She was sixty-five. (It is unlikely that she was sixty-five,
but I was fifteen, and so she seemed to me to be sixty-five.)

He was standing on a stair landing when I first saw him.
"That's Mr. Larrimar," the girls whispered, controlled distur-

bances of voices all about him. I did not think he looked like much. I was fifteen, and full of vain conceit about my powers of discernment. It strikes me now as odd that I discerned nothing about him that might give rise to any excitement—that a man universally admired (it is not too much to say adored), and about whom, furthermore, mysteries breathed, did not establish himself in my imagination, which was keen and overripe, as a romantic figure. He was slight and sandy-haired, his eyes were blue. He carried a bulging briefcase. I thought he looked like the Duke of Windsor, whom my father had instructed me to despise. I was at that time reading Sartre and Saint Augustine and Erich Fromm. I was infatuated with a Brooklyn Dodgers outfielder named Pete Reiser, who was most of the time benched due to injuries derived from slamming into the left field wall of Ebbets Field. I knew the receptionist at the Oldsmobile dealer where Pete Reiser bought his cars, and I spent many afternoons there, all of them fruitless. I was practicing being in love.

Six months later I was in love with Mr. Larrimar, and I remained in love, and in high excitement, for the next seven years of my life.

In fact David Larrimar looked nothing at all like the Duke of Windsor, although, when I saw a television movie about the duke, the actor who played the Prince of Wales looked so much like David Larrimar—deep lines etched from nostrils to mouth, thin upper lip, full lower lip, a fair broad forehead, narrow blue eyes—I startled myself by entertaining the thought that if ever this actor were to meet me, he would recognize me. In another movie, the same actor played a hired assassin. I watch this movie whenever I can.

David Larrimar became my English teacher six months after I saw him on the stair landing. He was told to expect great things of me. I was there when David Larrimar, looking only mildly interested, received this information. When his fine hands, which were entering something in his lesson-plan book, came to rest, he regarded me with the most direct blue gaze I have ever encountered. "Are you happy?" he said. The simplicity with which he asked me the question—which seemed to me the best question I had ever been asked, indeed the only question worthy of an answer—shocked me out of my shyness. "Yes," I said. I meant No. "We shall see," he said, smiling.

The first day of class, he wrote the name "Cholmondeley" on the blackboard and asked me—of whom great things were expected—to pronounce it. I tripped over all the syllables in an effort to please him. He gave me a chocolate-covered ant, for effort. To the girl who knew how to pronounce it, he gave one of his old snap-on bow ties, remarking that he no longer had any use for snap-on bow ties. He managed to imbue this remark with sadness and irony, as if a great history lay behind his discarded choices. He had only two rules, he said: No one was ever to use a semicolon in compositions, because no one under twenty-five knew how to use semicolons. Anyone who created a disturbance in class would be invited to leave the class for that day, and would be given a blank pass, after which he would be free to spend that period in any public space in school. David Larrimar did not believe in any form of punishment, except, he said smiling, "exile." As he was speaking, two beefy boys known to be troublemakers entered the classroom, hangdog. The dean of boys, who did believe in punishment but who didn't know how to administer it, always sent problems to David Larrimar, in whose presence they became, for no apparent reason, docile. Some of these rowdy outcasts later wound up in prison; David Larrimar sent them letters and pepperoni. On this first day of class, they sat silent, shuffling their feet, while David Larrimar talked about a poem by Christina Rossetti ("When I am dead my dearest. . . .") David Larrimar gave them each a chocolate-covered ant and gave one of them a snap-on bow tie when he shouted out: "She don't want no one crying for her when she passes away." "When she dies," Mr. Larrimar said. "Well, yeah," the boy said, "when she drops dead. I thought it ain't polite to say drop dead." "Meet it head on," David Larrimar said. "Say what you mean." "Well, right, I said when she dropped dead," the boy said. "I ain't afraid. And I ain't afraid of killing nobody neither." "Then don't say passes away," David Larrimar said. "Right. Got it."

Our homework assignment for the next day was to write about ourselves. "Call it *Portrait in a Mirror*," David Larrimar said. "Write what it is you see when you look at yourself. I won't be judging you," he said, smiling. "I'll judge only what's on the page. But I'll know if you lie. There is no such thing as an interesting lie. Anyone can tell the truth," he said drawling, leaving us in some doubt as to whether this was a good thing. "Only gifted people can lie," he said, leaving us with a small thrill of confusion. Why was he looking at me?

David Larrimar was forty and not married. He lied. He told one of his students, a girl, that he was married. I knew this to be a lie. I had done my research. He lived with his mother and father and his sister in a house with a screened wraparound porch, a block from the elevated line. The student to whom he told this lie, now the bossy mother of three children, is one of the people who call me to discuss him. She claims that this single lie poisoned her life for years. It is clear to me that she provoked the lie. I refuse to discuss him with her. I am not interested to know in what way she provoked him. I am not interested to know why he found it necessary to lie. He never told me a lie. He never told me the truth, but he never told me a lie, either.

I handed in *Portrait in a Mirror* two days late. I told all about a Harvard senior who had been in love with me and recited Browning to me and then married a girl from Vassar. I misspelled Vassar. I wrote all about the wedding and about how I then read all of Elizabeth Barrett Browning and how I cried and how I recovered ("he was such a foolish boy"). These were all lies. I was very careful not to use semicolons. I got an A.

The next composition I wrote was a short story about a man and his horse in North Dakota. In it I referred to insects as "little creatures of the night." David Larrimar crossed out "little creatures of the night" and wrote "bugs." He also wrote that I would be exiled to North Dakota—"or South, if you prefer"—if I ever turned in such horse manure again, unless I offered proof of having gone to a Marx Brothers movie. I got a C. After class, he asked me to stay behind.

"Why are you working for a Commercial diploma?" he

asked. All my teachers asked me that, even my steno teacher and my typing teacher. The reason was simple: My mother did not want me to go to college, where I might get fancy ideas put into my head. I passionately longed to go to college, but I longed even more—this passion was indistinguishable from fear—not to displease my mother, who suffered. The reasons for her suffering and its exact nature were not clear to me, but at night, every night, she came into my bedroom while I feigned sleep, and moaned. (Soon after I met David Larrimar, she moved into my bedroom for good.) I did not want to implicate my beautiful mother, who suffered so much, so my usual truculent response to this question was, "I don't want to go to college." Then they asked me why. "I don't want to," I said. Then they stopped asking.

"Why are you taking a Commercial Course?" David Larrimar said.

"Why did you ask me if I was happy?" I said, my forwardness surprising me so much that I dropped all my books, which David Larrimar picked up while I stood in stilled alarm.

"I think I'll have to take you to Mary's Venetian Gardens for pizza," David Larrimar said. "Do you know The Trout Quintet? You're reading *The Cloud of Unknowing*. Do you believe all that?"

"Yes."

"For example, do you believe there is a Devil?"

"Yes."

"That is not a mark of intelligence. Walt Whitman said 'Only that which everyone believes is true is true.' . . . 'Your hair is the color of sun-ripened wheat.' Would you call that good prose?"

"I don't know."

"We'll see," he said.

"My mother doesn't want me to go to college," I said.

"An impediment. However, our most important choices choose us. How do we know what is of overriding importance? Do you know the answer to that?"

"No."

"When we are overridden. Your passion is what makes you

beautiful, but it is only a shadow of what is to come. Your hair is the color of sun-ripened wheat.''

What could he know of my passion? What passion? No adult had ever spoken to me like this.

"We'll have pizza and you can tell me all about God," he said.

I could not tell if he was mocking me.

"I love God," I said. That was true—God was the only member of my family whose suffering I understood. But it was not because it was true that I said it. I said it because I wanted to say the word "love" in his presence. I had never before made such a declaration; my boldness humiliated me.

"That is the first time I ever heard anyone make such a declaration," David Larrimar said. "Are you always so direct?"

I had never been direct. I had always thought all the good questions were in books, and all the answers.

"I'd better get you to Mary's Venetian Gardens before long." Then he raised his sandy eyebrows, looked at me quizzically, as if he weren't quite sure what I was doing there, and I left, as awkwardly as I had ever left a room, as if walking were something new to me. I was conscious of every separate movement of my body, conscious of his watching blue eyes.

The next morning I ran to school. Steno class, typing, American History, lunch. The teachers' lunchroom was in a kind of glass booth, suspended above the students' cafeteria, and while I couldn't see David Larrimar there, I was sure he could see me. On my way to the food counter, where I bought a cupcake and a Dixie Cup (and immediately regretted the childishness of my choice), I was once again conscious that walking was a willed activity. I couldn't get my hips to behave correctly, and my shoulders seemed like autonomous strangers to me. I sat with other Commercial Course girls, some of whom already wore engagement rings, most of whom wore ankle bracelets inscribed with the initials of their steadies. The smart girls—the ones who took Academic Courses—sat elsewhere. I was, for the first time, embarrassed by the company I kept, and when one of the girls told a long and dirty joke, I didn't laugh.

But David Larrimar wasn't there to see my sober face (which

had trouble arranging itself; it too felt new). There was a substitute in English class, David Larrimar had the flu.

His absence obscurely frightened me. I wrote him a note, sitting at the blond desk that matched the blond twin bed in the bedroom my mother and I shared, while my mother applied cold cream to her face and hands and hovered. I cupped the note with my left hand, sheltering it from her inquisitive gaze—I guessed that this would be, for her, an occasion of suffering—and, in my haste to have done with it, and to begin so as to end the nightly ritual of rocking and moaning—I told him the truth: I told him I was afraid. I thought he might die (in which case, who would be left to ask me good questions?), but I did not tell him that.

Two days later, I got a letter from my mother in the mail. She wrote to say that some things were too difficult to talk about. (In fact she often went days without speaking to me, during which periods of silence she used the mails to communicate with me, though we slept four feet apart. During the time I'd spent Saturdays hanging around the Oldsmobile dealers, an act which she'd considered one of impropriety bordering on impiety, she'd used the mails [handing me her letter as soon as the postman delivered it] with a frequency that put an end to my visits, and then I spent Saturdays with her.) In the letter she now handed me, she said that she was noticing an inclination on my part to self-absorption and to secrecy, and that this was unwholesome as well as extremely painful to her. "I never had a mother," she wrote (she did, of course—her mother was old and ignorant, and, insofar as her ignorance allowed, kind). "And I give you everything, so it hurts me when you have time for Other People and not for me."

I took my diary to the Botanic Gardens and wrote in it that my mother was like a sponge, absorbing all the misery of the world; she was happy only when she was given offerings of pain. I wrote this sitting underneath a cherry tree. I had written beyond my knowledge of the thing, and so, feeling stupid and cruel and resentful of my own bewilderment, I took a piece of glass I found embedded in the dirt, sharpened it on a stone, and scratched it across my palm till I drew blood.

Every day after school I walked past David Larrimar's house, wondering in which room he lay sick, in an agony of apprehension lest he should see me, feeling blurred and unreal because I could not see him. The silence between me and my mother grew.

In David Larrimar's absence, I gleaned. He had had a nervous breakdown once; I did not know what a nervous breakdown was, only Mrs. Rochester came to mind, and he—fastidious and cool—would never shriek and never demand, I thought, in which I was partly right. He once left a classroom, they said, quietly and savagely insisting that it was unkind for students to lie and say bad things behind a teacher's back—no one knew to what lies, what bad things, he was referring: "We *wor*shipped him," a Senior Arista girl said, and I could see that she worshipped him still. He told his classes that McCarthy was evil, thereby putting himself at risk. (My mother greatly admired the Senator; my father, because he could not bear to see people's feelings hurt, admired the Senator's "principles," but took issue with his "harshness." My mother paid very little attention to my father.) David Larrimar often had students to his house. (Which students? I wished to know. What counted with him? kindness? intelligence? passion? passion for what?). One of his students was a Jehovah's Witness who refused to salute the flag. He sat with her at school assembly while everyone else stood, putting himself at risk. Her name was Dolores, and I envied her for what I supposed to be her passion. She was a year ahead of me, and she too was taking a Commercial Course. I searched her face for happiness (he sat with her while everyone else stood), but she looked dull and ordinary. Passion seemed to leave no visible mark.

Mary Guardini, the school librarian, was known to be in love with him. She was Catholic, as was I. She wanted to save his soul. In my experience, people who said they wanted to save souls for God wanted really to get their own claws in them. (My mother was forever praying for my happiness and my salvation, although I devoutly believed. I did wonder whether Original Sin had tainted me far worse than it had stained the souls of others; perhaps that would explain why she moaned at

night). Mary Guardini was gray, and she limped; she was far
older than my mother, who was beautiful. Sometimes David
Larrimar took her to concerts. Out of pity, I supposed. I was
beginning to understand that I was pretty.

When two weeks later David Larrimar returned to school, I
tried, chiefly by wearing ugly clothes, to efface myself, having
regretted writing what he could only regard as a silly, intem-
perate letter. When a girl named Shulamith Lipsky passed a
note to me during class, he said, his light drawl scathing,
"What's this? Hands across the water? Take your passes and
go out and play." I had wanted to be invisible, but not to be
exiled. I could quite happily have been invisible in his presence
—I understood this already—forever. I wanted to be the handkerchief he wore in his breast pocket, the sister he lived with,
the mother who cooked his meals, anyone but myself, but
always with him, an inanimate object, if need be, as necessary
to him as air.

While I was sitting disconsolately in my art class—a class for
which I had no aptitude and over which the teacher had no
control—David Larrimar walked in, causing the teacher to
blush. He smiled at me, in spite of my ugly clothes. After class,
with a formal nod to the art teacher, he took my arm, causing
me to become the cynosure of envy. Walking down the hallway, "Do you value subtlety?" he said.

"I don't know," I said. "Not in people," I said, not sure of
my meaning, but wishing to give the appearance of having
opinions.

"Good," he said. "Then I'll tell you my long-range plans. I
believe in long-range planning, don't you? It's an effective
antidote to suicidal impulses." My dismay must have shown on
my face, because David Larrimar said, "Suicide is just a subject, like any other—like geography. It's not part of my long-
range plans. We read 'Richard Cory' in class today. You should
have been there." Yes; but he had exiled me. "Do you think
suicide is an act of cowardice?" he asked. "Everyone else did.
Not an original thought in their heads." "I think that it is a sin
unless committed while not in sound mind," I said. What gray

Mary Guardini would have said; how far could being pretty carry me?

"That is not an original thought. Or a spectacularly kind sentiment."

"But it's what I believe. And I believe that it's contagious." Suicide was fashionable, that April: three men had jumped off the Brooklyn Bridge in the space of three weeks. I myself saw the glamour of it.

" 'April is the cruelest month,' " David Larrimar said, as if reading my mind. "Now that may be original, the idea that it's contagious. You must read Eliot. Not the *Four Quartets*, not yet."

"I don't think it's original. I think I got it from a book."

"And where do you think people get their original ideas from, if not from books?"

"Well, writers don't get their ideas from books, do they?" I had so far forgotten myself as to be able to talk.

" 'A poem should not mean, but be,' " David Larrimar said. "That's nonsense. It can be said of music, but not of poetry. All our ideas come from books. There are no original ideas. There are only original people." Among whom I was not.

We were standing in front of the attendance office. "Now for my long-range plan," David Larrimar said. "I am going to talk you out of God and into college. Tuesday night you will come to my house and listen to Beethoven. There will be other people there. I'll take you to Mary's Venetian Gardens next term when you are out of my class. People have petty minds."

"Why do you want to talk me out of God?" I asked.

"When you find your voice, you find it, don't you? Because God has a bad effect on you. Some people can believe in God and be original. You can't. And of course because he doesn't exist. Then we shall see what your passion leads you to."

I watched David Larrimar punch out his time sheet just as if he were an ordinary person.

What passion?

That was Thursday. On Saturday, shopping for my mother, I saw David Larrimar on his way to the laundromat. The sight of him carrying a laundry bag of soiled clothes titillated and embarrassed me. I ducked into a candy store for a chocolate malt. Once I had seen, from a car window, a girl with long hair sitting at a soda fountain, her feet naked, her toes curled around the foot rail. This had seemed to me the epitome of abandon—and, I supposed, impropriety. I slipped my feet out of my sandals and curled my toes around the foot rail, while I sucked the chocolate malt through two straws. I contemplated the unlikelihood of David Larrimar's carrying a laundry bag, his acting just as if he were an ordinary person. I felt as if I'd been witness to an exotic activity, and also that it had been vulgar of me to chance to see it. While I was sorting these feelings out, sucking noisily through the straws, David Larrimar appeared beside me. He asked for a vanilla malted. The candy store owner knew him, also a cause for amazement. I tried to slide my feet into my sandals without his noticing.

"What are your short-range plans?" he said.

"Grocery shopping," I said, while I waited numbly for clever words to arrange themselves in my head, which they did not. I had read *Prufrock* and *The Four Quartets*.

"May I join you?" he said.

I count that afternoon as among the happiest, and the most agonizing, of my life. It was like a day during which one is always conscious of the brilliant sun hiding behind the clouds, and always conscious of the clouds blotting out the sun, and conscious of being conscious, as if one had invented the sun, the clouds, and consciousness itself. I was conscious of being happy, and conscious of happiness as a great weight. I wanted desperately to act casual, but my happiness silenced me as effectively as pain silenced my mother, whom I did not wish to think about. It robbed me of small talk, of which I had never, in any case, had a large store. It did not help that the record stores were all blaring the same record, Number One on the Hit Parade: "Teenager in Love." In fact the air was like powdered gold, even under the elevated line, where long shafts of sunlight picked his slim figure out. He provided the talk.

When people ask me if I'd like to relive my life, if I'd like to be young again, I think of that afternoon of patterned sunlight. I think I will never feel the physical world enter my skin as it did then—the sun is never so bright now—and I think also in what agonies of embarrassment I said the simplest of everyday words: "broccoli," "half a pound," "veal cutlets." The words all seemed crude to me, as did I. I do not want to be young again. I prefer the dimming of the sun.

He picked out the broccoli for me. He waited patiently while I mumbled "six pork chops, half an inch thick, please," and he gave no evidence of noticing my awkwardness. He behaved as if all were harmonious, a golden April afternoon, ordinary, a pretty girl with a handsome man. "I wonder if they think you are my daughter," he said, more to himself than to me, as we left the dairy shop, where I'd been obliged to ask for half a pound of sweet butter, and that was the only thing he said that made me aware that he too was conscious of anomalies, and of the weight of the air around us.

I followed him without protest when, after announcing that the chocolate malted must have worn off by now, he led me up a flight of stairs to a Chinese restaurant with faded gold lettering and persimmon curtains under the el. He ordered soft-shell crabs for me, which I did not know how to eat. He said, "What are your long-range plans?" I tried to hide the crabs under the rice.

I had no long-range plans.

"To enter a convent," I said, which notion had never occurred to me.

He laughed aloud and accused me of teasing him, where-upon my long-range plan became clear to me. As it was to make him love me and to marry him, there was not much I could say, so I shook my head as two fat tears fell on the soft-shelled crabs.

"My God, I think you mean it," he said. "Do you mean it?"

"Yes. No. I suppose I'll be a secretary," I said, which is what in fact I did suppose.

"I won't have it," he said. "I won't have waste. I don't consort with secretaries. Clarify your long-range plans."

"And then I suppose I'll get married and have children."

"Stop playing with your food and listen to me. You are not going into a convent. You are not going to be a secretary."

"So can I get married and have babies?" His anger had the odd effect of putting me at ease. Besides, I was thinking: his babies.

"Let me tell you about Mrs. Horowitz's sister," he said. Mrs. Horowitz was chairman of the English Department. "Mrs. Horowitz's sister won an audition at the Met. Then she got married and now she doesn't sing."

I laughed. "But I don't have a voice! And anyway, maybe she's happier than she would have been."

"Tripe. All you know about happiness is how to give it. You have no idea where your own happiness lies."

"In giving it?" I ventured. The idea that I could inspire happiness was new to me.

"No formulas," he said. "Now you give happiness freely," he said, "because you don't know you're giving it. That's bound to change. Or perhaps not in your case, we shall see. I want you to read some books. Of my choosing. Will you? And no more uninteresting lies about Harvard seniors who were in love with you."

"You gave me an A."

"I gave everybody an A. You deserved an A for the composition I gave you a C for, though. I wanted to find out how complacent—how compliant—you were."

"Did you find out?"

"I found out that you accept what is given to you."

"Is that good?"

"Sometimes asking for more is more modest than asking for less."

Reduced to its simplest components, this conversation meant he loved me. That is what I told myself.

I was so finely tuned to my inner feelings during the months —the years—that followed, I scarcely wondered about his feelings at all, except as they related to me. I referred everything to myself. I believed that his celibate life could be attributed to one central and specific event, one mystery, which, if he declared himself to me, would shrivel and die in the blaze of love. When he tried to talk me out of God—and try he did—I debased my love for God by using it as an occasion to vent my

wit. Now I believe that all his elaborate teases and arguments were a way of talking himself, against the grain of his cynicism and despair, into God. I believe that he opposed God only in order to choose God. But as we talked—I grew less and less awkward, more and more expansive in his presence—I was conscious only of the relevance of irrelevant things. When he recited "The Pulley" to me, with an air of mockery, I thought only of the fine brown hair on my arms—did it displease him? I wanted so to be unlike poor Mary Guardini that I steered all talk away from God. I didn't want his soul for God, I wanted it for me. (So, perhaps, did Mary Guardini. When I saw her at his funeral, she looked like a shadow of her former shadowy self. I was still pretty.) I allowed him to teach me everything. All I know of music and of art I learned from him. And all I know of cowardice—my own.

His rooms were wide and white and high, a sun deck led off his living room; his bedroom, the threshold of which I never crossed, was white and high and narrow. In it there was a narrow bed, not even a print on the walls, only the constant whirr of the air conditioner, which, his narrowness notwithstanding, he never shut off. Only once, as I climbed the side steps that led to his separate apartment, did I see a figure through the screen of the porch below—his mother, a small bunched body that seemed busy even in repose.

To his rooms I frequently went, and through the months and years the pattern never changed, it remained consistent in its inconsistency; sometimes there were students and I was one of them—the privileged one, the one that was always there; and sometimes there were people I still referred to as grown-ups, and I acted as unofficial hostess, though no duty was ever assigned to me. I played my part well. I waited for a declaration. Sometimes I went to him alone. The air was weighty, then, with words unspoken. I never told him I loved him.

He had, from the moment I'd moved on from his class, given no thought to what he'd called the petty-mindedness of people. When I left his class, he, with perfect ease, made sure to see me every day. Sometimes he came early to school to peer in through a classroom door at me; sometimes he came to si

near me. How he carried this off without disapprobation and censure it did not occur to me to wonder. He was flaunting the unspoken rules, putting himself at risk. I did not wonder because I waited, in a tremble of anticipation, for his look, his glance, his presence. I lived like this for two years. When I left high school, everything but the all-important thing resolved itself. Now we were free to be alone, without risk to him. Without risk from other people. The risks he incurred from my presence I did not and could not measure: I waited for the declaration that never came; and all my energies centered around the waiting. I made no declaration—I knew he must know of my love for him; what was the need?

All impediments had been erased. The difference in our ages was not an impediment in my view—and my view was the only one available to me. He had caught me early enough to teach me to see through the eyes of others, but in the capturing of me he had made it impossible for me to see him through any eyes but my own.

And my mother's. But hers were so clouded with fear and suspicion, I dismissed any view she took of him as that of a jealous lover, which she was. My mother was my first jealous lover, and he was the fuel that fed the fires of her jealousy. She raised herself from the languors of her martyrdom to find out what she could. Aroused, my mother was formidable. I had of course acceded to his urgent implorings; I went to college, but in New York, both to placate my mother—who continued to share my blond room—and to be near to him. He was satisfied; she was not. Aroused, she was implacable. Her crystallized beauty—which so overshadowed my own common prettiness —was her ally. She made friends. She found things out. She presented me with the news that David Larrimar had "taken up" with a girl named Dolores, a Jehovah's Witness, upon whom he was urging college, which course her religion— which he was trying to talk her out of—forbade. Dolores, my mother said, was making her family miserable by insisting upon seeing David Larrimar, whom they regarded as a threat to the safety of her belief. These nuggets of information my

mother dropped in my lap; then she commenced another long silence.

Dull and ordinary Dolores! I'd never seen her at any of his gatherings. My mother lied. But I knew my mother never lied: a lie was a named, recognizable sin in the catalog of sins; and those sins written in stone my mother desisted from committing. Her gestures did not conform to love, but her habits followed the rules.

So I said to David Larrimar, as we sat on the sun terrace, placing myself against a background of wild climbing roses, feeling reckless and bold, "My mother has made friends with Dolores' mother." He received this information calmly, went in to make tea, and came back with it. He stood above me, pale and grave in the late summer sunlight, and said, "Do you think, then, that there is a new girl every year? Is that what they say? Is that what you think?"

All the old awkwardness returned to me, together with a new stubbornness. I didn't want questions. I wanted answers. I didn't want to reassure him. I wanted him to reassure me.

"That's what you think," he said, sadly; and then, when I might have seized the moment, he said, "You are so terribly unpossessive." He said the words with careful measure, as if they had neither positive nor negative weight; a shadow slanted across his face as he spoke.

I have had years in which to consider his light drawling words. I know—though most of my information comes from dreams—that they held within them a fatal reproach.

How can it have lasted so long? my friends ask. To fall in love at fifteen is not a fate I would wish upon my daughter. Who was the subject of this love? who was the object? Obsession is a form of self-love. One loves one's obsession as one loves oneself. David Larrimar was the object and the subject. So was I. We were both subject and object, and only death—a death he conveniently provided—can sunder such intimate ties, as lightning breaks the limb from the tree. (And new growths start from the raw amputation.)

I could have dispelled the mysteries by a single question. I didn't.

Perhaps it is arrogance to think I could have dispelled the mysteries by a single question. I love mysteries. He had always urged clarity upon us in the schoolroom, but I am at home with mysteries. I was bred to them. I was bred to mysteries and trained, as the vine clings to the trellis, to cling to silence.

He nourished me with mysteries. Once, when I visited him at school, he said, "They didn't know if you were my sister or my daughter or my wife. Of course I wish you were any one of those." I didn't say a word.

Mary Guardini talked to him of God, and so did Dolores. I let him do the talking. But he never said the words I wanted to hear.

If there was a central mystery, I did not unravel it. I was too busy hearing unspoken words. He never made a declaration. He never made a demand.

I tried to force his hand. I took a lover. It was time, in any case: I was twenty-two, my blood was hot. I had loved him for seven years. And my lover knew how to make the best of the business he'd prepared me for, sex. I continued to see David Larrimar all the time I saw my lover, a married man. And one weekend when I told David Larrimar how messy and intense and futile all this lovemaking was, he asked, "Do you see no way out?"

"Only if the man I love will love me," I said. I was drowning. I didn't know that he was. We were standing on a subway platform. "This is terrible," he said, "terrible." The train door closed on the word—"terrible"—and on his terrible face.

"There is more than age and God between us," he once told a girl who spoke to him of me. "There are some things harder, worse. Insuperable obstacles."

He must have known the words would get back to me. I never asked him what they meant.

I have never understood his silence, and I have never forgiven myself mine.

One day, inspired by a walk in the cemetery, I called him. "I have to see you," I said. "I have to talk to you. I have to ask you a question."

"No," he said, "not tonight, not now, no."

My married lover leaned against the phone booth. "What a fool you are," he said. "If he wanted to marry you, he'd have told you long ago. I tell you all the time, but you won't believe me."

"He's waiting for me to tell him so," I said, and I called again. He didn't answer.

Six months later, I married. I thought that marriage would be restful. I wanted to precipitate that explosion of feeling that we had never, between us, achieved. If that is what in fact I desired—I was led to marriage by my own sentient weariness —I did not nicely succeed. I heard of his death, an explosion of another sort, on my honeymoon in Carmel. I flew back for his funeral. I was pregnant, and I knew it: I have known Lucy well, since before she was born, from the moment of her conception; and I thought, as I looked at his reconstructed face, that she was his child, a result of everything spoken and unspoken that had gone between us.

They were all there: poor Mary Guardini, dull and ordinary Dolores, the beefy boys who seemed not to have changed at all.

He left everything to me—his diaries. But the diaries were only accounts of changing seasons, not his heart's seasons. They were bereft of human names. He wrote about the maple tree that overhung his terrace, its winy fragrance, the underside of its leaves the color of strong tea. But not about me, with whom under the maple tree he had so often sat. The diaries didn't solve the mystery; they deepened it.

I did not know, as I kissed his reconstructed forehead, that a resolve was forming in me: Words would become my medium, I would abjure silence. The only demand he ever made, and did not himself fulfill—*clarity!*—would become my watchword.

When I watch the movie in which the assassin looks so much like him, I am perversely thrilled by it (by him). Because he was I and I was he, I do not know who the killer was. I do not know who damaged whom. Because he was I and I was he—that is the nature of obsession, there is no space between subject and object, all the space is filled with the strong tissue of need—I sometimes think I have forgotten him. I could as soon forget to breathe.

When I met Devi—whom I did not recognize, but who was immediately, dearly familiar to me—I believed that I had fallen in love for the first time. That is how easily I forget David Larrimar. I forget my self. But—the screw turns round and round—I love mysteries and I hate mysteries—I have waited years for the denouement, for the clarity that David Larrimar promised and did not deliver. I waited all those years for David Larrimar. Doesn't it make sense that, robbed of a denouement with him, I should, nurtured to be stubborn, and proud, wait for Devi? I don't let go. I did once. And look.

Most of this is conjecture.

My husband was an interlude—an interlude which, however, produced Lucy (on whom, when the chips are down, I depend).

Of course some of the people who claim to have loved and been loved by David Larrimar say it is all very simple: He was gay. I do not believe this. Wouldn't he have told me? And when was life ever so symmetrical as that?

# *Part Four*

Love like Matter is much
Odder than we thought.

W. H. AUDEN, "Heavy Date"

# Chapter One

"Will you go for long, long walks with me? Will you tell me my life? How beautiful you are!"

"How beautiful you are, Devi. Yes. Long, long walks, how sweet London smells. How beautiful you are!"

Eileen carried our bags to the first landing; St. John helped her. Devi and I stood outside in the soft summer evening, holding hands. "How beautiful you are." "How beautiful you are."

"A walk now?"

"What about Eileen and St. John? I'm loopy from the flight."

"We will give them cause for scandal," Devi said; "I am ruthless, I want only you."

"Are you ruthless?"

"Happy. Happy?"

"Yes, Devi, very happy. There is green everywhere."

"London was parched before you came. St. John wants to kill me. You don't. I love you," Devi said.

"Yes."

"Yes?"

"I love you, Devi. When I was here last, there were still bombed-out buildings in Belgravia. And I remember, just minutes from town, a pasture—cows. That can't be here anymore. The sky is still enormous, though."

"All green pastures and magic woods," Devi said—we were walking in Belgrave Square—"and the buildings were all bombed out till you came. I've grown fatter," Devi said, "softer. Is it terrible?"

"A little fatter. Of course not terrible. And the gray at your temples suits you."

"Everything about me suits you, isn't it?"

"Of course."

"In our last lives," Devi said, "you were Cleopatra and I was the asp."

"And now?"

Devi only smiles. "We have been together from the beginning of time," he says. "Yes?"

"Yes."

We are walking back home, toward Chester Row. And St. John. What do I care? Devi loves me.

"For three months I didn't talk to anyone," Devi says. "And then, on the train to Oxford, there was a pleasant-looking chap. I thought, He isn't Angela, but I'll talk to him anyway. One has to speak. Or not?"

"When was this?"

"When the buildings were bombed out."

St. John is asleep. Eileen is lying on the couch in Devi's bedroom: "St. John sleeps in that funny little parlor thing behind the kitchen, Devi sleeps upstairs in his studio, you and I sleep here, in his bedroom."

"You can have the double bed, I'll take the couch. Who sleeps in the room next to this?"

"No one, apparently. Angela, you've done it again."

"I wasn't lying when I told you it was over. I didn't know. I didn't know until I saw him. I'm sorry you had to carry the bags up."

"He should have met us at the plane."

"Devi doesn't do things the way ordinary people do."

"This is going to be a strange vacation. Are you sightseeing, tomorrow, or Devi-ing?"

"I won't desert you, Eileen."

"You'd better not, you can't afford to."

"Good night."

"Good night."

In the moonlight the long white room with its sweeping arc of tall windows looked like the prow of a ship; and I drifted contentedly, at peace in calm and fragrant waters. The light streaming through my window was crystalline that morning; I awoke to an element that seemed foreign—neither air nor water is like this; imagine something that is not quite air, not quite water, hard and clear. Imagine swimming in air, feeling the currents wash against you in waves of light.

St. John is tall and fair and thin, he has a shuttered face, a monied voice. Eileen and St. John are talking pleasantly, their conversation rattles among the teacups.

". . . not a very good translation," Eileen is saying.

"They are talking about Celtic fairy tales," Devi says, as if they weren't there breakfasting like Happy Families. "Boring chaps, the Celts . . . Will tea do? Two lumps? St. John is taking time off from the City—while his money plays for him—to translate Celtic fairy tales."

"*Legends,*" Eileen says.

"Why is he translating Celtic fairy tales? Well you may ask."

"Actually, I'm taking Eileen to the City today," St. John says, "and I thought perhaps tea at Marlborough House with that chap at the Commonwealth Secretariat, I'll ring him up. Won't you join us, Angela?"

"No," Devi says. "She will not."

"Thank you, St. John, no."

"What will you do all day?" Eileen asks with a forced casualness.

"I don't know. Poke around the mews, maybe."

"Americans are always doing something," Devi says.

"Angela is American," Eileen says, her face flushed.

"No, she is not," Devi says. "She is pure Med, born to lethargy and pomegranates. Tootle off, you two."

"Are we going to meet for dinner?"

I am ruthless, I let Devi answer Eileen. "At the pub, five-thirty," he says; and Eileen kisses me good-bye. "Be good," she says, and then she looks confused; she starts to say something, changes her mind: "Be happy."

"What do you mean, St. John wants to kill you?"

Devi kisses me. "How could I have lived without you? In fact I never have. I had so many conversations in this kitchen with you when you weren't here."

"What did I say?"

"You listened. I talked. All my arguments with you have been arguments with myself, when you are gone there is no point in speech. You explain my life to me, though it is I who does the talking. I talk only to you. Talk without you is a nondecorative abstraction. Do you suppose it would be possible for me to love you, not for your consolations, but for yourself? Not for your sanity and goodness, just for you?"

"How would you tell them apart? me and what you call my consolations? How could you separate them?"

"You don't feel used?"

"I want to feel used."

"Will you look at my paintings?"

"Please."

"Not now . . . The trouble with art is that sooner or later someone wants it—wants what you've done to define yourself —and your definition of yourself is in someone else's drawing room."

"I thought that was the point. I mean, for example, you have a Hockney drawing in your bedroom."

"No, it's bad for me. The secret to growing old gracefully" —Devi pats his stomach, which is indeed paunchy—"is to want less and less, in the end to want nothing, certainly to want no praise. Yes?"

"Only saints want nothing—which is the same as wanting everything. It would probably be more modest to want a little."

"Shall I show in Paris then?"

"Why not?"

"To be damned or praised."

"The damning and the praise belong to someone else. They belong to the damners or the praisers. The work belongs to you."

"Do you accept criticism of your work with such detachment as you are urging upon me?"

"No, Devi, I don't. I love the praise. And I love the money."

"So you are asking me to be better than you?"

"Yes."

"Hmmm. The trouble is, people can't read the language of painting. So painters paint in the emotion—with no postscript saying, This was then."

"What's wrong with capturing the mood of the moment—for example, Vermeer?"

"What's wrong is, the moment you've captured it, it's fixed, it's no longer true. I paint people in desperate romantic positions—desperate emotional positions. I am not Vermeer—and the moment I do, I've created an emotional value judgment. I've departed from the exact and actual truth. Do you understand?"

"No. I keep thinking, Hopper. What's wrong with making emotional value judgments, which I'm not even sure what that means."

"Hopper is a case in point. His paintings are about the thing; they're not the thing itself. There ought to be a nonillustrative realism. But thinking like that gets me in a jam, paralyzes me in fact. Because a certain amount of manner and style is necessary. And the minute you talk about style, you begin to realize how many gestures you have because they're charming or pleasant or clever. So what you have—what I have—on canvas is not all of life, but a mannered example of something. I seem to be leading myself into a blind alley."

"How could you get all of life on to a canvas?"

"Raphael. All these too many ideas ruin my innocence. As a painter, I mean. I'm a decadent romanticist, and no way out."

"And as a consequence?"

"As a consequence I paint very little."

"So the ideas? . . ."

"Are a way I've chosen to stop me from painting? Yes, probably. Such hard work to arrive at no work . . . Do you understand about nonillustrative realism?"

"No."

"Think of it in terms of cinema. I can tell you what I mean only by giving you an example of what I don't mean. A film like *Mean Streets,* for example—the new romanticism of reality and truth. It's a fake. Films like that exist to spawn social mannerisms. They're about the thing. The thing itself is somewhere else. The real tough guys are outside looking in at *Mean Streets.* I'm talking about a flow I don't have. You flow. I think and think about all this, and I can't put it into words. We need another medium."

We need touch.

"But how I love not making sense when I'm with you. It tells me what I know. I've adopted beliefs and opinions out of desperation. Can you have beliefs without first having desperation? It's why I frequently sound ferocious and angry when I talk to you. It's because I love you that I sound ferocious and angry. We need another medium."

We need touch. Devi takes my face in his hands and kisses me on the mouth. "Do you mind my being silly?" he says.

"I mind not being able to understand."

"Only take me seriously and love me. How can you understand? I don't understand. How beautiful your hands are, shall I paint them?"

Devi and I met Eileen and St. John at the Duke of Wellington at six-thirty. Devi said if your regular had to be a tourist pub, what better than to go to it with tourists, and would I come to London and be a tourist forever? "Lovely," he said, stretching his legs, which were no longer so lean, "that you don't have to be *doing* every minute." He yawned. "Lovely to yawn with you," he said.

Eileen and St. John had gone first to the Grenadier, and Eileen was quite pretty in her enthusiasm for the vine-covered pub, the mews. "It all looks like a musical comedy," she said, her face shining. "I expect people to burst into song."

"And all built on the sweat of the Empire," Devi said, with perfect equanimity. "In fact I quite like it, too. It is pretty—I fancy it." Encouraged, Eileen said she'd seen a police station on Gerald Road—"do you call police stations something else

1

here?''—with a man-wanted-for-murder sign posted next to
window boxes—''do you call them something else here?''—
full of coleus and marigolds and black-eyed susans and pansies: ''It looked like a facade, like part of a stage set for *The
Student Prince*. . . . I've got my countries mixed up.'' Devi had
clearly made a decision to be pleasant for my sake, we would
hear no quick, angry speeches about Indian and Paki slums.

''Devi has made a decision to be pleasant,'' St. John said.
''I'm glad.'' (Devi and Eileen were getting a third round of
drinks. Pub protocol escaped me completely. ''Not to worry,''
Devi said. ''Leave all to me.'')

''I'm glad Devi has decided to be pleasant,'' I said. ''For
Eileen's sake.''

''Not for your own?'' St. John was pronouncing his words
with the careful articulation of someone who has had slightly
too much to drink.

''I can take Devi any way.''

Something very busy went on behind St. John's pale eyes,
which resolved itself in one sentence: ''I would die for him,'' he
said.

''And so would I.''

''He should have married you years ago,'' St. John said. ''He
is miserable without you, and he makes everyone around him
miserable as well.'' This was not what I'd expected, St. John as
an ally.

''You two look conspiratorial,'' Devi said, with a frown for St.
John and a smile for me.

''I keep thinking that if you all drink beer and I drink gin it's
not going to work out right.''

''Everything will work out right in the end,'' Devi said, and
favored Eileen with a smile, which she returned gladly.

''Angie? Why don't you just grab his cock? He's only waiting.''

''I can't believe you're saying that.''

''He's in love with you. It couldn't be clearer.''

''You've never been a fan of his.''

"I've never seen you look so happy. You look so decorative together."

"Decorative?"

"That's what St. John says. I agree."

"Only a fag could use the word 'decorative' in conjunction with love. Do you like St. John?"

"A lot."

"I do too. I was prepared to hate him. I did hate him. None of it seems to fit. I'm happy, Eileen."

"Well, take a chance."

"I'm scared."

"So is he. What's homosexual or heterosexual anyway? Just labels. Just concepts."

"I wouldn't call sodomy a concept." I didn't want to think about sodomy, about what he did in bed. "I can't believe you're talking like this."

"Do you mean you don't want him?"

"Of course I want him."

"Well, risk it."

"It's perfect the way it is. Whatever he wants, I want."

"You could cut the sexual energy with a knife. . . . Are you so afraid of being hurt?"

"This is funny. You've always been afraid on my behalf. I'm afraid of his being hurt. I want him to come to it by himself."

"Once I said he chose his suffering. Now I think you can help him bring an end to it."

"I could go on like this forever."

"No you couldn't. And neither can he. He may have deluded himself into thinking he could have a life without you, but his health is suffering; anyone can see that. How's his sex life, by the way?"

"Practically nonexistent, as far as I can make out."

"That's what St. John says. So you see . . . Your letters to Devi are all over this house. This place is like a shrine to you."

"You and St. John have gotten awfully thick."

"Why not? He's good company."

In fact he was, though prim, pleasantly proper, the effect of which was to make Eileen slightly vulgar.

"In New York Devi told me how he came to be a homosexual," I said. "He pinned two photographs to his wall, one of a naked man and one of a naked woman. His body responded to the picture of the naked man."

"How old was he?"

"Sixteen."

"I don't call that a choice," Eileen said. "I call that responding to the lure of the forbidden. I call that a way to be an outcast—effect, not cause, an effect of his wanting to place himself outside the grace of God. Anyway, he's nailed himself to a cross of his own construction. He probably made that story up, anyway. Do you think that's the way choices get made?"

"I don't know. All I know is you made me swear I wasn't in love with him before you agreed to take this trip with me. I'm surprised to hear you singing another tune all of a sudden."

"I know what I see. Devi is as beautiful as Lucy says he is."

Sooner or later Devi's beauty becomes for everyone who knows him a character trait, like goodness, or integrity.

"Are you telling me I've fallen in love with a pretty face? That's what Stephan says."

"Stephan," Eileen said, "is a moral idiot. It's time for you to make some demands."

"Devi told me tonight he couldn't bear weak women."

"Well, there you are. If you want the truth, I don't believe you're afraid of hurting him. I think what you're afraid of is garden-variety rejection."

"I don't feel rejected now."

"But this exalted mood you're both in is not going to last forever. Something has to happen."

"Something is happening. Without my intervention. I want it to go on happening, by itself."

"I think you're going to find that that's not possible," Eileen said.

"Every time in the past when I've pushed, Devi has fled."

"Push harder," Eileen said.

"And little things stop me."

"Such as?"

"Such as the housekeeper's door is painted lavender."

"Oh, for goodness' sake. Push harder," Eileen said.

Days passed in a blur of happiness. By unspoken agreement, Devi and I spent hours apart, during which there was a burst of renewed activity in Devi's studio; the fresh, exciting smell of paint and turps greeted us when Eileen and I returned from Harrods, the Tate. . . .

"Tell me all," Devi said.

"That Blake watercolor at the Tate, God creating man— *Elohim Creating Adam*—I love it. What's that in the Bible, Eileen? 'The whole creation groaneth in travail'—something like that. That's what it looks like, all the groaning and travail. It makes Michelangelo look just pretty. . . ."

"Heresy," Devi said, and placed me on his lap.

"And Adam looks just like God and they both look anguished. It can't be easy to be God."

"Angie's appreciation of anguish expressed itself in a huge and expensive lunch at the Tate," Eileen said. "She ate trifle."

"Which is heaven. Potted shrimp, on the other hand . . ."

"Not good?"

"Yuuch."

*Yuuch* was Lucy's word—at fourteen, she still maintained vestiges of childhood, I think on purpose. She was on vacation with her father in Paris. I hadn't spared her a thought in all these days.

"Tell more," said Devi; his chin was resting on my head.

"Angela ought to wear a sign that says *Deaf, Dumb, and Blind* —everyone stops to talk to her."

"Yes?" said Devi, whose arms tightened around me. "Who was he?" His chin rubbed my head a little too hard for comfort.

"A bag lady," Eileen said. "Do you call them bag ladies here? She had two umbrellas. . . ."

"Five teeth . . ."

"And half a pound of pink lipstick smeared on her mouth."

"Her husband was a waiter on the Empress of Scotland. . . ."

"You tell, Angela."

"Nothing much. She just said, 'Isn't the sun lovely, dear. You eat differently in the winter, don't you, dear.' She'd been born under a sun sign—born on the same day as JFK, and how she'd cried when he was killed. I told her my sign. 'An earth sign, but very nice indeed,' she said. I could make people die laughing, she was sure. And then she blessed us. I did feel blessed, didn't you, Eileen?"

"Where was this?"

"Kensington Gardens."

"I see that I shall have to come with you on your excursions," Devi said. "We can't have you blessed by all and sundry, only by me."

"What are you thinking of?"

Devi and I were stretched out on the sofa, doing nothing (a nothing in which a great deal was happening); Eileen and St. John had, in their easy, companionable way, gone off to the movies, Satyajit Ray. ("Gaga goo-goo over India, those two," said Devi, "of course they've never been.")

"I'm thinking how I'd like to be on the sea."

"Not happy here?"

"Silly. Of course. It's just that it's one of the regrets of my life that I can't swim. I learned once. You're not supposed to be able to forget, but I did. I loved floating on my back, it was like breathing in the sky. But I always panicked when it was time to get back on my feet again, I thought the physical laws would work in reverse and I'd go down headfirst. I always thought—I don't know why this urge to fly, it's so much more beautiful to swim—I always thought if I could swim I'd be a better person. A different one, at least. Maybe it's the other way around— maybe if I were a better person I could swim."

"One would have to trust," Devi said.

"Exactly. Only it doesn't necessarily follow. Because the person I knew who was most relaxed in the water—most trusting—was the most untrusting on dry ground. I don't know why I think good swimmers are generous people, there's no evidence for it."

"Who?" said Devi.

"My husband."

"He doesn't exist," Devi said, "he never did. I will teach you how to swim."

"When?"

"When we are married."

"What are you thinking, Devi?"

"That too often detachment becomes stasis, no? . . . What is the meaning of a red plastic chair in a green field near Oxford?"

"What's the meaning of that question?"

"All of my friends are ex-lovers," Devi said.

"Me?"

"You—here, come closer—are all my friends and all my lovers. And none of them. You are you. Your shoulders are tense, let me rub. I am painting a red plastic chair in a green field."

"What about the ashy mauve?"

"Bugger the ashy mauve."

"When do I see your paintings?"

"Soon. Be patient. I am."

"What are those pretty beads you're wearing?" St. John said.

"Emeralds. Unpolished. I got them in India, see the carving?"

"Yes, I see, emerald quartz. No one would know they were emeralds, that's unfortunate. For most people the reason to wear emeralds is to let other people know you're wearing emeralds."

"Balls," Devi said. "What makes it lovely is that nobody does know. Delicious. Angela reveals her secrets when she is ready."

"I'm neutral on the subject," Eileen said, "though sometimes"—a long hard look at me—"it takes Angie a long time to *reveal.*"

"No one can live every day with all this so much intensity," Devi said.

"What intensity? You're picking a head of lettuce." We were at the greengrocers, and, in fact, I had to hold on to my basket very tight, for fear that I would float away. "What could be more ordinary?" I smiled at all the shoppers. I felt sorry for poor Eileen, being American at Westminster Abbey.

"Picking a head of lettuce with you is like having an orgasm. Or breathing pure ozone. Imagine every day this excitement," Devi said. I couldn't read his voice.

"Everybody does this."

"Are you not excited?"

"If we did it every day it would not be exciting. There's nothing intense about brussels sprouts."

"How do people live when they are happy?"

"I'd welcome a chance to find out. . . . Washing the dishes."

"What about washing the dishes?"

"Would you call that an intense experience?"

"It would depend on whether you were doing the drying up."

"I'd be watching soap operas. I don't believe in drying dishes."

"What would I be doing?"

"Reading the newspaper and rolling cigarettes and muttering about my slothfulness."

"Domestic coziness?"

"Yes."

"What could be more intense than that?" Devi said. "Why do you have six packets of brussels sprouts?"

"I guess I'm excited."

"Well, if it doesn't work out," Devi said, "you could always write a novel about us. Or a screenplay. Al Pacino will play my part."

"How about me?"

"Anne Bancroft?"

"OK."

"I used to have a crush on Anne Bancroft. Now, of course, I
have a crush on Al Pacino."

"Oh, Devi."

"How funny you are. Is it so mean to tease you?"

"You'll have to pay for it."

"How?"

"Cook Indian food tonight and let Eileen go gaga goo-goo
over it. I hate brussels sprouts."

On the sixth day of our visit, four days before we were due to
leave for Italy, we drove to Oxford in St. John's Bentley. ("Eileen will go gaga goo-goo over Oxford, too, wait and see." "So
will I, probably, Devi." "That's different. I never mind what
you do. Whatever you do is perfect.")

Why do they call Oxford a city of gray? In that sweet city all
the stones of all the dreaming spires are pale gold (and when
all the bells rang, I drowned in honey).

*The university is a paradise. . . . Rivers of knowledge are there, arts
and sciences flow from thence; gardens that are walled in; bottomless
depths of unsearchable councils are there. . . .*

Eileen and St. John chattered merrily—"like two talking
*Michelin's,*" Devi said, though in fact Eileen was reading from
Wooley's *Clarendon Guide;* and St. John's plummy voice could
be heard saying, "But at Cambridge, there are sheep. . . ."

"Eileen will lose her wits in that guidebook and never find
them again," Devi said. "Soon St. John will be telling her the
story of how his great-grandfather dined at Hampton Court
and ate strawberries the size of tomatoes picked from a garden
that once belonged to Anne Boleyn."

"My great-grandfather, Eileen. . . ." St. John's mouth was
a perfect O of astonishment, the pupils of his pale blue eyes
contracted, when Devi and I began to laugh at him.

St. John parked the car on St. Aldate's Street. "Devi," I said,
"why does 'the High' sound so romantic?"

"When I read Henry James—you see, I pose as a country
bumpkin, would you have thought I knew James?—when I
read James, 'the Fifth Avenue' sounded heaven to me, some-

thing to do with the definite article, I think. 'Fifth Avenue' sounds just curt. Whereas 'the Fifth Avenue.' . . .''

"Makes it sound mysterious and very much your own. But it isn't the definite article that makes this place Paradise. . . ."

"You are the definite article," Devi said. We were not yet out of the car.

"Do you feel the need of a guidebook?"

"I have no appetite for facts. How did I know I would love this place?"

"Your feverish romantic imagination told you. It is a romantic city—'sweet city with her dreaming spires that needs not June for beauty's heightening.' All the friends you made in your lonely childhood when you read all the lovely grown-up books, all their ghosts are here, waiting for you."

"And it is June. And Peter Wimsey was here, he went to Balliol. How did you know I had a lonely childhood? Can we go to Balliol?"

"If Peter Wimsey was alive he'd be over eighty now."

"I have no doubt that he's alive. You know a lot."

"I shall make it my business to continue to astound you."

Eileen and St. John, striding purposefully ahead—"two walking *Michelin's*"—led us into the quad of Christ Church College ("Tom Quad," Eileen said, consulting her guidebook); and my capitulation was complete. Noble Tom Tower, and pinnacles, pale honey-gold, against a gentle blue-gray sky. Such an extravagance of subdued and peaceful riches; an enclosure womblike and expansive. Spacious day!

"And you sang in the choir here, Devi."

"Surely not," St. John said, "as Oxford is not Devi's university. . . ."

"That will do," Devi said, with a ferocious scowl. "Angela has no appetite for facts."

"What does it matter?" I said.

"Exactly," he said.

"Shall we punt on the river?" St. John said. "Shall we have a look at the hall?" I liked him very much.

"Yes," Eileen said.

"I'll drown," I said. "I don't want to climb stairs, either."

"No," Devi said. "No."

"We are beautifully lazy," Eileen said. "Maybe it's best not to approach Oxford with a guidebook right away." I loved her very much.

There was a haze over Christ Church meadow. A watery sun bled through the leaves of elms. We walked among the lengthening shadows, walked and walked. Someone was burning leaves. The sad, pungent smell of distant smoke (like incense to a forsaken god) and the cool dank smell of the river mingled with the fresh green smell of the meadow, and "all built on the blood and sweat of the Empire," Devi said; but his heart was not in his words.

"Surely the Cherwell and Thames owe nothing to the Raj," St. John said.

"What does it matter?" Devi said. "What does anything matter?"

Eileen paused to read a sign: "Christ Church meadow—where, according to the order of the Dean, no kites are flown, balls are thrown, pistols fired and no beggars allowed and no one of disorderly appearance."

"I was a beggar till you came," Devi said.

"I see kites."

"Ashy mauve?"

"We have a choice," St. John said, "owing to our late start. Evensong at the Cathedral or a drink at the Turl."

"Evensong."

"A drink at the Turl."

"The Turl."

The Turl.

"I have an errand to run," Devi said, and, such was my trusting happiness, his departure troubled me not at all.

"Was it a loss from your point of view? We didn't do any sightseeing to speak of."

"No," Eileen said, echoed by St. John. "It was beautiful. I'll come again." While St. John got our pints, she said, "To-night."

"Tonight what?"

"You and Devi. Tonight."

"You are the kindest friend I have ever had."

"I don't know about kind. I feel as if I'm standing on a precipice with you two."

"Precipice is an alarming word."

"Threshold, then. The fact is, I'm jealous. Love in the air."

"Not gone with the wind?"

"You're nuts."

Devi returned with a package: "I bought this off the High near Magpie Lane."

"You know, Devi, sometimes I don't know whether to believe you or not. What would you have said if you'd bought it on a street with a boring name? . . . Do you know Harriet Vane and Peter Wimsey stayed at the Mitre? . . . What's in the package?"

"Open it. I'd have said I bought it off the High near Magpie Lane. You really do believe in Peter Wimsey, don't you? You're going gaga goo-goo, you know."

"Oh dear. Do you mind very much?"

"How funny you are. Open it."

In the package was a Victorian camisole, with tiny embroidered roses—"for Lucy."

Devi took one look at my face and said, "How funny you are."

In the car, driving home: "But it would have been nice to see more of Magdalen," I said. Devi slapped his thighs—an uncharacteristic gesture—and laughed, and hugged me. *"Maudlin,"* he said. "You don't pronounce the *g.*"

"Really? Mary *Maudlin?* I'm sleepy."

"You're not Magdalen?"

"No, not maudlin, just sleepy."

"Sleep," Devi said. "We'll come again. But India first, I think."

"India?"

"You'll have to meet my mum. I'll come with you to Venice. But India soon, I think."

"Rest your head on my shoulder, Devi." He looked at me

quizzically and resisted the arm that was encircling his shoulder.

"You sleep," he said.

I pretended to sleep. Devi's arm encircled me, pulled my head to his shoulder. He reached for my sleepy hand, and placed it between his legs, where life was stirring. I gave a little grunt of pleasure, which Devi mistook for a snore. "She snores," he whispered, as if this were a good and remarkable thing.

I fell asleep in earnest when we returned. When I awoke, I found Eileen sitting in the kitchen, looking troubled.

"St. John's pissed," she said.

"What about?"

"I ate his cabbage soup."

"What about all the goodies we bought at Fortnum and Masons?"

"He doesn't care about the goodies; he wants his cabbage soup. Devi says he likes to play at being 'prole.' "

"You could have fooled me. Where is Devi? Was the soup any good?"

"At the pub with St. John. There's some left. He makes it with saffron."

"Well, the hell with him; I'm going to eat it. Do you think it's really cabbage soup he's pissed about?"

"Where Devi and St. John are concerned, I don't go in for motives," Eileen said.

"You could have fooled me."

"You two had better do it."

"That's what I think."

Devi returned: "He's placatable," he said, "though I'm only trying out of an excess of generosity toward the world in general. Why don't you tootle off to the pub, Eileen? We don't want his cabbage soup remorse souring our days."

"I'm too tired to tootle," Eileen said, and made off for the bedroom. "I'm going to read my guidebook."

"Everybody's grouchy," I said.

"Naturally," Devi said. "Our happiness sours their disposi-
tions. They will enjoy making up. It will give them the illusion
of virtue, all over a mess of cabbage soup."

"Which I also ate."

"And now what do you fancy?"

"Anything."

"I thought a walk. Unless you're too tired?"

"No. I'll just put a dress on."

"Wear that."

"Devi, it's a caftan. I sleep in this."

"You look like an Arabian princess."

"Well, I don't want to shock the natives."

"They'll think I rubbed my lamp and you popped out."
Devi's fingers were, quite without his appearing to know it,
fingering his fly.

I went into the bedroom to change. Eileen lay on the bed,
her face turned toward the wall.


"Aren't you going to ask where we're going?" Devi said, as
we walked. "You don't care?"

"Where are we going? I don't care."

"What are you thinking?"

"Nothing."

"Is that possible?"

"It seems to be. . . . St. John said he'd die for you."

"What impertinence. You, on the other hand, will live for
me, isn't it?"

"Yes."

I was thinking, in a lazy kind of way, how familiar these
unfamiliar streets were to me. "How far are we from Waterloo
Bridge?"

"Miles," Devi said. "Why?"

"I was thinking of a movie. Robert Taylor and Vivien
Leigh."

"How funny you are. You should be thinking of how much
you love me."

Near Victoria Station Devi hailed a cab, and said the name of
an unfamiliar street. "I've had it in mind to do this for a long

time," he said, "but no one will play with me." Devi's destination was an amusement arcade in Soho. I couldn't blame anybody for not wanting to play with him. With all of London at their disposal, why would anyone want to come to this tawdry place? I had a confused impression of gray bodies and glaring machines, the Coney Island of my childhood without the innocence, and without the sun, 42nd Street in less blatant dress, litter all over the ground—my shoe stuck to a piece of chewing gum—and an odor of unwashed bodies and cheap sweets. To come to this place we had to walk under an archway over which there were windows hung with red curtains, between which there was a lamp, offering dim light and cold comfort. I had a fleeting, disjointed impression, as we went through the dank passage, that we were already in Venice.

"Beat me if you can!" Devi said.

His forehead was knit in what might have passed for anger as he twisted the dials of the electronic tennis game—tiny blips, like a hospital heart-monitoring machine.

Devi won four out of five games. "Four out of five isn't bad," he said, as we wandered aimlessly through dark streets and cobblestoned alleys. "You didn't give the games to me?"

"I was famous in school for my lack of hand-eye coordination."

"Rubbish. And do you feel beaten because I've won?"

I knew the answer Devi required; it cost me nothing to say (it was true to say): "I don't feel I've lost because you've won."

"You are perfect," Devi said.

"Yes, but somebody's following us."

"Shall we give the old beggar a coin or tell him to bugger off?"

"Whatever you think."

"You are perfect," Devi said; and he gave the old man several coins.

"I don't take money from black men," the old man croaked, pocketing the money. "Scum, filth, taking all our pretty girls. Go back where you came from, nasty nigger boy."

"Here, now, that will do, sir." A bobby had appeared from a dark alley: "Let the lady and the gentleman be."

"Swine. Paki scum. Nasty nigger boy."

"The glory of Britain," Devi said. "I'm not bothered, love."

We walked to Trafalgar Square, which, at this hour of the morning, was almost empty; we sat on the terraced steps leading to the fountain, and listened to the muted sounds of the sprawling sleeping city for which I had formed such a vast affection; we might have been sitting in the country, except for the newspapers that blew around our feet. And listened to each other's silent thoughts. I watched the pulse beat of Devi's neck; I imagined the blood coursing through his veins, and I thought, If it is true that the only way to conceive of Heaven is to understand that it will be for us as happy—no more happy, no less happy—as our happiest moments on earth, then Heaven is this: Devi's pulse beat, the blood coursing through his veins. Vines.

"There is a point," Devi said. "No point without you and Lucy. If I took care of you? Should you like being taken care of? Would you stop work for a while? Is it very selfish? For me to make you the point? The pictures should be the point, but without you they are not. Would you," Devi said, "have a baby with me? Then there would be a point."

"Yes."

"Yes?"

"Yes to everything. Devi, have you thought about sex?"

"Thought? And thought and thought, of what else thought? Hold my hand, don't look at me. Do you love everything about me?"

"Yes."

"Ah. I thought . . . don't look at me . . . perhaps if I were to go to bed with you and another man, and I would be turned on by him being turned on by you being turned on by him. . . . No? It seemed to me not right, too. I can't see you in a pornographic movie."

"Can you see me at all? I mean, can you see us? Couldn't you —well, use me as you might use another man? Couldn't we do things that are—well, familiar to you?"

"I think it will just happen. And it will be familiar. I think better not to scheme and plan."

"Yes."

"Are you afraid?"

"No. Are you?"

"No. You don't frighten me any more. You never did."

"Happiness frightened you, Devi."

"It has happened in my imagination so often."

"Me too. When I was dreaming you, I thought you must be dreaming me."

"I was. I have always seen you. You were always in bed with me. Have you never known that when you called from New York I was sometimes in bed with a man? And always in bed with you."

"Why is it so easy this time, Devi?"

"I have decided to surrender. To myself." He laughed. "While you're still young enough to have a son. Better put a limit on the cigs." This time, when he kissed me, our tongues met. How sweet he smelled, how beautiful to be entered.

"When will it happen?"

"When it happens."

"Oh, Devi."

"How funny you are. I feel as if everything important has happened already, do you?"

"Yes. What's Gretna Green?"

"Why?"

"I don't know. It's where characters in novels get married."

"If you were a character in a novel you would know that we were on the Brompton Road, having left Belgravia behind us."

"Unless I were a character in a fog."

"Speaking of mist," Devi said—and in front of Brompton Oratory he unbuttoned his fly—"I must have a pee."

I watched.

Devi smiled.

"And now I want a taxi," Devi said; and, because everything that was supposed to happen was happening, a taxi appeared and into it we climbed, like happy tired children for whom the party has gone well.

As soon as we were in the flat, Devi slipped off his shoes and peeled off his socks. Imagine being married to Devi, imagine that gesture becoming commonplace. He disappeared into the bathroom and emerged wearing a blue velvet robe I had never seen; it stopped at his knees. "Put on your Arabian princess robe," he said. Imagine being married to Devi . . . the tendons on his brown calves . . .

We made tea holding hands. We drank tea holding hands.

I wish my body were more beautiful.

"What are you doing?"

"What I'm doing. Resting my head against your leg."

He spread my hair out like a fan over his knees. I had trouble breathing.

He will let me know when.

"Bed?" Devi said.

"Yes, bed."

He raised me to my feet and took me in his arms.


"Are you crazy?" Eileen said. She was sitting up in bed and smoking the Piccadilly cigarettes Devi had bought me.

"What are you talking about?"

"Do you know Devi's in the next bedroom?"

"Yes."

"You know he isn't sleeping in his studio?"

"Yes."

"Why aren't you with him?"

"He didn't ask me."

"Isn't that an invitation? Sleeping in the next room?"

"The invitation has to be clearer than that, Eileen. He kissed me good night—he didn't lead me to his bed, he'll know when he's ready, trust me. He is ready, but not tonight."

"It's morning."

"Well, that's another reason."

"What do you want him to do, rape you? Have some pity."

"Eileen, it's all right. I've frightened him before, I want it to be easy this time, it will happen. Too much has happened already tonight."

"Jesus."

"And I just want to sleep for a few hours, so does he."

"Did he say that?"

"He doesn't have to say anything. I know."

"You're crazy."

"Can I have a cig? I'm exhausted. So is he. So would you be if you'd walked all over London."

"Be exhausted with him. You're driving everybody else crazy, too. Both of you. You're afraid."

"No, I'm not. I'm happy."

"Happy is the next bedroom."

I knocked on Devi's door.

"Come in. Tired?"

"Very."

"Happy?"

"Very."

"Sleep?"

"Yes."

"I'm happy," Devi said.

We fell asleep in each other's arms, Devi in his velvet robe, I in my caftan. I did not dream.

It was midmorning when I woke up. Devi was gone. For a moment I did not know where I was; then the old terror returned: another departure in his perpetual departure. But Devi was coming in the door sideways, carrying a tray, singing, "Breakfast!"

Imagine being married to Devi; I moved my leg over to the warm depression left by his body and breathed in all the smells: tea and toast and apples and Devi's smell on the pillow and Devi here.

Devi drew a chair up near the bed, deposited the tray, and, for a moment looking acutely shy (imagine cradling his head, and not as a liberty), slipped into bed. Imagine being married to Devi; flank to flank.

"Not such good news," he said, handing me my teacup.

"What?"

"Dealer-wallah is coming over and I have to spend the day

with him. About Paris." Our feet were playing under the covers. "Pictures. And dinner tonight, business."

"Well, not such bad news."

"No, but what will you do all day?" His face brightened: "Will you stay in bed all day?"

"What are they doing?" I said, meaning Eileen and St. John.

"Eileen has already tootled with her guidebook and St. John appears to be applying himself to Celtic fairy tales."

The idea of my spending the day in bed separated only by two rooms from St. John (who would probably feel obliged to toss some plummy enigmatic words at me) did not appeal. Also I felt a rising restlessness divorcing itself from my exhaustion. "I never did see Magdalen properly."

"You'll go to Oxford?"

"What do you think?"

"Lovely to return to the scene of the crime. I wish I were going with you," Devi said, "I'll book my flight to Venice while you're gone." My hand shook—imagine Venice with Devi—and Devi mopped the tea from my chest and kissed the hollow of my throat. "I wish there were time now," he said, his voice muffled and urgent; but he was already out of bed.

## Chapter Two

At Paddington, just before my train pulled in, I thought I heard the stationmaster call my name over the loudspeaker, but I knew that in my excitement and exhaustion I must be hearing things, and forbore to call Devi, though just to think of Devi calling me back home to him made me realize with heart-turning joy how far we had come toward simplicity—toward bed.

Somewhere near Reading it occurred to me that Lucy might have called from Paris, but I warned myself against maternal hysteria; and I began to cherish the day, full of Devi, so present in his absence.

I wanted to be alone, to rest gently in my happiness, to allow it to expand, to let it completely overtake me. I needed a day of no voices; I wanted no kitchens, no words, not even other flesh. To be in love and to be in Oxford and to have the future before me; I was in love with a past I had never known, and it quieted me to breathe, in all the narrow intricate lanes and gracious walled gardens, the blessed bounty of the dead. I thought it serendipitous that Devi was engaged today, and proper; our souls could prepare themselves in peace—Oxford was a shining raiment, I clothed myself in it.

I love medieval cities; they do not clamor for attention; they possess their souls—their riches—in quiet; formal, courteous, they reveal themselves slowly, stone by stone, garden by garden; hidden treasures wait calmly to be loved and yield to introspective wandering.

A dream of North Africa wove itself into my dreaming thoughts: A twelve-foot-high whitewashed wall, a profusion of purple bougainvillea spilling over it; a sandy approach to the wall, lined with spiky cactus blooming with pale orange pears; a door of fretted wood, painted green, set in the high white wall; and once beyond the door, beyond the dry and stingy sands, the generosity: date palms and pomegranate trees, grape vines and lemon trees, morning glories, pansies, a riot of sunflowers, zinnias large as dinner plates, moonflowers closed and secretive by day, open like pearly trumpets and fragrant by night (and deadly: to sleep with a moonflower under one's pillow is to sleep without dreams, carried into the dark by waves of fragrance thick and soft as down; to sip their nectar is to sleep forever), and starbursts of yellow jasmine also deadly, and homely marigolds with their astringent weedy smell, and trees laden with great misshapen hybrid red fruit, tumorous and too heavy for the slender branches, the glistening wet-green leaves; and nasturtiums and anemones; and over all the unambiguous Mediterranean light. The wash and murmur of the endless sea. I spent my days in that walled garden once, leaving it seldom, leaving it to watch the sun set over the acquiescent sea, and I was unhappy there. But all my life I have wanted to live in a walled garden—before I lived there, after I lived there, even while I lived there, I wanted to live in a walled garden. And to select my own society. My husband would not let me sleep with a moonflower under my pillow. When I think of that garden I think of the tracery of shadows left on the whitewashed wall by the purple bougainvillea. My happiness was like that, then—imaged, a thing to come, a garden of the future, now.

The sweetness of the air of Magdalen's quad after the dust and noise of the High. "The auto machine," my guidebook quaintly says, "has made a desecration of the High," which is nonsense, of course; it's what they say about the hippies on the Ponte Vecchio, whereas in fact the Ponte Vecchio always belonged to beggars and to troubadours, and the High always belonged to the World, one has only to step into the quad to feel that one belongs to realms of endless time.

The cloisters of Magdalen, pillars: A sculpted man and woman embrace; climbing roses in full bloom twine around their joined forms. Single forms: men, animals—dry vines bearing no leaf or flower lock them in a brittle embrace. This is how it's meant to be.

In the softly scented deer park everything commingles: bells, birds, the dark brown smell rising from the river, the spicy fragrance of yellow and purple wildflowers which are woven into the meadow like the pattern of faded tapestry in a much loved house.

Down Rose Lane, in the Botanic Gardens, near a round pond, I see four little Arab girls, dressed in white, sedately playing with a ball; a fair fresh-faced English girl looks after them, what is her life like? Perhaps she is thinking this is all of life, looking after four little Arab girls, but life goes on and on —she does not know this yet. Perhaps she has never been in love. I want to give her a present; how easily one slips into the incomprehensible gesture.

Merton College—T. S. Eliot. Odd; I can remember all the lyrics to a thousand popular songs, yet all the poems I love are alive for me only on the printed page. Except for "Ash Wednesday." I can recite all of "Ash Wednesday" by heart. I knew someone who died of Alzheimer's disease, senile dementia, age: forty-five. The brain cells atrophy randomly, the doctors said. Randomly; but, during her long illness and to the day she died, she remembered birdcalls, and all the words to "Don't Sit Under the Apple Tree"—that, and nothing else, and nobody at all. *And the lost heart stiffens and rejoices.* . . . The sun warms my face.

Balliol—Peter Wimsey. If I could choose any man from any novel to marry, it would be Lord Peter Wimsey. And how unlike my Devi he is; how odd. Peter—impossibly rich, imperturbably urbane, an agent of British/divine justice masquerading as a silly-ass-about-town, a silk-lined aristocrat wearing the arrogance of caste lightly, possessed of that extraordinary self-assurance that being born to the English upper class confers— everything that Devi hates. And of course there would be nothing in it for Lord Peter, I wouldn't be at all his cup of tea. I couldn't even pour tea for him eighty years old though he is; I am not designed for Gracious Living, I am not lady enough, he

likes his women beautiful, they must know all of Donne and
Latin and Greek and God knows what else; why do women
never marry men who are like the men they admire in books
and movies? Perhaps the man who killed himself could explain
this to me, strange to be thinking of him so frivolously, but he
will understand, I will say a prayer for him. Prayer has after all
been heard.

The hall in Christ Church College smells of rancid mutton,
nothing is perfect, in fact everything is perfect, what else
should it smell of. Imagine, however, eating—dining—with all
those august personages staring down at one from their gilded
frames. Judges, bishops, Prime Ministers. And Viceroys. *Did*
Devi go to Oxford. Does it matter.

At the Bodleian I saw an illuminated manuscript: "With
Jesus hand I write this." No one would dare say that now. It
was easier to be humble, then, when everyone believed.

I'm tired.

I want to go to Evensong. I want to say a prayer. I'll call Devi.

On the way to the phone box, this thought formed: Give
Devi a night alone. He will see that I am patient, that I am not
afraid. And I have prayers to say. And he will not be overwhelmed by my intensity; how good.

"Devi?"

"Are you all right?"

"I'm wonderful. Tired. I thought I'd stay overnight. The
trains leave at funny times."

"Are you sure? Will you be all right?"

"Yes, of course. I love you. . . ."

But the connection was bad, and Devi's voice was lost.

"Devi?"

"Angela?"

"Devi?"

Static.

"Angela *something something* Angela."

I booked a room at the Eastgate; I went to Evensong; I
prayed. Early for dinner at the Elizabeth, I waited outside on a
bench—a waiter came to fetch me. How kind people were!

And I could see that men found me more attractive now. Because of Devi. Because he loves me.

From my room at the Eastgate I heard Great Tom ring 101 times.

I disregarded the sign at Sommerville that said "No Visitors." I felt the quad was mine by right, the right having been purchased for me by all those Oxford women who had fought so long and hard to be admitted for degrees. I paid them homage, those lonely scholars, celibate dons. And then I had lunch in a restaurant full of green ferns in hanging baskets on Woodstock Road, near the Radcliffe Infirmary: I wrapped a pastrami sandwich in three napkins to bring back to Devi.

# Chapter Three

"You are out of your mind," Eileen said.

"What does that mean? Where's Devi?"

"Do you care where Devi is?"

"Of course I care. What does that mean? I have a pastrami sandwich for him."

"You're out of your mind. You get him all primed and ready and then you disappear for a day and a half. You're torturing him."

"That's not true!" I started to tell Eileen my reasons for going to Oxford, but she would have none of it.

"I really think you're enjoying this game," she said. "Are you trying to get back at him?"

"I hate to say this, Eileen, but you're full of shit. Devi understands perfectly why I stayed at Oxford. It's what he wanted, too."

"Are you able to read his mind?"

"He's coming to Venice with us tomorrow, so I hope your disposition improves. Unless you'd like to stay here with St. John, so pale and prim."

"St. John is the best friend you have."

"Tell me another."

"He was in a frenzy all day because of you."

"Because I'm taking Devi away from him."

"Because he loves Devi and he thinks you should be married to him."

"Well?"

"Well, going to Oxford is not a step in that direction. It's a fancy version of blue balls. He was ready. And you left."

"He doesn't want a millstone around his neck. He needs to

know we can be independent of each other. I know he does. I didn't go to Siberia."

"Very highfalutin, but the fact is, you left. He *is* dependent on you, and you've given him every reason to believe you're dependent on him. You can't get somebody to screw up his courage and then leave just when you're supposed to stay."

"He doesn't like weak women."

"Going to Oxford was a sign of weakness."

"It can't be both a sign of weakness and a declaration of independence."

"Oh yes it can," Eileen said.

"Why are you home?"

"To see Act Three."

You bitch, I thought. "You're making a fuss over nothing," I said, close to tears. I had never been angry at Eileen before. "Did Devi tell you all of this?" Of course he hadn't.

"He didn't need to."

"So *you* read his mind."

"I know what I see," Eileen said.

At three-thirty Devi came home.

"I have a pastrami sandwich for you."

"Really? I wondered what the horrid smell was. Did you wear those high heels at Oxford?"

"Yes. They're not very high. Do you want the sandwich?"

"What did you do? Sit on a bench all day? You couldn't possibly have walked in those heels. The vanity of women."

I lit a cigarette. My hands were shaking.

"Of course you know," Devi said, "that every time you smoke one of those every expensive cigarettes you are killing a hundred Indians."

"What?"

"Your so-wonderful American Food for Peace sends cigarettes—without the warning label, of course—to Wogs and niggers in what you so delightfully call Third World Countries. So every time you light up, you're subsidizing lung cancer in a hundred Indians."

Devi had had three cartons of Piccadilly Filter De Luxe waiting for me when I arrived from New York; also he smoked.

"I didn't know," I said.

"Americans never know. I used to be amazed—appalled—at
the amount of food you and Lucy left on your plates, such
waste. Did your mother never tell you to eat your food for all
the millions starving in India?"

"Why didn't you tell me that you were appalled? Lucy
doesn't have a very good appetite. It isn't her fault."

"It comes as a surprise to you that Wogs are capable of good
manners?"

"Did you go to Oxford, Devi? How many brothers and sisters do you have?"

"What is this? Truth or consequences? Do you always deter-
mine the consequences?"

At four St. John came home and began to make the tea.

Eileen extracted some knitting from her traveling case.

"How did you spend your day?" St. John asked, serving me
first.

"Serving her first," Devi muttered.

"I sat on a bench for a long time," I said.

"Thinking, I suppose," Devi said, "romantic rubbish about
that ass Peter Wimsey. Creating playlets in your head."

"Thinking," I said, "of how much I love Eliot. And other
things."

"You don't *love* Eliot," Devi said. "Your fingers are yellow
from tobacco. You admire Eliot's work. Why do you admire
Eliot's work? A dried-up clerk and anti-Semite. You didn't
*know* Eliot to love him. Therefore you have no right to love
him, all romantic nonsense."

"I know all of 'Ash Wednesday' by heart."

"Why don't you recite 'Ash Wednesday.' I'll sing 'Jai Hind.'
I'm pushing off to the pub."

"Let me come with you."

"Suit yourself. Perhaps"—Devi kicked off his shoes—"I'll
walk over in your high heels." He slipped on my shoes and did
a little mincing pirouette in front of St. John. "Do you like this,
*bello?*" St. John gazed into his teacup. Eileen knitted.

"Devi, I want to come with you."

"Suit yourself."

Devi half-walked, half-sprinted, to the pub.

"Devi, I can't keep up with you."

"Your lungs are full of poison smoke. You know where the pub is."

But on the corner there was a group of young boys, and Devi stopped to talk with them. To laugh with them. So I got to the pub ahead of him.

"Waiting to be served?"

"I'm shy about getting drinks."

"Shy? You? Do you realize that in all these days you haven't once moved your arse to get a drink? You've only grandly said you'd pay for a round, making a show, smart enough to tell the women of America how to think, not smart enough to figure out how to carry a pint. An imperialist mentality. And now you make a spectacle of yourself by crying. I thought you liked the truth?"

A retired major bought us both a drink. "The thing about the RAF . . ." he said. Devi swiveled around so that his back was to both of us. I listened to the thing about the RAF.

"Blow your nose," Devi said.

"My wife was stricken with polio at the age of nineteen," the major said, and kissed me wetly on the lips.

Devi slammed down his pint and stormed out.

"May I buy you dinner?" the major said.

The pastrami sandwich was still in my bag. It stank.

"Where's Devi?"

Eileen was packing.

"No idea," she said.

"What are we doing about dinner?"

"St. John's taking me out."

"What about me?"

Eileen folded a pair of nylon panties with great care.

"If I were you, I'd salvage what I could."

"Thanks. I'll die of botulism eating a rotten pastrami sandwich."

"Are you drunk?"

"No, but I intend to be."

"Take a Valium."

"Fifty would be more like it. Does it give you great pleasure to know that you were right?"

"I don't know that I was right," Eileen said. "It might have turned out this way whatever you did."

"Then why aren't you kind?"

"I'm exhausted, Angela. You're an exhausting person to be with."

"That's not kind."

"It's true."

## Chapter Four

I climbed the steps to Devi's studio, there to wait for him in the dark. A wounded animal, an interloper. I carried a bottle of gin which I proceeded to drink, neat, from a glass dirty with traces of cadmium yellow. Gin and yellow. From the skylight and the long windows I could see rooftops, chimneys, lights; they belonged to people who had the gift of happiness. In the dark, Devi's canvases, most of them turned to the wall: four pictures of me—one of me sitting on a red plastic chair in a green field; in not one of the pictures did my face have features. On the floor was a Madras blanket in which Devi wrapped himself to sleep (it smelled of him), next to it a pair of *chappals*. I slipped them on. On every surface, old letters of mine.

"What's this? You?"

Devi tripped over me in the dark, where I sat with the Madras blanket wrapped around me, holding the bottle of gin to my chest.

"Me."

"Why?"

"Devi, what has happened? Please."

"I see we are in for a spot of melodrama, how dreary. Go to bed."

"Devi, we're leaving for Venice tomorrow. You're leaving for Venice tomorrow."

"I?"

"Yesterday you loved me, Devi."

"You badger, you badger, you badger. You talk, you talk, and you talk."

"Did you have me paged at Paddington, Devi?"

"What's this? Something from one of your movies? Who are you now, Greta Garbo or Celia Johnson?"

"I'm me, Devi, yesterday you loved me. Do you *want* me to throw myself under a train?"

"Anna Karenina. Bette Davis. 'The trains leave from Oxford at funny times.' Balls. Making dramas. When you swim you 'breathe in the sky.' What a way to talk. Balls. When you swim, you swim. When you are gone, you are gone. All melodrama. And always making comparisons, Michelangelo and Blake."

"Why do you remember every word I say if you don't love me? Why is it balls? You wanted a baby."

"I talk rot with you to keep you company. All this breeder chauvinism. All this wanting to perpetuate yourself—words, babies. Go away. Stop trying to make me," Devi said.

"It was what you wanted."

"It was what you wanted, trying to annex me, subverting my nature. I was playing your game. I am used to being colonized. Do you think you can change me after all these years? Who do you think you are? Bette Davis? *Go away.*" Devi kicked a hole in a canvas.

"Don't."

"And there. And there." Two more canvases.

"If I go away tomorrow we'll never see each other again."

"And what if we do and what if we don't."

"You said . . ."

"Turn off that fucking tape recorder that is your brain and listen to me. I do not love you. I do not want a bloody baby. A cute little American-Wog"—another canvas—"baby. Do you corrupt Lucy with all this romantic bullshit too? She should be taken away from you. I do not want you. And what is all this coyness? You dress behind closed doors. Do you think I care if I see your body? You come to bed robed. . . ."

"Because I was shy."

"Shy. And why can you never be passive?"

"You don't *like* weak women."

"I don't like aggressive American bitches. I don't like frauds."

Devi, drunk already, took a swig of gin.

"The amount of money Stephan owes me is exactly the amount of money the painting is worth. The painting in your living room which every day you see. I could live half a year on that. Were I not buying you cigarettes and gin. Fortnum and Masons. Lucheon at the Tate. You and Stephan are exactly alike. Did you plan it? The swindle? The painting? My painting in your house. Did you put your white capitalist-imperialist heads together? And if you're going to blubber get out now."

"I'm not blubbering. I'm laughing. It's too ridiculous to call me a capitalist-imperialist. What the hell swindle, Devi?"

"How did you go to Oxford?"

"What do you mean?"

"What class?"

"First."

"Third isn't good enough for you."

"I came back second."

"Tickets to Venice, do you think I am rich? Where are you going?"

"To get my checkbook. You can have the money for the painting."

"Heartbroken, and you reach for your checkbook. Sit down." Devi shoved me, hard. "The ultimate capitalist solution to all problems of the heart, a checkbook. And don't talk. Where were you fifteen years ago?"

"You said we were together from the beginning of time."

"The ultimate impertinence, quoting myself to me. And you believed I meant it. I was mad. I speak to no one when you are not here. I told you what you wanted to hear. If you make me a character in your story—the boring soap opera of your life—you have to expect romantic crap from me. *Crap*. How many men have you been to bed with since I left New York? Why aren't you married? What, no words? Are you ill? How many? None. That is what you and I exist for, to keep each other from happiness with other people. I could be fucking now."

"Who?"

Devi slapped my face.

"Now will you go?" he said, and he was crying.

"No."

Devi struck three matches before he could get one to light.
The sputtering light of the match drew sparks from the diamond I wore on the fourth finger of my left hand. The ring
Devi had given me, from his mother, he'd said. The ring Stephan had bought in India, and with which he'd paid for Devi's
painting, Stephan had said. I believed Stephan.

"Take this for the painting," I said.

"What painting?"

"Take back the ring."

"You never know when to stop."

"Will you let me lie down with you, here?"

"Imbecile."

"Then take back the ring." I offered him my outstretched
palm, the ring resting on it.

"Let me tell you," Devi said, "what gay men do with rings
and their cocks."

"No."

"And you love everything about me, I thought you said."

"I'm so tired, Devi."

"Take my *chappals* off."

"Take your ring."

He did. He flung it across the room, where it fell among a
pile of drawings.

"I love you, Devi."

"No you don't. If you did you'd know what to do. You
wouldn't talk."

"Tell me what to do."

"Go to bed."

"Can't I sleep here? With my clothes on?"

"Still you talk."

"Tell me what to do."

"Go to bed."

"Won't you tell me that you love me?"

Devi kicked another hole in another painting. He savaged
the painting of the red chair in the green field, my faceless face.

"I'm going now."

On the way down the stairs, I tripped and twisted my ankle,
and cried out in pain.

"Bette Davis," Devi said.

I stumbled in the dark of the landing and knocked a vase off a bookshelf. Devi laughed, and shut his door.

"You should have kissed him and said nothing," Eileen said.

"You heard?"

"Who could help it?"

"And you know everything and he knows everything and I know nothing, is that right? Was St. John listening too?"

"I've packed your bags," Eileen said. "The cab is coming at seven."

"What a good mommy you are. I don't like anyone touching my clothes, thanks. Now if you'll stop giving me advice I'm going to bed."

"I don't have anything more to say."

"Time to get up, girls," Devi said. I held my hands like fists to my eyes, the gesture of a child who doesn't want to see or can't bear to be seen; I would never see him again. "Wake up."

My caftan was gathered up around my thighs, my knees were tight against my chest, I hope to hell he saw. I hope he god-damn saw. Everything.

St. John carried our bags to the cab. He drew back slightly when Eileen kissed him on the cheek. His pale eyes regarded me without expression. "He does, you know."

"Does what?"

"Love you."

"Tell him about it. . . . I hope your marriage lasts forever," I yelled out as the cab pulled away.

"I'm not going to Venice with you, Angela."

"You're leaving me alone in Venice?"

"I can't stand it anymore."

"*You* can't stand it?"

"Your imbroglios. I need some peace. There's too much wear and tear."

"Wonderful word, imbroglios. What about your imbroglios?

# *Chapter Five*

I am flying over Paris. Thick gray clouds cover Paris. Perhaps Lucy is just now walking down one of the streets hidden from my view; I see Lucy in Montmartre; I see Lucy at the Ritz; I see Lucy at the Tuileries; the airplane groans and rolls in waves of clouds. I want Lucy, who is hidden from me, who is perhaps now holding her father's hand. (If I listen hard enough perhaps I will hear her voice.)

The clouds are gone as if scooped away by giant hands to reveal a blue expanse as brittle as enamel.

I am flying over the Alps to be in a city where the sundials are inscribed *Horas non numero nisi serenas.*

He—Devi—found a copy of Ruskin for me at Blackwell's: "Let us consider for a little the significance and nobleness of that early custom of the Venetians . . . that there should be but one marriage day for the nobles of the whole nation, so that all might rejoice together, and that the sympathy might be full, not only of the families who that year beheld the alliance of their children, and prayed for them in one crowd, weeping before the altar, but of all the families of all the state, who saw, in the day which brought happiness to others, the anniversary of their own."

The anniversary of their own happiness. Devi: "breeder chauvinism . . . territorial rights . . . annexation . . . imperialism . . . capitalism . . . corruption . . . legal possession and possessiveness."

"Imagine the strong bond of brotherhood thus sanctified among them . . . the greater deliberation and openness necessarily given to the contemplation of marriage, to which all the people were solemnly to bear testimony; the more lofty

What about your divorce from Jim? What about your suicide attempt, what's that, your idea of fun?"

"You talk too much, Angela, you make me tired."

"Oh good. Sisterhood is powerful."

"You need help."

"And that's why you're not coming to Venice with me. Where are you going, by the way?"

"Home. I'm standing by for a flight."

"You're not my friend."

"I am your friend. But I can't bear to see you like this, and Venice would be all postmortem."

"That's not my definition of a friend. I'm sorry I'm so boring. Unlike you, when you left Jim."

But that was unfair. Eileen had lost more than Jim. She had lost her baby. I had Lucy.

Nevertheless, I said: "Right now it's up for grabs. Who I hate more."

Eileen said: "You use words like 'hate.' . . ."

"Go to hell," I said.

I paid the taxi, grabbed my bags, and resisted Eileen's attempt to kiss me good-bye.

and unselfish tone which it would give to all their thoughts. It was the exact opposite of stolen marriage. It was marriage to which God and man were taken for witnesses, and every eye was invoked for its glance, and every tongue for its prayers."

The irony, of course, being that Ruskin's own marriage was said to be white.

Sansovino says, "And when the form of the espousal has been gone through, she [the bride—*vestita, per antico uso, di bianco, e con chiome sparse giu per le spalle, conteste con filia d'oro]* is led, to the sounds of pipes and trumpets, and other musical instruments, round the room, dancing serenely all the time and bowing herself before the guests—*ballando placidamente, e facendo inchini ai convitati.*"

This practice—the opposite of stolen marriage, communal weeping before the altar, espousal to the sound of pipes and trumpets, the bride in white, her hair, thrown down upon her shoulder, interwoven with threads of gold—ended in the Year of Our Lord 943.

Apparently this plane has no intention of crashing.

My hotel is wedged pie-shaped into a piazza that is a village unto itself: a foundry, a church, a barbershop, a beauty salon, a taverna, a trattoria, and of course a palazzo, and around a vine-covered passage a theater, La Fenice. I have no wish to wander very far. All my human needs can be satisfied here, except those that can't. For example, tonight there is a concert, Vivaldi and Purcell, in St. Mark's Square, five minutes from here. This cannot possibly be as good as it promises to be—a concert on the Grand Canal, in an open-air drawing room where no one reproaches you for speaking or for not speaking, for silence or for action. And if there is any chance that it will be good, I have no wish to go. Of course I do go. It is good—though the musicians have minimal attachment to notions of harmony and synchronicity—but my heart refuses to rise to the lovely, absurd occasion. Absurd to be alone in Venice, a gondola built for one does not exist. Of course I am not thinking. I refuse to think: *Oom-pah-pah* goes the band in the square. May I have a *limonada,* please? Florians. In *Summertime*

Katharine Hepburn met Rossano Brazzi here; Devi is right: I
live in a perpetual soap opera, and one that is not even my
own. Imagine falling in love with Rossano Brazzi, not I. How
easy it is to get lost here. If God is looking, which I don't think
He is, I must seem to Him like a rat in a maze; no matter how
hard I try I cannot return to my hotel without walking through
an alley under a clammy overhead passage oozing with centu-
ries of slime. Perhaps from the Year of Our Lord 943. If I walk
the right way from the square, I pass the church of San Moise. I
like its baroque facade—it looks as if it were made by a de-
mented soft ice-cream machine, a glob here, a trickle there,
and here a whirl. How could I have imagined us in Venice. Of
course at the Accademia, I see paintings of camels in St. Mark's
Square, so any mating is possible—as, for example, the An-
nunciation took place in San Marco, as did the Ascension;
Christ suckles on the Grand Canal—no juxtaposition is too
strange. But suppose I were to say to him, Look, Devi, look at
that little boy in the orange rubber raft rowing past the house
where Mozart once stayed. What would he reply? "Bette Davis." Of course it is all loot here, that can't be denied. We
would hear it for Byzantium, you can be sure. Whereas I am
not so interested in loot (the interior of the basilica—all those
heads bobbing up and down to see the mosaics, the jewels, and
the gold—bores me, to tell the truth) as I am in *The Dream of St.
Ursula*, Carpaccio: How still the young girl lies upon her bed
while the angel brings tidings of her future martyrdom. Her
head rests on her cupped palm, her eyes are closed, she
sweetly dreams the angel in the muted morning light, and
scarcely a wrinkle in the red and white bedclothes to show for
the sad tidings. The canopied bed is solid and untrembling in
the presence of an angel. Poor Ursula, whose slippers, neatly
placed, do not protest this imposition of trumpets. What rubbish, Devi would say. Or would he. Who knows what Devi
would say? Of course when all is said and done I prefer—to all
the Veroneses and the Titians and the Carpaccios and the
Giorgiones and the Tintorettos (though there is one Tintoretto, women comforting one another, that I love)—a pregnant Madonna, *anon.*, second century, hung on top of a stair-

well, badly lighted, of course, in the Accademia, her secrecy, surprise, delight. Devi once said it was all right, in matters of art, to know what one loved and not to know why one loved it; this does not apply, however, in matters relating to vaporetti, where knowledge is essential: It took me half a day to find out how to go to Burano; everyone thought I meant Murano, really it should be easier than this. And then it was too late. The only thing that really gives me pleasure is to walk, in the early hours of the morning, to the markets of the Rialto; once I said to Devi I should have been born in Italy and had twelve babies, and he laughed; but I am happy here, buying food for meals it is true (*the waste,* Devi would say) I will never prepare; after all, one can't just come to look, and it is quite possible that I might have had twelve children had my mother not married my father, had my father not left Italy. But then who would I be. Or not. Dreaming. On Sunday the priest presses a button just before he elevates the Host, and the church—empty but for three old women and one Tintoretto and me—is filled with the scratchy, stuttery sound of a jittery old recording of the "Hallelujah Chorus." In English. In Venice. And all this time I want to be in the Turner painting at the Tate. The one I love of Venice, though better actually to be here, one would suppose. But not.

On my fourth day in Venice my fever reached 104. The concierge sent for a doctor, who asked me, in his lisping Venetian accent, where I'd been, what I'd done, what I'd eaten. And something about the American Consulate and Trieste: "One is informed that last night you drank three espressos. Correct?"

"Yes."

"With a fever of a hundred and four? Fahrenheit."

"I didn't know I had a fever."

"What did you think was the matter with you?" Suddenly he looked suspicious and alarmed and began to knead my stomach. "When was your last menstrual period?" Did he think I'd come to Venice for an abortion? The fool. To be that Madonna, smiling, secretive, glad. "Ten days ago," I said.

"Ah."

Everything was hazy; the famous Venetian mist surrounded

his bald head like a nimbus. I told him my daughter was coming in a day or two, I could not go anywhere, least of all Trieste. (Bonjour, Trieste.)

"Perhaps it was the little fishies from the Canal," he said (I'm sure he said fishies); "sometimes they bring the fever."

Perhaps it was the little fishies.

The problem, now that I was well, was Lucy. There was an air traffic controllers' strike in Italy, news of which had been given me by the concierge, who came in waving the international *Herald-Tribune*. "Unruly! We are an unruly people!" he said, making no attempt to contain his delight; for him chaos in the Italian sky was bliss. Lucy was no longer in Paris; her father had left no forwarding address. There was nothing for it but to wait.

In an old guidebook I read: "What if some terrible natural catastrophe, an earthquake or a deluge, had wiped Venice off the face of the world, say about the year 1500?" and this sentence served to galvanize me, to connect me to the real world. Now everything arranged itself simply. I took the Murano-Burano steamer from the Fondamente Nuove, and I felt for the first time that I was really in Venice, rooted in concrete and watery reality. There was a world outside of me: its shapes and contours did not conform to the shapes and contours of my pain. This observation struck me with the force of a beautiful revelation while I was spooning up a chocolate ice; I laughed at myself. I wished—but not for long—for Eileen and her guidebooks; then I hardened my heart against her.

I liked the rough, inelegant pastel exteriors of Burano, the stocky, dark-suited old men who stood in groups on the main street of the fishing village. Their talk and their games were as incomprehensible to me as my grandfather's, but also as familiar. An old lady with a black shawl, her face wrinkled (her flesh a network of canals) glared at me, and then I saw that she was blind. The sun was out. I had lunch in what appeared to be a men's social club, not a woman in sight; I heard pool balls clicking in the next room (but they took American Express). There was a sudden summer shower. I heard Vespers at the

church of San Martino (a Tiepolo crucifixion in the sacristy).
Little children in crocheted bonnets and rain slickers, and
prepubescent girls wearing lumpy dark skirts over delicate lace
petticoats that dipped beneath the mended wool in delicious,
provocative waves, and a few stale-looking women and one old
man sang the "Our Father" and "Ave Maria," led by a stringy
nun with a high true voice.

This outing made me quite extraordinarily happy. The
world was not Devi, nor was Devi the world. Nor for that
matter was I Devi, nor for that matter did my sorrow affect one
whit the sweet singing of children in the summer rain.

"There was a telephone call for you," the concierge said.
"From England. The call came through successfully." He said
this reproachfully, as if it were evidence of some depravity on
my part.

"Did they leave a message?"

He shrugged, brushed some lint from his striped coat.
Amazing how they had the energy to loot Constantinople. And
what was Devi doing, calling me here, why? If he rang again I
would not answer.

On the sixth ring I snatched the phone from its cradle.
"What is it?"

"Mommy?"

"Lucy?"

"Mommy, I'm in London."

"How? Why? Where?"

"Daddy said it was the best thing to do because of the
strike."

"Where are you? I love you, Lucy."

"Daddy's home. I'm here."

"Where?"

Lucy's voice rose and fell, it was as if I were simultaneously
listening to her and holding a seashell to my ear. A word, and
then a *woosh*.

"I'm at Devi's," she said.

"Where?"

"Devi's. Because of the strike."

"I want you to come here."

"Because of the strike," Lucy said.

"Take a train," I said.

"We're having such a good time, Mommy."

"No you are not. Come here."

". . . makes Indian food," Lucy said, "and he's painting me
. . . water shortage."

"What water shortage. What."

". . . shower together because of the water shortage," Lucy
said. ". . . long walks . . ."

"Walk yourself to a train, Lucy. I want you in Venice."

". . . Mommy."

"Lucy? Lucy, I'll take a train to London. . . . Lucy? . . ."
But the line was dead.

I called the concierge. We are an unruly people, he said.


The next day the air traffic controllers went back to work; no
space on flights to London for a week.

The day after the air traffic controllers' strike was settled, the
railway workers went on strike.

I could not get through to London by phone.

My fever returned, 101. Fahrenheit. I spent a day on lovely
lost Torcello; someone had put daisies in the ruined church of
Santa Fosca. (Like it or not, the world is a reflection of our
pain.) As my gondola slid silently through marshy lagoons, I
imagined planes and trains crisscrossing endlessly as Lucy and
I sought to find each other.

My hatred for Devi raged.

# Chapter Six

"Mommy! Mommy!"

Lucy ran to me, she found me among thousands in the middle of St. Mark's Square. Stephan loomed behind her.

"Oh, Mommy, isn't it wonderful? We're at Florians. Isn't it wonderful? When we didn't find you at your hotel, I told Stephan you'd be here. Oh, Mommy, isn't Venice wonderful? I was so scared when I couldn't get you on the phone. I dreamed of planes crisscrossing in the night. And here we are."

Stephan said: "It occurred to me that you might need rescuing. Devi pretended to be a Chinese laundry every time one called. At great expense. So I flew to rescue you."

"He took the Concorde," Lucy said.

"But I rescued my niece instead."

"Did you need rescuing, Lucy?" She was meeting my eyes with a clear, straight gaze.

"We only joked about taking a shower together," Lucy said.

"Is there anything else I ought to know?"

"In the fullness of time," Stephan said.

"Never mind the fullness of time, I'd like to know now, please. What else did he do?"

"Mommy, he's so sad when he's not having fun."

"I consoled him with a check," Stephan said. "Have you had dinner, dear?"

"Lucy, are you in love with Devi?"

Lucy met my gaze. "I'm glad Stephan came for me," she said.

Stephan took us to Harry's Bar, where Lucy had two enormous hamburgers and a Tiziano—champagne, grapefruit juice, and grenadine. Then he led us to a *motoscafo* that took us to the Cipriani Hotel. "I took the liberty of changing your hotel," he said. "I thought you needed gardens." An anxious silence formed around his words. I will never forget the look on Lucy's face as she waited, poised on the abrupt edge of adult sadness, for my response; she looked as if she might grow old in that silence.

"I need gardens," I said. "I love you both. I put myself in your hands."

"In mine too?" Lucy said.

"One is happy to be of use," Stephan said.

The Canal was still vibrating from the red sunset when Lucy climbed in bed with me.

"Mommy?"

"My darling?"

"Do you smell roses?"

"I smell you."

"Will everything be all right?"

"Are you all right?"

"Yes. Stephan acts as if he thinks something terrible happened to me."

"He thinks Devi made love to you."

Lucy gave this some thought.

"Is that why he's spending all this money on us?" she said.

"That's not kind, Lucy."

"I know Stephan's kind," she said, "but he'd like it less if he thought nothing much had happened. He'd find me less interesting."

"Well, I'm grateful to him. He saved us."

"From what?"

"I'm not sure I know. But I'm glad you're here."

"Me too," Lucy said. "Devi is so beautiful."

I had left behind in London a raincoat, a nightgown, and a gold chain. Several days after we returned from Ravello—where Lucy had fallen in love with a young waiter—a package arrived from London: a gold chain, and a raincoat. The raincoat was not my own, however, it was Devi's. No nightgown. In the next mail, a letter from Devi: "Thought I'd keep your raincoat to keep warm in. Have mine in exchange. I enjoyed your visit, and do apologize if I was occasionally offensive, no excuse except maybe that I live so shuttered (introvert) an existence that I am frequently unaware of the normal boundaries of civilized hetero exchange. Hope you returned with your psychic bone structure intact. You must admit I did lay on some decent weather. . . . D." The most remarkable thing about this remarkable letter—which I tore up immediately, bearing in mind that there are no inanimate objects—was that Devi had not sent Lucy his love.

Lucy never again referred to England, although she prattled on prettily for months about Venice and Ravello. What she held in her heart about Devi I did not know—for which silence between us I held Devi responsible.

Occasionally, that fall, as we sat comfortably together in the evenings, I would look up from the book I was reading to find her searching my face carefully, tenderly, warily—as if to see if the invalid had recovered.

I had recovered. Devi's abominable behavior was strong medicine indeed.

I had recovered. I had not recovered. I longed to tell Eileen, from whom I had not heard since our return from Europe, that I was cured. I was cured. I was not cured.

To Stephan, pleased, as well he might have been, with his rescue mission, I announced that I was cured.

I did not write to Devi. I called my silence renunciation—an active and noble sacrificial state. I was not prepared to admit that even my renunciation of Devi was a form of control. I told myself I'd given Devi control. In fact, allowing him to have control gave me ultimate control—I wanted, still, to win. I wanted to play the game so as to make him comfortable until he could no longer be comfortable. I was playing to win. I seldom asked myself if the prize was worth the struggle.

I believed, still, that Devi could not live without me.

I believed that my greed, my heedless grasping, had damaged his equilibrium, the delicate balance of his peace. So I forced myself not to write to him—not understanding that my silence, my waiting, was a way of perpetuating this drama. My passivity was coiled and alert. It is one thing to tell yourself that the courage to wait is greater than the courage required to act; but that is true only if one waits expecting nothing—and I still expected everything.

(But I had once been a girl adored by a man who never claimed me. I had been well taught, taught to wait and taught to expect. My expectations—I still believed in that porch in Kansas, that villa on the Med, in happiness with Devi—gave the lie to my renunciation, so-called, a renunciation which served me well in that it allowed me to play with other men. Which I did. Never forgetting Devi. Always comparing. Always waiting.)

I tried to be honest with Father Caldwell (my disastrous visit with Devi had restored me to formal religious obligations), who tried to ask the right questions, but I never got all the dimensions in, I said what came to mind, which meant I spoke the half-truth of the ephemeral moment. Obsession dulls the intelligence, obscures the light.

And then the Stuntman—whatever his limitations, lack of ingenuity was not one of them—found me in New York; and I played, for a while, in earnest.

# Part Five

*Love and religion are invasions of one's privacy.*

Virginia Woolf

# Chapter One

"It would help," Father Caldwell said, "if I knew more precisely what you thought about Devi."

"But I don't think about him. Not in the way you mean. I don't analyze. He says I do. It's one of the things he holds against me. I don't think I think. I think I only feel."

"Thinking, as you know, is an intensified form of feeling."

"Why does he stay alive, I often wonder."

"It has been said that despair is the sin that lives for nothing and remains alive only because there is nothing it would die for."

"I know it has been said."

"What do you think."

"I think he loves and he hates. Therefore he doesn't despair as I understand despair."

"What does he love? What does he hate?"

"Me."

Father Caldwell—I refused to call him Eugene—lit a cigarette. With a black Magic Marker he made a diagonal mark on his wrist; this was his fifth cigarette of the day. He kept count.

"Do you believe that his loving you, or his hating you, keeps him from despair?"

"Sometimes I do. I realize it's presumptuous."

"Nevertheless, presumptuous or not, you have to act, I think, on that belief. Prayerfully, of course."

"You mean that I may be dealing with my own egoism. I see that. But it gives him something to do, loving me and hating me. He doesn't do much of anything else. He doesn't paint much. I also think he's capable of violence, and that he's afraid of that. So maybe the kindest thing for me to do would be to

stay with him and let his violence roll over me. To prove to him
that he's not a killer. . . . I take a lot on myself, don't I?"

Father Caldwell sighed and reached for another cigarette.
He changed his mind and unwrapped a Tootsie Roll lollipop
instead.

"I find that disconcerting," I said.

"What do you find disconcerting? Your inclination to masochism? Your giving yourself so much importance in Devi's
life?"

"No, your sucking a lollipop."

This was not Confession as I had known it as a child. We sat
in Father Caldwell's office, a ramshackle affair. Occasionally
the phone rang. Later, after we prayed together, and after he
gave me formal absolution—an act which always seemed
slightly to embarrass him—we would go to Chinatown for
dinner, and he would be Eugene. Gene to my daughter. Sometimes, over hacked chicken in peanut sauce at the Szechuan
Dumpling Palace, I fantasized about going to some dim church
in Queens that advertised Bingo Wednesdays, there to say my
confession to a priest who had never heard of Teilhard or of
Jung, and who would tell me to Go and sin no more, five Hail
Marys. That was, however, the trouble. Where Devi was concerned, I did not know wherein lay my sin—although it did
seem to me that my loving him added to the general sense of
shame and futility that suffused his life.

"I don't understand this about masochism," I said. "It
seems to me I make his suffering sharper when I am present in
his life."

"And your own suffering?"

"My own, too. But also my happiness. I can't always tell the
difference between suffering and happiness, you know."

"On what grounds would you ask him not to write or call
you?" This was my latest idea.

"On the grounds that it's been an awfully long time. Almost
five years now. I can't go around loving people for five years.
It's just stupid. It ought to be over by now."

"Why ought it to be over? How, since you do not seem to

know exactly—at all—what is at work in this relationship, do you know this?"

"Well, put like that . . ."

But in his last letter, Devi had said I'd put my hooks in him. Hooks! How could I love a man who said those words to me? And in my purse I had the letter before that one, the one that said, "How can I thank you for all the love and energy you've pumped me full of, witness to which I'm still alive and walking, occasionally thinking, feeling, responding. Why does it always take me so long to get around to saying I love you?" This was the Devi I loved; how could I not love this man?

"This relationship has not kept you from other men," Father Caldwell said.

"No."

"No."

"Not entirely."

"Nor has it kept you from loving your child."

"No."

"And he has not been a source of concern for Lucy?"

"That's what I don't know."

"Why not ask her?"

"It's not as simple as that, Father." I sometimes wondered whether celibacy blunted a crucial part of his intelligence. "Lucy's growing up—and away. There are things one doesn't ask." There was a slackness around Father Caldwell's jaw that I persisted in believing was a result of his not understanding the flesh.

"Has your relationship with Devi interfered with your friendships or your work?"

"Unless you count Eileen."

"Do you want to talk about Eileen?"

"What is there to say?"

"Do you want a truck to run her over?" Father Caldwell asked.

"No."

"Then, given your nature, which tends not to be charitable, I think we can safely say you love your enemies within the meaning of the rubric."

"Which would be stretching things a bit."

"It has been said that God exists to be used."

"Like taffy?"

"Now, you alluded to vows." Father Caldwell extracted another cigarette from his World War II cigarette case and made a stick sign on his wrist with a Magic Marker. "Vows," he said, regarding his cigarette, "are in my experience frequently the cause of immobilizing guilt."

"This is the vow: I trade my happiness for Devi's. If I choose to remain celibate, Devi will be satisfied. Even, if you'll excuse me, with another man. As long as he's happy. It's a trade-off."

"Let me understand you. What exactly are you giving up?"

"Sex."

"I'm not sure God is handing out awards for that nowadays. Perhaps you're just ready for a stretch of celibacy. In that case, why bring Devi into it? What you are really saying, it seems to me, is that you are prepared to sacrifice your happiness for Devi's."

"Isn't that what I said? And I wish you'd pronounce his name right—it's *Davie,* Father, as if it were Jewish. And why not? That's the way it used to be. For example my Aunt Milly gave up chocolates when I had my tonsils out."

"And how would your sacrificing your happiness help your daughter?"

"I see what you mean."

"Even if you could renounce your happiness, which is arguable, since it has always seemed to me"—another lollipop—"an involuntary act."

"Yes."

What I didn't tell Father Caldwell was that I was engaged in magical thinking. If Devi could really love another man, I thought, he would come around to loving me. With his body.

"Did you give up the man with whom you were living for Devi? The person who performed stunts?"

"The Stuntman? No. I stopped living with him because he was a drunk. But he was jealous of Devi, which made Devi wild. Every time Devi called, he hung up. And I didn't do a thing

about it. How could a stuntman be jealous of a queer like me,
Devi said."

"You could have managed that more tactfully," Father Caldwell said.

"Yes."

"More gracefully. With grace."

"I know. The thing is, I didn't really love him. The only
reason I let him stay with me at all was to break the pattern."

"When you think in terms of breaking the pattern, the pattern is still governing you," Father Caldwell said. "It wasn't
fair to him to regard him as part of a pattern, or as the inter-
rupter of a pattern. You must come to each person new, as
each person *is* new, and himself, and not part of your pattern."

"Which you were good enough to point out to me at the
time."

"However, that is in the past. As for this vow of yours. God is
not the Chase Manhattan Bank. You cannot take happiness out
of your branch and deposit it in another. You cannot deposit
happiness to Devi's account by withdrawing it from your own."

"But I shouldn't stop praying for Devi's happiness?"

"Pray for his happiness and his salvation. Remember Augustine when you are inclined to despair: 'Therefore hadst Thou,
O God, regard to the aim and essence of her desires and didst
not do what she then prayed for, that Thou mightest do for me
what she continually implored.' Continually implore. All
prayers are answered. We do not always recognize the answer
when we see it. I should stop praying for your own unhappiness, the sincerity of which prayer I would in any case question."

But I had so prayed. I hadn't asked to be actively unhappy, I
had asked God to let me bear Devi's pain.

"The way to bear another's pain," Father Caldwell said, "is
to be happy."

"I don't think I understand that."

"Prayerfully consider it."

"I seem to spend a great deal of my life considering happiness and very little of my life achieving it."

"You are one of the happiest persons I know," said Father

Caldwell, and I took umbrage. "Objectively speaking. You have roses in your cheeks. Your daughter loves you. Your laugh is real. Your work goes well. Objectively speaking: In the long disease that is your life most of what you consider problems are really solutions"; and I took umbrage: conundrums. But I could see that Father Caldwell was hungry for his dinner. So I didn't say aloud the thought that had just occurred to me: I trick myself into thinking that my suffering is redemptive. Whereas all my suffering has done is to cause others to suffer: Eileen, Stephan, perhaps Lucy, certainly Devi, whom I am trying magically to control by my piffling attempts at redemptive suffering, the drama of which I enjoy. And Devi—so beautiful!—has been for me the God-bearing person; and is. So if Devi is the God-bearing person, I am causing God to suffer. Father Caldwell was more interested in hacked chicken in hot sauce than in God at the moment. The first time I ever had dinner with the man who killed himself we ate at a Chinese restaurant. I do wonder, I am obliged to wonder, whether I enjoy high wire romance more than I enjoy the payoff; a pathology. (What is the payoff?)

On the way back home to Lucy I considered Devi's violence, which I persisted in believing was a form of love. A declaration of war is an engagement. It was as much the closeness born of violence (flesh against flesh, spirit against spirit) as the potential danger to life and limb that frightened Devi. When all was said and done, what was apparent was true: Violence proclaimed a fierce rage for union that indifference would have disavowed.

But the more Devi injured me, the more he resented me; and the more he resented me, the more he injured me. So was I—the source of his misery—"good" for him or not? Father Caldwell could not help me unravel this.

I went to a cheap hotel on the Cape. I wanted to feel mesmerized by the pull of the tides, lost in some primeval mystery outside myself; the sea, I thought, would provide answers. I imagined porches, rocking chairs, walks on the beach, a dining room with views of the sea and quiet courteous guests, solid and graceful, absorbed in their own concerns. It rained. The only other guests were a newly married couple who exchanged no words, a large untidy woman with four raucous untidy sons, and an elderly man who spilled his soup and muttered to himself and glared at the boys. I shared a bath with him; one morning I found his false teeth on the bathroom sink. I had brought Augustine's *Confessions* to read, also Eliot. How it rained. I read Nero Wolfe mysteries and a sensational biography of Marilyn Monroe instead. The walls of my room were painted pink; the ceiling was a dingy gray; the floors were barn-red cement. All the furniture in my room-without-a-view was flimsy except for a Victorian dressing table, painted white; one of the brass handles was missing, and in its place was a piece of dirty rope. No outlet in the room would accommodate my radio. (I had thought: Beethoven Quartets.) I slept with a chair propped against the doorknob, insurance against mad killers on the prowl. I was sure there were bats, I could smell their dung. I decided to give up smoking and ate pounds of sour balls. Also I smoked. Late one night, after a trip to the bathroom, I looked down the dim hall—twelve varnished oak doors—and I panicked. Fearing for my life (this is a place where murders happen, young boys in sneakers go berserk and find their prey), I went to the public coin phone in what for no apparent reason was called the library, and telephoned Devi.

St. John answered.

I had had several glasses of gin, along with sour balls and cigarettes, having spent the night composing letters (never to be mailed) to Eileen:

"Is Devi there?"

"It is three A.M."

"Is Devi there?"

"I am afraid not," St. John said.

"Well, tell him I'm trapped in a loony bin," I said.

Two weeks later Devi called:

"St. John said you were in a loony bin or some such," he said; "I knew that wherever you were you could take care of yourself. I never really understand what goes on in your head, but I suppose you don't mean harm. Since you seem to be enjoying yourself, I hope you carry on." He hung up.

("Would you call him supportive?" Father Caldwell asked. "That is a word I intensely dislike," I said.)

I searched for an appropriate sacrificial gesture. None came to mind.

Again Devi called. Without preamble, he asked, "Shall I come to New York? Or shall I go back to India?"

And immediately I answered: India. Wanting him in New York.

From India came letters: travelogues, witty, warm, charming, barbed ("communal baths, beautiful brown bodies, the West has spoiled me for these simple pleasures. . . .") And one drawing: his mother, sleeping; her toothless mouth is puckered, her sari is in disarray, her hair escapes its neat confines, bangles adorn her fleshy arms, which are drooping in the abandonment of sleep. Above this figure is another, floating in undefined space. This figure too is Devi's mother; but its face is featureless, the contours of its body are blurred. Is Devi's mother dreaming? Is Devi dreaming of another mother? The mother he wishes he might have had? The one who rocked him and crooned to him and adored her darling boy? The drawing is profoundly disturbing.

I break my silence and call Devi:

"Devi, thank you for the drawing. Is your mother dreaming? Were you dreaming of another mother?"

"You attach yourself to meanings," Devi said. "I messed up one sketch and did another, that's all. What rubbish."

"Oh. What did you learn in India?"

"That I liked to talk to servants."

"Only that?"

"That was quite enough. Enough to make my mother weep for shame. It is four A.M."

"Did you see your brothers and your sisters?"

"What brothers? What sisters?"

"Are you coming to New York?"

"Do you think I am rich?"

# *Chapter Two*

"Welcome to the wounded healer," Father Caldwell said. I could see at once that he was troubled. I was shakier than usual. The taxi that took me to the rectory had struck a Puerto Rican man on a bike. I did not think the man had been much hurt, but, thinking only of what I wished to discuss with Father Caldwell, I had only faintly protested when the driver—muttering imprecations against city cyclists in general and against Puerto Rican cyclists in particular—had sped off without assessing the damages. Now I entertained visions of concussions, hemorrhages, internal bleeding. . . .

"I'm glad to hear that," Father Caldwell said. "I have been concerned that you were too absorbed in what you regard to be an unselfish love. I don't know if you understand that the less you value yourself the more absorbed you become in yourself. Masochism serves no one's interests, least of all a sadist's. I have been concerned that you were hardening your heart against others."

"Not too self-absorbed to wonder if I haven't helped to kill a man. I suppose I could have stopped the cabdriver, but he was an angry man. Do you think Devi is a sadist? Sometimes I think I am the sadist."

"How is Lucy?" Father Caldwell said.

"Fine. Settling in at college. Happy."

"How much time do you give her in your thoughts and prayers?"

"Plenty. And hours on the telephone. I miss her."

"How often do you see your father?"

"Twice a week. Sometimes more."

"How many dinner engagements have you broken in the last month?"

"Three or four."

"With what reason? With what excuse?"

"No compelling reason. I lie."

"And what do your friends think of this?"

"That I am careless and lazy. The truth is I would almost always rather watch a television movie than go out to dinner, but one can't tell them that. So I lie. And after all one can only accommodate just so many friends in one's life. Usually they forgive me, not always."

"It is difficult," Father Caldwell said, choosing his words carefully, "to distinguish between an unselfish love and an idolatrous one."

Sometimes I think it takes forever for information to travel from Father Caldwell's head to his heart. I myself had put this proposition to him years ago.

"I suppose," I said, "an idolatrous love could be unselfish?"

"An obsessive love is bound to interfere with your relationship with God. As it has with your dinner engagements."

"I think what you mean, Father, is that I confuse Devi with God."

"That is an unhappy possibility, yes."

"Do you think I enjoy my pain?"

"I believe your pain is real," Father Caldwell said. And, he said, "I think also that you are engaged in magical thinking. You believe that if Devi has a successful love affair with a man, he will come around to loving you in the way you wish to be loved. You wish another to live as you live. You cannot accept the gifts he brings you."

"So I offer him my own?"

"You bring him gifts he has no use for," Father Caldwell said.

"A gift you have no use for is no gift at all, just a burden," I said.

"Possibly," Father Caldwell said.

Over dinner, he said, "I would like to know more about the man who killed himself." Usually, over dinner, we discussed movies, novels, the latest pronouncements of the Holy Father, and television, to which Father Caldwell also was addicted.

I told him all I knew.

"You do not know much."

"I only know that he was the first man—the first person—who made me feel that I was interesting and good."

"Not excepting your father?"

"I don't think my father comes into this."

"Have you telescoped them?"

"Who?"

"Devi and the man who killed himself."

"Do you mean, Do I get Devi and him mixed up? Yes. But isn't that natural? They are the only men I have ever loved."

"And both are mysteries to you."

"Yes . . . And he always played Schubert's Trout Quintet for me, and a record by Kathleen Ferrier—'Blow thou wind southerly, southerly, southerly/Carry my lover home safely to me.' And a song about a girl with soft down on her white arms. I was embarrassed about the hair on my arms—look, there isn't even much of it at all."

"What about the person who did stunts?"

"The Stuntman I didn't love. I loved his lovemaking. And he was good company. When he wasn't drunk."

"He was Catholic."

"Is that relevant?"

"Everything is relevant," Father Caldwell said.

"The thing about the Stuntman was that he was handsome and good in bed."

"What is good in bed? Bearing in mind that we are our bodies, which means"—Father Caldwell blushed, he was about to express a truism with a cliché—"that 'good in bed' means a mating, a meeting, of souls."

News to me.

Father Caldwell never reproached me for having had what another priest might have called illicit sex. "The consequences of the act and not the act itself . . . ." he intoned, how I wished he would simply tell me to cut it out.

"I don't know about souls," I said. "Do you want details?"

Father Caldwell looked pained. One could not accuse him of prurience. He lit a cigarette.

"He was athletic in bed," I said. "He didn't go in for kissing much. We laughed a lot together. He got along well with Lucy. I liked to show him off at parties, he was always the most interesting man at a party."

"Do you prefer that to your being the most interesting person at a party?"

"I thought we were talking about souls?"

"We are."

"It sounds more like we're talking about personalities."

"You make these arbitrary distinctions," Father Caldwell said. Then he said—I never knew whether his questions were the gropings of a blind man or the utterances of one of God's fools, or (the thought alarmed me) the result of the Sexuality Workshops or Sensitivity Training courses he often chose to attend—"Did he make your body feel loved?"

"He made my body feel used. Occupied. The man who killed himself didn't, and Devi doesn't, and I had begun to think I had abandoned my body, that it was nothing but weight."

"So when your body is rejected you feel as if it's you who are abandoning it?"

I did not know the answer to this question, which seemed to imply a degree of unconscious complicity I did not want to think about, so I said, unkindly, "Sometimes I get the feeling that you regard me as your most interesting patient, Eugene," by which I wounded him. He began to talk to me of a television rerun of the *Forsyte Saga*. "Eugene," I said, "I think that I will go to London."

"Yes," he said. "It is time. Finish it. Settle it. Resolve it." He reached for a cigarette, but not for a Magic Marker. "Perhaps," he said, "it would be wise to bear in mind that desire creates its own object."

Was Devi my own creation, my invention? nothing more than the object to which my floating desires had attached themselves? How lost to us are our own intentions.

# *Chapter Three*

Long ago Eileen—who no longer called me—had asked me to ponder the relationship between the sanctity of the flesh, the Incarnation, and human love. It was of course an amazingly simple equation, how could I ever have failed to grasp it: Because God had become man, love enabled one intuitively to perceive the divine image in material creation; for me, Devi was the apprehension of the eternal moment—he had been from the moment I saw him. Devi was the God-bearing person. Now Eugene was asking me to consider whether my love for Devi was idolatrous, a pretty pickle, and whether I wished to abandon my body, an even more difficult question to confront. Strange that all my friends envied (when they did not scorn) the consolations of my faith; I myself was vastly troubled by this question, to which there seemed to be no ready answer. To which the only answer seemed to be Devi, in the flesh: England.

I wanted, before I left for London, to make peace with Eileen. But every time I tried in my mind to approach her, the word she had spoken—her summary of my life—stopped me. "Imbroglio. Your life is one imbroglio after another," she had said. I knew I was not a restful person; but that word: Imbroglio. One day I repeated the word to myself a hundred times, to divest it of its bad magic; when it became merely a cacophony of silly syllables, I called Eileen. She said hello; I hung up. It gave me—Eugene is right when he says mine is not a charitable nature—pleasure to think that I was Eileen's obscene phone caller. I called her several times; each time, after her hello, I hung up. At last I wrote her a letter in which I reproached her for being careless of friendship. "I suppose

you're laughing at me," I said. "Because it's clear that you
don't care." She replied: "Let's have dinner," she said; "I'm
not laughing."

So we had dinner at a French restaurant in Soho. Eileen
brought a bottle of *spumante*. "To friendship," she said, toast-
ing me. "To friendship," I said.

I tried to interest Eileen—as a token of good faith, and
because I was much immersed in the question (no act has a
single motive)—in Father Caldwell's talk about abandonment
of the flesh. She'd been a nun, after all, therefore, one supposed, an authority. As I talked nervously, I sensed there was
something different in her manner, and that that something—
illusive—had little or nothing to do with me.

"I don't want to talk about your problems in the context of
the Church, Angie. A church that doesn't ordain women
doesn't know anything about what you call the flesh when you
mean sex."

"It's your Church, too."

"No longer," Eileen said.

"That can't be true."

"You live in a dream world. I'm telling you it is true. Not
everyone can be like you, doing whatever you want and still
professing loyalty to the Church."

"Don't you miss God?" I said, deciding to ignore Eileen's
disapprobation of the way I lived. I had never been Catholic
enough for Eileen.

"She is not found in the Church," Eileen said.

"*She?* God is She? Since when?"

"Your problems have to do with your mother," Eileen said.

"And what problems are those?" We were eating salmon
mousse.

"Your imbroglios."

"Fuck this," I said.

"I'm willing to be your friend, Angie, but no God talk, and
no Devi talk."

"So have you seen any good movies lately?"

"And you ought to know," Eileen said, "that I've had an
abortion."

"But not an imbroglio."

Eileen ignored this. "How does Lucy feel about the Catholic thing?" she said. "And about the way you live?"

"Odd that you should call it the Catholic thing, given that you were a nun. My daughter is not censorious. Why should she be?"

"This isn't going very well," Eileen said. "Let's start again. Tell me about your real life."

"My life consists of friends—those that remain loyal to me—and Devi and what you call the Catholic thing and Lucy and work and soap operas. Which do you want to talk about? Tell me about your real life. Tell me about your abortion."

"Have you decided on an entree?" Eileen said.

"Remember how we used to plan menus? I saw a shop the other day called the S & M Meat Market. Near my Aunt Milly's house. And outside it there was a dairy truck called Instant Whip. It reminded me of an S & M menu Devi planned once—rack of lamb, mashed potatoes, beets, frozen whipped pudding. . . ."

"Do you want to know the truth?" Eileen said.

"Sure."

"Your life is glamorous. And I am a secretary in a methadone clinic. You have never understood that."

"I have never understood what."

"You have never understood my life. How can you speak of my abortion so casually?"

"How can *you*? My life is not glamorous."

"*I've* never interviewed a movie star. I see junkies all day long."

"Of what possible use is a movie star? Eileen, you were my best friend."

Eileen began to cry. "I've lost a child, I've had an abortion, and you carry on about God and Devi and movie stars."

"I loved you, Eileen." I wanted to hold Eileen's hand, I wanted to tell Eileen I loved her still. I wasn't sure I did. I remembered the night we'd sat together in her glass house while it snowed and snowed and Eileen held me to her so that I could hear her baby's heartbeat. "Are you happy?" I asked. Idiotic question; she was crying.

"You make too much of happiness."

"That's what Devi says."

"No Devi," Eileen said.

"There's still some *spumante* left," I said.

"To your health," Eileen said.

"And yours."

"Devi sent me a drawing," Eileen said.

"He sent *you* a drawing?"

"When I wrote to tell him about the abortion."

"You told him about the abortion?"

"I thought he'd understand."

"I hate you," I said; and I left Eileen—who worked in a methadone clinic—alone to pay the bill.

I called Lucy at Smith to tell her—who else to tell?—about the dismal evening I'd spent with Eileen. I left out all the details.

"Naturally she's dismal," Lucy said. "Wouldn't you be if you'd had an abortion?"

"How do you know about Eileen's abortion?"

"She told Devi and Devi told someone who told Stephan and Stephan told me."

"So how come nobody told me?"

"Probably nobody thought you'd be sympathetic." What with my mother's death and God knows what at Smith, Lucy seemed to have developed a mulish mind of her own.

"Damned right, I'm not sympathetic. Why should I be?"

"If I had a baby now, it would ruin my life," Lucy said.

"In which case, you'd better take care," I said. "Anyway, you're not Eileen."

"I like Eileen."

"I doubt that."

"I wrote her a letter after I heard about the abortion."

"What did you say?"

"Condolences."

"For her or for the baby she killed?"

" 'Kill' is a dumb word. She wrote me a very nice letter back. I'm going to see her when I come to New York."

"She's an appalling person," I said. "You can't know how appalling. You can't imagine how much she's hurt me."

"How?"

"I don't want to go into it."

"So you expect me not to see her and you won't tell me why?"

"Take my word for it."

"I can't take your word for it. That's not fair."

"All right. Do you want me to tell you all the terrible things she said and did? Starting in London?"

"I don't want to hear about London," Lucy said.

"Why not?"

"I don't want to hear about Devi," Lucy said.

"Well, just beware of Eileen, is all I can say. She's good at betrayal."

"My life is separate from yours," Lucy said, as if this were news. "You make me friends with Stephan and Eileen and then you tell me not to be friends. I can't be angry just because you're angry."

"Stephan's still my friend."

"I hope so," Lucy said. "After what he did for me in England."

"And what exactly was that?"

"I've got to work on a paper," Lucy said. "I think we've used this conversation up." Just what Eileen had said.

"Will you call me soon?"

"Sure," Lucy said.

I spent the weekend with my father, who was sinking rapidly into senility. "Esther?" he said. My mother's name. "Angie, daddy." "She's dead." "Yes. Mommy's dead." "Angie's dead," he said.

Lucy called, quite as if we'd never quarreled, to tell me about her latest boyfriend, a dental student.

"He says the reason my teeth are yellow is that I had tetracycline when I was a child."

"Your teeth aren't yellow."

"Well, he should know."

"Tell me what you like about him," I said.

"He's normal," Lucy said.

"What's normal?"

"Boring," Lucy said. "But handsome."

"Rich?"

"How did you know?"

"I guessed."

"You wouldn't like him," Lucy said.

"So?"

"I don't really like him, either."

"So?"

"I think I'll ditch him," Lucy said. "Tell me about the parties you went to this week."

"I had dinner with Sylvia. I had a drink with the Stuntman. I had a drink. He had six. And who's your favorite movie star, because I'm going to interview him."

"Not *him.*"

"Him."

"What a glamorous life you have, Ma."

"I do, don't I? And three parties next week besides."

"Do you think it's retarded not to be in love when you're my age?"

"No. Just as long as there are plenty of guys in love with you."

"What do you think of someone who calls a cat Cat. That's his cat's name, Cat. He thinks it's original."

"I wouldn't ditch him for that alone," I said.

"Love you, Mommy."

"Love you, Angel."

"You hang up first."

Five minutes later Lucy called me back (collect). "Mom? I've been thinking. My life wouldn't be ruined if I got pregnant. It would be changed, but it wouldn't be ruined."

"Just be sure to use your diaphragm," I said. I never have

known how to leave well enough alone. Only it never used to
be a problem between me and Lucy, what to say next, what not
to say. "Oh for Pete's sake," she said, and hung up.

Eileen was using Lucy to get back at me. Why else would she
want to see Lucy, and how dare she come between a mother
and a child. I did not want to be discussed by Lucy and Eileen.
Stephan agreed with me, though he said he thought Eileen was
too boring to do anybody any harm. I wondered how elastic
Lucy's loyalty was: Would she countenance talk from Eileen
about my "imbroglios"? I remembered fondly the days when
Stephan had swept down upon Lucy, like some benevolent
maternal bird, to take her away, to rescue her; how I'd protested! Now I only wished she were within his grasp; I saw
precious little of Stephan nowadays, sad, really.

I was thinking all these things, and wondering, at the same
time, why the movie actor was late—did he think he was roy-
alty? I'd consented to interview him only to establish credit
with Lucy, who was still young enough to be impressed by him,
as was most of the world, come to think of it. . . . I was
thinking all these things when the movie actor walked into his
receptionist's office, and I stood up to greet him, and everything fell out of my purse and onto the floor. "Does neatness
count?" I said foolishly, as we scrambled around on our knees,
both in search of my lipstick, which had lodged itself behind a
leather couch. Odd, I'd never gotten a buzz from him on the
screen, but now that we were eye to eye, on our knees, I saw
the point. He was at once fine and strong, golden from the tip
of his blond head to his tawny cowboy boots; he exuded male-
ness. Even his skin was rich, as if years and more dollars than I
could imagine had gone into the making of him, the only one
of our current movie stars whose appeal did not rest on the
fact that he was just like everybody else, only slightly magni-
fied. He was larger than anybody else, but he was not like
everybody else. Odd that this had escaped me on the screen. I
was still on my knees. I perceived in his golden looks—which
on the screen had struck me as merely bland—a vivid goodness; I always attach character to beauty, perhaps because

Lucy, who is beautiful, is also possessed of a vivid goodness.
. . . And of course thinking of Lucy brought me to my feet
again, dear me, perhaps people are right when they say beauty
is a curse. Think of people ascribing all that goodness to you
just because God has blessed you with symmetrical features.
Which his, in fact, were not, they were rather haphazardly
arranged, but the effect was like that of an English garden—the
deceptive appearance of beauty without artifice. I am not
known for writing flattering interviews; I saw myself being led
down the garden path.

I operate on the uncharitable principle that all actors are
mentally deficient unless proven otherwise (I could name any
number of actors who radiate intelligence on the screen and
who are, in real life, dumb as twigs), and with this thought I
attempted to arm myself. I armed myself further with the fact
that he had been married three times; good people stay married (don't they?).

It has been my experience in life that people do read each
other's minds though they are not consciously aware of the
process. The actor wished to speak about goodness. People
very often introduce the subject of goodness when they are
with me, which is not because I am good. I am preoccupied
with the subject, which I doubt any truly good person would
be. Good must seem natural to truly good people. With me,
however, it is of perpetual fascination. So he had me hooked.
(Hooked—a word Devi used of me; even distractions from
Devi—all this talk of goodness evoked activity in my genitals—
led me back to Devi, the pity.)

So the actor wished to know if he was considered frivolous.
Was acting frivolous, given that millions were starving in Ban-
gladesh, etc.? He was interviewing me! We were reclining on
two couches set at right angles to each other in his inner office.
Should he go into politics? Did politics inevitably corrupt? I
was flattered. I neglected to turn my tape recorder on. I could
just hear my editor say, There's no news in goodness, goodness is boring. Nothing so rare as goodness could possibly be
boring, of course, but one can't expect editors to understand
that. From which you can see how he blunted my honed jour-

nalistic instincts. A sex object discussing entry into politics is a
story, one any editor or writer however dim would recognize in
a second, and I wasn't even scribbling. (I was not above thinking—sometimes when I catch my mind watching itself I do
wonder if Devi isn't right: Perhaps I do play parlor games in
my own head—that if I paid him the compliment of treating
this as privileged information, I'd be sure to be allowed to
cover his campaign, thereby raking in the bucks. My own goodness is a very muddied stream.)

"Why do you think I should be interviewed?" he asked. If
he'd said, "What's in it for me?"—which is what he was, albeit
gracefully, asking, my tape recorder would have been activated
in a hurry. "I can't think of a single reason," I said, which was a
form of disguised hustling. I wanted him when he was ripe and
needy—which now, having had six box office smashes in a
succession, he was not. I wanted him on the campaign trail.
"What good would it do anybody to read about my private
life?" he asked. "None at all that I can see," I said, thinking,
with perverse satisfaction, of my editor's reaction to what she
would, with reason, call my lack of professionalism, thinking
also that his views on ecology (standard left liberal), which
were well known to all, were boring. His wife, the cultural
editor of a news weekly had told me, rinsed out paper towels
and believed salvation lay in recycling aluminum cans, what
could be more boring? Having determined to our mutual satisfaction that there was no point in an interview, the movie actor
said, "What about lunch?"

We had lunch at Paone's, which interfered with my notion of
his goodness, given that everybody who ate at Paone's was
well-heeled and smelled rich—old rich—and carried with him
an invisible aura of power. Everybody at Paone's is somebody,
usually the kind of somebody you've never seen or even heard
of but whose access to influence in high places is practically
tangible. He was the only actor in the place; I was the only
female. The proprietor knew him well. Covering his campaign
would be fun.

"Do you mind if I smoke?"

"Not at all. I'm happy to breathe it in. I promised my wife I wouldn't, but once or twice a year, when I'm feeling particularly happy, I inhale a cigar."

"I'm dieting."

"I'll diet with you. We'll have the same number of calories."

The actor had a whispered conversation with the proprietor, who took his order, and soon before us there was: a plate of young asparagus vinaigrette for him, a plate of cannelloni for me.

"I don't think this is fair. I thought you said the same number of calories?"

"I'm assured this is low-calorie pasta."

"And low-calorie ricotta?"

"You have a point," he said; and, after further negotiations with the proprietor, a plate of mashed potatoes (not on the menu) appeared before him, every bit of which he ate so as to keep up with my calories. (I regarded this as an act of gallantry. Lucy—to whom I duly reported all—regarded it as manipulation. "He's off," she said.)

My cannelloni and his asparagus and mashed potatoes were followed by veal marsala, accompanied by a white wine the bouquet of which was designed to put one in mind of money as well as sex and spring in sylvan places. After two glasses I put my hand over the glass to signify that I'd had enough, which I hadn't. It was a wine nobody could ever have enough of. He poured the wine through my fingers, causing my brain to go into further decline. From that point on, I do not remember what we talked of—not politics, and not acting, I'm sure of that. We laughed a lot. He made me feel clever. I flirted, not quite against my will. He created the illusion that nothing I could say was wrong, that everything I said was amusing—catch Devi doing that. He—known for his seriousness of purpose—set himself to amuse. It worked.

After lunch—he made a point of saying he was two hours late for an appointment with John Kenneth Galbraith—he motioned to the proprietor: "Do you still have that teak box?" he said.

The teak box appeared as if by magic (in fact by the snapping of fingers): Cigars. "Today I inhale," he said. Well, I ask you.

When I reported this to Lucy, she said, "He's a phony." Yes; but romantic gestures count for something, even if they're contrived. Especially if one is starved. When I told my editor that, for various personal reasons I declined to interview the movie actor, she said, "You're a fool."

After three days of concentrating on the problem, I decided that both my daughter and my editor were right, which time has proved. But oh I had liked feeling female and attractive, of such do my diversions from Devi consist. Though whether they are in fact diversions is arguable. Because all the time I was diverted, I kept reminding myself I was diverted, which is, as Devi once said in another context, like trying to walk on both sides of the street at the same time.

A few weeks later, the editor, having decided to forgive me, called to ask me to interview a movie star, a hot new movie star, a blond, who made her home in Paris. Born in Brooklyn. I was feeling miserable and brittle—the proximity of Paris to London did not escape me; and it had been weeks since Father Caldwell had said, Resolve it, it is time.

"I love it," I said. "Where does she get that accent from?"

"What would you do if you were born in Brooklyn?"

"I was. You don't hear me peppering my sentences with *alors.*"

"She was born in the *bowels* of Brooklyn," the editor said.

"As was I."

"You're sure to hate her. Be as malicious as you like."

"There's always the chance I'll like her."

"Not if I know you."

"Do you think I'm uncharitable?"

"I think you know bullshit when you hear it."

"That's one way of putting it. Can I stay at the Ritz?"

"You don't come cheap."

"I have college tuition to think about."

"Think about that while you interview the blond. She's very very rich. I promise you, you'll hate her."

"How, rich? From three movies?"

"Find out. Use your seductive charm."

"If I like her, I'll say so."

"You won't," the editor said. "The password is 'bile.'"

So I called Devi and told him I was coming to London. He was cool; but he didn't say no. I was cool, too. I didn't want Devi to feel I was hurling myself at him; I didn't want to frighten him with protestations of love. I didn't want to back him into that corner of his nature from which he would attack me like a trapped animal.

It was time, anyone could see that. I wanted it resolved. I felt Lucy drifting away from me, judging me, and I suspected the reasons lay in Devi, though neither my intelligence nor my intuition could grasp how. And I did not want a life of diversions. I wanted a life. My own churning thoughts about the redemptive powers of suffering were beginning to sicken me, they struck me as morbid and sentimental; and I struck myself as being worse than bad, as being fake good. Perhaps it was true, what people said, that I used Devi to give myself a vacation from sex, that I needed to devote myself entirely to work. (Perhaps it was true, what Father Caldwell never said, that deep in my heart I regarded sex as sin.) I dismissed these glib ideas as so much nonsense—one loves because one loves. I dismissed these glib thoughts a little too facilely for my own comfort.

If I loved Devi because he was inaccessible, I'd damn well make him accessible to me—I'd go to London. And then we'd see.

How had I damaged him, what did he mean? Time for clarity. I was energized. And at the same time so sad.

As Devi always knows when I am applying my concentration to him, he called to ask me when I'd arrive in London.

"It's cold and miserable here," he said.

"And you?"

"Cold and miserable. I always am. I always was. Perhaps I'll go to Spain and leave the flat to you."

Silence. He *could* not keep my life on hold.

"But all my journeys end nowhere," Devi said.

"So will you be in London when I come?"

"I expect so."

It struck me that I had proffered no comfort to Devi, I who had assumed the role of comforter. Devi thought my gifts of consolation were acts of aggression. Nevertheless he asked for them. This time he had asked and I had not given. Something had shifted. So recently energized, I faced the future now with weariness, with a kind of blank curiosity. As if my life were happening to someone else.

Stephan, whom I now regarded as a source of comfort, was —certainly not by design?—unavailable to me. Perhaps he had another clamorous young lover, thin? Every time I called him, I got his answering machine, which referred me to a number in Southampton, which I did not wish to call. I had grown used to Stephan's being the pursuer. I am stubborn in my ways, and I wanted Stephan to love me again. Perhaps he'd made a pact with Devi? Nonsense. He'd always side with me as opposed to Devi. Scrambled brains, I had, and Devi, exerting his long-distance influence, was scrambling them.

"I understand that Stephan has settled down with one lover," Devi said. "Rich bastard."

"Nonsense. He would have told me. Lucy would know."

"Do you think everyone tells you everything?"

"Yes."

"He's old and ugly."

"Stephan?"

"Stephan's lover. Who must therefore be even richer than Stephan."

I was preparing to go to Paris when I heard from the rich Park Avenue boozer with whom he lived—to whom he had gone when I ditched him—that the Stuntman was dying. I responded to this news by considering how much money he'd cost me while he'd lived with me. I called Lucy, who burst into tears and announced that she was coming down from Smith on the first available bus. His heart was going, his brain was going, and his liver was hardly functioning at all. My liver was in good form, but the same could not be said of my heart and brain. My coldness frightened me, my brittleness frightened me. I had not found the mother I hoped to find in memories, the mother who had loved me beyond words, before words—I had not found her because I had never looked for her; and now a man with whom I had lived was dying, and my eyes were dry as bones. Was it I who had written to Devi that the nature of love was to multiply and expand? My own seemed to be curling in on itself, shriveling.

"Of course," as I said to Stephan, "it's true that he was awfully expensive. He once called a vibrator an obscene toy, and that's what I sometimes thought he was to me—an obscene toy that cost me a lot."

"Why obscene?" Stephan said.

"I wish I could think of something besides money now. Don't tell Lucy. She thinks money is vulgar, it's her new idea."

I had finally called Stephan in Southampton, and he had responded with kindness and alacrity: He drove to me at once.

"I depend on you, Stephan"—and the look on the old dear's face was a lesson: Stephan was gratified by my love, which, dammed in so many directions, still flowed to him, taking me by surprise.

Stephan and Lucy arrived at practically the same moment. Lucy hugged me: "Are you glad to see me, Mommy?" she demanded, as if there could be any doubt. Doubt is infectious. There were pale blue circles under her eyes: "Aren't you glad to see me?" Whereupon I burst out crying, and Stephan— amazing how practical he is, when you come to think of it— poured me a double vodka. Lucy called the hospital for the Stuntman's condition (critical) and the Park Avenue boozer. You'd think I'd call her something other than the boozer now that the Stuntman was dying. While Lucy was out of the room, I took the opportunity to ask Stephan—who seemed remarkably unspiky as well as unreproachful—in fact one could almost call him serene (though, self-absorbed, it did not occur to me to wonder why his mind and body seemed so much at rest): "Do you think Lucy is beginning to sound like Eileen? Because I think she's imitating the way she speaks, so finicky. The words themselves have nothing to do with the way Lucy says the words, if you know what I mean." In fact I had no reason to believe Lucy and Eileen saw each other, though I knew they corresponded about Lucy's Comparative Religion course, which ticked me off no end, and about which correspondence Lucy was uncharacteristically reticent.

"My dear," Stephan said, "any resemblance between boring Eileen and my niece exists solely in your head. But the child does have to establish herself as separate from you. Having an interesting mother is a mixed blessing, you know."

So avuncular; I found myself slipping back into old conversational patterns with Stephan: "How would you know that having an interesting mother is a mixed blessing, Stephan?"

Stephan, refusing to return barb for barb, sighed.

Lucy returned to the living room and—touch erasing doubt —reclined against me. "He tried to pull the tubes out of his arms," she said. "He's on a life-support system. She"—the Stuntman's Park Avenue paramour—"wants to pull the plug."

"No," I said, surprising myself by the ferocity of my feeling, and hoping that principle wasn't all that governed my feeling.

"I agree, no," Lucy said. Well, thank God for that; this was not going to provide an occasion for a quarrel.

Lucy had gotten this story out of the Stuntman's lover (I could not stop thinking of him as the Stuntman, a term used affectionately between us; and I could not do more than envy the simplicity of Lucy's feelings, while I was surprised by the strength of them): They had decided to marry (Lucy's lip trembled), and, when they took their blood tests, his revealed so much liver damage due to hepatitis that his doctor ordered him into the hospital that very day. He blustered; he didn't want to go to the hospital, but his fiancée (Lucy stumbled over the word) insisted. That was three days ago. Now he was dying.

How can everything collapse at once, I wondered. From marriage to funeral day. He'd never asked me to marry him.

"She was his last hope, he said. That's what she said."

Well, I suppose she was. If you can't find salvation in will or grace, where else to find it than in money? And in the company of one whose vice is identical to your own? I never represented salvation to him, I never offered salvation to him, I never gave him love. All there was between us was sex and laughter, affection. He was my obscene toy, a diversion. Lucy loved him, he was kind to her, but perhaps he hadn't known that Lucy loved him—after all, it came to me as a surprise that she did. On the other hand, perhaps it was Lucy he had not wanted to leave when he'd protested that he hadn't wanted to leave me, perhaps all along he'd felt the force of Lucy's love. Can anyone be loved and not know it?

"What can we do?" Lucy asked.

"I don't want to see him the way he is now," I said; which was true, but not for the reasons Lucy generously supposed. I had no delicacy of feeling. As far as I was concerned, he was already dead.

"Is it OK if I do?" she asked. I thanked God that Lucy could not read my mind.

"It will be ugly."

"It's OK. I didn't love him as much as you did," Lucy said.

She went. Stephan, who seemed to have grown both sturdier and more imaginative since we'd last met, went with her. The Stuntman didn't recognize Lucy. He called her Louise, his sister's name. Stephan brought her home in a limo, made tea for her, and, with the application of many kisses to me, which I received guiltily, she went limply off to bed.

"So?"

"Terrible. Everything gone. The brain, now, apparently. Your child is brave."

"Stephan, I'm scared. I don't feel a thing. Except for about the money. I just don't want Lucy to know."

"He must have seemed like a father to her," Stephan said.

"For six months? That's all it was."

"He was here every day for six months."

Well, yes. Here. Unlike Devi. Unlike her father. The Stuntman was the man Lucy had quarreled with over the bathroom, the man in striped pajamas warm from sleep she'd stumbled into in the hall.

"But will she love him years from now, Stephan?"

"She loves him now, when she needs to."

"Maybe she didn't love him as much as she thinks she did."

"Sufficient unto the day," Stephan said, "and perhaps you loved him more than you're allowing."

"No," I said, "I didn't. The first time I went to bed with him in New York he said he'd already 'taken care of' two women that day. You don't love a man who says things like that."

"Let Lucy believe what she needs to believe. Your feelings aren't important now."

"Yes. I love you, Stephan."

"One tries to be of use," Stephan said, a blush suffusing his face.

In the middle of the night, I called the hospital. I pretended to be calling from California. I pretended to be the Stuntman's sister, Louise. So I got the news first: The Stuntman had died.

"What can we do?" Lucy asked.

"We can call his mother and his sister; probably nobody's thought of doing that."

Nobody had. The Stuntman's almost-widow, wife-to-be, called me to complain about the size of the hospital bill—she was putting two children through school, she said, she couldn't afford a dead man's bills. I said I couldn't be expected to sympathize with her, and I hung up. A friend of the Stuntman's called to tell me the Sheridan Pub was opening early on Sunday morning to hold a memorial service for the Stuntman, drinks on the house for his friends; he had it in mind to put the Stuntman's ashes (which he called his "cremains") in an empty vodka bottle and place the bottle on a garbage scow on the East River, "the way he would have wanted it." I said I couldn't be expected to take part in such a barbaric ritual, and I hung up. I called the Stuntman's sister, who said that as far as she was concerned, he'd been dead for a long time, but that, as he'd been baptized Catholic, she'd like a Catholic service in New York, and would I arrange it. I said yes. She said she couldn't be expected to approve of our having lived in sin; and I hung up. I called Father Caldwell.

I told Lucy none of this. I told Stephan all.

"Interesting," he said. "We do that with one of our own,

sometimes. It's totemistic. He died for them, that's what underlies the Sheridan do. It's a celebration."

"That's disgusting."

"Of course it is. But he's dead and they're still alive, so they can go on drinking. It wasn't them, this time."

"It will be one of them soon enough."

"That's what the do is designed to make them forget. They're offering him up as a sacrifice, so they can go on drinking. And they're hedging their bets with ashes in a vodka bottle. It's a farce. They can't deal with the reality of it."

"A sacrifice to whom?"

"Their thinking doesn't go that far," Stephan said. "It's primitive behavior."

"It's disgusting behavior."

"Of course."

"One of us is getting older and wiser, Stephan. I think it's you." I was just getting older.

The memorial service was held in Father Caldwell's church in the Village. The Park Avenue boozer wore a lynx coat and a black veil. She was supported by another boozer. She was sober. The Sheridan Pub contingent came in, all tipsy—"pixilated" was the word that came, unwanted, to my mind—and prepared, one could see, to giggle, which they did the moment Father Caldwell, looking impressive in his vestments, rose. We all had mimeographed sheets with Scripture readings, drawn heavily from Ecclesiastes and doom-and-gloom and judgment prophets, the point of which I did not see. Even a condemned man gets to hear "The Lord Is My Shepherd." The church was very cold, no music. The woman in front of me, whose hair was a rat's nest, could barely contain her guffaws when she was instructed to remember the Four Last Things. When the community, such as it was, was obliged to read a particularly dreary passage from Ecclesiastes, she burst into maudlin tears, interspersed with hiccups, indistinguishable from giggles, whereupon Lucy left the church, anger and pain fighting for equal time on her waxen face. I followed her. She sat on the steps, where also was sitting a wino who had pissed his pants. Lucy and I clung to each other, like two shipwrecked orphans, Lucy's love going in two directions, toward me and toward the Stuntman, mine going in only one direction, to Lucy, who said, "We have to go back in. We can't leave him to them." I reminded myself that honesty was not always the best policy, and supported her—so fragile, so strong—to a back pew. When it was all over, the wife-to-be, almost-widow, established herself at the head of a reception line, which I did not join, having no wish to embrace her lynx coat.

"I call that stern, Eugene," I said to Father Caldwell. "Not even one Psalm? What about And death shall have no dominion? What about God's mercy, for example?"

"Don't rely too heavily on God's mercy," said Father Caldwell, a man of many parts. "He is also a God of judgment, which you tend to forget."

You always let me off the hook, I thought, but forbore to say so. "A little comfort might have done," I said.

"Considering God's judgments is a way into thinking of God's mercy," Father Caldwell said; "make the leap."

"Were you offended by the laughter?"

"I was impressed by the terror," Father Caldwell said.

"Since when does terror express itself in giggles?" I said.

"You must come to me soon," Father Caldwell said.

"Mommy's tired," Lucy said, quivering with cold; "this has been too much for her." And she kissed Eugene, and crossed herself with holy water as we went out into the watery sunlight of midafternoon.

Not knowing when to leave well enough alone, greedy, I asked Lucy if anyone had thought to tell Eileen about the service, to which Lucy, whose magnanimity was making me ache with guilt, replied, "Why? This doesn't belong to her. This is ours." I turned away from my child, so she could not see the victory written on my face.

Stephan was waiting on the steps, in the company of an old and rather ugly man, not thin. "We've prepared a meal," he said, and ushered us into a limousine, where Lucy rested inertly against me, and I felt triumph compounded with self-loathing: She belongs to me; she loves me well enough to

attribute her own fine feelings to me. God bless Lucy, mine.
My thoughts were taken up with Eileen—my lack of charity was
an open book to Father Caldwell, who had apparently decided
to take a hard line with me. I considered the alarming thought
that my duplicity was restoring me to the safety of Lucy's love;
I considered the thought that Lucy's love for me was, in its
current blindness, large enough to allow her to suppose I was
good. This was confusing. Somewhere on the East River Drive,
I considered Stephan's use of the plural pronoun ("We've
prepared a meal"), and I began to regard his old and rather
ugly (not thin) companion with curiosity bordering on jealousy. We drove to Sutton Place in silence.

"Now, Dearheart," Stephan said to his companion, who
hauled himself less than limberly out of the limousine when we
reached Stephan's building; and he offered him his hand; dear
me. Lucy, who even in her pain was gathering information and
exuding a diffuse tenderness, said, "Come, Lucas"—for that
was Dearheart's name—and offered him her hand, on which
the veins were remarkably pronounced, a symptom of exhaustion; the vines.

Stephan's drawing room, which I had not seen in months,
was now all chintz and clutter, it lacked only a dog on the
hearth for perfect domesticity. "Come into the kitchen with
me, my dear," Stephan said. His serenity was coming into
focus.

"OK, Stephan, tell."

"He is the love of my life," Stephan said.

"Rich?"

"A man to whom no worldly success has accrued."

"So what's to love?"

"He has a great and tender heart," Stephan said.

"I didn't know you went in for that."

"You are setting the tone for the day," Stephan said. "Believe me and be kind."

"I know. The tone I'm setting stinks. I think my kindness has
deserted me."

"Remember Lucy."

"I do. I'm cold to the marrow."

"Life has dealt with you harshly," Stephan said.

"Not really. I haven't known what to do with the cards. Are you happy with him?"

"Yes."

"I'm glad," I said; and I was. "Will you tell me more?"

"Another business presses," Stephan said.

"What are we eating? Nursery food?" He was piling buttered rice and lamb chops on plain white plates. If Lucas had brought Stephan to simplicity, he had done what no one else had managed to achieve. My heart was indeed kindly disposed, but my mouth, lagging behind, continued to prattle mischievous nonsense. "What other business presses?" I asked when we were alone, and when I no longer had to pretend, for Lucy's sake, to be grieving for the Stuntman.

"I see that I must prepare myself for another rescue mission," he said.

Lucy had told him of my proposed trip to London.

Stephan's use of pronouns had changed. Imagine not referring to himself as *one;* it did lend credence to his claim that the kind and ugly man was the great love of his life. I liked this change in Stephan. But I perversely missed the bad old days, when he would have said, "One sees that one must prepare oneself for another rescue mission." Sincerity was robbing Stephan of his idiosyncrasies; true love was robbing him of colorful speech.

"No Concorde flights, this time, Stephan, please. I'm not ungrateful, as you know, but this is my battle, no charging around on white horses, please."

"Battle is not a word used in conjunction with love," Stephan said sententiously. His complacency vexed me.

"Struggle, then, if you prefer."

"Whatever happened to the rich boring doctor? The one with hair on his knuckles." Stephan too reverted to old patterns.

"Are you prescribing him?"

"You are getting no younger, my dear."

"In any case my financial future is secure. You are leaving me your Renoir when you die."

"The small Renoir, my dear."

"Oh, I get your drift. Dearheart gets the big stuff."

A look of real pain came over Stephan's face, causing me at once to regret my thoughtless words. Lucas must be nearing seventy.

"I'm sorry, Stephan."

"Lucy gets the major Renoir," Stephan said; and my acquisitive soul thrilled at the same time as my gratitude spilled over.

"Let me at least pay for Brown's Hotel," Stephan said. "To which you can repair after your daily battles with that boy. Let me be of use."

"No thank you, Stephan dear. If I wanted to stay at Brown's, I would. I don't."

"May one know," said Stephan, hurt pride influencing his pronouns, "what you hope to accomplish?"

"I don't know. I only know it's time."

"Time for what? He is a dangerous man."

"Dangerous to himself. I don't know time for what. I just know it's time."

"Nothing I can say will change your mind?"

"Nothing."

"You grow more stubborn as you grow older."

"I wish you wouldn't keep saying *old.*"

"None of us is getting younger," Stephan said.

"Oh, Stephan, don't be pompous. Nothing bad is going to happen to me."

"I shall book a Concorde just in case," Stephan said.

"Save your shekels, Stephan. None of us is getting younger."

Lucy's pity for me warmed and warmed, and only occasionally was my warmth blighted by the chill that came from my knowledge that I didn't deserve her pity. The night Lucy left for Smith I found a note on my pillow: "Dear Mom, Sometimes I argue with you awkwardly but that's because I don't know if my ideas are my ideas or yours. So I have to find out. So if I was rude, I'm sorry. I love you, Lu." But she hadn't fought at all, nor had she once been rude. And no mention of Eileen. ("A temporary aberration," Stephan said. "A pulling away from you to get back to you. And boringness can be seductive. Eileen is so boring one is misled to believe there is more there than meets the glazed eye." I found myself defending Eileen, a welcome sign to myself that I had not grown altogether scaly and hard. But of course I could afford to be generous—Lucy didn't love her anymore.)

I lay awake and tried to conjure up some love for the Stuntman. All I could think was how much money he'd cost me, a sign to myself that I had grown altogether scaly and hard.

Three days before I was to leave for Paris, I had a coughing spell, followed by a muscle spasm in my diaphragm, and then by a searing pain in the region of my stomach, for which I took four Gelusils and twenty milligrams of Valium, which did no good. I called my doctor, who prescribed codeine. "And are you smoking again?" Yes.

The codeine did not begin to touch the pain.

In the middle of the night, I fell out of bed and bruised my thigh. The next morning I walked ten blocks to my doctor's office, sweating.

"The codeine isn't working."

"You're gray," he said.

"I feel like hell. I hurt."

Howard, my doctor, has healing hands. His hands searched. "Does it hurt when you move like this? Like that? Try this position. Now this." For half an hour, naked, I performed convolutions. At last, "Ah!" he said; and called his colleague: "Arthur, have a look at this. Here. A pinpoint."

"Hard to find those," Arthur said.

"Hard to find what?"

"You have a tiny hole in the wall of your upper stomach."

"Is that bad?"

"How did you get here?"

"I walked."

"You walked with this pain?"

"You *walked?*" Arthur said.

"Is the pain bad?" I said.

Howard and Arthur exchanged looks.

"Hypochondriacs can never tell," Arthur said, "the real thing from the fake."

"How bad is my pain?" I asked. "On a scale of one to ten."

"Let me put it like this," Howard said. "If you had terminal cancer your pain would be no worse, and I'd inject you with morphine."

"So now what? You're not telling me I have cancer?"

Arthur left the examining room. "Dr. Cohen's going to have a job convincing her that all she's got is a rupture," I heard him tell the nurse. "She *walked* here. . . ."

Howard has healing hands and tells the truth.

"Nothing that a few days in the hospital and Demerol won't fix," he said. "We'll strap you up."

"I can't. I'm flying to France tomorrow."

"Lift a suitcase and I won't answer for the consequences," Howard said. "You ought to be in bed."

"I can't."

"With a will as strong as yours, why can't you stop smoking?"

"What about the pain?"

Howard called his nurse and swaddled my middle with yards of broad adhesive tape. "It's the best I can do," he said, "if you won't go to the hospital."

I began to cry. "I love you, Howard," I said. "What about the Demerol?"

"I wish you'd learn to love yourself. No alcohol, no Valium while you're on Demerol," he said. "No lifting, no abrupt motions. You have a remarkable tolerance for pain."

"When it's real," I said.

I flew to Paris in a blur of Demerol, Valium, and gin.

The blond movie star took one look at me and said, "My God, you're ill," and led me to the bed, fur covered, of her apricot-and-cream guest room. I slept for twenty-four hours, and the next day I interviewed her with her doctor in attendance.

Afterward—she drunk on Pernod, I crazed by Demerol, Valium, and gin—she called her faithless lover in New York; I called Lucy. Wonderful what mascara can do for heartbreak (hers). We went then to the Lipp, to meet, she said, "some amusing, decadent people—all the good people are dead."

The next day Aldo Moro's body was found. My new blond friend and I went to services at Notre Dame. All the world was there; and all the world was crying.

My father never used a four-letter word or told a dirty joke in his life. As sincerity had changed Stephan, so had senility changed him: The last time I'd been to see him, he'd sat in his rocking chair and sung a song of—I think—his own making:

> "Oh Hell, Oh Hell,
> Oh Hellen, please be true.
> Oh Hell, Oh Hell,
> Oh Hellen I love you.
> Your cunt, your cunt,
> Your country is divine.
> Oh Hell, Oh Hell,
> Oh Hellen say you're mine.
> Fuck you, Fuck you,
> For curiosity,
> Oh Hell, Oh Hell,
> Oh Hellen do love me."

Pleased with himself. ("Esther?")

This led me to wonder about his love life with Esther, my mother (dead).

Once my father told me that he and Esther said the rosary together every night before they went to bed. This remark—offered in a moment of greatly unusual candor—nagged me on my flight from Paris to London. Can one say the rosary and afterward make love? Cunnilingus after decades? Can sex be hot and holy? Because that's what I wanted; or thought I did. Difficult to talk about sex with Father Caldwell; perhaps I didn't understand sex at all. Sex with the Stuntman was heat and lust ("Say the words . . . say what I'm doing to you now

. . . tell me where my mouth is . . . give me . . ."), until it became merely athletic (he loved booze more than he loved bodies); and not, really, even hot enough to suit me. This I should have anticipated from the first night I went to bed with him in New York, when he boasted: "I've taken care of two women already today." Were those the words of a man who was truly hot? *"I've taken care of . . ."*? I liked to hear the words for everything I did, we did, for every part of our engaged bodies. (Suppose I were to say to Father Caldwell, "Father, I like to hear him describe my . . ." I couldn't, even in my imagination, say those words to my confessor. Would he have said, "I think that qualifies as love . . . under the meaning of the rubric"?) Could one say "With my body I thee worship" and then say, "Tell me—say the words—what your hand is doing now"? *License my roving hands. . . .* I tried, as my plane flew through the rosy gloom, to picture sex with Devi; I could not.

What did I want to save Devi from?

What did I want Devi to save me from?

# Part Six

This is the use of memory:
For liberation—not less of love but expanding
Of love beyond desire, and so liberation
From the future as well as the past.

T. S. ELIOT, "Little Gidding"

# Chapter One

"Angela, Buzz for the housekeeper, either on her own bell or on mine. She will let you in. . . . I'm working, will phone midday, back this evening. Keys on the kitchen table, Cheers. (Use the room behind the kitchen.)"

I found Devi's note underneath the door knocker. This appeared to be a good omen—nobody in New York would dream of leaving a note under a door knocker. I rang the housekeeper's bell. Her door was the color of clover. She was fat and sullen and old, and had no English. Trust Devi to have a fat and sullen and old French housekeeper. This appeared to be a bad omen. I managed to convey to her that I could not carry my bags, and she panted and heaved up the stairs, casting scornful backward glances at me (I pointed to my stomach and grimaced, and she grunted in disbelief or derision); she deposited my bags in the kitchen, stood for a moment regarding my flat stomach with contempt, said something guttural and incomprehensible, and waddled out, shaking her head and clucking. She hated me.

(Later I said to Devi, "The housekeeper was awfully nice, she carried my bags. I don't think I thanked her adequately." "A pound note would have been adequate thanks," Devi said; "the obvious solution always escapes you.")

The room behind the kitchen, which had belonged, when last I was here, to St. John, bore no trace of him. It was a room with no personality. Perhaps it had looked like this even when St. John lived here. (Where was he?) For certainly his colorless personality offered no clues to his character. The sheets were not clean; whose smell is this?

Hours till Devi should arrive. I pondered—no abrupt moves

—what to do. I opted for a walk. I found myself on the seedy edge of Belgravia, near Pimlico. I remembered I had forgotten my Demerol. I went into a disreputable-looking restaurant (Ali Baba's Mid Eastern Continental Cuisine) to ease my throbbing body. I had a cup of sweet mint tea, and (because I felt sorry for the lugubrious proprietor) a sickeningly sweet dessert, which added to my discomfort. I went to the bathroom, where cockroaches scurried. The sink was full of vomit, to which I contributed my own.

Thank God, a taxi.

Back at Devi's, after the Demerol had taken effect, I showered. (The towels were not fresh.) The adhesive tape was beginning to curl and turn black at the edges; also the pink flesh beneath it itched. (And Devi has mocked me for getting undressed behind closed doors, "So coy.")

Midday. Time for Devi's call. No call.

Cautious as a thief in the night, frightened as a child, I prowled. In the fridge there was nothing but a greasy margarine wrapper. Empty cupboards, no tea. I feel like a prisoner here. Shall I go away? (But it is time.) Afraid that I will be caught out. Afraid the pain will come again—and the fear is as bad as the pain. On the kitchen table there is a motorcycle helmet, a pair of black leather gloves. On the kitchen bulletin board there is a sketch of a naked man, muscular, sleeping on his back; a sketch of a man entering a woman from behind, her breasts pendulous, their bodies forming two perfect ellipses; a snapshot of St. John, overexposed; a scrawled verse from an ode of Horace, who evidently preferred plain bread to honey cakes; a felt-pen drawing of a toy soldier; a sketch of two poodles with people's faces, one sniffing the other's anus (*I want to go home*); an Indian rupee; a picture of John Travolta cut out from a magazine. I have come all this way.

I climb the stairs to Devi's studio: A large acrylic landscape; the beach at Kerela. On a chair, a pastel sketch of a naked brown boy. Three pen-and-ink drawings of a woman, two full-face, one in profile. The woman is me. A photograph, ancient, large, of an Indian man, wearing Western clothes, looking as if he were going to a costume ball and feeling foolish (Devi's father?). A photograph, ancient, small, of an Indian woman in a sari (Devi's mother). On a scarred table, a copy of the *Kamasutra*. It opens to well-worn pages: "On How a Woman Can Make Love Like a Man." I snap the book shut and return it to its place. ("The obvious solution always escapes you.") One might question why.

The phone rings as if in an empty house. A man with a working-class accent, a young voice, asks for Devi. *If this boy comes here and goes to bed with Devi I leave.*

The phone rings again.

"Devi?"

A voice I remember from the past, an impeccable upper-class accent—which owes, however, nothing to the speaker's geographic origins or his antecedents, but which is entirely a result of temperament and of a vast desire to succeed, in which desire he has succeeded. "Hello darling." Mark. Who thought he was in love with me in India. Who in any case lusted after me. He and Margaret, his aristocratic wife, long to see me, they are on their way. Stephan has told them I am here. Damn Stephan, who wishes only to be of use. Devi will have much to say on the subject of this invasion; damn him, too, and his house, in which there is not even tea.

Mark is nervous, as well he might be: I'd slept with Mark one drunken night in Bombay; it seemed easier to give in than to entertain his ceaseless importunings, also there was a certain lascivious curve to his upper lip. . . . Margaret did not know of this, which is why Mark is nervous. . . . The next day Mark sent my husband, who lay stricken with amoebic dysentery, a case of Teacher's Scotch, presumably he thought that was what I was worth. (Duty free.)

Margaret—sixty now; none of us is getting any younger—runs up the stairs, her hair a tangled mane of orange and white. "Darling!" she says breathlessly. "You were the only woman in Bombay who walked into a room with ideas of her own. The new liberationists will never understand us, darling —we figured it out all on our own. How much better to prefer the company of men. We knew that. And you liked me better

than you liked Mark. No one else does. Darling, how marvelous to see you!"

Margaret is all this time standing up, I think she will twirl like
a dervish in her rainbow-colored silk cape, under which she
wears jeans and a low-cut blouse of Indian fabric; I wonder if
she is deranged. Mark, meanwhile, is setting out cartons of
*hummus,* olives, *taramasalata,* also paper-thin Black Forest ham,
and raisin-nut salad and feta cheese and two bottles of young
white wine. Oh, Devi will not like this. Mark is foraging for
silverware and dishes while Margaret is saying: "It is all nonsense about the pill and about love children and abortion.
Absolutely marvelous to have one's menstrual period, lovely
to get angry at your husband when you have premenstrual
stress, biological rhythms are all that count. I knew that before
the libbers came along. You knew that, darling. Now they talk
about rape, but they ask for it, don't they, wearing miniskirts
and transparent blouses." Margaret's cleavage—a ragged di-
vide between withered breasts—is clearly in evidence. "It's all
individual, you see. Did it all on my own. So did you. Individual. Human liberation. I was shackled to other women at Oxford. That's why I left, you see. Of course de Beauvoir wrote
my book. I was too busy living. Imagine. Giving up the slavery
of children for that bloody fucking Sartre. To be a slave to
him." Mark and Margaret have one child. Margaret—too busy
living—has never had a job.

"Now what is it all for? I have alienated my son, who loves
only Mark. Mark likes only people who are amusing and only
people he can con." She speaks as if Mark were not there; and
then she cries. Margaret is drunk.

"Don't be bloody silly," Mark says. "Of course I like amusing people. It isn't possible to dislike people who like you. And
you have not alienated Jamie."

"Your bloody fucking charm," Margaret says. "Thank God
for you, Angela. You loved me better than you loved Mark. You
were the only woman in Bombay who walked into a room with
ideas of her own."

All this time I have said nothing.

"All I did in India was arrange flowers in vases, Margaret."

"Don't be bloody silly. You were the only woman . . . You like me, Angela," Margaret says. "Most people like Mark better."

"Bloody nonsense," Mark says. "No one I like and admire doesn't like and admire you more. I am the man you made me."

Mark is afraid that I will tell Margaret he and I have been to bed together.

"That was years ago, in Manchester," Margaret says. "Now you *are* the man you are, it's all bloody silly, and people like you better."

"How was your flight, darling?" Mark asks. He watches me carefully, as if I were a cobra coiled to spring. What a wicked man he is to think that I would tell Margaret, who used to be beautiful.

I am in the grip of a vast lethargy. Why don't I kick them out? They do not belong in my story, or in Devi's, they are nothing to do with us. I feel as if I am watching a play in which characters from another play have wandered in by accident. (Once I said to Eileen, when the curtain went down on a bad play, "I think there's been a mechanical failure. This can't be the end." "It was a mechanical failure for the curtain to go up," Eileen said dryly. Really she is not so boring as Stephan thinks she is; and why am I thinking of her?) In fact I am enjoying this diversion. I dread Devi's walking in on it, but perhaps Devi will enjoy the spectacle; who knows? The fact is I am terrified of being alone with Devi. And the further fact is that I am enjoying Mark's discomfort, it reminds me that I had a life before Devi, that men loved me and lusted after me. I am also enjoying this visible reminder of my past sins. It will help me not to bully Devi with my love, this reminder of my past sins, it will keep me humble. Who am I to whip him into shape? Of course none of this may account for my tolerating Margaret and Mark, perhaps it is only Demerol that governs my actions. Devi will call me Bette Davis, of that I am sure.

Margaret, the ravaged beauty, says, "Pernicious, this about lesbians. Girls used to have crushes on other girls and took it for what it was. Now they think they're homosexuals. I quite understand bisexuals. But homosexuality deprives one of the truest *meant* relationship. . . ."

"I think bisexuality is boring," I say; "like Switzerland."

Devi is standing in the door.

"Where, I wonder, is the bread knife?" Mark asks. And then he greets Devi as charmingly as if this were his house and he the host.

Devi returns Mark's greeting perfunctorily. He picks up a bottle of cognac, from which Margaret has been drinking. It bears an airport duty-free label. "Presumably you bought this for me?" he says.

"Darling! I didn't know you were Indian!" Margaret exclaims.

"Won't you have some feta?" Mark says.

"We lived in Bombay. . . ."

"How very interesting," Devi says. "You have had your Indian Experience."

"And you?" says Mark. "Have you gone back, then?"

"No."

"I find that the most interesting thing about contemporary life is . . ."

"Yes, tell me, please," Devi says, looking—glaring—at me. "I do so love to hear English intellectuals on the subject of contemporary life."

Devi has not yet greeted me. Where Devi and I are concerned, time does not exist.

"Are you Angela's friend?" Margaret asks. "You're giving her a bloody fucking rude welcome, she is wonderful. She is the only woman who walked into a room in Bombay . . ."

"Yes, do tell me I'm rude. I quite like hearing I'm rude in my own kitchen. It makes a change."

Margaret is carrying on, another diatribe about the "libbers."

Devi is wearing a loose Indian shirt, a vest, and khaki pants. His beauty is undiminished.

"You, my darling, are young," says Margaret to Devi. "I am an old woman. I *can* be rude. Angela is my oldest friend. I love her, you see."

"Young? That's relative, surely." Devi's accent is now BBC. "I am just younger than you. I may be allowed, I assume, to have my own opinions."

"I speak," Margaret says, "from my experience and my perceptions."

"Who else's? Your perceptions are the only ones available to you. I should love to hear them, but I must go to the laundry. And I must wash this proletariat grime off myself. . . . Perhaps some other time."

Mark, pouring oil on troubled waters, offers Devi food and wine, not understanding that Devi is bound to hate anyone carelessly rich enough to squander money on fancy food.

A tiny insect comes to rest on Margaret's breast. Mark casually brushes it away. This gesture—this proprietary gesture, this tender reflex gesture that says *husband-wife*—excites me to envy so profound I feel that I shall weep. And all the while they are quarreling. If only Devi would touch me like that—there—all pain would go away.

And Devi leaves.

Searching for a neutral topic after Devi left (no laundry bag in hand), I said: "Moro's body was found when I was in Paris."

Mark says: "It's an occupational hazard for politicians."

"But it was a symbolic death, the churches were full."

"An old fart," Margaret mutters. "Darling."

"I can't pretend the bloody terrorists are worse than Moro, can I?" Mark says. "They're all the same people. If you are a pacifist you are permitted to deplore Moro's death. If not, you have no right to speak."

Then he talks about the IRA, the PLO, and Welsh coal miners. How could I ever have thought this man was interesting? Margaret agrees with Mark, with everything that he says; it is only about their lives that they quarrel.

Margaret understands that she is drunk and lurches off to bed, Devi's bed. (I will pay for this.)

Margaret is cracked. (But: "How is it possible to dislike anyone who likes you?" Who said that?) I pity her. My loving feeling for her is adulterated by contempt.

Mark carries on about Welsh coal miners, assiduously avoiding all references to the past; his knuckles, however, as he holds his wine glass, are white: fear.

"You were rotten in bed," Mark says. "You simply lay there."

"I was thinking of England."

"Why your husband put up with you I'll never know."

"That's right. You'll never know. And I'd cool it with the Welsh coal miners, if I were you. Devi has a violent temper, Welsh coal miners are not his thing. Why not practice now for his arrival? Tell me about your latest venture in the world of finance."

Mark, who could not resist talking about his money and success, told me about his latest venture in the world of finance, Welsh coal miners far from his mind.

Margaret, looking blanched and chastened, rejoined us: "Terribly sorry, darling, no idea I was so pissed."

Devi returned.

"We're still here, you see." This was Mark.

"You'd hoped we'd buggered off." This was Margaret.

"I did wonder if you'd still be here, yes."

Mark switched on his charm. "I so much like the drawing of the toy soldier. How was it done?"

"Felt pen on hardboard."

"I collect toy soldiers."

"How very interesting."

"How was it done?"

"Felt pen on hardboard."

"Might I persuade you to part with it?"

"No."

"On hardboard, is it?"

"I can't say hardboard more than three times, can I?"

"Won't you have dinner with us tomorrow at Simpson's?"

"No."

"Perhaps at Shezan?"

"No."

"Darling, you must," says Margaret to me.

Reluctantly I agree.

And so life has once again offered me a diversion. Perhaps all conversation is a diversion. Devi has often said so. But if so, from what does it divert? My heart is not in Aldo Moro. It was, in Paris; then it was real. Talking about it here is not real.

I go to sleep—these sheets smell of mildew; I do not dream of Devi.

I do begin to doubt the seriousness of my purpose.

What mission am I on?

Afterward: "Devi, I'm sorry."

"Oh, why? Are you trying to get me to demand an apology? I won't, you know. I have no wish for an apology from you."

No wish for anything from me.

"But you were invaded."

"Not at all. You have every right to entertain guests. I thought you might use the kitchen as your salon, and your bedroom—your own apartment, don't you see? I'd thought of staying with friends and letting you have the run of the flat. Silly to squander money on an hotel. That was surely the reason you came here, wasn't it, to save money on an hotel?"

"Yes," I said; meaning No.

"Ah."

"I don't want to entertain."

"No? An American girl rang you up, by the way. Very cheerful . . . How are you, anyway? You're looking well."

All this time Devi has not sat down. His beauty is undiminished.

"I've never looked worse."

"Yes, now that you mention it . . ."

The Demerol is wearing off.

"You're not very fit, are you?" Devi says. "You don't take exercise, and if you're going to be greedy, you might as well be honestly greedy. You say you eat all the time, but one never *sees* you eat. Did you model yourself after Margaret, by the way?"

"I keep a ledger."

"A ledger?"

"I keep count of calories in a ledger."

"Amusing. In a revolting kind of way. Even as to food you are a capitalist. Did you model yourself after that woman?"

"I learned from her in India."

"What."

"That I could have opinions of my own."

"Surely you were born knowing that. Strident and aggressive. You. Her. Two women in my house at the same time. I thought I behaved very well. Why are you drinking wine and milk?"

"I hadn't noticed that I was. What is it you hate about me most, Devi?"

"Your schizophrenia. And all your cigarettes. I steeled myself against your stubbing out cigarettes half-smoked and smoking with your meals."

"What schizophrenia?"

"No discussions, Angela. Beware of people carrying ideas. Beware of ideas carrying people. So. How are you?"

"How are you?"

"As you find me."

"Doing?"

"Apprenticing to a landscape artist. 'Please, may I plant a pansy here?' I fancy it. An occupation fit for a queen."

"And did you say, 'Hello, I'm Devi, a happy homosexual, and may I have a job?' Where's St. John?"

"Something like that, yes."

"Where's St. John?"

"Not here, as you can plainly see. And I teach. At St. Katharine Docks."

St. John is gone with the wind.

"What about painting?"

"Nothing you'd want to hang on your wall. Small things." Liar.

"I haven't painted since you've been gone." Liar. "My life is my art. See? See how I walk, isn't it beautiful?"

"Devi, how about sitting down?"

"I don't like sitting."

"I don't like crouching, but I've got a muscle spasm. . . ." I crouched on all fours. The pain was intense. On a scale of one to ten: Unbearable.

"Could you give me my purse? The pink pills?"

"A muscle spasm as a result of overindulgence? Can you talk in that position? You can talk in any position. I quite enjoy watching you." Devi swallowed two Demerols—"to keep you company . . . I like the way you write, a certain fluid grace. I don't like what you say. I'm not very interested in your work."

"Could you give me a Demerol?"

"What is it that anybody needs to say that's so important? I only talk when you are here, to keep you company."

"Devi, I need a Demerol."

Devi lies down on the floor and puts a Demerol in my mouth. "Would you like a cigarette?" he says. "I've bought you a carton of Piccadillies."

"Why?"

"You wanted them. . . . If it's art, one doesn't use it to pay the gas and electric, if you use art to pay bills it is by definition no longer art. I prefer my kind of whoring. Are you here to work, by the way?"

The muscle is still held in its vise of pain. From this position I talk. Devi's face is directly below mine, its perspective distorted by my pain.

"Devi, I have to breathe in through my nose and out through my mouth to ease the pain," I say, every word intensifying the pain—which, as quickly as it appeared, now goes away, leaving only a faint throbbing. I sit up. Devi remains on his back. He is talking, talking, talking, about the futility of words.

"How do you communicate?" I say. "No words? No art?"

"Why communicate?"

"Don't you ever want to? . . . If you're a whore, what am I?"

"A whore. Perhaps it becomes you better. You do it more gracefully than I."

"Devi, could we sit on chairs?"

"You said, 'I only lie about small things.' That made my hair stand on end. I thought about it for three months."

"Nobody thinks about what I say for three months."

"Who is to say what things are small?"

"Devi, I'm sitting on a chair. If you'll help me up."

"I'm going to the pub."

"I'm going to bed."

"Good. I bought three paperbacks for you."

"But you hate words."

"But I love you."

"How else could I support Lucy, Devi? I'd make a lousy waitress."

"You chose. At some point you made a conscious decision that words were your medium."

"A despicable choice?"

"No. Simply an unimportant one."

"Did I hear you say you loved me?"

"That's the trouble with words."


Devi returned after midnight. I was sitting up in bed reading *One Hundred Years of Solitude,* and feeling not up to it. "This book gives me an inferiority complex," I said; and Devi spilled six more packs of Piccadilly cigarettes on to my lap.

The phone rang.

"Where would you like to go?" I hear Devi say; his voice is sweet. "What would you like to do?" His voice is tender. Whoever is on the other end of the phone I wish to kill.

"Thanks for the cigs, Devi."

"I'm not ready for bed yet. Talk to me."

Devi sits on the bureau, where he has arranged brandy, wine, and coffee.

"A joint?" he asks.

"Ummm."

Brandy, wine, coffee, a joint. Demerol. Devi talks: He wants to erase-efface the ego. Erase-efface, dear me, how he carries on. I have never laughed at Devi, but now laughter is welling up in me. I douse the irresistible urge with words:

"Only somebody with an enormous ego or an ego very much infatuated with itself would go on and on about its own destruction." Or maybe, it occurs to me (sobering thought),

someone with no ego at all. "Oh Devi, you do go on and on.
You do think of yourself all the time, don't you?"

"Yes," he says. "I do. Do you think I should get a haircut?
When Stephan was here he said I looked like the Wild Child.
What d'you think?"

"No haircut."

"Actually, I ought to get a haircut. . . . You're better than
most," Devi says, and leaves his perch on the bureau to put his
head on my lap. What gesture is appropriate? He has frozen all
my gestures. Fierce love returning, I place my hand on his
coarse and wavy hair.

"Devi?"

"Hmmm?"

"Is it OK to laugh at you?" In fact I want to cry.

"Oh, yes, that's all that can be done with me. Far better"—
he is now kneeling beside the bed, rolling another joint—"far
better than your hysteria, your possessive love, your manipu-
lating."

"I never manipulated. I was never devious, I was never
cunning."

"I felt manipulated. . . . Do you want to come with me day
after tomorrow and see my students' work? Talk to them about
art? . . . When you tell me I am angry, I am angry. When you
apologize, I feel that you have done something for which to
apologize. . . ."

Poor Devi, he is telling me that he is what I make him feel; he
is afraid I am creating him. Is this what he means when he says
I have damaged him? Surely my powers are not so great.

"I sometimes talk to this bed where you are lying; there is
never anyone to talk to."

("The obvious solution always escapes you.")

Keep me in your life, love me! I want to say. But the word
"love" no longer resonates with desire. But what if I stop
loving him? Will I damage him more?

"Yes," I say. "I'll come with you the day after tomorrow. My
grandmother used to call the day after tomorrow 'next tomorrow.'"

Our laughter—we are smoking our third joint—spirals upward.

"Devi, I have two questions: Could you live without a book
or a poem?"

"Yes."

"Liar. And in which bathroom do I shit? This one or the one
upstairs. Do I move at your convenience?"

This seems immensely funny—what good grass; we hug
each other laughing.

"How I love you," Devi says.

"Say it again."

"Let me count the ways."

"Why were you so mean before?"

"Why not? You use me as an hotel. . . ."

"Oh that's bullshit. You know that's bullshit. You treated me
like a stranger."

Devi's face darkens. I know what he will say before he says it.
(Let him for once disappoint me. Let me not anticipate him.
. . . Am I getting bored?)

"*You* define friendship," Devi says, just as I knew he would;
"*you* define love, always *you*. You define *me.*"

"Boring boring boring, Devi, half of what you say is pretend.
Fuck off."

"No histrionics? No fights? Is this you?"

"I only like fights when they lead to bed. As foreplay."

"You're laughing at me."

"Yes."

"I like you this way," Devi says; and he laughs too. "You
have to tell me when I mean what I say. I'm out of practice."


In the morning Devi is easy and cheerful, as ordinary as
bread. I am not bored.

"I quite liked your friend Margaret," he says.

And he goes whistling off to work.

I peel the adhesive tape off; odd, I feel no pain.

# Chapter Two

"The sight of all those stairs gravely walking upstairs forever and ever is calculated to seriously shock a man of nervous temperament, and is a thing to be avoided by one of uncertain or unsteady vision."—*Vanity Fair,* 1911, on the occasion of the installation of an escalator in Earl's Court Tube Station.

I had that day an engagement to have tea in Islington with the Stuntman's mother, which appointment I was not letting Devi in on, Devi having chosen not to mention the Stuntman since my arrival, Devi having chosen to act as if he had never existed —with which game I played along.

I spent the early part of the day making my way slowly from Belgravia to Cheyne Walk.

"A perfect day for walking," the housekeeper, who seemed suddenly to have acquired English, had said; by which she meant it was not pouring rain. In fact—I have noticed this phenomenon before, but hesitate to speak of it, since it seems mildly nuts, even to me—the weather put me in mind of a log-cabin quilt, bands (ribbons) of weather: snappy sunshine in Belgravia; in Pimlico a white hole in the silver sky where presumably the sun was; in Chelsea and on the Embankment a pewter sky, the air sweet and moist. By the time I reached Cheyne Walk, the inside of my head felt something like a crazy quilt, which perhaps had something to do with last night's brandy, wine, grass. And Demerol.

I love London.

I stopped at churches on the way, partly in anticipation of a visit with the Stuntman's mother, a pious widowed Roman

Catholic who, though she deplored my having lived In Sin with
her son, had at one time believed that I might bring him back
to the Church, fat chance.

I especially love Cheyne Walk, though Devi makes terrible
noises about its chichi trendiness, never mind that he lives in
Belgravia, hardly prole.

At Albert Bridge I found a cab—the vast extravagance of a
taxi to Islington (where the Stuntman's mother lived above an
eel-and-pie shop in two tiny, impeccably clean and cluttered
rooms) owing to my fear of escalators and my sure knowledge
that a ride on the Tube would be rewarded by a muscle spasm.

The flat smelled like a charnel house. We had our parsimoni-
ous tea, during which I heard many words about Saint Jude,
and was shown pictures of the baby Stuntman naked on a
bearskin rug. The Stuntman's mother showed me a picture of
her taken long ago by Cecil Beaton; for she had married into
money, though her husband had lost it all—or so she said—
"on alcohol and the dogs," which seemed highly improbable
to me; but I have known stranger things to happen. We talked
about the Stuntman—I reported that he had been respectably
employed, a lie, and that he had gone to Mass, also a lie. This
lightened her grief considerably. Living above an eel-and-pie
shop, she needed all the cheer she could get, so I felt little
guilt. And, cheered by me and grateful to me, she gave me a
pink-gold brooch with seed pearls and a bit of lovely old lace. I
kissed her dusty cheek good-bye. "Write me! Pray for him!"
she said; and duty done, I went in search of a taxi.

No taxi.

I walked to Angel Tube. One look down the escalator was
enough. I must wait for a taxi.

No taxi.

I waited at a busy intersection for an hour, panic rising. Here
I shall stand, I thought, until my flesh is reduced to a mound of
ash, and no one will remember me. Why had I lied? Why had I
accepted the brooch? What possible justification could there
have been for bringing false comfort to an old lady with whose
son I had done unholy things in bed? Here I shall stand, where

the High Street meets Pentonville Road and City Road, forever.

In an effort to distract myself, I went into a hole-in-the-wall
shop where a lazy orange cat lay on the counter and bought a
picture of the fire of London for Lucy, who would not love it.

Next door, a dim café, where I ordered a ham sandwich and
had a muscle spasm. The counterman brought me a glass of
sweet red wine—"You look ill"—and did I know his cousin in
Newark.

"Can you call me a taxi?"

"Hold on a bit and I'll drive you there myself," he said.

"Where is there?" I said; he called me a private taxi and
would not accept any money from me. Perhaps he thought I
was dying. I felt as if I were. The taxi cost twenty dollars in
American money, and I arrived at Devi's house exhausted and
violently self-reproachful, hating my body, prepared for the
worst.

"How was your day?" beautiful Devi said, "my love?"

"Good," I said.

"How spent?"

"Walking, and tea with the American girl"—whose identity
was still a mystery to me—"in Islington."

Sometimes Devi's lack of curiosity is a boon. He asked no
questions about the American girl with the perky voice who'd
rung his house and asked for me.

"How was your day?"

"Nasty," Devi said equably. "A stupid woman who thinks
she knows all about gardens, why does she employ a gar-
dener?"

Well, of course; women are the caretakers of the world, easy
to blame them when the garden grows wild—or when they
wish to tame it. I told Devi about the escalator and the taxi,
omitting to say how much the taxi had cost.

"And you say *I'm* mad," Devi said.

"I never said any such thing."

"Mad," Devi said.

"Well, but functioning. I got here, after all."

"Functioning within your madness. The way Stephan functions within his."

"Why bring Stephan into it? You think I'm mad because anyone who could love you must be crazy, which proves that *you* are mad."

"Is that something you wrote for a woman's magazine? Have a joint," Devi said.

"In what way am I mad?"

"Divest yourself of all things," Devi said. "Divest yourself of Lucy, friends, and work." He was rolling another joint.

"That's mad. What's that paper you're rolling the grass in?"

"A page from the Bible."

"Jesus."

"Ezekiel, actually."

"Why should I divest myself?"

"Talk to me," Devi said.

"Do you want to hear a quote from Tagore? I found it on a plaque in a church and I wrote it down."

"Read me a quote from Tagore," said Devi, who was once again supine on the kitchen floor.

" 'We are not beggars. Pain is the hard coin which must be paid for everything valuable in this life, for our power, our wisdom, our love.' And in the same church it said the vicar died 'whilst fire watching.' How about sitting up?"

"Balls," Devi said. "Christian masochism, exalting suffering. Balls."

"Rabindranath Tagore was not a Christian, Devi."

"Balls," Devi said. "Going in search of pain."

"That's exactly not the point. The point is that since suffering will come to us whether we search for it or not—who searches?—we might as well make use of it."

"Capitalist rubbish," Devi said. "Even pain is a commodity you put to use."

"May I remind you again that Tagore was an Indian?"

"What if I said to you that your Catholic Church was made for fortyish divorcees?"

"What if I said to you that my Catholic Church was made for freaky fags?"

"Yes, yes. For them, too. I'd agree." Devi rose and disappeared into the drawing room.

"What are you doing?"

"Lighting incense for you. Because you can't believe in God without the trappings."

Devi hands me a picture, an insipid picture of Saint Francis of Assisi surrounded by pink flamingoes.

"Where did you get this junk?"

"What does it mean, to be part of the Body of Christ? How can you allow yourself to be discriminating, belonging to your silly Church? Nevertheless," Devi says, "I wrote to Stephan on the basis of your Christian intervention. To thank him for his check. I didn't mail the letter."

Devi, whose beauty had gone a long way to convince me of the reality of God, also convinces me of the reality of the Devil, for whom I sometimes think he speaks.

Now so stoned as to be unavailable for ordinary human conversation, Devi is lying on the velvet drawing room couch.

I too am stoned. "I like that Kantha cloth hanging," I say.

"Don't remark on everything," Devi says. "Noticing is the first step toward analyzing. You analyses are as insipid as this picture of Saint Francis" (which he tears in half).

The phone rings.

"For you, I suppose," Devi says.

A woman asks for Devi.

"A woman with an Indian accent is asking for you, Devi."

"My sister. Tell her I'm not at home. Ring off."

"How do you know it's your sister? How many sisters do you have, Devi? How many brothers?"

"What it is that I hate about you is your ambition," Devi says.

"My ambition is to stay alive."

"I want to go through life leaving no mark."

"I'd say you were well on your way."

"I despise your too many words."

"I know you do."

"Why do you stay when I treat you like this?"

"Because I love you. Because nothing you can do to me can hurt me."

At that stoned moment it seemed to me I had found a key: If I did not allow Devi to hurt me, Devi would not be the hurtful, hurting person he is. I would prove to him that nothing he could do would hurt me. I would submit to anything. At another moment, I might have called this masochism. But I didn't want to be hurt; I wanted, for his sake, not to hurt, even if he inflicted pain. That is what I thought. I love him because he loves me and doesn't love me. That is what I also thought. Like the man who killed himself, he loves me and doesn't love me; I am familiar with this.

"Mad," Devi said. "What do you love about me?"

"What there is to love."

"I want to tell you a story about butter," Devi says.

"Tell me a story about butter."

"Common Market. Britain sold butter to Russia which sold it to Poland which sold it back to Britain. At twice the price. Is that mad?"

"I'd say so. If you have your facts right. Russia, however . . ."

"It's mad," Devi said. "And you have so often told me that I talk pretentious crap when I say the people inside the asylums are sane and you people outside who run the world are crazy."

"You were. You are. Talking pretentious crap."

"Madness."

"Russia, however, is not part of the Common Market."

"I wouldn't have celibacy as a gift," Devi says. "I am having sex. Teilhard is unreadable—conversion through the mails, I wish you'd stop. I am having sex. Often. Are you?"

I am silent. Devi is right: It is not good for me to be alone.

"I am not running the world, Devi."

"Shall I count for you the ways in which I am having sex?"

"No thank you, Devi."

"So much of sex is masturbation. Lonely people should masturbate together." Devi gives me an appraising look. "I am coming to think," he says, "that masturbation is better than sex."

"No." But a mild excitement disturbs my marijuana torpor.

"No? I am growing disappointed in men."

"In males? Mankind?"

"Men. They only want to talk about themselves. The moment you say the word *I* . . . Women, they are wonderful. They always listen. I was in my element in your house, Angie."

"You've never called me Angie before."

"I've never loved you so much before."

"When you say lonely people should masturbate together . . ."

The doorbell rang.

Margaret and Mark.

"Devi, *please* come with us."

"Stoned," Devi said.

"I don't want to be with them, Devi, please."

"Discuss contemporary life with Mark."

"I hate Mark."

"Christian charity. Stay home with me."

"How can I? They've come all this way."

"You are stoned, you are mad, and you are not very clever," Devi said.

"Tell me you love me. Wait up for me. . . ."

"Toodle-oo."

"Mark has shaved his legs," Margaret said.

"What for?"

"He is in love with a woman who does not like hairy legs. She is twenty-three. He has never been unfaithful to me before."

"I am not unfaithful, Margaret. I have never been unfaithful to you."

"I believe him, Margaret. But why did you shave your legs, Mark?"

# *Chapter Three*

At breakfast, Devi said: "The shavings the sculptor leaves on the floor are more important than the sculpture. Not to try is the way to succeed. . . ."

"I don't understand modern sculpture."

"That is one of your minor charms. . . . For example, the bazaars in India have not been designed by Corbusier. And yet in every way they please the senses. . . ."

"Like the New York skyline, hodgepodge and perfect—no one could have planned it. . . ."

"Yes. And Chor Bazaar."

"Yes. And bargaining in the bazaar, choreographed conversation."

"A way to become involved and yet to remain distanced," Devi said.

"That, as you once said in another context, is like trying to walk on both sides of the street at the same time."

"Hmmm. Are you good at it?"

"Becoming involved and remaining distanced?"

"Bargaining."

"Yes. I especially loved it in North Africa, all those cups of sweet tea, the ceremony. The tea got sweeter as the price went down. My husband thought bargaining was a form of swindling. He gave the dealers the first price they asked for."

"Depriving them of their pleasures," Devi said.

"Yes. And thinking he was fair."

"You were graceful at it," Devi said.

"How can you know?"

"How funny you are. . . . How were Meg and Mark?"

"Boring."

"Good."

"We ate well, though. I used to think they were exciting when we lived in India. Now for the life of me I can't see why. Last night Mark said, 'Yesterday is past, tomorrow is yet to come, live for the moment.' Imagine. He talks like a fortune cookie. I must have been out of my mind."

"You were younger then."

"Maybe some people have to be transplanted in order to be interesting." But what had interested me in Mark—and in his son—was sex.

"He's sexy," Devi said.

"No he isn't, he shaves his legs."

"Oh," Devi said, stretching, "my creaky old bones. I creak in bed. 'Try this position.' Creak. My knees crack. And you'd think after all the gardening I'd be limber."

"That doesn't matter when you're in bed with someone you love. Like cellulite."

"What is cellulite?"

"Something we Americans have invented, fat you can't see."

"What will capitalism come up with next."

"I myself don't believe in cellulite."

"You believe in God, whom also you can't see."

My belief in God is not unrelated to my love for you, Devi; but I did not say this out loud.

"A twelve-year-old boy hanged himself in church before you came," Devi said. "He was doing a skit. He was pretending to be some martyr. He was pretending to hang himself with a rope wrapped around his chest and neck and looped over a rafter. He'd done the trick fourteen times with no hitch, and the fifteenth time he died. The chest was supposed to take all the weight. So how is there a God?"

"Usually they say earthquakes."

"Earthquakes? Have another cup of tea."

" 'If there is a God, why does he permit earthquakes?' "

"To which you answer?"

"I don't know. If there is no God, why isn't the universe all dark brown? A poet said that."

"Not a very good answer," Devi said.

"I suppose."

"What does it mean to be part of the Body of Christ? What about urine?"

"What about urine?"

"Morarji Desai drinks his own."

"Yes? So? Horrible."

"So could you drink the urine of someone you loved? If it was inert? If it was clear and sweet?"

"Devi, please, not while I'm drinking tea. . . . How would it be clear and sweet?"

"If one drank lots of water first. I've drunk my own."

"Devi, please, I'm drinking tea."

"You forget I'm Indian."

"I forget nothing. Not all Indians drink their piss."

"Not everyone says to me, I love every part of you. As you did say."

"How do you remember all the words I say?"

"I forget nothing. . . . Would you like to wash my socks? Would you get off on it?"

"Oh dear. Are we about to have a fight?"

"How funny you are," Devi said. "How beautiful you are today."

Devi, beautiful, sat contemplating the beauty no one else could see.

"One of them paints with accurate simplicity," he said.

"One of what?"

"One of my students, whom today we are to see, have you forgotten? Already we are late."

"Too late to take the Tube?"

"Too late to take a taxi."

"I think I'm going to have a muscle spasm."

"I'll bring a taxi round," said Devi, astonishing me.

"Do you want to tell me what to expect? I'm nervous. Will they hate my being there?"

"They are illustrating an article."

"Whose? What?"

"Yours."

"I thought you hated my too many words."

"No fights," said Devi; "how funny you are."

The taxi takes us to St. Katharine Docks. On one side of the river, old warehouses have been renovated at great expense: shopping arcades, flats; those who live in them can see from their arched windows the Thames, and the yacht basin, and have, for their added convenience, the Dickens Inn nearby, also a huge and fancy new hotel. Lucy would love it here. I love it here. I am already weaving a romance: a flat on St. Katharine Docks. And Devi goes so far as to buy me a pint and a plowman's lunch at the Dickens Inn (not commenting on its somewhat excessive charm), pointing out the sights without so much as a word about the inequities of capitalism. Even the guards at the Tower of London do not excite him to wrath. (No "all built on the blood and sweat of the Empire.") Lighthearted, he is treating me as fondly as he would a child.

"Do they just wait for you? Your students?"

"As they are squatters, they squat."

On the south side of the river, old warehouses present a blank and dreary face. The dreariness is punctuated by clotheslines, pots of flowers; here and there a recessed door is painted orange; red; blue. . . . It is to one of these red doors that we go, and we are greeted by the smell of paint and turps. A dozen young men and women sit or stand at easels and at tables in a huge space where the stone walls sweat, the floor planks are rotten—and everything is flooded with cool river light. A baby wearing only diapers crawls on the splintered floor: "Mama, Mama," she says to me; and Devi introduces me to "Brian, we teach together, we have totally antithetic ideas about art, good for the kids to be confused now, as they certainly shall be later." Brian is wearing a blue French workman's smock, he smiles shyly at me—he is handsome, perhaps twenty-five, and I like him immediately. The men and women (boys and girls) nod gravely and courteously to Devi, who smiles sweetly back. Then they return to work.

It is odd: I am in Devi's life.

Devi takes my hand, and leads me to a girl with long black

hair who is hunched over a rough table, drawing in pen and ink; on the table is tacked a story of mine, which she is illustrating. She tosses her hair and smiles at Devi flirtatiously; he, holding my hand, returns her smile with one of great neutrality, and, for long moments, regards her work. "Perhaps too baroque?" he says gently. "Remember" (astonishing me), " 'in the beginning was the Word.' The illustration must serve the word, no?" "Yes," she says, biting her lower lip with her teeth; "the trouble is, the baby distracts me, and when I'm distracted . . ." "When you're distracted, you get baroque, yes. Good. Good that you should know that. This is Angela." He relinquishes my hand and wanders off.

"I'm Linda," the girl says.

"Is the baby yours?"

("Mama, Mama," the baby is saying, this time to another girl; the baby is sitting in a puddle of pee.)

"Yes, the idea is that we take care of her communally, but I get distracted. . . . Devi talks about you constantly."

Devi talks about me constantly.

"He says you have a baby too."

"My daughter is seventeen."

"Are you distracted?"

"No. But then I've never had to worry about communal care."

Linda, whose pearly teeth are once again biting her lip, looks puzzled; she thinks she has not heard me correctly.

"You take care of her alone?"

"I did, yes."

"And you weren't distracted?"

"Well, I wouldn't say distracted. Absorbed in her and then absorbed in work, by turns." This was not exactly accurate, but really how silly this poor child is. "She's in college, now," I say. "Oh you must be pleased." Linda's baby is patting the puddle of pee with a fat dimpled hand; Linda thinks that the baby will never grow up, that she will never be free of her.

"Actually I miss my daughter," I say.

"You miss her?" Linda sighs.

"But it is true," I say, knowing that I have sounded smug,

"that when they're little they are always *there*, it's hard to work."

"Oh she's often off with the others," Linda says. "But I get distracted."

"What's the baby's name?"

"Rowena."

"It's nice," I say, thinking how awful it is.

"Her father chose it."

"Is her father here?"

"I think he's that one," Linda says, pointing to a man with long blond hair in a ponytail. "We think, you know, that he was the one. Anyway, he chose the name."

Rowena is tugging at Devi's trousers and saying, "Da-da, Da-da." Devi gently releases her hold on him and returns to me and Linda, thank God.

Linda tosses her hair and smiles coquettishly at Devi, who says, "Carry on," and—to me—"Come see, here." An ungainly boy in denim overalls is regarding his work dolefully. When he sees Devi, his face, an unfortunate one, lights up. "I don't know what to paint," he says. "Look at this, sophistic and simplistic." His hands, even while he speaks, are vainly trying to cover up his work (his nails are bitten to the quick). Devi grasps the boy's wrists and quickly scans his work. "It's good," he says. "Good?" "Only perhaps without enough regard to the edges of the canvas; you haven't quite defined your space." "It isn't any good," the boy says. "I shouldn't worry," Devi says. "Only bear in mind that you are troubled by a technical problem; your vision is secure." "It is?" "What do you like to read?" says Devi, he who hates words, "Tennyson," the boy says shyly; "and Tolkien." "Try *The Book of Common Prayer*," says Devi, he who does not believe in God; "for its soothing effect if for nothing else. But you will find it ennobling." "Ennobling?" The thought that he might in some way be ennobled comes to the boy as one of life's great and beautiful surprises. He blushes—which does nothing to ennoble his acne—and looks at Devi with slavish devotion and humility, a look that says, I am not worthy.

"Tell me the truth, Devi. What do you like to read?" I ask.

"*Peter Pan,* the Bible, and *The Oxford Book of English Verse.*"

"And which is your Bible?"

"*Peter Pan,* of course. . . . See how they all love you. I am wonderful when I am with you—come live here and teach with me."

"Teach what?"

"Teach me to be wonderful."

"That girl will never make an artist."

"Quite right," Devi says. "You were jealous of her."

"Yes."

"How funny you are."

"That boy, though . . ."

"Yes?"

"He needs to be fed and cared for." I am jealous of him.

"You are Candida," Devi says. "Now play with the baby, like a good girl."

Happy, I play with the baby ("Mama, Mama"), who is trailing the nipple of her bottle in pee. (Am I too old to have a child?)

Brian offers to take us home in his Mini, thank God. Devi invites Brian and Rita to dinner.

"Who is Rita?"

"His girlfriend. They live together. I like her. I like her better than I like him, he's wet. The worst thing about them is their relationship. I don't know why I invited them to dinner, what do you think?"

"Why not? . . . In New York the person you live with is called your Significant Other. I got that once on an invitation, engraved—'B.S.O.'—I had no idea what it meant: Bring Significant Other."

"What will capitalism come up with next."

"Then there's the composer who introduces his girlfriend as the 'dedicatee' of his latest score."

"What people you know. You need me."

"I've been telling you that for years."

"How wonderful I am when I am with you."

# Chapter Four

"Devi talks about you constantly," Rita says.

Devi is at the stove. ("If my mother—that bitch—can cook, why shouldn't I?")

"Oh, good, curry," Brian says.

"Gaga, goo-goo over India," Devi mutters as he stirs. "The trouble with Indian food is it always makes your asshole itch the next day."

In an extravagant mood I have bought Boodles gin, which we drink neat.

Soon Brian, unaccustomed to gin, is talking about the economy, "How hard it is to live."

"I can't remember when we had steak last, Bri, can you?" Rita is a salesclerk, her monthly salary would not keep Lucy in junk food for a week.

Devi has not provided cutlery for the curry, which puts Brian and Rita at a disadvantage.

"I try not to think about how hard it is to live," Brian says, eating curry with his left hand, to Devi's obvious displeasure. "I think of the people in Ireland, how terrible it is for them."

"Does it give you a buzz to think how terrible other people's lives are when you are enjoying your own?" says—who else?—Devi.

"I think how terrible it is for them."

"Why not do your work and leave the Irish to the Irish."

Rita says, "In Wales . . ."

"No sad songs for Welsh coal miners, please," Devi says.

"Why not?"

"If you cared about Welsh coal miners, you'd be in Wales, wouldn't you?" Devi says. "Not here."

"What nonsense," Rita says. "Do I have to live in South Africa to care about South Africans? To care about racism?"

"You say nonsense and you eat my food."

"Stop looking for a fight, Devi," Rita says; "we don't need to be entertained. Why are *you* here? Why aren't you in India, helping the oppressed?"

"My views entertain you? *I* am oppressed. Marxism . . ." Devi says; and he and Brian are off about capitalism and Karl Marx, the relationship of art to which.

Rita wants to have a baby. Rita and I talk about babies.

Before they go, Rita and Brian invite us to dinner at their house in Hampstead Heath tomorrow night.

I gird myself to face Devi's anger. He has been shouting at Brian all night.

"How wonderful I am when I am with you," Devi says. "I never get angry at them when you're not here. I need you as an ally. How they whine. Two Yorkshire flower children hustling art and politics, a way to escape their own embittered hearts."

"Why are their hearts embittered? What were you so angry about?"

"Their relationship is the worst thing about them. . . . Why the Irish? Why Welsh coal miners? Why not Indians. So cute, Welsh coal miners, How Green Is My Valley. Why not homosexuals. Oppressed because they don't have steak."

"I'll wash the dishes."

"No, you won't. I'll do the washing up. You go to bed and pray for me."

I cannot tell, from Devi's face, whether he is now angry at me. He is not: "Am I not wonderful when I am with you? To bed, Angie, perchance to dream. I love you. And you must always find me lovable, agreed?"

"Agreed."

But the next morning Devi's mood was black.

He was sitting at the table chipping away at some hash.

"Why should we go there tonight? Ostentatious to invite us. What is this? Noah's Ark? Two by two? And two nights in a row? . . . What are you doing?"

I was looking into the fridge, not seeing anything, thinking of Devi's war with himself, with me, endless; he was like a crazed rat in an intolerable cage—like two rats, the happy Devi and the angry Devi (the good Devi and the bad Devi); he will manage to erase-efface himself with all his contradictions, the question is, How long can I stand it? I have sworn that I will take anything from him. He must not be allowed to believe that he can kill me. (I want another to live as I live. I damage him.)

"Isn't tea enough for you? Your excesses have to be paid for by someone else, you know."

"Nevertheless I'm hungry."

"You were born hungry."

"I suppose so."

"What nourished you?" It is impossible to tell from the tone of his voice whether the question is a trap.

"A man I loved, books, a honeysuckle bush outside my window, a mulberry tree."

"Romantic rubbish, a honeysuckle bush. Neurotic romantic rubbish. Why not have spare opinions? Secure simplicity. 'How was the movie?'"

"How was the movie?"

"And the answer is 'good,' or 'bad.' Eradicate excess. No more words. Last night, too many opinions."

Most of them his.

"Tell me about your husband," Devi said.

"No."

"No? What is this?"

"Secure simplicity."

"Tell me about your love life."

"No."

"Tell me about sex."

"I don't talk about sex."

"You talk about sex all the time."

"Not this morning."

"In love someone is always diminished."

"Then it isn't love."

"Why aren't you married?"

"Cut it out, Devi."

"You were in love with a man who killed himself."

I spilled boiling water from the kettle on my hand: "God-damnit!"

"Did you kill him? With your possessive love?"

I had sworn I would take anything; not this.

"Why are you crying?"

"I burned my fucking hand."

"Good. If it's the right one, you won't be able to write for a while."

I headed for the bedroom, but Devi grabbed my arm and forced me to sit down. I had a muscle spasm.

"Drink your tea," Devi said.

This is only pain, I thought; it will go away. His pain is worse.

"I don't expect nourishment," Devi said; "better to be an honest hedonist . . . Well?"

"Well, what?"

"You're not going to take issue with me?"

"I have a muscle spasm."

"The result of dissipation."

"Nevertheless it hurts." The Demerol was in the bedroom.

"Wipe the sweat off your face," Devi said, handing me a napkin on which marmalade was smeared, "and talk to me."

"I can't talk."

"A novelty . . . What's that you're wearing?"

"Robe."

"Reduced to monosyllables. Will wonders never cease. I'm off to work," Devi said; "some of us do, you know. Work. Not always off on hols. Paris."

"That was work."

"I thought you couldn't talk? Did you go boohoo when Moro died? You did. You said to Brian you condemned all terrorists. What's the difference who kills whom? Or what. In India they die because you eat steak."

"I didn't say *condemn.* Terrorism is the ultimate sin against the Holy Spirit because it is despair."

"On the subject of sin your tongue is loose."

"Devi, I love you."

"Yes? I'm off to work. Among the pansies."

I got down on all fours and crept toward Demerol.

Hours later, I took a taxi to the Tate. I looked only at the Blakes and Turners, and at an oil I loved for reasons that were obscure to me: *The Cholmondeley Sisters* (twins?), propped up against white pillows, wearing ruffled white headdresses, holding on their laps two newborn babies clothed in red, stiff and formal—the sisters and the babies too. The sisters' expressions are almost, but not quite, identical. Twins giving birth to cousins who might as well be twins. No loneliness in that house of mirrors. So why do the women look grim? I am enchanted by this doubleness, perplexed by the sisters' unsmiling mouths.

In the gift shop of the Tate I bought Lucy a poster of a Turner, and a tote bag. I debated with myself whether to buy Devi a present, and decided against. On the way home (home?) I stopped at a jeweler's and bought Lucy a gold Dunhill lighter, secondhand.

"What's that?"

"A lighter for Lucy, secondhand."

"Wonderful. To fuel her addiction. Lucy smokes?"

"Lucy smokes. So do you, I notice."

"But I don't pretend to be a Christian."

The doorbell rang.

"Off to your room," Devi said; "it's Jake." Cinderella.

Into the kitchen came a man of sixty or more, Indian.

Devi shut my door securely.

Who is this man? And why can't I go into the kitchen to get the gin, which I have bought. Why am I here, invisible? To whom would I be an embarrassment? To a lover? In his present mood, Devi would flaunt a lover. A colleague? He'd introduce me. A brother! ("How many brothers and sisters do you have, Devi?") Petty to want the gin, which I have bought. The hell with this, I am going to a hotel. What is it that I do, what is it that I am, that turns Devi into the Devil?

I hear the murmur of their voices. A laugh. A door slamming.

"Come out, come out, wherever you are."

"Come in here, Devi, I'm lying down."

Devi comes into the bedroom obligingly, sits on the bureau. (There are, in this room, three chairs. To say nothing of my bed.)

"Who was that man?"

"Jake. A cousin."

"An Indian named Jake? A blood cousin? Or cousin as in India, to mean close friend?"

"Jake, a cousin."

"How many cousins do you have, Devi? How many brothers?"

"He's had a heart attack. The doctor told him to cut down on sex. So I'm getting cut out. It will all go to his wife now. He'll bugger her now."

"I don't believe you."

I turn on my stomach and fall asleep.

"It will all end in sleep," I hear—I think I hear—Devi's voice say as I drift off.

Hours later Devi woke me up gently; then—understanding that I was fully awake and only pretending still to be asleep for the pleasure of his hand on my shoulder—he shook me roughly.

"Time to get ready for your soiree," he said.

"Are you ready?"

"I'm not going."

"Why? If you're not, I'm not."

"Then ring them up and tell them so," Devi said.

"Why me? You should."

"Not I."

"Rita's making a special dinner, she told me."

"Eat for two."

"If you're not going, I'm not going, and I'm not calling, either."

Devi yanked the pillow out from underneath my head, exited, and slammed my bedroom door.

He's off to the pub, I thought; whatever did I hope to accomplish? Is loving him a sin? It brings him so much misery. Is it presumptuous of me to think of myself as the source of his misery? The evidence is confusing. Could I love him without making demands? But what demands have I placed upon him lately? To try to hold him to a dinner engagement with his own friends is hardly a voracious demand. Would my prayers do him more good than my presence? But it is always he who breaks the silence, though he says he hates my words.

I was writing a letter to Father Caldwell ("I do what I want to, Eugene, whether I want to or not, and then I give myself fancy reasons for doing it") when Devi, without knocking, walked in.

"To whom?"

"The letter? To a friend."

"Of course a friend. What friend?"

"My confessor."

"What do you have to confess?"

"I was telling him about the weather."

"You lie not beautifully."

"I know."

"Do I want to read it?" Devi said.

"What kind of question is that?"

"In England husbands used to have the right to read their wives' letters."

"You're not my husband, however."

"But I am taking you out to dinner, what rights does that give me?"

"Where are we going to dinner?"

"To Brian's house."

"Oh. I thought you weren't going. Do you want to read the letter?"

"Is it about me?"

"More about me. Also about you."

"Then not."

"Why not?" Now I was as eager for Devi to read the letter as I had earlier been to hide it from him. After all, to all my questions only Devi could provide the answers.

"I am afraid," Devi said.

"Oh, Devi, afraid of what?"

"How can you love me. Get dressed."

"How deep is the escalator at the Hampstead stop?"

"No escalator, a lift."

"But we'd have to ride the escalator to get the train there."

"More than one, it's on the Northern Line, we'd have to change."

That does it, I thought. He'll never agree to take a taxi all the way to Hampstead. I'll get a speech about starving tonga drivers, and then he'll go to the pub; what had I hoped to accomplish?

"We'll take a taxi," Devi said.

In the taxi, passing Regent's Park, "I wish I could describe in words the quality of that light," I say. "The shadows on the grass. Henry James said 'summer afternoon' were the most beautiful words in the language. Monet . . ."

"Why? Why James? Why Monet? It's hubris to think that people need help to see. Vanity. One of your seven deadly sins. A cretin could see the shadows on the grass without your help."

"Why don't you make up your mind whether you're going to be nice to me tonight or hateful? Because I feel like I'm being bounced on my head."

For the rest of the long ride, Devi said not a word.

From the open windows of the tiny house in Hampstead Heath, voices floated out to us: "Soutine . . . more expression in a side of beef . . . Warhol . . . decorative . . . earthworks . . ." Devi, scowling to begin with, looked more and more ferocious as Rita's footsteps approached the door; I was sure he'd leave—he was not disposed to talk of art.

Rita greeted me with a kiss. Devi grunted.

"You look Heathcliffian tonight, Devi," Rita said. "Cheer up."

Devi grunted.

Madras-covered mattresses all over the floor, candlelight and incense.

Devi: "What's this?"

"Gin," Brian said, smiling shyly at me.

"To impress our American guest?"

"This is Billy," Rita said, nodding to a boy in the corner who was holding in his hands a human skull with a peacock feather in its eye socket.

"May I hold it?" I said. The skull, so smooth, was comforting (it will all end in sleep). Billy—who he was and what he did was not made clear—said, "Death isn't all it's cracked up to be. A fellow in the hospital says, he says like this: 'I've had enough of this,' and he rolls over and dies. Simple as kiss your aunt goodbye."

Brian says: "I don't think it will come that easily to me."

Devi, lying with his eyes closed, on the floor, says, "That's a form of vanity."

"What is?"

Devi doesn't answer.

In three days I am flying home (what had I hoped to accomplish?). "I'm afraid of planes," I say. "Imagine knowing you were going down. A minute would be too long."

"Bless your heart," Rita says; "I'll pray for you."

"Vanity," Devi says. "Make up your mind whether to be afraid of planes or of dying of dissipation. You can't have it both ways."

"Will you Rita? Oh, I'm glad."

"Funny about church—I never go," says Rita, "but when I die, I want everything, last rites, the Mass, everything. I shouldn't feel right if I didn't."

"You'll be in no condition to feel anything."

"You know what I mean."

"I'd accept absolution from you, Rita," Brian says. "Does it really matter who does it? Does it have to be a priest? God is a God of mercy."

"Also a God of judgment," Rita says, and I agree: "I want the whole works, too. It's not something I like to think about, but He is also a God of wrath, and I've given Him plenty of occasion."

"You, as usual, have it backward," says Devi, who is contriving to drink his gin while lying down. *"Not* quick to wrath."

"I agree with Angela," Rita says.

"Naturally."

"Call me Angie."

"The Crucifixion bit has been overdone, that," Billy says.

"And the baby will be baptized," Rita says.

"Are you really having a baby? How wonderful! I haven't seen one child on Devi's street. It's so nice to see kids on bikes here. . . . When?"

"I want to have a baby, but I can't get maternity leave," Rita says, "and it's hard enough to live."

Devi balances his glass of gin, which he has replenished, on his stomach (no longer hard and flat): "You see this stomach? No womb. So I can't have a baby. Unfair, uneven distribution of goods. How women carry on."

Rita subdues her chortle with a gulp of gin. "Be responsible and adopt one, Devi," she says.

"Vanity."

"In this case," Rita says, "you can't argue that uneven distribution of goods is a capitalist conspiracy. There are some problems Marx can't solve."

"Producing future commodities for the labor market," Devi says.

Rita says, "Is that what you see when you see a kid on a bike? A commodity for capitalism?"

"In America there was a big court case because men got insurance money and leave for hair transplants, but corporations wouldn't give medical insurance or leave for maternity. We won."

*"You* won? As I am not likely," Devi says, "to have either a hair transplant or a baby, what is there for me? Why can I not get leave for something that doesn't result in a product? Angela?" He glares.

"Of course," I say; lying. What would Devi get leave *from*. To do what? "What did you think I'd say?"

"I was hoping you'd agree," he says, all mildness. Devi doesn't know when I am lying.

When Rita goes into the kitchen, I follow her. Brian follows us.

"I don't know how to say this, Angela," Rita says, "but stay here tonight, please. He's dangerous."

"Who?" Brian says; and Rita answers, "Your innocence is unbelievable. Unforgivable. Devi is dangerous. Anyone can see he's mad."

"It's terribly hard to be gay," sweet Brian says. "And we're all a little mad." He has a point.

"Go back to the men," Rita says.

"I wonder. Do I make him nuts because he's gay, or is he gay because he's nuts? Or would he be nuts no matter what. He was so kind at St. Katharine Docks. And sane."

"Well, what does it matter *why*. I'm afraid of him."

"But you like him."

"That's what I don't understand," Rita says. "I do. We borrowed money from him once—a hundred quid—and he's turned against us ever since. We paid it back."

"Would he have turned against you anyway? Did he use the money as an excuse?" When it comes to money, Devi is pathological. But then so many people are, and we don't call them mad. "Why are you afraid of him?"

"That's what I don't understand," Rita says. "Everyone who loves him, he hates."

"Yes."

"Will you stay, then?"

"You won't have much of a friendship left with him if I stay, will you?"

"It doesn't matter, really. He'll find a way to feel betrayed no matter what anybody does. Bri thinks I'm hysterical. He doesn't understand why I should be afraid of Devi. But then Brian's a man—they never do."

"I don't think you're hysterical. But I don't think I'll stay, either."

In the parlor, where we eat with our plates in our laps, Billy and Devi are discussing "rational suicide"—"a contradiction in terms," I say.

"A sin," Rita says.

"My old mum was an invalid for years," Billy says. "She wanted to die, we didn't have the wherewithal. She'd have been happier dead. Life isn't all it's cracked up to be."

"She probably thought *you'd* be happier with her dead," Rita says.

Brian—incapable of attributing unkindness to anyone—mutters, "Not at all, not at all."

"How sentimental men are," Rita says. "They don't have logical minds."

"And yet you love us," Devi says.

"What choice do we have?"

"You could always kill yourself."

"Or go bowling."

"I want a good death," Brian says.

"Vanity."

"What is a good death? You mean a dignified death, Bri. I mean dying in a state of grace. I don't go in much for dignity."

"Vanity and balls, I'm going off to the pub," Devi says.

"Conversation never seems the same without Devi," Brian says.

"I for one don't miss him at all," Rita says. "His conversation isn't all it's cracked up to be." I long for Devi to come back. No matter what his mood.

"Too late," he says, when he returns, "for the Tube." As if it were our fault.

When Rita and I kiss good-bye, she says: "Devi has always held you up as a kind of artifact. A Lady Journalist. We were terrified of meeting you. . . . Will we see you again?"

"I don't know. Everything depends on Devi."

Billy—who lives God knows where—drives us home. No words.

"If you'd stop smoking, you'd stop wheezing up the stairs," says Devi.

"I see you've made your decision. To be unkind."

" 'Hateful' was your word. Have some brandy. What did

they think they were doing, gin. And cake. They can't afford gin, 'How hard life is.' "

"On the other hand, there was only one piece of meat in my shepherd's pie."

"Good night, Angela."

"I haven't finished my brandy."

"Good night."

But I sat in the kitchen and finished my brandy, and then I tiptoed into Devi's bedroom. He was snoring. I knelt and kissed his outflung hand. I rested my head on his chest. I was flooded with peace. (I love this body more than I will ever love another.) "We will be cosmic specks together, some day"— when had he said that to me? "Cosmic specks, we'll find each other and dance." Damn the stillness and damn the dance. I love his flesh, I do not want a cosmic waltz. On his stomach there are stretch marks, of which he is ashamed. Carefully, I pull the sheets away. I kiss the marks on his brown flesh. His arm—does it know what it is doing?—encircles me. Half-dreaming, half-awake, I am keeping vigil for a child. I cover him and steal away.

In the morning, the door to Devi's room is open; he is gone. I kneel by his bed. On his bed there are damp spots. (Did his arm know what it was doing?) I kiss the damp spots (there is nothing of his that I do not love), and crawl into his bed. Let him find me here. Let me rest here forever. I am very tired. I know that he loves me. I know that I have damaged him. I want to be his wife. I should have left him alone.

The bright afternoon sun wakes me up. (His bed smells of my perfume—and of something else, stale.) I dress and walk to Kensington Gardens. (In his house, nothing needs care: The tiny fridge is empty; there are no plants. Who lives here?) On a bench in Kensington Gardens, I read this plaque: "In loving memory of Yvonne Maud Jenson, 1897–1972." How often, I wonder, in the seventy-five years of her life, did Yvonne Maud Jenson cry? How many times did her heart crack? How long life goes on! *(After all.)*

How can I begin to understand his moods when I don't

understand my own? For today I am happy; though with what cause? The cherry trees are in bloom. The sky is gray; the whole world looks to me like a pewter bowl full of bright blooms and tender moss.

I walk among the mews of Southwest Ken—pastel houses, tubs of merry flowers—and I am happy, well-disposed to all inhabitants, no matter color, creed, or race. Or sexual preference.

Tomorrow I will leave. (And what have I accomplished?)

# Chapter Five

"Your day?"

"Good."

"Tell."

"I saw a butterfly—three butterflies—in Kensington Gardens. And I thought God copied butterflies from art nouveau. It was a while before I realized it must have been the other way around."

"A decadent perception if I ever heard one," Devi said; but he was not cross. "Stay longer, a few more days."

"Why?"

"Why not? I've gotten theater tickets for tonight."

"What play?"

*"Candida."*

We went to the pub.

"You were voted the most beautiful girl—woman—to come to the pub in the past five years."

"Who voted?"

"The major and me."

"Not what you'd call a crowd."

"Beggars can't be choosers," Devi said.

"I'll stay," I said.

At the saloon, the barmaid and I chatted easily; I could see Devi was glad that she liked me. I could see that he thought I was beautiful. No one else thought I was beautiful.

The next day was Sunday, and Devi said we'd go to Mass at Brompton Oratory.

"Why Brompton Oratory?"

"Because I cherish memories. And because I have plans."

"A mystery day?"

How shy I was in church with Devi. When we exchanged the greeting of peace, Devi kissed me on the mouth. I prayed silently for Devi while he watched me (did he read my mind?); indistinguishable from praying *to* Devi.

"Lousy homily," I said.

"And yet your face is glowing."

"Well . . ."

"Because you ate the Body of Christ." Outside the church, in full view of pastor and parishioners, Devi embraced me, kissed me, tongue in my mouth.

"What now?"

"A stop at Queens Gates Gardens. I have to deliver a note to a chum, and then to Gloucester Road Tube, no escalators."

"What mysteries." I loved not knowing. Wives seldom know.

I waited outside while Devi disappeared for five minutes into a house at Queens Gates Gardens. At the Gloucester Road Tube station we took the Circle Line to Victoria.

An escalator down to the Victoria Line. "I thought you said no escalators."

"No escalators at Gloucester Road. An escalator here."

"I can't, Devi. I can't go down that escalator. Please, I'll pay for a taxi. Let's go home."

"You have just eaten the Body of Christ," Devi said, "hardly enough time for it to be digested."

"Oh so fucking what."

"Do this for me," Devi said.

"I can't. . . . Well maybe I can if you go ahead of me. Let me take a tranq."

"Tranqs take twenty minutes to work," Devi said. "What good is your religion?" But he stood in front of me, facing me, as we rode down the long escalator.

"I can't talk."

"I'm just chatting you up to distract you"—and, backward, he moved six steps down. Six steps between us, "Devi, I'm going to die." He walked up toward me. "Hold on to me, tight," he said.

"I can't take my hands from the rails."

He put his arms around me: "You're crying."

"This fucking thing will never end."

"Of course it will end."

The Victoria Line to Euston. A long walk through a tunnel, during which I could not catch my breath. "Drunk on the wine?" Devi said.

"I hate these fucking goddamn things. You can't make love to me, and I can't go on escalators."

"It's almost over," Devi said.

At Euston there was a long escalator up to the station. "Devi, no."

"You can't go *up* escalators?"

"Up or down. I'll pay for a taxi."

"I'll walk ahead of you."

"Behind me. So if I fall . . ."

"You won't. I'll catch you."

At Euston Station Devi bought me coffee; I had a muscle spasm.

How kindly he regarded me. As if the mess he saw before him were not the work of his hands. Did he know what he was doing?

"Are you in pain?"

"What do you think? I'm scrunched up because I like to sit this way. I'm crying because moisture is good for the skin."

"It goes against your nature?"

"What?"

"What we have done?"

"What have we done, Devi?"

"We have between us subverted your nature and mine. You know that."

"So what now?"

"I thought we'd go to the Midlands to see some friends."

"Who?"

"But now I think no. They have," Devi said, "a repulsive child."

"I want to see them anyway."

"How can you know that?"

"They're your friends."

"No," Devi said; "I think no. You look ill. We'll go back home."

"Taxi."

"Why not?" Devi said; "but you go alone. I'll have a word with my friend in Queens Gates Gardens."

"You're leaving me alone?"

"You were going to leave me, weren't you? To go back to New York?"

"Devi . . ."

"If you want to talk to me do it on the escalator," Devi said. I took a taxi home.

When the taxi stopped at a red light, I saw, through a blur of fine rain, a billboard: "Try Faggots—It's a Saucy Delight."

The world insists upon conforming to the contours of our pain; and mocking it.


"Devi, we have to talk."

"What if I wanted a night out with the boys?"

"What are you talking about?"

"If I married you. Would you marry me?"

"*Would you* is not the same as *will you*, Devi."

"I don't want to marry you," Devi said.

"What do you see ahead of us?"

"Live for the moment."

"Oh, Devi, a talk, Devi, not a fortune cookie. This has been going on for five years. You say I damage you. How do I damage you? What do you want me to do?"

"I have been thinking all these five years. I don't know. Why are you my only friend?"

"Tell me what to do."

"Love me."

"I do. You know I do. How do I damage you? How can I love you without damaging you? Tell me what to do."

"I don't know. You don't damage me."

"You say I do."

"I know."

"I don't know what to do, Devi."

"Can't we just go on? As we have?"

"I don't know. You say we stop each other from loving other people."

"Love diminishes."

"Love multiplies and expands."

"On the evidence of these five years?"

"We always come back to where we started from."

"I damage you," Devi said.

"You don't."

"You would be married to someone else by now."

"I don't know that."

"Do you want to be married?"

"Only to you."

"I damage you," Devi said.

"Can you imagine our never seeing each other again?"

"I think that I should die," Devi said.

"So then it goes on."

"What if we were to be casual friends."

"There is no such thing as casual friendship. Impossible. And where we are concerned, absolutely impossible. There is nothing between friendship and love. No middle way."

"Loving friends?"

"On the evidence of this week in London, I'd say that was impossible."

"So nothing is possible," Devi said.

"You want less, I want more."

"I'd say it was the other way around," Devi said.

"What do you want?"

"You."

"How?"

"Anyway I can keep you."

"The way you keep me is by being alive."

"That presents an alternative."

"No. That wouldn't end it."

"What shall I do?"

"I don't know. Bring us into the real world. Tell me about your brothers and sisters. Tell me about your first love affair."

And Devi, like a child reciting his lessons, did.

"I love you," he said. "I have loved others more."

"Is that true?"

"No, Angela, it is not. Have you loved others more?"

"No." But I had loved a man who killed himself. Devi, so trusting, yielding, now, had reason, had he only known it, to distrust me. I lied. And I knew, even as we spoke, that there would be other loves for me. Devi, for all his strange and hurtful ways, loved me—could this be true?—better than I loved him. Devi was ironbound to me; I was bound to him elastically.

"Love is a prison," Devi said.

"No," I said; but wasn't this in fact the case. For him.

"Marry," Devi said. "Adopt me. Keep me as a pet."

"You'd bite the hand that fed you."

"Yes."

"We used to talk about living together. A week is just time enough for us to quarrel. You don't think we should do it? Live together for a year?"

But even as I said this, I felt great weariness. A year of weeks like this. (And yet, I thought, it remains true that I love him now as much as I have ever loved him. I will always love him, and I will love again.)

"When we are old," Devi said, "not now."

"How old?"

"When happiness no longer matters." By happiness, Devi meant sex. Would I ever be that old?

"I don't see my old age without you," Devi said.

"Nor do I"; and this too was true. Nor, however, could I foresee a lifetime of waiting. Perhaps my plane would crash. (I decided, at this moment, to go home by ship.)

"We settle nothing."

"No."

"Will you wear the ring again? My mother's diamond ring?"

"Yes."

Having settled nothing, we watched television until we fell asleep, wrapped in each other's arms, old history.

When Devi woke, he said, "Why can't I be a brother to you?"

This question required no answer.

# *Chapter Six*

There was a man, once—an unimportant man—who told me I was making a conscious effort to be kind and loving, I wasn't loving with my heart but with my will. He wished to be adored. "I like my men flawed," I'd said. "I like my women not to see my flaws," he said.

"Flaws can be endearing."

"But I don't want to be endearing," he said. "I can practically see you overlooking flaws, as if you were jumping hurdles in your mind."

(I was at the time of this conversation washing dishes in his kitchen, during a commercial break in a television film I had long waited to see. This he took to be a conscious effort on my part to be solicitous—he was above TV and had removed his set from the broom closet only at my behest.)

"I don't get points for trying?"

"If you have to make an effort to be kind," he said, "it doesn't count."

(Our relationship did not flourish.)

But Devi I'd adored. Will didn't enter into it.

I agreed with Stephan, whom Dearheart had so beautifully changed: "To love judiciously is not to love at all."

*Did* I agree with Stephan? No one could accuse me of loving Devi judiciously. And look at us.

Devi I'd adored. But not loved perfectly. For, as Father Caldwell said, I wanted him to live as I lived. ("Marry me.") As Father Caldwell said: Devi's gift for loving me was insufficient to my needs; so I offered him my gifts, which he did not want and did not need. Or was in any case incapable of accepting. Which naturally made him mad.

So what to do.

I have formed the habit of loving him. Now it is partly a matter of will. No matter what he does—to me or to himself—I will love him. I owe him that. (Perhaps if he were not so beautiful.)

Of course this is nonsense. Will enters into it this far: I will not let him believe (but last night he was so sad, so sweet) that he can do me violence. I owe him that.

These thoughts I had while Devi was away at work, the morning after he'd placed his ring on my finger. These thoughts did not get me far.

Would nothing ever happen, the seesaw never stop. I wanted to be thrown in the air, flung on the ground, anything.

Devi said: Be passive.

I was passive now. Or patient? Not patient. I wanted the seesaw to stop. My presence was an act of aggression.

He wanted me not to leave.

I could love him silently, in my prayers. (This thought I dismissed. Fake-good, just like me.)

It will all end in sleep, Devi said.

I went to sleep.

I dreamed of him. And of the man who killed himself. I awoke, these words sounding in my head: *He is my only love.*

Who is my only love? Devi? The man who killed himself? I can no longer tell them apart. And I call Devi mad.

I wanted to be in the real world of real people.

I walked to Harrods to look at fruits and vegetables, which had this virtue: They were real.

La Merced in Mexico is like a cool cave that smells of over-ripe mangoes. When I was contemplating divorce I spent hours there, among the stalls of fruits and vegetables and herbs. I liked the sweet thick smell of rotting fruit; it gave me pleasure to walk in sandals on concrete slimy with decaying greens. The only part of nature I really love is that which I can eat; I leave summer afternoons to Henry James. I like that which is inert.

"I beg your pardon, madam?" Talking to oneself in Harrods is a sign of decay. I bought three aubergines to establish myself as a sane person with a purpose, and then I wandered among the hams. I was looking forward to the cheeses when I perceived that a man was dogging my footsteps. Stephan's oft-repeated words—"Let one be of use"—came into my mind. Well, let him take his pleasure in following me, I thought; no harm can come to me here, and if he gets his kicks by trailing after strange women, I might as well provide a practical service. I was looking at fresh fish when he sidled up to me, his breath hot upon my neck.

"Hello, Angela," he said. "Care to have tea?" Billy.

"I didn't recognize you."

"I live near here," he said, which I took to be a lie.

"I would like tea," I said, which was also a lie. In fact, his face revolted me, it looked waxen and dead, rather like the fish, in fact. I remembered how he'd fondled the skull at Rita's house; his hands were pinker than his face, pink and fat as hams. I wondered if it was really tea he had in mind, and my spine prickled; what would it be like to be handled by those pink and fleshy hands, which had caressed the skull so lovingly?

I said to Billy, as we walked to his flat, which was in Knightsbridge (he hadn't lied—odd how I'd come to think of lying as the natural way to behave), that he didn't talk very much—he'd done nothing but hum a little tune since he steered me out of Harrods, applying his fat hand hard to my elbow. "Conversation isn't all it's cracked up to be," Billy said.

"What do you do?" I asked.

"Psychiatric social worker," he said. His voice, thin and sweet, was the only pleasant thing about him. A light dawned. Billy's was the Cockney voice I'd heard on the telephone at Devi's house. My God. Billy was the psychiatric social worker Devi had written me about.

"Is anything what it's cracked up to be?"

Billy just smiled, a revolting sight. I imagined his salmon-pink hands flipping white bodies over in hospital beds.

"Do you like your job?" I asked, eager, with a distanced curiosity, to see to what extent I was prepared to debase myself. He had not meant tea.

"It's a job," Billy said; and I thought, This man Devi preferred to me in bed.

"How do you feel when they die?" I said.

"Death isn't all it's cracked up to be," Billy said. This man Devi preferred to me in bed.

We walked without words, Billy humming his jaunty tune, while I considered the sin I was about to commit. Lucy kept insinuating herself into my mind. I prayed that she would never be old or wicked enough to do what I was about to do. Old and wicked are variations on unhappiness. With what notions of redemptive love, of redemptive suffering, I had come here. Only to wind up in a seedy bed sitting room in Knightsbridge to fuck a man called Billy whose last name I didn't even know. It once again struck me that all my so-called redemptive suffering had done was to cause others to suffer: Devi, whose nature I insisted upon warping out of shape (that he was complicit in this game made me no less culpable); and perhaps—almost certainly—Lucy, who needed a father (who needed, in any case, to understand the normal channels through which normal love flowed); Stephan, toward whom my attention had so woefully lapsed (Stephan had long wished, and acted upon the wish, of assuming me as his burden, and I, choosing to make another person, Devi, my job, had not assumed the burden of Stephan by gracefully allowing him to be of use); perhaps—almost certainly—my father, to whom I had been less than dutiful. And I supposed God came into it too. As Devi—Devi's damnable beauty—had convinced me so intensely of the reality of God, Devi was still—damn him!—the God-bearing person; which meant that my obsession, tarted up as redemptive suffering, had injured God, too.

(I have fancy thoughts to distract me from my essential silliness. The fancy thoughts, however, are not silly; I don't act on them, however, and that is why my nature is frivolous and flawed.)

Billy's room smelled of anesthetic, though perhaps this

smell emanated from him in close quarters; perhaps from me. On his window ledge there were three skulls, on one grimy wall a detailed anatomical drawing—the heart, when you think of it, is a most improbable organ, ugly with all its tubes and valves, a hideous machine, no more beautiful than a kidney or a liver. When I was a child I got it into my head that the heart looked like a rose, I used to imagine its flutterings were the opening and closing of petals. Billy had never been young enough to have thought of the heart as a rose. I wonder what funny little ideas Lucy has had in her head, ideas she will never share with me, if only because she will not remember them. One remembers images of innocence only when one has lost one's innocence, and innocence can be lost again and again and again, proof of which is that I am sitting on Billy's gray and dingy bed. The separation from Lucy I fear, if it happens, will not be of Lucy's devising, it will be of my doing, and that is perhaps what I have always feared: that I am not good enough for her; there has never been any reason for me to fear Eileen, or to feel superior to her. How can I feel superior to anyone? I am sitting on Billy's bed.

And that is the only furnishing in this room, aside from a greasy chair whose squashy guts are spilling out through rusted iron loops, and a felt-covered table which lists and on which there is an electric kettle and several tins. Billy plugs in the electric kettle and offers me a tin of biscuits, which I refuse. The tea, when he serves it to me in a thick white cup, is dark and bitter. "Forgot milk," Billy says. "Milk isn't all it's cracked up to be," I say; Billy nods solemnly. There is a pink fringed lampshade on the ceiling light, which Billy has turned on against the gloom of a rainy afternoon. Now everything is salmon-pink—his hands, the teacups, my hands, the skulls on the window ledge. He could murder me in this room; but he wouldn't, he hasn't the energy—I wonder if that was what Devi called sweet in him, this lack of passion and conviction. There is nowhere for me to rest my teacup except on the window ledge, among the skulls. Tucked behind one of the skulls is a bottle in which a bug is preserved. Billy understands my mute question. "Mayfly," he says; "lives for a little while and dies. Just like us. Bang. Not important."

"So is it your memento mori?"

"What's that, then?"

"Your reminder that you will die."

"No. Wouldn't have that. Not important enough, death. Just like to look at the little bugger."

"I suppose you think life's not important, either?"

Billy shrugs. He thinks my question is stupid.

It is very cold in this room, and very stuffy. I am going to do what I am going to do because it is the closest I will ever get to Devi. I am going to do what I am going to do because I want all these years of love and yearning to end in one putrid explosion of flesh. This is where my ideals have carried me—to a degradation I could not have imagined. I said I would not let Devi kill me, but I have chosen an instrument that will do just as well, better. (I do what I want to—whether I want to or not.)

Billy takes one of the skulls—a small one, that of a child—and runs his hammy hands over its cold surface. "What about it?" he says. His eyes turn inward as I undress. He stares at me as if I were a mayfly in a bottle, his eyes slightly out of focus. I climb under the clammy rough wool cover—there are no sheets—and avert my eyes as Billy undresses. The cold seems to have entered my bones. I feel nothing but cold.

His hands are cold. He flips me over effortlessly and puts his fat hands through my hair as I lay with my face pressed against the mattress which smells of stale encounters. His fingers caress the contours of my skull. He hums his jaunty little tune, his breath catching when his fingers linger on a chosen spot. Then he draws my knees up to my chest, and enters me from behind. He is very gentle, very rhythmic and slow, and I am nothing but cold. There is a vast shuddering of flesh, then a fluttering, as of many birds; in the rain-darkened room our faces swim like fish in a salmon-pink sea. I am cold.

Billy lies still in the narrow bed. I climb over his motionless body and put my clothes on. They feel clammy and smell of anesthesia, sweet-sick. "All right, then?" Billy asks, addressing his words to the ceiling. Whether or not I answer is of no concern to him. He is only an instrument.

I survey the room, wishing to remember it well—I will not return to the scene of the crime—while Billy hums his little tune. I think that he will have forgotten me before I close the door.

Outside the rain beats hard and there is no protection. No taxis, either. I have no idea what time it is. I walk all the way to Belgravia, where else is there for me to go?

# Chapter Seven

Devi: "Where have you been?"

"To Harrods. And walking."

"In such weather?"

"Yes."

"So you can discuss the English rain when you go home? Is this a romantic notion, dripping all over the floor?"

"Shut up, Devi."

"Dry yourself off and put your robe on. Put my robe on."

I did. My limbs seemed to be acting independently of my brain. It is warm and bright in Devi's white kitchen.

"You need a fire. You should be sitting in front of a fire. . . ." Devi takes my damp hair in his warm brown hands.

"Shut up, Devi. Don't do that to my hair." These are not the words I want to say.

"What is that you're humming?" Devi asks.

"I don't know."

"What mood is this?"

"I'm cold."

"Wet through and through, I should think. You need a spot of tea."

"No tea."

"What then?"

"I don't care."

Devi searches my face carefully. "Since when do you not make choices?" he asks. "Since when are you mute? Say words."

I shake my head.

"In two days you shall go home," Devi says, a note of wonder, and of fear, entering his voice.

"Yes."

"What shall we do tomorrow?"

"I don't care."

"Perhaps I shall come to New York with you."

I say nothing.

My silence alerts Devi, he is giving off waves of fear. "Perhaps I shall come to New York with you," Devi says again.

"I would like some tea."

"Where did you have dinner?"

"I didn't."

"Have some port," Devi says; he cuts two slabs of bread and two thick slices of ham and cheese, which he places before me.

"I can't eat this."

"You have found out."

"Found out what?"

"The cable."

"What cable?"

"Now you will want to go home."

"What cable?"

"A cable came for you." He is watching me closely.

"Lucy?"

"Not Lucy. I opened it."

"May I see it, please?"

The cable is from Uncle Dominick: YOUR FATHER IN COMA. DOCTORS SAY NOT SOON. ADVISE HOME IN TWO WEEKS.

"Thank you."

"Thank you?"

I am only cold.

"What do we do about Lucy?" Devi asks.

"Nothing. I'll figure it out tomorrow, Devi. I'm going to sleep."

"Finish your port."

"No."

"This is hysteria," Devi says, hysteria rising in his voice; but it is not: I feel nothing.

"You love your father?"

"Yes."

"Then?"

"Then nothing. I want to sleep."

"You love your father?"

Perhaps this cold is calm, but I know better. Devi expects melodrama, he thinks I thrive on it. Hysteria would be a decent response; I feel nothing. It is Devi who grows more and more agitated.

"Where were you today?"

"Harrods. And walking."

Devi reads the cable to me as if I were an idiot child.

"Yes, Devi. Now I want to sleep."

Sleep is not possible. The cold that has entered my body has entered my heart. My father lies dying, and this has no measurable effect on me. I think about the man I did not marry—"witty, coordinated, kind, uses all that comes to hand." Margaret, Mark—people parading through my life and not entering it. No more important, when it comes to it, than Aldo Moro was to me; no less important. All symbols. (Of what?) This afternoon, I was entered, and not entered. I wanted to be entered and I want to be rooted; and Devi cannot enter me and I cannot be rooted in him.

I have forgotten human bodily reality. Devi is a phantom of my imagination. Once Father Caldwell—who has his moments —said that, just as language embodies consciousness, the flesh sacramentalizes the spirit. I did not know what he meant. I see now what he meant: I have crucified my body—by squandering it and by offering my squandered virginity to Devi, who has no use for it. No flesh has touched my spirit for years. And this is why I do not understand the flesh and I do not understand the spirit, and why my father's dying has no measurable effect on me. Devi is a phantom of my imagination; and I have enshrined him. The Devi who is real I refuse to believe in; I have always denied him the right to be real.

Devi, in his blue velvet robe, his brown tendoned calves as beautiful as ever, enters my room; and my vaginal muscles contract, a reflex.

"Auden says that without communion with the dead a fully human life is impossible."

"Words," Devi says. "In extremis, you resort to words."

"Perhaps you can tell me what else to resort to. In any case it is my father who is in extremis, not I."

"I am dying too, Angela."

"Well, die."

"What?"

"Whether you live or die is of no matter to me, Devi. I have accounts to settle with the living and the dead, and it doesn't matter to me in which category you fall."

"I am dying, Angela."

"In fact it is my father who is dying, and not making such a fuss of it as you are."

"Say again."

"Say what again?"

"Say that whether I live or die is of no consequence to you."

"It does not matter to me whether you live or die, Devi. I fucked Billy today."

"You what?"

"You heard me."

"This is hysteria talking."

"Look at me carefully, Devi, and tell me whether I am being hysterical. Does it matter to you whether my father dies, by the way? What does matter to you? How many brothers and sisters do you have, Devi? The truth."

"You need a drink," Devi said; and I laughed. To think that Devi would offer such a conventional solution. To think Devi—who assigned to me every evil property under the sun, when he wasn't ascribing to me every property owned by Candida and the Virgin Mary—would not credit my having slept with Billy.

Devi returned bearing a glass containing a bluish, milky fluid: "Drink this."

"And will I, like Alice, grow smaller? Will I disappear, Devi? Would you like that, Devi?"

"Drink this."

A sudden vision of my father lying with tubes in his arms. I pushed Devi's outstretched hand away, spilling half the liquid on the counterpane.

"Drink this," Devi said.

"No."

"Do what you're told," Devi said, his voice harsh.

I hated Devi. I drank it. Then I was falling—like Alice; only it was Devi who was growing smaller. And then all was blackness; a velvet tunnel.

*What is he doing? Where is Daddy? What is he doing.*

Devi was making love to me. Entering the deep dark tunnel I was in. Entering me. Another man has been here. Devi is entering me. He is making love to me ravenously. I am not participating. This has happened in my dreams. It was not like this in my dreams.

It was the middle of the night, and Devi, in his blue velvet robe, was sitting cross-legged at the foot of my bed.

"What happened after I drank what was in that glass?"

"You fell asleep."

"I fell asleep. I want to be alone, Devi."

"I've phoned Lucy."

"Why? I don't want you to call Lucy."

"I've phoned to Lucy, but she wasn't there, so I rang Stephan."

"Why?"

"To tell them."

"To tell them what?"

"That your father is dying. That you are no longer in control of yourself."

"You take a lot on yourself."

"Stephan is taking Lucy to Newport."

"He takes a lot on himself."

"You might as well stay here."

In my tunnel of love.

The phone rang in the drawing room.

"Mommy?"

"Oh, Lucy! I'm coming home, Lu."

"Mommy, I need you."

"I need you."

"Stephan says you shouldn't fly. He's booked passage on the QE II."

"Five days on the ship, Lu, too long. I can't."

"Mommy, I want to be here with Stephan, I do."

"Don't you want me?"

"I want you. We'll meet you at the boat. It's better, Stephan says."

Stephan got on the phone. "I've booked a first-class cabin, dear. You sail day after tomorrow."

"There's a ship the day after tomorrow?"

"And you will be on it."

"I'm taking the Concorde tomorrow, Stephan."

"Your doctor will not allow you to fly."

"I have a daughter."

"Let me take care of her, Angela. Let me be of use."

"I can't abandon her, Stephan. Besides, I need her."

"She needs you, Angela, but not as you are."

"I don't know how I am."

"Of course you don't."

"I do know how I am."

"Mommy? Mommy, promise me you'll sail. Stephan says I can see the ocean from my room in Newport."

"But don't you want me?"

"But Mommy, please. What if the plane should crash?"

Stephan's voice: "Angela? For once let someone take matters out of your hands. Lucy has got it into her head that your plane will crash."

"Be good to her, Stephan."

"I want to be of use."

"Mommy?"

"OK, Lu."

"Don't cry."

The next morning, "Devi," I said, "I know what happened last night."

"What happened last night?"

"You made love to me."

"What is this? *Rosemary's Baby?*"

"You didn't make love to me?"

"I love you, Angie."

"My father calls me Angie."

"Drink this," Devi said.

"No."

"Why are you packing your bags?"

"I have a daughter."

"And you love your daughter more than you love me? I'll come to New York with you."

"Don't call her 'your daughter'. She has a name. Just keep your hands off Lucy." Some instinct made me not tell Devi that I was sailing on the QE II.

"I have just begun to use you and you are leaving me. This house is a tomb without you."

"Will you marry me, Devi?"

Devi said: "Yes."

"I will marry you if you tell me that you made love to me last night."

"I love you, Angela."

"Where are you going?"

"To buy a sausage roll for your flight. Some paperbacks for you to read."

Our prayers are always answered, Father Caldwell said.

Before he left, Devi booked a flight on my plane—which was of course not my plane. I still had my plane ticket; I could change my mind.

("Let someone take matters out of your hands for once." I would not bully fate.)

Devi returned with a sausage roll, how ridiculous, and paperbacks. "I have a Mini outside," he said; "we'll drive."

We were ten minutes out of Greater London when Devi said, "I forgot my passport."

As also he had left no word for the housekeeper.

I would not bully fate.

Devi braked. Cars behind us screeched.

"Devi, what?"

We were in the middle of the road, he had not even pulled over to the side.

"The housekeeper could bring the passport," Devi said; "or we could go back home and fly another day."

Horns honking behind us, Devi proceeded. Then, again, he braked.

"What if I wanted a night out with the boys?"

"We'll miss the plane. What about your passport?" I knew Devi would never get on that plane. I knew it was over. Who had ended it? Me? Devi? In whose hands were matters now?

"Perhaps I would need no nights out with the boys."

"You made love to me last night. What are you doing?"

"Back for my passport."

We would die before we got there—it would all end in sleep. The way Devi was driving.

"Now what, Devi?"

"I'm driving you to the airport. I can't marry you."

"Oh."

"*Oh?* Is that all you have to say, *oh?*"

"I love you, Devi." I did. There are habits it is hard to break.

"It's Lucy I think of," I said. "I think of Lucy. I feel such pity and rage. Her daddy's dead. . . ." I meant, of course, my daddy, as good as dead.

" 'Pity and rage,' what words. I can't marry you, your words."

"You made love to me last night."

Devi was driving ninety miles an hour.

"Help me," he said.

"It will all end in sleep."

He braked, swerved violently; my head hit the windshield.

"Angela. I'm mad."

"Are you?"

"Will you promise me something?"

"Yes."

"If I am really mad—if ever I can't walk or talk or live—will you come to me?"

"Yes."

Devi drove.

"Did I do this to you, Devi?"

"What sanity I have I owe to you."

"Is that true?"

Devi drove.

# *Chapter Eight*

At the airport, Devi bought me cigarettes and gin. Strange that he should be crying this time, not I.

"My father never loved me," he said.

"I know."

"I'm sorry, Angela."

"I know."

"I get it mixed up. I don't know whether I am I or I am you."

"Yes."

"Do you believe I love you?"

"Yes. You are so beautiful, Devi."

"Only you think that."

The whole world thinks Devi is beautiful. What is true is that only Devi thinks I am beautiful.

"Shall I wait with you?"

"Better not."

"Good-bye, Angela."

"Good-bye, my Devi."

He kissed me, a briny kiss.

His mouth. Oh beautiful Devi. Good-bye, good-bye.

I slept in my clothes, in the hotel near Heathrow; thinking that in English novels this is always a sign of impending mental disintegration. In English novels heroines who sleep in their clothes and don't brush their teeth before they go to bed are on the brink of nervous collapse. But I was no heroine. And I was no victim—just an actor in a drama, an actor who had wanted to direct the show. And who had paid less than full attention to all the other actors in the drama; a sin. How Devi would have hated my thoughts: "A heroine in an English novel," he would have muttered; "everything is grist for your word mill."

I fell asleep in the unwashed body two men had entered ("What happens to the tails of the sperm?" Lucy had asked me when she was little; "where do they go away to die?"); two men —and my body felt unused.

In the morning, on my way to Waterloo, I felt (unwashed) like a heroine in an English novel (neither Jane Eyre nor Mrs. Rochester, neither claimed nor unclaimed, neither loved nor despised, neither virginal nor ravaged—just a body without a will, traveling away, traveling toward). A body in a state of suspended animation.

All the answers lie in the flesh. Devi has broken into my controlling dreams; the fantasy has become flesh, he is embodied. And I am leaving him, going home to live my father's death; and to settle (a lifetime's work) my accounts—Stephan, Eileen, my mother. Lucy. And to pay attention, to die the life I have been living, never again to live in a state of perpetual ungratified desire, never again to love idolatrously the object created by my desire. I sailed toward these goals; knowing well that I might be sailing to fictitious shores.

I remember little of that voyage but the sea, the primeval pull and ebb of the gray-green waters . . . and the information that came to me in dreams. Father Caldwell appeared to me in dreams. God wants not suffering, but trust, he said. All is grace, he said. All is grace. Adrift on that vast and patient space, afloat on the moon-pulled yielding tides, it seemed to me that all was grace; my graceless life could not refute the evidence of the accepting sea. All is waiting and all is work; all is change and all is permanence. All is grace. Would I, could I, recapture grace by not greedily grasping for happiness? The swelling ocean stills all greed.

There are people it is impossible to love without damaging them. I can love Devi only by not loving him. He is not I and I am not he. There are oceans between us.

Lucy and Stephan were waiting. My life was waiting, too.
"Receive your gifts with grace and praise," Father Caldwell
says; "be still."

Sometimes I dream of the man who killed himself. I shall
dream of him all my life.
Sometimes I dream of Devi, his beauty undiminished, call-
ing for my help. These dreams make me intensely happy.
There is no one to guard my restless sleep.
Sometimes I dream I am in a walled garden.

In this story there are no villains.